The Best American Mystery Stories 2003

GUEST EDITORS OF
THE BEST AMERICAN MYSTERY STORIES

1997 ROBERT B. PARKER
1998 SUE GRAFTON
1999 ED McBAIN
2000 DONALD E. WESTLAKE
2001 LAWRENCE BLOCK
2002 JAMES ELLROY
2003 MICHAEL CONNELLY

The Best American Mystery Stories™ 2003

Edited and with an Introduction
by Michael Connelly

Otto Penzler, Series Editor

HOUGHTON MIFFLIN COMPANY
BOSTON · NEW YORK 2003

ISSN 1094-8384
ISBN 0-618-32966-8
ISBN 0-618-32965-x (pbk.)

Printed in the United States of America

MP 10 9 8 7 6 5 4 3 2 1

Contents

Foreword

EACH VOLUME of this series of *Best American Mystery Stories* has certain peculiarities and certain similarities as it is being compiled. Some of these similarities will be immediately evident to those who have read several editions.

First, and perhaps most important, is that one will be struck by the extraordinarily high quality of the fiction between the covers. Whether by established authors, lesser-known writers, or first-timers, the excellence of the prose cannot be denied. It is not surprising, then, to realize that many of the stories selected for these books were first published in literary periodicals, which sometimes have a very small circulation. It is these little magazines that search for experimental work, often accepting material that would be unlikely to find a wide mainstream audience. Frankly, some of it is awful. Experiments that, if successful, should never have been attempted, or, more likely, were poorly conceived and had no chance of being successful. But sometimes they work, and they are wonderful. Most are not mysteries in the way we usually think of them, but some slip into the genre because of my very liberal definition of "mystery" (any work in which a crime, or the threat of a crime, is central to the theme or plot). Most volumes of *BAMS* have one or two of these.

Another similarity of the books in this series is the apparent ubiquity of Joyce Carol Oates, who remains one of the brightest colors in the rainbow of American letters. She has appeared in six of the seven annual volumes of *BAMS*. Nobody makes it into these books based on their fame or popularity, and she is no different.

It is about the work, and she simply will not be denied. "The Skull" made it into this book, but another of her stories, "Angel of Wrath," was nominated for an Edgar Allan Poe Award by the Mystery Writers of America. It could have gone either way.

Yet another similarity from book to book is the range of subgenres of the very broad category of mystery. Styles have ranged from very hard-boiled to quite cozy, but an even greater range has been from the very structured detective story to capers to character studies to espionage fiction. There have been stories of policemen and stories of criminals; they have been set right next door and also in the farthest corners of the globe. There have been happy endings and those that almost force a sob. It seems reasonable to say, then, that one similarity is that every book is so different from every other one.

There are similarities that the reader can never know, however, because they have to do with the actual compilation of each volume and the personal contact I have with authors. As you might expect, most are delighted to have been selected for the honor of being included in these wonderful books. Two didn't want to be included. (E. L. Doctorow didn't say why, and his excellent story found its way into *Best American Short Stories* last year; T. Coraghessan Boyle said he wasn't a mystery writer and didn't want to be identified as one, though he had written a splendid crime story.) My favorite response, however (and it's happened *every* year), is from the authors who are excited to be included but who never realized they had written mysteries.

No, no, I explain, a mystery is not merely a detective story, which is just one subgenre of this rich and diverse literary form. Then I give them my definition and they say, well, then, they guess they've written a mystery. Each of those stories has dramatically enhanced the volumes in which they appeared, and if you have previous volumes in this series, it might be an interesting exercise to figure out which are those stories. (Hint: all were published initially in literary journals.)

And that reminds me. Back in the Age of Enlightenment, when I first got into the world of publishing, publishers kept books in print practically forever. Nowadays, it is very common for publishers to let a hardcover edition go out of print within a year of publication. Houghton Mifflin deserves a little recognition and a lot of credit for keeping virtually every book in this series in print. The accountants would probably tell them it is not an economically wise practice, but they do it anyway, which is definitely cool.

Speaking of cool, Michael Connelly did a terrific job as guest editor, which should be no surprise except that until a few years ago he had never even written a short story, and now he has developed a great affection for this difficult but rewarding form.

Also, as I can never fail to do, a sincere word of thanks and admiration to Michele Slung, who did so much of the preliminary reading for this and every volume. Her skilled speed, intelligence, and taste make it possible to produce these projects on time. It's not just reading the 1,000–1,200 mystery stories but going through many, many hundreds of magazines and finding which of the fiction falls into the mystery category. Title alone will not do it, and if you don't believe me, check the table of contents for "Thug: Signification and the (De) Construction of Self" and decide if it leaps out at you as a crime story. Ditto "Aardvark to Aztec," "Home Sweet Home," and "That One Autumn."

The process is the same every year because it seems to work pretty well. After I've selected the top fifty stories of the year (in my opinion, anyway, which is all anyone can offer), the guest editor reads them all and picks twenty favorites. The others are listed in the back of the book as "Other Distinguished Mystery Stories of [the year]."

Although we read every consumer periodical and hundreds of little magazines, as well as all anthologies or short story collections with original material and electronic publishing sites that offer fiction, we recognize that we might miss something worthy. Therefore, if you are an author, editor, publisher, or someone who cares about one, you are encouraged to submit stories. The original publication or a tearsheet is fine, or a hard copy if it appeared electronically. The date of the initial publication is vital, as well as a contact address. No unpublished material will be considered, for what should be obvious reasons. Please understand that no submissions can be returned. If you require an acknowledgment of receipt, please enclose a self-addressed postcard.

To be eligible, a story must have been written by an American or a Canadian and first published in an American or Canadian periodical or book in the calendar year 2003. The earlier in the year I receive material, the more warmly I regard it. Stories received after January 1, 2004, will not be considered.

Please send submissions to Otto Penzler, The Mysterious Bookshop, 129 West 56th Street, New York, NY 10019. Many thanks.

O.P.

Introduction

I DRIVE A TWO-SEATER. It's a drop-top sports car built low to the ground for better control and handling. All right, it's an automatic with a pushbutton, electronic top. But that's not the point. The point is that when the top's down and I'm sailing through the curves along the bay, the wind cutting in behind my shades, I can't think of a better car to be in. Sure, it's so small, I can't fit more than one suitcase into it. But again, that's not the point. The point is performance and beauty. In a word, velocity.

The point is this is why I love the short story. Velocity. Room for one suitcase only. The short story deals with issues and themes large and small. But it does it succinctly and quickly. The short story is a car for the short track. Put the top down and power into the curves. If you're going a long distance, get yourself a novel. Take the freeway and get yourself an SUV.

I drove seven SUVs before I ever tried a sports car. I found the difference amazing. You have to dig in to write a novel. You have to cover all the angles. You need a trunk big enough to carry a lot of baggage and extra supplies. Conversely, the short story is lean and mean and built low to the ground. Its ideas burn on high-test. They are spare and to the point.

What happened to me happened to many novelists I know. You push a few books out there, get them on the shelf, and get a bit of notice. Then comes the big question: "Have you ever thought about a short story?" One thing leads to another, and you leave the big car in the garage, and you're out running around in a candy-apple-red sports car. It's fun. It's a change of pace. Nine out of ten doctors recommend it.

In these same pages last year James Ellroy said he wrote his first short story only to pay off a debt. After that, he repeatedly returned to the short form. Me, too. In fact, my guess is that the debt I paid with my first short story was to the same guy — but that's another story. The point is I reluctantly tried it and then liked it. I ended up happy for the coercive genesis of it. I got hooked. I found the short story gave me balance. Elements of character and action and intrigue were all there. But in a spare form I found invigorating. I like the short story because you can conceive and complete in hours or weeks instead of months or years. It is a form I am sure I will always come back to. It has become part of how I evaluate and then execute my ideas as a writer.

This is not by any means to say that the short story is the easier road to take. The novel and the short story are simply different animals. Or, I should say, beasts. In the spare style of the short story is the bedrock philosophy of less is more. This makes the labor over each paragraph, each sentence, intensely important. Every word must count in the short story, so the pressure of the writing experience is ratcheted down tightly on the author.

What you have here in this collection are the examples in which the author has met that pressure and come out with a beauty. Each one of these stories has a well-tuned machine under the hood.

What I have tried to do here is put together a collection that showcases the power of the short story. These stories run from the traditional to the experimental, from deadly serious to deadly satirical, from established writing masters to voices I am betting you have not heard before but will likely hear again.

Each story is a sports car that handles superbly as it takes you to a destination you haven't been to before. Pay attention to the nuances of the ride, the telling details of character and place and emotion and experience. Watch the way a man struggles with language and a new country, the way a man sees his long-lost daughter in the reconstructed face of a murder victim. The way a woman extracts justice after being betrayed. On and on. The way you never know how somebody is going to act or react.

These aren't shiny sports cars. No way. There is a lot of road grit on these pages. There is violence and betrayal and justice meted out without the benefit of the justice system. There is also sympathy and hard-edged romance and a haunting sense of hope. I think that is why the mystery story is so important. It can carry all the in-gredients, even if the car will hold only one suitcase.

We live in uncertain times. And as I write this it looks as if they are only going to become more uncertain. The mystery story is no antidote. But it certainly can act to reassure, to help make some sense of the world. Maybe only in a small way, but that is still better than in no way.

So let's begin. Time to take a ride. You are in luck here. I think you will find everything you are looking for in these pages.

MICHAEL CONNELLY

The Best American
Mystery Stories 2003

DOUG ALLYN

The Jukebox King

FROM *Alfred Hitchcock's Mystery Magazine*

AUGUST 1960. Worst heat wave since '43. The year of the riots.
No clouds. The sun cruising a sheet-metal sky, scorching Detroit's mean streets all day long, hammering the heat down to the
ancient salt mines beneath the city.

By noon the auto plants were like ovens. People said the temperature at Ford Rouge hit a hundred and thirty up near the steel ceil-
ings. Overhead crane operators had to rotate down to the factory
floor every half hour, panting like dogs, their clothes soaked.

Welders were working half blind, squinting through steamy vi-
sors, torches slippery with grease and sweat. And the painters in the
infrared booths? Hell on earth.

But the assembly lines never stopped. Never even slowed down.

Nightfall brought no relief. Black tar bubbling in the streets and
alleys like grease on a griddle, black folks boiling out of their tene-
ments and rowhouses. Restless and surly. And thirsty. Very thirsty.

Brownie's Lounge on Dequinder was buzzing by seven, jammed
tight by ten. Selling Stroh's beer by the gallon. Straight up. No
glasses. Shop rats guzzling the brew out of the pitchers. Getting
high, feeling mighty. Ready to hear some blues.

John Lee Hooker's trio came on at nine, kicking out jams on
Brownie's postage-stamp dance floor. Big John wailing on his old
Harmony guitar, James Cotton on harmonica, and a pickup bass
player.

No drummer. No need for one. If you can't feel the beat when
John Lee stomps his size 13 Florsheims on a hardwood dance floor,
you'd best lie down. You might be dead.

Around midnight the crowd finally started to thin. Working men had to be up at four. Making Thunderbirds, making Fairlanes, making that overtime pay. The best way for a blue-collar black man to rise in this life. The UAW saved the crap jobs for blacks, but the bosses didn't care if a man worked double shifts for time-and-a-half. Turning out Fords for Cadillac money.

By one-forty A.M. Brownie's Lounge was down to a die-hard handful of customers.

Four white kids, blues fans from the University of Detroit, applauding wildly as John Lee closed his show with Smokestack Lightning.

A few couples still grinding each other on the dance floor, ignoring the beat, rocking to a rhythm of their hearts and loins. Hot to trot.

A few hookers gabbing near the door, too whipped to stroll the Cass Corridor for trade.

And at the bar? One old white man. A stone killer.

Moishe Abrams had wandered in a little after one, parked his wide ass on a stool at the end of the bar, his back to the wall.

Brownie spotted him instantly. Hard to miss Moishe. Most of Brownie's regulars were black or beige, plus a few white hipsters. Blue collar. Or no collar.

But Moishe? A surly old white dude with coarse features. Built like a cement block, squat, square, and hard. Old-timey gray suit, wide tie, porkpie brim. Still dressing like swing was the thing.

But nobody ever joked about Moishe Abrams's clothes. Not to his face. Not even behind his back.

Carolina was working the counter. A big woman, milk chocolate skin, a smile wide as a grand piano. She dressed like a man: tuxedo blouse, bow tie, and slacks. But nobody ever mistook her for one.

Brownie stood in the shadows of his office doorway, keeping an eye on Moishe. Watched him guzzle his first drink, then knock back another just as quick.

When Moishe swiveled on his stool to watch the band, Brownie motioned Carolina over to the waitress station. Leaned in close to her, keeping his voice low.

"The white dude at the end of the bar? He drinks free. On the house."

"You sure?" Carolina frowned. "He's already pig-drunk and he's throwin' down bourbon like Tennessee's on fire."

"I don't care. Give him whatever he wants, no charge. And say yessir, nossir. He likes that."

"Fine by me, long as he knows I'm not on the menu. Who is he, anyway?"

"He's the local jukebox king," Brownie said.

"King? You mean he's some kind of singer?"

"No." Brownie smiled. A good smile. "Moishe's people own the jukeboxes. All of 'em. In every joint in Detroit. And the cigarette machines and the candy machines and even the damn slot machines in the blind pigs. They also own pieces of half the bars in Motown, including mine. You get my drift?"

"He's mobbed up? That old dude?"

"Moishe damn near *is* the Mob. Used to be muscle for the Purple Gang during Prohibition. Ran whisky in from Canada, drove trucks right across the ice on the Detroit River in wintertime."

"Must've been crazy," Carolina said, glancing sidelong at Moishe. Curious now.

"Oh, he's still crazy. Only nowadays he collects vending machine money and the vig for loan sharks. When Moishe comes round, you'd best have his bread ready. Slow-pays get stomped. Or just disappear. So, you make nice with Moishe, sugar. While I figure a way to get his honky ass out of here."

"Got it covered," Carolina nodded, sauntering down to sweeten Moishe's drink with her wide smile. Leaving Brownie to worry. And wrestle with his conscience. Because he hadn't told Carolina everything.

Sometimes Moishe Abrams killed people. Just for the hell of it.

Brownie saw Moishe cut a guy in a blind pig once, five, six years before. Bled the poor bastard out on a barroom floor over some stupid argument. Over nothing, really. On a hot summer night. A lot like this one.

Brownie was only a bartender then. Hired help.

He mopped up the blood, then helped the owner load the stiff into the trunk of the dead man's '54 Lincoln. They left the car in an alley off Twelfth. Keys in the ignition.

End of story. A black man knifed to death on the Corridor? Do tell.

But that was then. Brownie wasn't a bartender anymore. The Lounge was his place, and these were his customers, his people. Which made Moishe his problem. The trouble was, he still remembered the look on the old man's face, sitting at the bar calmly ordering another drink with a dead guy on the floor a few feet away.

He looked . . . No, that was the thing. Moishe didn't have a look. Empty eyes. Nobody home. He'd killed that dude like it was nothing. Maybe because he was black. Or maybe just because.

Leo Brown — Brownie to his friends and everybody else — was no coward. Running a blues joint on Detroit's Cass Corridor, trouble just naturally came with the territory. Drunks, brawlers. He'd even faced down a stickup man once.

But Moishe? Down deep, where it mattered, Brownie was afraid of Moishe Abrams. Scared spitless.

He didn't like the feeling. Didn't like feeling small. Especially since he had an easy answer. The gun in his office. A Colt Commander, .45 auto. Nickel-plated. Loaded.

He thought about getting it, jacking in a round, walking up to Moishe, blowing his freakin' brains all over the wall without saying a damn word to him. Solve the problem that way.

Permanent.

He liked the idea, the simplicity of it. The courage it would take. But he knew it wouldn't end anything. It would only bring on more trouble. Which made it a dumb move. And despite his easy drawl and laid-back style, Brownie was no fool. In some ways, he was an educated man. He owned books and read them. Didn't have much formal schooling but he listened to people. All kinds of people. And he remembered what they said. And learned from it.

But he'd never heard an easy way to manage Moishe Abrams. The old mobster was about as predictable as a weasel on amphetamines.

So Brownie took a deep breath and forced down his fear. Slipping off his tailored jacket, he hung it on the hook beside his office door. Wondering if he'd ever put it on again. Then he strolled casually over to Moishe.

And smiled.

"Mr. Abrams, how you doin' tonight?"

Moishe didn't look up. "Get lost, blood."

"You remember me, Mr. Abrams. Brownie? This is my place. Can I buy you one for the road? We're gettin' ready to close."

"It's early."

"Nossir, it's almost two. Word is, beat cops are checkin' up and down the Corridor. Writin' tickets for after-hours."

"No beat cops are gonna roust me."

"Hell, I'm not worried about you, Mr. Abrams. More worried about them. You bust 'em up in my place, it's bad for business. Mine *and* yours."

Moishe glanced up at Brownie, looking him over for the first time. Tall, dark, and slender. Even features, liquid brown eyes, wide shoulders. Well dressed. Soft-spoken. "You tryin' to give me the bum's rush, Brownie?"

"Nossir, no way. Couldn't if I wanted to, and we both know that. Now, how about that drink?"

"I'll take the drink, but I ain't leavin'. I'm stuck. My damn Caddy overheated, and I'll never get a cab this part of town, this time of night."

"No problem," Brownie said. "I'll drive you home." And instantly regretted it. "My car's outside, it'd be my pleasure."

Moishe considered the offer. "What kind of a car?"

"'Sixty Studebaker Hawk. Emerald green. Brand spankin' new."

"Hawks are pimp cars," Moishe grunted, knocking back the last of his bourbon in a gulp. "Beats walkin', though. Let's go."

Grabbing his jacket from his office, Brownie thought again about the gun in his desk. Decided against it.

If Moishe spotted the piece, Brownie'd have to use it or lose it. Mix it up with a pro like Moishe? Might as well jump in the ring with Joe Louis, try to land a lucky punch.

Brownie's Stude hummed to life, rumbling like a caged cat. After a few blocks, the radio warmed up, WCHB, Inkster. Long Lean Larry Dean murmuring between soul tunes in his silky baritone.

Moishe switched it off. Glancing over his shoulder, he checked the road behind him, his eyes flicking back and forth like bugs in a bonfire. Paranoid. The price of being a prick.

Neither man spoke, Moishe stewing in his sour, boozy silence, Brownie not about to make conversation. Be like gabbing with a gut-shot bear.

"Stop," Moishe said suddenly. "Pull over here."

Surprised, Brownie eased the Studebaker to the curb. Moishe lived out in Grosse Pointe, a good five miles farther on. Here they were only a few blocks from downtown in the dead of night. Empty streets, eyeless windows.

Moishe climbed out. "Take off," he said, slamming the door.

"You're very welcome, Massa Abrams," Brownie said. But very quietly. To himself.

As he circled the block to head back to the lounge, a car suddenly gunned out of an alley, pulling up right on his tail, staying just a few feet behind his rear bumper.

Prowl car. City cops. But they didn't turn on their gumball flasher. Hit him with the spotlight instead, checking out his car.

Half blinded by the blaze, Brownie braced himself for the roust, wondering if they wanted grease money or just to bust his balls. Black man, new car. Must be up to no good, right?

Or maybe not. For whatever reason, they didn't pull him over. Just tailed him for half a mile with their spotlight glaring through the Stude's rear window, reminding Brownie he was the wrong color, wrong part of Detroit, wrong time of night.

Like he needed reminding.

The sweet scent of coffee woke him. The rich aroma dragging him back from the land of dreams. Brownie opened his eyes. Blinked. Breathed deep.

Black coffee. Fresh. His bedroom door opened a crack, and Carolina stuck her head in.

"Brownie? You awake?"

"I am now. What time is it? And how'd you get in here?"

"It's a little after noon. I showed up for work, Eddie gave me a key, said to get my young butt over here, get you up. Couldn't call you. Didn't want to talk over the phone."

"Why not?" Brownie asked, snapping fully awake. "What's wrong?"

"That old guy you left with last night? He's dead, Brownie."

"What do you mean dead? Dead how?"

"How you think? Somebody did him in."

Brownie shook his head, trying to clear it. Felt like a fighter who'd walked into a sucker punch. He remembered wanting to pop Moishe bad, even thinking about the gun in his office.

For a split second he wondered — no. He'd dropped Moishe off downtown. Alive and well. Maybe a little drunk. Or a lot drunk. With Moishe it was hard to tell.

"What the hell happened to him? Exactly."

"Hey, don't bark at me. I don't know anything about all this. I just tend bar, okay?"

There was something in her tone. He glanced at her sharply.

"Whoa up. You don't think I iced the old dude, do you?"

Her hesitation said more than the shake of her head.

"No, of course I don't think that. I got coffee on. You want some?"

"Yeah. There's Canadian bacon in the icebox. Better fry us up some eggs, too. It's liable to be a long day."

He showered quickly, chose a dark blue Sunday-go-to-meetin' suit from his closet. The jacket fit a little loose in the shoulders. Room enough for a .45 auto in a shoulder holster. Too bad the gun was still in his desk back at the Lounge.

But it was all for the best.

When Brownie stepped into the lounge, two men immediately rose from their barstools. Both of 'em wearing off-the-rack suits from Sears, Roebuck. One white guy, one black. Cops.

"Leo Brown?" the white cop asked. The black cop didn't ask Brownie anything, just pointed at the wall.

Brownie raised his hands as the black cop patted him down for weapons, found nothing, then spun him around. He was a big fella, half a head taller than Brownie, probably outweighed him by a hundred pounds. Sad, deeply lined face. Like a blue-tick hound.

The white cop was smaller, freckled, maybe forty. Whitey showed Brownie an ID. Gerald Doyle. Lieutenant. Doyle did the talking.

"Tell us about last night, Leo. What happened between you and Moishe Abrams? Did he start trouble in here?"

"There was no trouble," Brownie said, straightening his lapels. "Moishe came in about one, had a few, hung around till closing. Couldn't get a cab, so I gave him a lift uptown."

"To what address?"

"No address. He got off at a corner, Clairmont and Twelfth."

"Twelfth Street? *That* time of night?" the black cop said skeptically.

"You guys know who Moishe was, right?"

"We know," Doyle nodded. "So?"

"So you know he could get off any damn place he wanted in this town, any time at all."

"Maybe," Doyle conceded. "I hear he had a piece of this joint. That so?"

"Moishe was the jukebox king. Worked for the people who own the jukes and cigarette machines."

"We know who he worked for," Doyle said mildly. "But that isn't what I asked you, Mr. Brown. Did Moishe own a piece of this place?"

"Not exactly."

"What the hell does that mean?"

"What bank do you use, lieutenant?" Brownie asked.

"Me? Detroit National. Why?"

"Five years ago I was a bartender. Had about ten grand saved, needed a loan to buy this place, fix it up. Where do you figure I got the money? Detroit National?"

"I guess not," Doyle said, smiling in spite of himself. "So what went wrong last night, Brownie? You a little late payin' Moishe the vigorish?"

"I told you what happened. Nothing. I mean, look at me," Brownie said, turning right and left, showing both profiles. "Do I look like I been alley dancin' with Moishe Abrams?"

The two cops exchanged a look; then the white cop shrugged. "Maybe not, Leo, but you left here with him. Which makes you the last one to see him alive."

"No way. It was around two when I dropped him off. A prowl car pulled out of an alley on Clairmont, tailed me a dozen blocks or so to make sure I got out of the neighborhood. Check with them."

"We will. But even if that holds up it won't get you off the hook, Brownie. If you know anything —"

"All I know is, Moishe was half in the bag, and he was a mean drunk. Mean sober, for that matter. And it was a hot night. I'm not surprised somebody got killed, I'm just surprised it was Moishe. What happened to him anyway?"

"Cut," the black cop said, bass voice like coal rumbling down a chute. "Somebody opened him up. Sending a message, most likely."

"What message?"

"Move over," Doyle said. "Moishe was mobbed up with the Mo-town Syndicate, the old Purple Gang. I hear there's a new bunch crowding them. Sicilians from Chicago. Which means you're in a world of trouble, Brownie."

"Why me? I don't know a damn thing about this."

"You're still in the middle, like it or not. And if the Sicilians whacked Moishe to send a message, who do you think the Motown mob is gonna use to send one back?"

"Have them Italians been around to see you?" the black cop asked.

"I've heard they leaned on some people in the neighborhood," Brownie admitted. "Haven't gotten around to me."

"They will. When they do, you better call us, hear? Maybe we can help you out."

"Talk to y'all about mob business?" Brownie smiled. "Yeah, right. Why don't you just shoot me in the head right now?"

"Maybe we should." The black cop smiled, a wolf's grin that never reached his eyes. "Might be doin' you a kindness."

"We've wasted enough time on this moke," Doyle shrugged. "We got two more homicides to check out before lunch. One of 'em might interest you, Brownie. A guy got himself beaten to death a few blocks down on Dequinder last night. Makes you wonder who was mad at him, doesn't it?"

"Nobody had to be mad at nobody, lieutenant. It was a hot night. People get edgy."

"Want to take a ride with us, take a look at your future?"

"No, thanks," Brownie said, shaking his head. "I'm doin' fine right here."

"So far, you mean," the black cop snorted. "You ever hire blues singers?"

"Blues is what I do. Uptown places get the names, Jackie Wilson, Sam Cooke. The blues suits this neighborhood a little better. Local folks like it."

"Ever book Jimmy Reed?"

"Can't afford him. He's The Big Boss Man."

"Too bad. Ol' Jimmy does a tune that oughtta be your theme song. 'Better Take Out Some Insurance.' In your situation you're gonna need it. *Big* time. I'll see you around, Brownie. Hope you're still breathin' when I do."

After the law left, Brownie stepped into his office and closed the door. Didn't turn on the light. Stood there in the darkness trying to make sense of what the two cops had said.

Some dude stomped to death on the Corridor? No news. Happened about three times a week.

Moishe murdered a few blocks from where Brownie dropped him off? Damned hard to believe. Partly because the old man seemed invincible. Partly because it was too good to be true.

The white cop had one thing right, though. With trouble brewing between the mobs, the middle was a bad place to be. Might as well sack out on the Woodward centerline at rush hour.

Switching on the lights, he opened his top desk drawer. Eyed the nickel-plated .45 Colt Commander a moment, then closed the drawer again, leaving the gun where it was.

Truth was, he didn't like guns much. Kept the .45 strictly for show. But one crummy pistol wouldn't impress the Syndicate or the Sicilians either. They had plenty of guns of their own.

Three Motown Syndicate hoods showed up an hour later, shouldering into the club's dimness out of the afternoon heat.

He knew who they were, sort of. Tony Zeman, Jr., was royalty. Son of Big Tony Zee. Tony Senior was a Motown mob boss when Capone was still a bouncer. He was in a wheelchair now, people said. Lost a leg. Diabetes. Life whittling him away. Maybe as a payback for the way his goons carved up other people.

Tony Junior looked more like a preppie than a hood. Short, sandy hair, pasty face. Suit from Hughes and Hatcher. Wingtips. Buffed nails. Brownie had heard Junior was in law school. Which would make him more dangerous than his daddy ever was.

His bodyguard was a pushy little fireplug of an Irishman everybody called Red. Fire-haired, freckled, bad-tempered. Risky business to be around.

Brownie didn't know the third guy at all, Spanish-looking dude in a gray suit. Pocked face.

"Mr. Zeman," Brownie nodded, not bothering to offer his hand. "How you doin'? You want to talk in my office?"

"Forget it. We'll sit here," Red said sharply, marching to the end of the bar where he could watch the door. Moishe's favorite spot. Even took the same damn stool.

Brownie told Carolina to take off, took her place behind the bar, shedding his jacket so Red could see he wasn't armed.

"Would you gentlemen care for a taste?"

"We're not here to drink, Mr. Brown," Junior said. "You've got exactly five seconds to tell me what happened to my uncle."

"Didn't know Moishe was your uncle," Brownie said. "Sorry for your loss. But that's really all I know. He came in 'round one, had a few drinks. I offered him a ride home, dropped him off downtown. At Twelfth and Clairmont."

"You dumped him there?" Red butted in. "By himself?"

"Moishe told me to get lost, so I got," Brownie shrugged. "A prowl car tailed me out of the neighborhood, but I expect y'all know that already, since you've got more lines into Detroit P.D. than Michigan Bell."

"Did you see anybody hanging around when you dropped him off?" Junior asked.

"Nope. Not that time of night. And nobody followed us."

"How do you know that?" Red asked.

"I don't, but Moishe did. He checked. About a dozen times."

"Like he was nervous?" Red pressed. "Expecting trouble?"

"More like he was bein' Moishe. He was a careful man."

"Not careful enough," Tony Junior said, looking Leo over. Reading him. "Have any strangers been around to talk to you, Leo? Maybe about changing jukebox companies?"

"No. Maybe they're saving me for last."

"So you know who they are?"

"I've heard they're Italians from Chicago. Serious people. But it doesn't matter. Y'all fronted me the money when I needed it, Mr. Zeman. I'm not forgetting that."

"Glad to hear it," Junior said, leaning in. "Just so you know — I may be taking over the jukebox business. My uncle was . . . a good businessman. But he was old-fashioned. I've got new ideas. For instance, you should make some changes, Brownie. Get with the times."

"What kind of changes?"

"For openers, lose the blues on your jukebox. Put on new music. Run some beer specials, hire some rock bands from the college, get a younger crowd in here. Put in some girls upstairs. You're sitting on a gold mine here, Leo. Together we could turn it into a real moneymaker."

"I like it the way it is," Leo said evenly. "I don't get rich, but I make my payments on time. And that's all you've got to worry about, mister. This is a neighborhood joint. Local people come in to hear some blues, forget about life awhile. White kids and hookers would bring trouble, and I don't like trouble. The big bucks won't mean much if I have to blow it all on bail."

"Maybe you didn't hear what the man said," Red said, doing a movie version of a badass stare. "You hard of hearing, blood?"

"I hear just fine," Leo said, ignoring Red. "The thing is, my uncle's alive and well and livin' in Alabama. Yours is downtown coolin' on a slab, Mr. Zeman."

"Are you trying to threaten me, Brownie?"

"No, sir. I'm just sayin' maybe you don't understand how things work down here. If I was you, I'd be a lot more worried about who waxed Moishe than tunes on a jukebox. It's the kind of thing you have to be sure about. Especially since a whole lot of people could get killed for nothing if you're wrong."

"We know who killed Moishe," Red said. "Them Italians."

"No," Leo said, shaking his head slowly. "I don't think so."

"Why not?"

"If the Italians took him out, they'd put it all over town so everybody'd know how bad they are. But I haven't heard anything about it one way or the other. How about you? You hear any noise about Moishe gettin' waxed? Like who did it? Or why?"

"No," Tony Junior admitted. "We've talked to a few people. Leaned on a few more. Nobody knows anything. Including you."

"I don't know who killed Moishe, but I might have better luck finding out than you will."

"How do you mean?"

"This is my part of town, Mr. Zeman. I know who to ask, how to ask. People will talk to me who won't talk to you, you know?"

"Why be helpful?" Red sneered. "What's in it for you?"

"Stayin' alive, for one thing. If you start up with those Italians, I'm liable to get caught in the crossfire. On the other hand, if I can turn up the guy who did Moishe, it oughtta be worth something, right?"

"It might be," Tony Junior nodded warily. "Like how much?"

"We just call it even. My loan's paid off. Sound fair?"

"Not quite," Junior said. "My dad taught me any deal should cut both ways. Something to win. And something to lose. So you've got twenty-four hours, Brownie. After that we start taking people out. With you at the top of the list."

"Me? Wait a minute, I didn't —"

"Save it, Brownie. You're right, I don't know how things are down here. And I don't care. Maybe you people think I'm too young to take over from my uncle. Too green. Maybe you even think you can con me. Is that how it is?"

"No, I —"

"Shut up! And listen up! You've got one day to give me the guy who did Moishe. Or you're the guy. You got that? Or should I have Red take you out in the alley and explain it some more?"

"No need," Brownie said, swallowing. "I got it."

Brownie didn't waste any time. Five minutes after Tony Junior and his goons left, he was in his emerald Studebaker retracing the route he'd taken with Moishe the night before. From the club to the corner of Clairmont and Twelfth.

Easing the Stude to the curb, he scanned the area, remembering. Moishe hadn't asked to be brought here. He'd spoken suddenly when he ordered Brownie to pull over.

As though he'd forgotten something. Or remembered it. Okay. What could Moishe remember about this corner?

A newsstand in the next block carried the morning papers, the *Detroit Free Press,* the *News,* a few magazines. But it hadn't been open yet. Hell, it was after two A.M. Every damn thing was closed . . .

No. Not everything. Brownie parked the Hawk at the curb and climbed out. The steamy afternoon hit him like a blast from a furnace door. Instant sweat.

Dropping a dime in the meter for an hour, he strolled down the narrow service alley that led to the loading docks in the middle of the block behind the shops.

There. A wooden staircase led to a second-story warehouse above a print shop. No lights showing. Naturally. The windows were painted flat black. Trotting up the steps, Brownie rapped twice on the gray metal freight door, then twice again. And waited.

The tiny peephole winked as somebody inside checked him out. Then the door opened. Just a crack.

"We're closed."

"I know. I'm Brownie, I own the Lounge up on Dequinder. Tell Fatback I need to see him. It's important."

The door closed a moment, then opened to admit him. Bass,

Fatback's bouncer/bodyguard, patted Brownie down for weapons, then waved him through.

Inside, the blind pig was empty, chairs stacked on tables while an ancient janitor mopped the hardwood floor. Skeletal microphone stands stood on a small stage in the corner. The only difference between this joint and Brownie's was a liquor license and the gaming tables. Roulette, craps, blackjack. All illegal.

So were his operating hours. Fatback's place opened around midnight, stayed open till five or six. Or around the clock if a serious game got going.

Fatback was at the end of the bar, sipping a Vernors, thumbing through his cash register receipts. His nickname suited him. Five-foot-five, 360 pounds, with a full beard, Fatback looked like a black Santa Claus in a China blue sharkskin suit. Custom tailored, it fit without a wrinkle. Brownie pulled up a stool next to him. Fat kept counting.

"We've got trouble," Brownie said quietly.

"What trouble? I'm just tryin' to run a business."

"I dropped Moishe Abrams in front of this place last night," Brownie said, shading the truth. "I know he came in here, Fat. What the hell happened?"

Fat glanced up at him, then shook his head. "What always happens with the jukebox king?" he sighed, jotting down the tape tally in a tiny notebook. "Trouble happened. And thanks a bunch for dropping him off. Why didn't you fire a couple of rounds through my front door while you were at it? Gimme a friendly warning."

"I figured you'd notice Moishe soon enough. Did he get in somebody's face?"

"Mine, for openers. I didn't want to serve him, he was already loaded. Told me if I didn't he'd toss my damn jukebox out the window and me with it."

"Sounds like Moishe. So?"

"So I gave him a bottle. What else could I do? Didn't figure he'd cause much trouble. I was dead wrong about that."

"Why? What went down?"

"Nothin' at first. Place was pretty quiet. Couple of card games, some craps goin' on. The kid they call Little Diddley was playin' guitar, but nobody was payin' him no mind. Too damn hot to

dance. Moishe yelled at Diddley to quit singin' them blues. Little D
don't know who Moishe is, tells him to screw hisself. I told the kid
to pack it in for the night just to save his damn life." Fatback shook
his head, remembering.

"Then Moishe decides he wants to play some cards. Butts into
Charlie Cee's game. Them studs been at it all night, serious money
changin' hands. Seven, eight hundred bucks every pot. Moishe an-
tes up a grand, plays awhile. Loses his ass, naturally. He's too drunk
to pitch pennies, to say nothin' of playin' cutthroat poker. Then
Moishe claims Charlie Cee's cheatin'."

"Sweet Jesus," Brownie whistled. "What happened?"

"All hell broke loose. Charlie came out of his chair with a piece.
Me and Bass jumped in, cooled Charlie down, and hustled
Moishe's ass out of the place. Might cost me my jukebox, but it's
better'n havin' Moishe kill somebody in here or get killed his own
self."

Brownie was staring at him.

"What?" Fatback asked, annoyed.

"You haven't heard, have you?"

"Ain't heard nothin' about nothin,' Brownie. I just rolled in here
ten minutes ago. Why? What's up?"

"Moishe bought the farm last night. Somebody cut him up. His
body turned up on the street a couple of blocks from here. His people are lookin' to bleed somebody for it."

"Aw, man, you got to be kiddin'," Fatback moaned. "Who his
people lookin' for?"

"You. Or maybe me. They don't much care. They just wanna
burn somebody quick. Any chance Moishe waited outside for Charlie Cee, maybe mixed it up with him?"

"Nah. I bounced Moishe around three-thirty. Cee's game didn't
break up until seven or so. I closed up, and me and Cee went over
to my woman's in Greektown for breakfast."

"Cee was with you the whole time?" Brownie pressed.

"Yeah, damn it. The whole time, just me and . . ." Fatback broke
off, frowning.

"What is it?" Brownie asked.

"Just thinking. Half a dozen people saw Charlie Cee and Moishe
get into it. But I'm the only one can cover for Cee after."

"Sell Charlie out? That's pretty cold, Fatback."

"Hey, me and Cee ain't family, you know? If somebody's gotta get whacked over this, better him than us. Got any better ideas?"

"Not yet," Brownie said, rising. "Hang loose, I'll get back to you. Gonna be here?"

"Got nowhere else to be," Fat sighed. "Might want to knock extra hard if you come back, though. I'm gonna lock this place down and turn my jukebox up extra loud. Any way you figure it, I probably won't have it for long."

Outside, Brownie stood at the top of the stairway looking around. According to Fatback, Moishe got tossed at three-thirty. What would he do next? Where would he go?

Nowhere. The answer came to him as surely as the turnaround in an old blues tune. Moishe would never accept getting bounced by a black man. He'd look to get even. And right away. So he wouldn't go anywhere. He'd wait for Fatback or Charlie Cee.

Where?

Only one place. Against the warehouse wall in the shadows of the loading dock. Concealed there, you could watch the door and the stairway and make your move when somebody showed.

Trotting down the stairs, Brownie quickly scanned the area. Spotted the signs almost immediately. Polka dots. Dark droplets, more brownish than red now, spattered across the cardboard boxes that littered the alley floor.

Dried blood. Easy to miss if you weren't looking.

Damn.

Brownie nudged the loose boxes around with the toe of his shoe, half expecting to find a body beneath them. He didn't. Instead he found a battered chipboard guitar case. The name Little Diddley was crudely lettered on the side in white paint. Spattered with polka dots.

"The kid's real name is Jonas Arquette," Fatback said. "Calls hisself Little Diddley 'cause he tries to sing like Bo." They were in Brownie's Studebaker headed down Eighth as the steamy dusk settled over Detroit, darkening the streets without cooling them a single degree.

"Diddley worked for you long?"

"Few weeks. Came up from New Orleans a month or so back, scufflin' for gigs. Boy sings pretty good, plays a mean guitar."

"And works cheap," Brownie added dryly.

"That, too," Fatback grinned. "But it's not like I'm rippin' him off. I gave him a gig playin' after hours, got him a room over at the Delmore Arms where most of the players stay. Figured the kid could make some connections, maybe get hooked up with somethin' steady, you know? And this is how he pays me back. Gets into a jam with the damn jukebox king. Might as well head for the morgue and pick out a slab for hisself."

"Maybe he's already there," Brownie said, wheeling the Stude into the Delmore Arms parking lot. "Cops said they found a stiff in an alley on the Corridor last night, beaten to death."

"You think it was Diddley?"

"They didn't mention a name. Let's find out."

Fatback slipped the Delmore desk clerk a five for a key to the kid's room. He and Brownie rode four floors up, the rickety elevator rattling like a cattle car on the Rock Island Line.

Didn't bother to knock. Fat silently unlocked the door, and the two men warily edged into the dark room. Brownie switched on the light.

"Aw, man," Fat breathed. A body was on the bed, a tangled mess wrapped in bloodstained sheets. Fatback held a pudgy finger to the kid's throat, shaking his head. "He's alive. But not by much."

"And not for long, no matter how you figure it," Brownie said, gingerly picking up Moishe's bloody razor from the nightstand.

Fat glanced at the razor, his mouth narrowing. Then he slapped the kid. Hard. "Wake up, Jonas! Come on."

Diddley's eyes snapped open, flicked from Fat to Brownie and back again, dazed, terrified. Tried to sit up, then fell back, groaning.

"What happened last night?" Fat asked. "What'd you do?"

"Nothin', I swear," the kid rasped. "It was crazy. I was headin' out like you told me; old dude jumped me. Never said nothin' to me, just come out of the dark with a razor. Moved like lightning. Must've cut me five times before I knew what the hell was happenin'."

"Then why aren't you dead?" Brownie asked reasonably. "Moishe is."

"The old dude's dead?"

"You know damn well he is," Fat growled. "You did him."

"No," the kid said, wincing, remembering. "I was holdin' my guitar in front of me, just tryin' to stay alive. His razor stuck in the case. I grabbed it, swung at him a couple of times, just lookin' to back him off me, you know? He took off runnin' one way, I went the other. Came back here. Snuck in. Guess I passed out. Damn, I gotta go back. I lost my guitar."

"Relax, I've got it in my car," Brownie said. "You stay still or you'll start bleedin' again."

Turning away. he motioned Fatback over.

"Now what?"

"He's cut up pretty bad," Fat shrugged. "Needs a doctor."

"If we take him to a hospital like he is, Moishe's people are gonna hear about it five minutes later. We might as well shoot him now, save them the trouble."

"Maybe he's got it comin'," Fat said evenly. "He's the one that mixed it up with the jukebox king."

"It wasn't his fault and you know it. Moishe didn't know who the kid was and didn't care. After you bounced him, he jumped the first black man who came down those steps. Could've been you, me, anybody."

"That's Diddley's tough luck."

"And ours, too. Diddley works for you, Fat, and I dropped Moishe off at your place. Tony Junior's mob is so paranoid they'll figure we set Moishe up for the Italians. We can hand the kid over to 'em gift-wrapped and still get killed."

"So? What do we do? Dummy up, hope this blows over?"

"Can't. We found the kid, it's only a matter of time before they do, too. Do you know a doctor who can keep his mouth shut?"

"My brother-in-law's a medic, ex-army."

"He'll have to do. Get him over here, patch the kid up. But no hospital."

"You got somethin' in mind, Brownie?"

"Hell, no."

Brownie sighed, wrapping the bloody razor in his handkerchief, slipping it into his pocket. "All I know is it's too damn hot to think straight, and I'm tired of bein' pushed around. I'm ready to push back. How 'bout you, Fat? You up for some trouble?"

"Do I have a choice?"

"No," Brownie grinned. "Come to think of it, I guess you don't."

*

Waiting in the air-conditioned lobby of Churchill's Grill, Tony Zeman, Jr., felt a twinge of unease. He'd sent Red for the car five minutes ago. What was the holdup? He was about to head back into the restaurant when his black Lincoln rolled up out front. A pudgy black valet in a blue blazer opened the rear door and stood aside, smiling.

But as Tony climbed into the Lincoln, the valet scrambled in after him, closing the door, seizing his wrists with one hand as he jerked Tony's pistol out of its shoulder holster. "Don't do nothin' sudden, Mr. Zeman," Brownie said, gunning the Lincoln into traffic on Woodward. "We just want to talk."

"What the hell is this?" Junior blustered, eyeing the gun in Fatback's huge fist, trying to conceal his panic. "Where's my driver? Where's Red?"

"Back at the bar answering a bogus phone call. By the way, Red's way too dumb to be your bodyguard, Mr. Zeman. You need to hire better people."

"I'll look into it," Tony Junior said grimly. "What do you want, Brownie?"

"To give you a present," Brownie said, nodding at Fatback. Fat took a handkerchief out of his valet's blazer and laid it carefully on Junior's lap.

Junior hesitated a moment, then peeled back the linen to reveal the bloody razor. "My god."

"You recognize it?" Fatback asked.

"It's my uncle's. Where did you get it?"

"Bought it from some street kids. They took it off a body they found in an alley on Eighth last night."

"What body?"

"The guy your uncle beat to death before he died of his wounds. The guy who killed him."

"Who was he?"

"I don't know his name, but with your connections you should be able to find out easy enough. He's down at the city morgue. Unidentified body number fifty-four."

"Was he a professional? Was it a mob hit?"

"Not likely. No pro would have taken on your uncle one-on-one with a blade. Looks like it was a street scuffle that went bad for both of 'em. You know how your uncle was when he was drinkin,' right?"

"I know how he was," Junior nodded, "but I don't know about you. Why should I believe you? How do I know you're not —"

"— working for the Italians?" Brownie grinned. "Because you're still breathin', young stud. If we were with those guys, you'd already be dead. Instead . . ." Brownie eased the Lincoln quietly to the curb and stopped. "We'll be getting out here. And congratulations, Mr. Zeman. You're the new jukebox king. Can I offer you some friendly advice?"

"Like what?" Junior said, swallowing, still half expecting a bullet from his own gun.

"The guy that turned up in the alley? Nobody knows what happened to him. You might want to put the word out that you happened to him, Mr. Zeman. That it was your people who took him down. Show the Italians how quick you can take out the trash."

"I'll think about it," Junior said, climbing warily out of the car, sliding behind the wheel.

"And my loan?" Brownie pressed. "We're even now, right?"

"I'll think about that, too," Tony yelled, mashing the gas.

The Lincoln tore off into the night, tires howling. Leaving Brownie and Fat standing at the curb. Next to Brownie's emerald green Studebaker. "Jukebox king," Fatback snorted. "You think you can trust that punk?"

"We can trust him to look out for number one," Brownie said. "Junior's in law school, so he must be at least half smart. And taking credit for the stiff in the alley is a smart move. If he goes for it, the kid's off the hook. And so are we."

"What loan were you talking about?"

"It doesn't matter. He'll weasel on the deal. I owe him six large, and those white boys are killin' each other over jukebox quarters."

"Them quarters add up."

"To what? Bleedin' out in an alley? All I know about jukes is what's on 'em. John Lee Hooker, Muddy Waters, they're the real jukebox kings. People will be playin' their music a hundred years from now. Nobody'll care who got the quarters."

"We might care. If it was us."

"Meaning what?"

"After seein' Junior up close, I ain't sure he's smart enough to hang onto the jukebox business, Brownie. Or tough enough."

"You want to be the jukebox king, Fat? Like Moishe? Look what it got him."

"Okay, maybe not a king," Fatback conceded. "Too risky. I ain't sayin' we should try to grab up the whole thing. But maybe we could take back the action around the Corridor. In our end of town."

"Like . . . jukebox princes?"

"Yeah, that's it," Fatback said with satisfaction, his vast face brightening. "Jukebox princes. Listen here, after you close up tonight, why don't you come on down to my place. We'll shoot us some pool, drink some beers. And figure out how to be jukebox princes. What do you say?"

"Gotta admit it does sound interesting," Brownie nodded, mulling it over. "Jukebox princes? Yeah. Why not?"

CHRISTOPHER CHAMBERS

Aardvark to Aztec

FROM *Washington Square*

MIRANDA WHEELER was against adultery in theory. She had been raised uptight and proper, if not churchgoing, her parents nominally Episcopalian or the like, and she had occasioned to sin far more in her mind than in practice. Though not a classic beauty like of film or supermarket fashion magazines, she was not bad to look at with almost always a pleasant smile. Her body attracted male notice and comment even now at thirty-one, and after one kid, causing her some embarrassment and an uneasy glow. Fit and curvy in all the right places, she carried herself with an awkward charm, as if her body were a new pair of shoes that did not quite fit. She worked during the school year as a teacher's aide at Laurel Elementary, where little Duff Jr. would enter fourth grade in the fall.

Miranda ran into a clown outside the Krusty Kreme. She watched through the cracked windshield in disbelief as he stumbled in sad comedy in front of her car, tripping on his oversize shoes to sprawl with a sorry thud full length onto the sun-faded hood of the Nova. His orange wig lolled against the windshield for a moment like an obscene, alien fruit. Miranda stopped the car. She got out and touched hesitantly the gaudy shoulder of the prone buffoon, his Hot Now — Indulge! sandwich board underfoot. The manager appeared, sweating profusely, and most solicitous of Miranda. He fired the clown after determining he was unhurt. Miranda felt awful.

She offered to buy the clown, whose name was Josh, a cup of coffee at a neighboring franchise. And so Miranda sat at a concrete picnic table overlooking the frontage road, eating Krusty Kremes and drinking coffee with a surprisingly charming, though unemployed, clown. They talked about little or nothing as the world drove by. She could not remember when she had last laughed so.

When school let out the following week, Miranda drove Duff Jr. to her parents in Jackson for a break so she and Duff could work some things out. In the days that followed, Duff left for work, and Miranda cleaned the empty house and read paperback novels, waiting for Duff to come home. Some evenings they would fall asleep watching garishly colored classic films on their new big-screen television. As the days passed, she found herself thinking, and smiling at the memory, and wondering what had become of the clumsy clown.

Miranda's husband, Duff, a former high school athlete, was senior sales consultant at a local car lot. Duff spent his days lounging among clean, expensive automobiles in a clean, well-lit showroom, getting people into cars. What would it take to get you into this car today? he'd ask. He typically draped the jacket of his pricey suit over a chair, rolled up the starched white sleeves of his shirt, and loosened the knot of his power tie. People are drawn to the appearance of success, he told Miranda, they are made comfortable by the image of a man at ease in his surroundings. And when they are comfortable, they buy.

Duff surreptitiously snorted cocaine in the stalls in the employee restroom throughout the day. He did not approve of illicit drug use in general, but had found the occasional toot gave him an edge in a keenly competitive marketplace. This was not recreation. This was business. Life or death, success or failure. No different than the gridiron and the steroids old Doc Highfield slipped to a few select starters on Laurel High's state-champ football team in the glory years of the late seventies.

Josh, local college boy and ex-clown, working his way down the blistering street, came hopefully to Miranda's door, as to all the others, peddling his encyclopedias. Miranda had just finished a lawyerly murder mystery when the knock came at the door. She peered judiciously out at the traveling salesman. Stared in disbelief. He shimmered like a mirage in the heat on her stoop.

"You're that clown," she finally said, though his shoes fit, proportional, and his hair was no longer orange. She invited him in. They could not afford a set of encyclopedias what with Duff's erratic sales record and her own meager unemployment check, but it was unbearably hot outside. The dead of June, most languorous month.

Josh stood inside the door, settling into the air-conditioning, his sweat cooling pleasurably. He accepted her offer of a cold drink.

From the kitchen, Miranda, pouring iced tea, called out to him. "Sweet or unsweet?"

"Sweet, please, ma'am," he replied. This being the South, certain social graces endured.

"So, selling encyclopedias now?" Miranda returned to the room.

"Yes, ma'am." Josh took the glass from her hand, thanked her, and drank deeply.

Josh was downright shy without the clown costume. The outfit had afforded him a *joi de vivre* which he was unable to muster as himself, and so he sorely missed his old job. He had not yet mastered the art of small talk, and made up for the lack of it with politeness and his unconscious youth. The conversation that ensued was borne by Miranda then, who tended to talk quickly and without stop when nervous, non sequitur ad infinitum. When she finally paused, she felt a bit lightheaded from her oratory. She fanned herself with a brochure. Josh's glass was empty, the sample case of *Encyclopedia Americana*s forgotten at his sneakered feet. Miranda looked at Josh as if truly seeing him for the first time. He was of indeterminate ancestry, sunburned, tall, and handsome in an ungainly sort of way.

In considerable silence, they sat upon the sofa, which had come to Miranda from her parents. She'd covered the horrible thing — upholstered in Civil War battle scenes, a dark brocade — with a cheery yellow blanket. Miranda reached out and touched the boy's face, a gesture more maternal than seductive. And yet he shivered involuntarily and she felt the shiver course through her like a fond memory, or a low-voltage electrical current. For Josh, this moment seemed his highest dream come true. A full-grown woman in a cool faint before him, her cotton summer dress slightly askew. This was not *Playboy*, or *Hustler* even. She was real. Flesh and blood, as they say. There was a moment more of silence. Trembling, Josh wound up and reached out to touch lightly a coffee-colored mole on the low inside of Miranda's left leg. She sighed in spite of herself.

"No. Please, don't," she said, "stop." But she did not move away.

"I'm sorry," he said. "It's like I'm under your spell." Josh looked away, as if to fight his awful urges. He was painfully aroused, and lyrics from pop songs suddenly true came unbidden into his mind. A high-fidelity system gleamed in the corner, bought on credit from Circuit Circus. "Nice stereo, ma'am."

"Call me Miranda," said Miranda. She stood unsteadily and walked across the room. Inhaled deeply. She drew closed the draperies. The cheap sandals on her feet felt awkward and cheap. She kicked them off, sending them sailing into a lamp and Duff's La-Z-Boy, respectively. Miranda selected Vivaldi's *Four Seasons,* a recording by the Atlanta Philharmonic. As a child she'd studied briefly the violin, and she still loved the strings. She returned to the sofa slowly, her bare feet gripping the shag, the great hopeful swelling of the first movement all around her. Spring, was it? She had been in school for physical therapy, spring semester, when she got pregnant with Duff Jr.

Duff cringed at the ringing of the phone on his desk. The conversation was brief and hushed. He covered the mouthpiece with his hand, and warily eyed the office door.

"Listen . . ."

"Yeah, but . . ."

"Aw, man . . ."

"All right, all right . . ."

"But . . ."

"O.K. All right. Friday."

"Friday. I swear." Duff replaced the receiver, clenched his teeth, and mopped his beaded brow. "Son-of-a-bitch."

He searched his shelves for something small to break, hefted but replaced unharmed his golfing trophy, a dusty Salesman of the Week plaque. He picked up the framed glossy of Miranda and little Duff Jr. He gazed upon his lovely wife and his only issue, chip off his block. There was one thing he could do. He fogged the nonglare glass with his shaky breath, buffed it to a shine with his shirttail, and replaced it to its place of prominence on his desk.

Duff straightened up, the old fighting spirit rising in him. It was time to sell cars.

Miranda sat beside Josh and kissed him abruptly on the mouth. Then looked him eye to eye.

"I'm not, I don't ever, don't do things like this," she said truthfully. "I can't, well, you know. But if you want, if we're careful, we can, maybe, sort of. Only so far."

"Okay," said Josh.

He was on her at once, eager to please, his hands and his mouth here and there, careful, lightly and firm, grasping, finessing. He had studied for this moment. Miranda pushed aside her awkward childhood, her rumbling guilt. Plenty of time for that later, she thought. Time only now for this traveling heaven. Josh knelt on the floor and kissed her on both knees, and then the mole that she always had hated. His mouth moved up her leg, his hot breath saying something profound to her on a cellular level, though his words were too muffled to make out. Miranda thanked god she'd taken a shower that morning, and buried her hands in his hair, guiding his enthusiasm onward and upward.

Duff, across town in a stall in the men's room at Jeff Davis Honda, snuffed with vigor. He licked his finger, and wiped the paper bindle clean of its powdery residue and paused. He peered at the small, unfolded piece of paper, the glossy image of a fleshy cheek or inner thigh, a curve of breast perhaps. The Frenchman folded his gram bindles from the pages of skin mags. Pervert, thought Duff, dropping the piece of paper into the toilet bowl. He rubbed his gums, depressed the handle of the toilet with a polished wingtip, and exited the stall.

In his office waited a distinguished professor from the college and his youthful second wife, teetering on the brink of a new red D'Accord LX. Duff consulted his granddaddy's pocket watch and sniffed again, admiring the smooth, ancestral sweep of the second hand, and savored the metallic drip at the back of his throat. He'd give them another five minutes. Enough time to call the wife. He would close this sale and knock off early, play the back nine at the public course, and maybe celebrate with happy hour at Maxi's Lounge.

Duff called home from an empty office, and got his own voice on the answering machine. Annoyed, he hung up on himself. In the next office, the professor and his wife discussed options and finances in intimate whispers. Duff counted down, took a deep breath, and burst in beaming.

"Good news, folks," he began. "I just talked to my boss, and he says I can knock two bills off the luxury package. This one time." Duff paused significantly to let the full import sink in. "You can't tell a soul," he went on with a conspiratorial wink. "I'm taking a beating on this. Because I know you want to get into this car today. What do you say?"

They signed the papers, the tweedy intellectual and his young missus. Duff awarded them the keys and firmly shook their hands, a little extra squeeze for the little lady. What does she see in this stuffy old fart, he wondered, a typical pinhead up on his Dante and Shakespeare but unable to change a flat or sink a ten-foot putt. And they looked happy. Duff hustled them out the door, chalked his sale up on the big board, and headed for the links in his Interlude demo. En route, pumped up victorious, he called home again on the cellular, this time recording a message on the machine.

"Miranda, baby. Made a big sale, and hard working on yet another. I'll be late, so don't wait up. Oh yeah. Don't forget my dry cleaning. Love ya." A kissing noise.

Miranda, sufficiently satiated and repositioned by this time, heard Duff's distant disembodied voice in the other room, and paused in her ministrations, her head in Josh's lap. The machine clicked *off.* Like in a dream she was. She had forgotten the dry cleaning. She had forgotten much of the past ten years in the recent throes of Josh's tireless exuberance. Indeed, she had almost forgotten. How much fun. It had only seemed fair to reciprocate.

The erstwhile clown was now sprawled back on the yellow-blanketed sofa, limbs outstretched as if he'd been hit by a bread truck. They were nearing the moment of truth, the fork in the road that Miranda recalled from her brief honeymoon, dates with Duff, and a few other early intimate encounters with males of the species. She had never much liked this part of things, so was surprised to find an odd thrill in bringing this polite young man to apparently new heights of ecstasy. He did not touch her, as if he were afraid of breaking the spell, and she felt in complete control of him by virtue of simple manipulations of his proud appendage. The mixture of power and pleasing was an intoxicating one. But, the decision.

On the one hand, no pun, there was the imminent mess to consider — her hand, the sofa cover, her dress, perhaps even her hair. And further then, the evidence of guilt, feelings of foolishness, and deep regret intensified by the chore of cleanup. Her idly stroking hand stopped as she pondered, and Josh returned reluctantly to the world.

"Please," he implored in a voice weak with want. "Miranda, oh, please."

"Mmm," said Miranda. "Okay . . ." And she, eyes closed, again hungrily, as if savoring the last fresh forbidden pastry in the box. He whispered endearments in quick, shallow breaths. Miranda persisted, and, and, and, oh, primly swallowed.

Josh, overwhelmed, hugged her, and kissed her, but Miranda only tucked in his shirt and pushed him gently toward the door.

"That was so, I mean, I think," he stammered, "I think I love, and must see you again. Oh, Miranda."

"Don't be silly." Miranda handed him his sample case, and opened the door. The breathtaking heat walloped them. "This should not have happened, and never did. I hope you sell some encyclopedias. And never give up on your dreams. Now go."

Josh stepped back onto the stoop and attempted again to express his jumbled feelings.

"Miranda, I understand, but I must, you see . . ."

"Good-bye, Josh."

The door closed on him and he was left alone in the heat of the afternoon. The sweat began again on his brow, and down below this new ache. Josh got into his car, dazed, and drove home. He could no longer sell encyclopedias today. He needed to think. He had plans to return to State in the fall, to finish that degree in Marketing, again pursue the perpetually cheerful, perky coeds, and so on. But all that seemed dull now in the wake of this moment with Miranda, his first true taste of earth and heaven. A future without Miranda seemed no future at all.

Josh paced the floor of his efficiency down by the tracks, clutching the fateful lead he'd received with the others just that morning —

Leach, Miranda and Duff, one child, address and phone. He authored great fantasies in which he rescued Miranda from her suburban limbo, from the boorish Duff who no doubt took for granted his inimitable wife, forcing her to cook and deliver dry cleaning for him, to live in a modest ranch house, its walls decorated with duck-hunting prints in gilt frames.

In Josh's elaborate fantasies, a balding, pot-bellied Duff wore a dirty, sleeveless undershirt and needed a shave. Poor Miranda, distraught in a simple blue dress that accentuated her fine form, was torn between her vows to this ruffian and her true new love for Josh. Our hero appeared on the scene righteous and reassuring, sometimes here quoting scripture, and the greatest of these is love, and there dispatching Duff with an honest haymaker to his stubbly chin. Sometimes he, Duff, merely belched drunkenly from his La-Z-Boy, and dismissed them both without looking away from the Braves game.

From here the fantasies soared. Josh and Miranda living, scantily clad, in a beach hut on Dauphin Island or some equally exotic locale. Josh and Miranda with their own Chik-Fee-Lay franchise, working side-by-side in sanitary whites, pores slick with vegetable oil, returning home nightly for endless lovemaking in their high-rise condo. Josh and Miranda et cetera. Yet all the while, understandably, tragically, Josh overlooked one important character, young Duff Jr., who was at the moment engaged in electronic mayhem at Mamaw and Papaw's in Jackson, unleashing an awful, vicarious firepower, joystick clutched in his innocent paw, the inevitable carnage piling up.

Duff ordered the chicken breast sandwich and grinned at the waitress in her faux French maid's uniform. He tipped her a dollar for his next Coke and bourbon. He wondered how old she was, and idly wondered, if he were single again. Oh, but, he did love Miranda, he thought, mildly maudlin. The commission on the D'Accord would hold them to the end of the month, and keep the Frenchman off his back for a while. Though Duff would still be into him for almost a grand.

He had hoped to sell most of the last eight ball to cover his own, and maybe make a little on top. But it had been a tough week on the sales floor at Jeff Davis. And he'd traded one gram to a black guy in the service department for a snubnose .38 Special. He didn't quite know why. Except perhaps that the Frenchman, a gap-toothed goon who'd played left wing one season for the Winnipeg Jets, gave him no respect. The revolver made Duff feel dangerous, like a body worthy of respect. He knew he would never use the piece, but the comfort of its weighty little bulk, its combat grips, in the Honda's glove box put some resolve in his step.

Miranda brushed her teeth and gargled with minty-fresh mouth-wash. She appraised herself in the mirror. A few gray hairs amongst the brown, crow's-feet at the corner of her dark eyes. She missed Duff Jr. and Duff, who was never home, it seemed. She tried to smile, and only shook her head saying no, no, no, no, no, never again. I must put this out of my head, and never, never again. She wondered if perhaps she should have bought the encyclopedias for Duff Jr. Or the first volume anyway. Perhaps she could call Josh. But she knew that would not do. She needed to get away. A weekend on the Gulf. A real family vacation. She resolved to make her appeal to Duff and collect her son from the folks.

Josh tried to watch the television, but he could not concentrate. His mind runneth over with Miranda. He turned off the set. He tried to recall her words, but they were lost already, and she herself was fading with them. He could not see her face complete. Perhaps the eyes, her crinkled smile. He could see her dress, the vague shape of her, but only clearly the mole, and the sweet, woodsy smell of her. He had to see her again, if only to commit her forever to his memory. He sat at his little desk to write. He poured it all out onto page upon page. His great, illicit love. The sun sank, but the heat remained in the near dark, lingering like a villain. Josh, freshly showered, dressed in his best white tee and khaki chinos. He pulled on the orange wig for courage, and strode to his car.

Duff finished the tasty chicken breast sandwich, one last Coke and bourbon. He paid with a credit card, and halfheartedly invited the waitress aside for a blast, a snort, a pick-me-up. She politely de-clined, the way she always did. And Duff left alone. Some relieved, if truth be told. Savoring his lonesome liquored blues. In the park-ing lot, a quick line for the road. He dreaded to go home these days, and as often wondered why. How could this have come to pass? he wondered. And so, vintage Black Sabbath in the optional tape deck, Duff pounded the dashboard as he drove, the righteous beat of his yearned-for youth, and wailed along with the awful words.

Miranda showered and dressed in jeans and a t-shirt. The yellow throw off the sofa and into the washer with an extra splash of cleansing Tide. She remembered Duff's dry cleaning, and rushed off in the old Chevy. The dry cleaner would close soon. The heat of the day, only slightly diminished, came in through the car's open windows like a free sample of hell. A strange glow of sunset about the town. Otherworldly, Miranda thought. And as she maneuvered through the evening traffic, she willed them all together in a beachfront timeshare. Duff, herself, and spunky Duff Jr.

Josh drove a secondhand Mustang, ragtop, car of his dreams. Bought and paid for. In the back seat, his livelihood, a carton of *Encyclopedia Americana,* volume one. Aardvark to Aztec. Gold-embossed blue leatherette. Riding shotgun, his letter explaining himself to Miranda, handwritten on lined yellow paper, folded neatly in thirds. He would give it to her inside the complimentary copy of volume one that he'd neglected in all the excitement to leave this afternoon. Tucked arbitrarily into the page for Amaryllis. A flower and name from some forgotten studies. A pretty word, illustrated, for this thing between them. The rest would be up to her.

Miranda, Duff, and Josh, three residents of one town, on the road. Theirs was not a small town, but not big either. It is certainly conceivable that three cars leaving different places for the same destination could cross paths, perhaps even collide, given the poor driving skills of most on the road. But they did not. Duff arrived home first, parked in the drive, and noticed that the Chevy was gone. A late-model Mustang in fair condition pulled up across the street. A convertible with the V-8 option. Duff looked in the rearview mirror, but could not clearly see the wild-haired driver in the feeble light. That dent in the front left quarter panel would sure reduce the trade-in value. No one got out of the car, and Duff began to sweat. A henchman of the Frenchman, he wildly imagined. He tried to calm himself, but took the pistol from the glove box nonetheless, and slipped it into the waistband of his slacks.

*

Josh sat in his car, his heart pounding wildly. He watched a well-dressed man get out of a new Honda and walk toward Miranda's door. The man stopped and turned to peer across the street. Josh was sitting motionless in the dark car praying when he was momentarily lit up in her headlights. Stricken, you might say. Like an armadillo on the centerline.

The old Chevy approached, pulled in the drive, and parked beside the Honda. Miranda emerged from the car with a load of dry cleaning. Duff walked out to meet her.

"The Gulf, Duff, this time of year," she began.

Josh got out of his car and stepped into the street.

"I must," he called out. "Just one moment, please. This cannot wait." He used his firmest voice.

"You leave her out of this," Duff yelled in reply, brushing past Miranda. "I told him Friday."

Miranda looked at Duff, and Josh. She put a hand on Duff's arm, to steer him into the house.

"It's some crazy kid. Let's go inside."

Josh stepped closer.

"You think I'm scared of you?" said Duff. "Think again, punk." But Duff was scared — scared of losing, scared of pain, scared of growing older in a world devoid of meaning, a world inhabited by violent ex-hockey players and their psychotic, orange-haired thugs.

Miranda took Duff's arm. He shrugged her off a bit roughly. She dropped the dry cleaning. She felt suddenly very small, in the midst of big, big events spinning ever out of control around her.

"I have something for you," Josh called to Miranda, continuing on.

"No," said Miranda.

"I got something for you, too, you fuck," replied Duff.

Miranda afterwards recalled being knocked to the parched lawn by the scuffle, the smell of the soil, and Duff's stiff, clean shirts blue-white in the dim streetlight. The clumsy sounds of struggle, and exhalations. And then a gunshot. How strange, she thought, that she knew immediately it was a gunshot, having never heard one before, except at the movies and on TV. And like on TV, the porch lights came on, up and down her street, and soon there were sirens in the distance. The world became new, her life important. Newsworthy.

Miranda stood then, and gathered herself and the dry cleaning.

She walked over to Duff and handed him his shirts, but one. He stood as if struck deaf and dumb.

"Go call an ambulance, honey."

She knelt next to the young man who lay wide-eyed on their lawn with his hand wetly to his stomach. She cradled his head in her lap, gently straightened his wig, and pressed a clean white shirt to the dark wound.

"Go on, Duff."

And Duff went dumbly. The front door closed behind him, and the sirens came louder.

"I'm dying, aren't I?" said Josh.

"Yes," said Miranda, who believed in being truthful at times like this.

"I had to see you again."

"I wish that you hadn't."

"The first volume," said Josh, "is yours to keep, and, I think, I love you."

Miranda picked up the book from where it had sprawled on the lawn, and with it, the letter and all it contained.

"Thank you, Josh," she said. She brushed gently the blue leatherette. "Everything's going to be all right."

But she knew that everything would not. Those were only words from a song she used to know. Miranda once more touched his face. She held him as she would Duff Jr. until an ambulance came and took the boy away. She went inside, carrying *Aardvark to Aztec*. On the empty front lawn, a blue-white shirt, darkly stained, forgotten.

Miranda made a pot of coffee for Duff, and for the cops when they arrived. In the living room they asked Duff the perfunctory questions, sympathetic of a man in defense of his wife and his home. One had played ball with Duff back at High. They talked. The old, good times. The wanton state of kids today. Firepower and home defense. A compliment on the elaborate martial pattern of the sofa.

Miranda, meanwhile, sat on the back steps, thinking about Australia, its climate, economy, quality of education. She smoked one of Duff's cigarettes, the first volume of the encyclopedia in her lap, heavy with facts and possibility. She thought and smoked, and carefully burned the handwritten letter in the barbecue grill, gently feeding it into the small blue flame one page at a time.

CHRISTOPHER COOK

The Pickpocket

FROM *Measures of Poison*

MY NAME is Christian Richelieu. A good name, all in all, and famous on both counts, though neither appreciably influenced my life.

That I don't believe in a Messiah practically goes without saying. The notion that a Saviour will rescue us from loneliness and despair would amuse me if not for the misery. But the yearning I see etched on troubled faces in the street is sincere and I don't laugh.

The cardinal at least was French, like me, and being a politician and a pragmatist, he did not wait but sought solace in this life. Perhaps he found it. Who knows? Still, he was first a great moralist, then a tireless sinner, and I am neither.

I am simply amoral.

So much for my name, which is more interesting than my appearance. In looks I am suitably ordinary, an advantage in my profession, and that's all that needs saying.

I have been a pickpocket since I was a boy when Moses Marchant taught me the trade. A native of Algiers, Moses had reached his twilight years by then. He was a stoop-shouldered pied-noir who emigrated to Paris just after the war and lived in the same rundown tenement building as my parents near Place d'Italie. He smelled of patchouli and belched garlic and smoked a filthy clay pipe. He muttered constantly.

Moses lived on the floor above us. I used to watch him in the stairwell, shuffling up the steps in a cloud of tobacco smoke mingled with an incomprehensible amalgam of mumbled Arabic and

French. My parents were young and my grandparents were dead, so Moses represented for me that decrepitude of old age so difficult to comprehend in youth. Indoors and out, he wore a tattered burgundy fez.

I must have been fifteen or sixteen when Moses took an interest in me. Cataracts had ruined his eyesight and he was crippled from the arthritis that put him out of business, but he was a good teacher, very thorough and demanding. If I sometimes seem critical of the way others behave nowadays, it's because Moses taught me that pride in one's work gives purpose in a world abandoned by both God and man. He preached that tenet tirelessly and I've never found reason to disagree.

Back then the practitioners of my trade respected the craft. In the argot, we called ourselves *voleurs à la tire,* which means "pulling thieves." When we met one another in the street we tilted our heads in mutual and silent recognition. We were courteous. In those days the civilized world had not yet begun its decline. Even a pickpocket took pride in his profession. He acquired his skills by hard work. It required self-discipline. Initiation demanded a price, a commitment. Frankly, we considered our vocation a kind of art.

In the beginning, Moses made me practice in his apartment. Day after day I played truant from school, learning the tricks on a dummy constructed by stuffing an old suit with a blanket. Then Moses pulled on a red velvet smoking jacket I had never seen before — it smelled of mold and mothballs — and I practiced on him. It was tedious work, very demanding. Moses was especially critical and boxed my ears when my attention wandered. "Learn to concentrate!" he scolded me. "A man who controls his mind controls his destiny." Naturally, this was difficult. The adolescent mind is a wild horse. But I tried and with time my ears became less tender. The idea of controlling my destiny appealed to me. Even now, after all this time, it attracts me.

After six months, Moses began to drill me in public. He insisted I pick his pockets on the Métro, in the markets, on street corners. Finally he permitted a real pick. He called it my baptism.

I lifted the wallet of a hulking giant of a man in Gare St. Lazare during rush hour. He was running for a train and Moses stepped in front of him. The man tripped and fell, cursing. I helped him to his feet and he angrily pushed me away. In the men's room I opened the wallet and found six hundred francs, a faded picture of his wife, the telephone numbers of several prostitutes listed with their going rates, and a packet of condoms. I kept everything but the wallet and photo, though his wife was not a bad-looking woman, with blond curls and a sad smile.

That was long ago. I will turn sixty-three next month. The work is exacting but does not wear a person down like physical labor or an office job with its politics. I could retire today if I wished. I have been careful with my money, certainly more careful than others.

To tell my life's story would take too long. Besides, most of it is humdrum, the same as any other life. I was married but we argued and divorced. My two children are grown now. They lead conventional lives and I see them but they have their own concerns. I live in an apartment. I have been betrayed in love and have acted badly myself. I am quite selfish. I vacation on the coast, watch my weight, eat fish instead of meat, and exercise by walking in the Jardin du Luxembourg. Gravity has exacted its customary dues and my lower back often aches. My prostate acts up, nothing unusual at my age. I live alone but have a mistress who complains and several close friends. I appreciate good wine and enjoy music. I lead a quiet life. I don't expect much from others and have not been disappointed. So, as I said, it is an ordinary life in almost every respect.

It is the work — my work — which is of interest. No doubt, it seems romantic in a way. No boss, no set hours. Plenty of time to think or daydream. Living by one's wits, a real challenge. While all that is true, it is still work. It is my profession, my trade, full of demands like any other. I do not let myself forget that. The person who forgets, who becomes lazy, who practices the craft by habit, lands in jail. He becomes his own victim.

Still, the idea of my livelihood intrigues people. They want details, the more exotic the better. I have overheard victims of pickpockets actually boast of their misfortune, having received a kind of vicarious thrill. But as with any job the extraordinary events occur infrequently. Between, there are protracted lulls, even monotony.

How then to dispassionately describe my vocation? Perhaps it would be easiest to recount three incidents which I readily recall. Each in its own way better describes what I do than anything I might otherwise tell.

*

The first incident concerns the things people carry. Most of what I find in wallets is routine: credit cards, photos, ticket stubs, receipts. If contents are a gauge, then the average life is remarkably mundane, even more so than mine. No wonder so many feel restless! Pockets also contain scads of things I never take — passports, lighters, pens. If I was a burglar, I might be a millionaire. People are surprisingly careless with keys.

But on occasion something catches me off-guard. In a wallet at Gare de Lyon only last week I discovered a small bag of heroin. Once at Musée Picasso I was flabbergasted to see I'd filched the ID card of an FBI agent. He was part of an American tour group. I left the museum immediately, having heard enough about those cowboys to give wide berth. Another time I reached into a pocket on an escalator in Les Halles and felt a gun. That provoked another well-timed retreat. I know how to calculate risks. Violence does not interest me.

Everything but cash goes into the nearest safe trash can. Moses twisted my ear that first day in Gare St. Lazare when I kept the prostitutes' numbers and the condoms. "You think they'll visit you in jail?" he asked. "Show some sense!" Disgusted, he took his cut of the money and threw the other things away. He had forgotten the carnal desires that surge through a young man day and night. Just think how many flames three hundred francs might quench! But I learned the lesson. The trash can gets all but the cash. It is an unfortunate policy, I know. People who lose their wallets are terribly inconvenienced. Replacing official papers and credit cards is a bother. All the same, it is an absolute necessity and part of the self-discipline. To permit sympathy to override this requisite is to invite disaster.

Of course, most in the trade these days keep the credit cards and fence them. For several years after Moses died, when credit cards came into common use, I did, too. But now such fraud has become big business. The people you meet in that line seem sleazy. They run in packs and can't be trusted. Among those thieves, there is no honor. I avoid them. This may sound strange, but whenever thieves become organized they also become corrupt. Better to work alone.

The incident I have in mind occurred at the Centre Georges Pompidou several years ago. The curators had put together an exhibit of Brassaï photographs that I admired. While leaving the gallery, I bumped into a man and reflexively picked his trousers pocket. I wasn't even working that day. In the toilet I was disappointed to see less than twenty francs. If the pick had required effort it wouldn't have been worth it. From the condition of the wallet, I gathered the man was either mindless of appearances or down on his luck.

What caused me to look further I am not sure. But tucked carefully into a corner of the wallet was a folded sheet of paper. I opened it. It was a letter written on hospital stationery and dated the previous year. I read it. It was from the man's wife. Apparently she had written it just before dying. She did not say but it appeared she had a cancer. She had sent her husband a last love letter.

What she wrote was very moving. She described her love for him and said his affection had made life worth living. That same deep affection now made death manageable. She had endured great pain, that much seemed obvious. The final weeks had been a torment. She regretted to die so young. She worried over failings. There was so much left unaccomplished, so much she had postponed. Then there was the physical pain, to which she only alluded. Yet she spoke of when she first met her husband and remembered their first tender kiss. She mentioned a vacation they once took to a beach in Spain. She repeated her devoted affections in every paragraph. This dying woman even managed a private joke, adding, "Ha! You know I'm only kidding!"

Over and again the woman expressed concern for her husband. She urged him to be brave and reassured him that wherever she was after death, she would still be with him. He would never be alone. Their love, she wrote, would conquer death. A trite sentiment, perhaps, but in her letter it seemed plausible. Despite my own opinions on such matters, I found myself believing her. Who possesses the nerve to deny a dying young woman? If she had been my wife, I would have agreed to anything. Her signature was barely legible, a weak scrawl.

Upon finishing the letter, I was overcome with remorse. My hands began to tremble. I sat on the commode and gazed at her signature. Then I began to weep. I knew the letter must be returned to its owner. I carefully refolded it and placed it in my pocket.

What might have been simple became complicated. The man no longer lived at the Montparnasse address in the wallet. I posed as a friend and a neighbor gave me his new address near Gare de l'Est, an unsavory area. But he had moved from there, as well. I finally got another address from the concierge and found him in a fourth-floor walkup in the ghetto of Aubervilliers. With each move he had found cheaper quarters in a more dilapidated building. I supposed that since his wife's death he had fallen into that kind of decline only an unimaginable grief might cause.

When he came to the door I explained myself in a rush of words. I mentioned finding the letter on a bus seat. It looked important, I said, and very personal. Beginning with the hospital, I had tracked him down. I began to perspire and my voice cracked. It was the profound emotion of that letter, no doubt, which I had somehow absorbed. For a moment I lost my head and even said that my own wife had died of cancer not long before. That wild statement was intended to establish motive for all my trouble, I suppose. Surely my efforts to find this man would appear peculiar and invite suspicion.

But he had no such reaction. Instead, he took the letter and broke down sobbing. He was a young man, poorly dressed. He held the paper to his chest. Thank you, thank you, thank you, he cried. He wailed and whimpered like a child. Between the deep sobs and groans, he wiped his nose on a coat sleeve.

I stood in the doorway feeling quite awkward with all the commotion. While the letter from his wife had touched me deeply, his shameless grief now struck me as pathetic. His wife — who was, after all, the one dying — had asked him to be brave. She would always be with him. Their love would conquer death. Yet there he was completely without courage, a broken man.

I saw then how thin he was, the wretched lines of despair eating deeply into his narrow face, and the gloomy disheveled apartment strewn with litter and smelling of decay.

Without saying a word more, I turned on my heel and left. I beat it double-time, taking the stairs three at a time. I needed some fresh air.

Afterward, I realized why my policy of dumping everything into the trash is a good one. What people carry is their own concern.

As you might expect, I do much of my work on the Métro. A salesman has his territory, I have mine, and any territory has its downside.

The city underground is nothing like the one above. Without question, the Métro is a cheerless place. The trains burrow through the tunnels like huge distended worms, their bellies full of commuters, disgorging and engorging the contents at each stop. The people remain silent and disengaged, their sensibilities dulled by the crowds, the noise, the constant motion. The place is dark and humid, a world of hollow shadows and impersonal fatigue, and it smells like a sewer. The boys who spend their days there hawking newspapers resemble rats. In those pinched faces the pale eyes peer furtive and sly. These repulsive creatures scurry from car to car in search of crumbs. The passengers lift their feet and avoid them.

Perhaps I am too harsh. In truth, at times some Métro stations assume the festive milieu of a carnival. Music, gay and loud, echoes through the corridors and up and down the stairwells. Accordions, guitars, saxophones, trumpets, you hear them all. North African *marabouts* offer to tell your fortune. For a few francs more they'll improve your love life and increase your sexual stamina. Angry young men deliver orations about famine, drought, war, unemployment. Puppeteers perform. Feet stamp, lovers smooch. Beggars without legs rattle their cups on the *quai*.

And the peddlers! Legions of vendors wangle peanuts, floral bouquets, and cheap jewelry. These immigrant salesmen have big dreams. From the subterranean atmosphere of beggary and vagrancy there is no direction but up. There in the Métro, budding entrepreneurs become inured to thievery and vice, good training for a career in business.

Altogether, this teeming, clamorous world is not unlike a raucous scene from Dickens or Hugo's lunatic rabble in the Court of Miracles. Ironically, there is little violence. Petty graft prevents serious crime, as any policeman knows. When violence does rarely occur even the most hardened hustler is shocked.

In any case, this underground circus exists and I work there. For a short time, it is intriguing. It appeals to one's fascination with the perverse, like a freak show or blue movie. Repulsive though it is, one cannot help but watch. Of course, the novelty wore off for me long ago. Now when it begins to irritate me, when my eyes grow dim and my skin feels clammy, I seek sunlight. I work Right Bank streets and tourist sites.

I mentioned the Métro musicians, which reminds me of a particular incident I wish to relate. Like the vendors, these musicians are everywhere — in the stations, the corridors, the trains. Some are superb. I think of a courtly old man who plays a violin in the Châtelet station, or a somber young woman in a blue evening gown who sets up her harp at St. Michel.

There are bad ones, too, naturally. A man who played the trumpet once got on the Number 4 line and punished everyone from St. Placide to Les Halles. People held their ears and griped. They got off the train just to escape. On that same line, a tall blond woman with enormous red lips performs as a one-person band. She wears high heels and puts her hair in a beehive. She plays accordion and sings while blowing a harmonica, kazoo, and steel whistle. A tambourine hangs from one arm, a bracelet of bells jangles on an ankle. She is awful but people applaud her energy so her purse overflows with tips.

But the particular musicians I have in mind are a group of South American Indians who frequently appear in the Montparnasse station. They play that eerie, wind-driven music from the Andes. Two bamboo flutes, a guitar, a mandolin, drums, and a gourd rattle. They usually perform during evening rush hour when the money flows best. For fifty francs they sell a recorded cassette tape. They call themselves Andes Wind.

I first heard them from a stairwell in the station. The music was indescribably sweet, both joyful and sad, simple and complex at once. The sound called to me. Irresistibly, I was drawn toward it. Finally I saw them near the central escalator — seven smiling men, short, stocky, with dark skin and thick black hair. Some wore colorful woven ponchos, others beaded cotton jackets. I took a position against the wall and listened. I soon entered into something like a trance.

How is it that some kinds of music make a person feel happy and sad at the same time? Those Andean songs spoke to me that way. I was overcome by a deep melancholy yet felt completely at peace. Though I am not by nature maudlin, now and then the poignancy of profound melancholia has the effect of a purgative. For more than an hour I listened.

In the end, I moved away from the wall to the front of the crowd, as near the musicians as possible. I basked in the exquisite illumi-

nation which swelled over them and flowed through all who listened. It really was quite extraordinary. An open guitar case cluttered with coins and paper notes lay on the floor at their feet. I first
put in one twenty-franc note, then another.

The band finally took a short rest. One of the flute players, a
heavyset fellow who wore long hair in a ponytail, edged through
the crowd accepting donations and selling cassette tapes. When he
gave change, I noticed he carried a large wad of bills in the left
pocket of his beaded jacket. He stopped near me.

On impulse I spoke to the young man and mentioned how the
music seemed quite special. I said it struck me as otherworldly, ce-
lestial, even mystical. I felt a bit embarrassed by my enthusiasm, especially the triviality of my words, but they were sincere and he
agreed with a simple naturalness that put me at ease. I noticed then
that his face emanated the same quality of deep, meditative seren-
ity with which the music resonated in my breast. When he gazed at
me, it seemed for a moment as if something preternatural passed
between us. In my experience, the event was unprecedented. Then
someone touched his arm and he turned away.

I faded into the crowd and left. I went for a long walk down Rue
de Rennes and along St. Germain, still listening to the ethereal
modulations of the flutes reverberating in my head. The curious
sensation stayed with me for the longest time.

When I stopped for couscous in a Tunisian café, I stepped into
the toilet and counted the money. It was a decent take, almost a
thousand francs.

I wondered if the serene young musician had lost his composure.
I hoped not. But he really was so careless and the temptation was
too great. Even artists should show a little responsibility.

The final incident pertains to the current state of my craft. Forgive
me if I complain. It dismays me to watch the people in the trade today, especially the younger ones. They are clumsy and unprepared.
They have no self-respect.

Practice, much less real apprenticeship, never occurs to them.
One need only see them work. One morning they decide to become a pickpocket, that evening they grab for a wallet. These im-
postors have no idea what is required. They lack subtlety. Instead of
skill they depend on violence. If their victim protests they pull a ra-

zor or knife. They pick on the elderly, on single women. They work at night. Naturally, their takings are small, so they double their efforts. Soon everyone feels frightened.

In my opinion, this decadence parallels the decline in the culture. We French are a democratic culture built on aristocratic forms. Hugo warned against erosion, Spengler predicted it. Who listened? Now the debasement of form has become a popular pastime, a disease we import. We send the sun to the west, it sends darkness back.

No doubt some will express astonishment to hear a pickpocket deploring the loss of values, quoting Hugo and Spengler. Such incredulity merely reflects the decline to which I refer. Nowadays we presume only intellectuals and the upper crust are literate, and the latter I seriously doubt. It wasn't always that way. In my generation, even thieves and pimps read books, went to the theatre, listened to Mozart as well as Piaf. I knew a burglar who was a closet poet. Genet became a famous author. So much for stereotypes.

But occasionally a young pickpocket completely surprises me. I recall one day when I had worked the tourist crowds on the Right Bank. Tourists are easy marks for the most part, especially Americans. I always know where an American keeps his wallet. He touches it too often. He is so excited to arrive in the City of Lights that a kind of elation overcomes him and he neglects to think. The brochures warn him but he ignores the precautions.

He is a strangely naive creature, this American. Everything takes him by surprise. He expresses great optimism and is continually disappointed. He considers pessimism a weakness. But he is well organized. In that respect he surpasses even a German. Such a view contradicts orthodox notions, but it is true.

On the day to which I refer, my work had gone especially well. It was the height of tourist season. Sidewalks along the Rue de Rivoli were crowded. Wallets leaped from their pockets. My fingers had never felt so nimble. Near the Louvre, I went from one mark to another. It was like picking grapes. At one point I went home and emptied my pockets, then returned to the street.

In the mid-afternoon I passed an hour in a café. Things were going so well, I had become nervous and needed to calm my nerves. I went back to work and found nothing had changed. I was at the top of my game. Nothing was safe. My fingertips had eyes.

Normally I keep a sharp watch for undercover cops. They are easy enough to spot, like unmarked police cars. Still, one must look for them. Some are cagey and hide behind posts or doorways. That day I felt so confident that when I saw one standing near the Hotel Meurice, I passed behind him and took his wallet.

Such insolence! How audacious! I never would have dared but was possessed by a kind of euphoria, like a golfer who follows one hole-in-one with another. My only regret was that I could not loiter to watch him discover the casualty. I felt tempted to approach him and ask for change just to see his face. But I showed some common sense and resisted. I had had my pleasure. Why tempt fate?

At the intersection of Rue de Rivoli and Place des Pyramides I saw a young man bungle a pick. The pigeon was a stout German tourist wearing loose trousers and a Hawaiian shirt. He started across the street when the signal was still red and jerked the young man's hand. That sort of mistake denotes a novice at work. Never depend on a mark to behave predictably. The German jumped back to the curb and yelled, pointing into the crowd.

But the young man had disappeared. On that score, he performed admirably. I followed him along the sidewalk for several blocks. He turned right onto Rue d'Alger, leaned against a plastered wall, and lit a cigarette. His hands were shaking.

When I approached him he almost bolted. He thought I was an undercover *flic*. He denied the entire affair, claimed he hadn't been near the Place des Pyramides all day. He was adamant. In that way, at least, he showed good judgment. He had reason to be afraid. He easily could have ended up in jail.

I smoked a cigarette with him. He calmed down. We talked. He was a handsome kid, dark hair and blue eyes with long lashes. He had the angular and delicate boyish features so many women seem to favor in men. At the same time, his bearing exuded a certain brazen confidence that appealed to me. He wore a gold earring in his left ear.

It turned out the young man was from Lyon, had recently arrived in Paris, was determined not to work in a deadly nine-to-five job. I took him over to the Au Chien Qui Fume on the Rue du Pont Neuf and bought him dinner. He evidently had not eaten in some time.

Afterward we walked in the Jardin des Tuileries and I gave him some pointers. It was basic information: how to recognize an undercover cop, not to try anything on an elevator where there's no escape route, never work the same place two days in a row. These I had learned from Moses Marchant long ago. For me they had become second nature. Repeating them brought back fond memories of Moses, and I began to consider taking on the young man — his name was Sebastien — as an apprentice, much as Moses had done for me.

But something Sebastien said turned me against the idea. He said he intended to get rich quick and retire to Corsica. Before the age of thirty, he said. He was quite serious. He wanted to live on a boat and lie in the sun all day sipping pastis.

If there is a single greatest danger in my trade, it is greed. A greedy person takes absurd risks, puts himself in peril too often. Inevitably, he gets caught. Before that happens, he is apt to hurt someone. He is in too much of a hurry. Usually such impatience results from ambition and youth. But ambition can be too large and youth can fail to mature. That dangerous mixture was the weakness I detected in Sebastien. In the end, I kept my thoughts to myself and wished him luck. We parted by the garden gate at Place de la Concorde and I walked home.

The day had passed magnificently. Never had I worked with such precision or felt so much the master of my craft. As for Sebastien, I had not let nostalgic sentiment carry me away. I had made a wise decision. I whistled all the way home. There I put Bach's *Violin Concerto in A Minor* on the stereo, opened a bottle of La Bacholle Gamay, lit a cigarette, and stretched out on the sofa.

As soon as I relaxed, the most unusual feeling came over me. I sat up and went to my coat, which lay draped over the back of a chair. I reached into the pocket where I had put my afternoon earnings. The pocket was empty.

At first you could have tipped me over with a feather. I felt dizzy, forgot to breathe, took one step sideways, staggered, caught myself. Once I found my breath, I fell into a rage. I paced up and down swearing. I pounded my fist and slapped my thighs furiously. Such an outrage! I cursed Sebastien, then cursed myself. I kicked the door, the sofa, the chairs. I even bit my fist like a madman. It was quite a scene, with no one to see it.

Finally, I settled down. For a while I stood by the window shaking my head with disbelief. I watched the passersby below on the street. I smoked a cigarette. I smoked another.

Then I began to laugh. It was marvelous. He had really fooled me, that young man, a remarkable performance.

In the end, I lay back on the sofa, finished my wine, and listened to Bach.

I had lost half a day's take. But what can you do? The world is full of thieves.

JOHN PEYTON COOKE

After You've Gone

FROM *Stranger*

I LOVED IT so much I was cradling it in my hands, fondling its stock, bracing its chamber between my thumbs, staring into its barrel like you'd look into a lover's eyes, in search of some kind of truth. It stared back at me deeply and gave me the ultimate truth: *Yeah, you got it right, Grant. I'm your trusty Glock. You can count on me. I'm going to kill you.*

I kissed its muzzle. My tongue tasted oil; and I could smell powder traces on my fingers. I'd cleaned it out after being down at the firing range all afternoon, blasting at all those black hanging targets, trying to get rid of all my black thoughts but only making them blacker. It was all I could do to keep from turning my Glock on myself then and there.

I didn't want to go out that way, in front of everybody. I wanted to have some privacy and leave a note — three notes, maybe, addressed to different people and taped up on my bathroom mirror. One to my landlord, saying sorry about the mess and take what you want. Another to Captain Feliciano, telling him thanks for your support when the going got tough, but face the facts, guy, I'm a screwup. The last to Mom, saying love you lots and none of this is your fault, even if you did put Poncho to sleep.

I loved my Glock so much I was laying four of its six inches on my tongue, forming my lips around it, hooking my thumbs around its safe-action trigger. There's no such thing as a safety catch on a Glock — you have to apply direct pressure in the right spot, or the trigger acts like a safety and refuses to fire.

My thumb was in the right spot. The rest ought to be cake.

I was telling myself that if I was a real man, I'd do it.

I was sweating bullets, staring down at the trigger cross-eyed. The last thing I'd see would be the knuckly creases on my thumb parting ever so slightly.

I depressed the safe action so it wouldn't be safe anymore — and I wouldn't be depressed anymore.

I did it. I squeezed the trigger.

It should have fired. But it didn't. It jammed on me.

For the first time in my career, my Glock had let me down.

And now my hands were shaking and my heart was beating so fast I thought I was going to have a heart attack. If I tried again, I was going to screw it up. And I didn't want to fail.

I set the gun down. My stomach churned in disgust. With fumbling fingers, I tapped out a cigarette and lit it on the third match. It felt good to have that smoke in my lungs. The nicotine got my mind to thinking — maybe the ol' Glock was giving me a sign, that I needed help, that something was terribly wrong with me. And you don't argue with a Glock.

I didn't know where to begin. The brass always encouraged us to use the departmental psychiatrists — but everyone knew what that was about. I couldn't count on total confidentiality. Whatever was wrong with me might get leaked to IA. It might get subpoenaed in some future court case if my policing skills were called into question, and such a case was not outside the realm of possibility. It might simply get spread around as interprecinct gossip: *Officer Grant's a loose cannon. Yeah, you can't trust Tom Grant as your backup. The guy's nuts. Let's find him a nice desk job and pull him off the streets.*

I couldn't turn to the department. No sir, not on my life.

Facedown on the kitchen table in front of me lay the *Village Voice*. One of the classified ads on the back page caught my eye:

> LONELY? DEPRESSED? SUICIDAL?
> CALL THE 24-HOUR HELP LINE!
> 555-HELP 555-HELP 555-HELP

It looked like what I needed. Help was only a phone call away. Even though it was two in the morning, somebody would be there on the other end of the line to talk me down.

I picked up the phone and called.

"Hello?" A man's voice, exceedingly mild, somewhat sleepy.

"Um, yes, is this the help line?" I croaked.

"Yeah, sure." He cleared his throat. "How can I help you?"

"I — I just tried to kill myself."

"Really?"

"Yes, really."

"What happened? Why didn't it work?"

"My gun jammed."

"Oh, you're using a gun? What kind?"

"What kind? Does it matter?"

"Of course it matters. What kind of gun do you own?"

"Well, it's a Glock."

"Mmm," said the guy on the help line. "What model?"

"It's a seventeen-L. Semiauto, six-inch barrel."

"What does that use? Nine-millimeters? Forty-caliber Smith & Wessons? Or forty-fives?"

"Nine-millimeters," I said.

"How many in the clip?"

"I've got seventeen in the clip and one in the chamber. The one in the chamber jammed. I'm going to have to start all over."

"How much does a gun like that cost?" the help line wanted to know.

"I don't know what it costs now. I got mine, what, four years ago, when I joined the academy. It set me back about eight hundred."

"The academy?" he said. "You mean the police academy?"

"Yes, I'm a policeman."

"How interesting."

"Listen, I'm serious about this. I'm going to take my Glock apart, clean it all up, reload it, and try again. Probably one chance in a billion that it'll jam again."

"Probably," the help line said.

There was an uncomfortable silence.

"Aren't you going to try to talk me out of it?"

"Why should I?"

"I thought that's what you were there for."

"If you want to kill yourself and you thought I was going to try to talk you out of it, why would you call?" he asked.

"I don't follow," I said.

"Why don't you do it right now, while I'm on the phone?"

"What?"

"You heard me. Talk to me while you're unjamming your gun or whatever it is you have to do. I'll wait. Get it all nice and ready, and then do it. Just do it. I want to hear it."

"Listen, maybe I dialed the wrong number, buddy."

"No, you didn't. You dialed five-five-five-H-E-L-P, didn't you? That's me. I'm the help line. You got what you wanted."

"I still don't understand."

"Who cares whether you understand? You're about to kill yourself. In a few minutes, no one's going to give a damn about you anymore. You'll be gone, and we'll still be here. It's not for you to understand. Are you beginning to see my logic?"

"Not exactly."

"How are you going to do it? Side of the head? In the mouth? Through the chest?"

"In the mouth."

"Good," he said. "That's best. Side of the head, there's too much chance you'll turn yourself into a vegetable. Through the chest, you're not guaranteed to hit the heart. You might only wound yourself, pass out, and wind up in the hospital."

"I don't need your advice," I said. "I want help."

"Help? You want help? What do you think I'm giving you?"

"Not that kind of help."

"I didn't specify what kind of help in my ad, now, did I?"

"No, but —"

"Everyone always *assumes* I'm here to rescue them. I'm not. You want to kill yourself, that's fine by me. I can't abide suicides who get halfway there and then can't finish the job. Some of them only need a little push to be on their way. So I put the number in the paper. I want them to call me at that moment of crisis, when all they need is a little encouragement."

"You're sick."

"Ho-ho!" he said. "You're the one who's already tried to kill himself once this evening, and you want to do it again. Which one of us do you think is sick?"

"Wait a minute," I said, and began to laugh. "I see what you're doing. I can see right through you. You're smart, you know that? You really take the cake. You're using reverse psychology, just like my mother used to do when I was a kid."

"Oh?" the help line said. "Just how am I doing that?"

"By pretending you want me to go ahead and do it, acting like you get some kind of kick out of other people dying while you hang there on the line. You think all we're doing is feeling sorry for ourselves and looking for someone to hold our hands and tell us it's okay, tell us we're somebody special, tell us there's a brighter day dawning somewhere over the rainbow."

"Stop wasting my time. Are you going to do it or not?"

"See?" I said. "Instead of giving us soothing words, you give us abuse. You try to make us feel even more worthless, because you think we're going to react against it and tell ourselves we're really okay. We listen to you and think you're a jerk, but we say to ourselves, 'Hey, why should I listen to this guy?' and before you know it, you've cured us of our mania and sent us on our merry way. Isn't that how it goes?"

The voice on the help line gave a rude, audible yawn.

"Hello?" I said. "Are you still there?"

"I've been making a sandwich. You were saying?"

"Never mind what I was saying. I'm onto you, and it won't work. Maybe with some other schlemiel, but not with me, man."

"What won't work?"

"The reverse psychology trick. You've just proved to me what a lousy world it is that we live in. I don't want any part of it. I'm going to clean my gun up and blow my brains out."

"Do you really mean it this time?"

"Of course I mean it!" I shouted. "If you want to hear it for yourself, just stay on the line. It won't take very long."

"You promise? You're not just pulling my leg?"

"I promise. Cross my heart and hope to die."

"That's the spirit! Where do you live?"

"Oh, no," I said. "I'm not telling you. Now you believe me, and you want to send somebody over. Somebody from my precinct, maybe, or an ambulance or some goddamn social worker."

"No," he said in that calm, level voice of his. "No, I want to come over. I want to see it for myself. Maybe I can even help you do it. That is, if you really want my help —"

"I can take care of it myself, thank you very much."

"I'm not so sure. You sound chicken to me."

"Chicken?" I said. "Why don't you go fuck yourself?"

"What's your name?" he asked, unfazed by my suggestion.

"Tom," I said.

"Tom what?"

"Just Tom, okay? I don't want you reporting me."

"I'm not going to report you. You can trust me, Tom. My name's Ray. I'm your friend Ray. I'm here to help you."

"Lot of help you've given me so far, pal."

"I have," Ray said. "Only you just don't appreciate it. Now why don't you tell me where you live? I want to come over."

"As long as you promise not to interfere," I said.

"Oh, I won't," Ray said. "I wouldn't dream of it."

I gave him my address. He said he lived only fifteen blocks away and could be there in ten minutes. We hung up.

I laid out some newspaper and started cleaning my gun.

"Why a nine-millimeter?" Ray asked from across my kitchen table. He was my age, with an altogether too intense look in his eyes. "Why not a revolver? Revolvers never jam. You never would have had this problem. You never would have had to call me."

"If you must know," I said, carefully reloading seventeen live rounds into the clip, "I really believed the nine-millimeter was the way to go. Right after I joined the academy, the department had just changed regulations to allow us to carry something more powerful than a thirty-eight."

"Thirty-eight Special," Ray beamed. "Standard police issue."

"Yeah, in the old days," I said. "Most of us supported the change, but the old-timers were opposed. They kept nagging at us that semiautos were unreliable and prone to jamming."

"See?" Ray said. "They knew whereof they spoke!"

"They were so scared of the change, they drummed up other reasons. They thought that we youngsters would lose control and empty our clips into every unlucky punk who crossed our path."

"Did they switch?"

"No. They kept their thirty-eight Specials. Switching would be like ending a love affair. Most of us under forty went for the nine-millimeters, though. We were the ones facing the front-line action. The gangstas were outgunning us, with AK-forty-sevens, sometimes. We had to be on as equal a footing as possible."

"Thus the Glock," Ray said admiringly. "It *is* nice, Tom."

"Thanks. My Glock and I have been through a lot together. I had to use it once to stop a sixteen-year-old kid who was armed with a beautiful silvery Colt Double Eagle ten-millimeter."

"Do tell!"

"The kid had just robbed a liquor store. I identified myself and asked him to drop his weapon. He refused to do so. He wanted to go out in a blaze of glory, I guess, and I had little choice but to oblige him."

"Good for you," Ray said with a gleam in his eye.

"Ever since, I wished he could have got a bead on me and let fly. Anything to make it seem less like an execution. But to do that, he would have had to have had at least a few shells in his gun. Once the kid was down, we examined his Colt, and we found his magazine just as empty as mine was after I'd shot him."

"Oh, too bad!" Ray pouted his lips. "Poor Tom!"

"It only takes a second holding that trigger down to let all those slugs come spewing out. I thought I only let him have a few, but the count we did of his chest came up seventeen."

"Wow!" Ray said. "And you didn't get in any trouble?"

"Of course not," I said. "It was all okay. I'd done what I had to do to protect my fellow officers and the citizenry. My captain, Captain Feliciano, said, 'Good work, son,' and gave me this big slap on the back. 'Don't sweat it,' he said. 'He was asking for it, and you gave it to him. Go home and take a nice long shower. You'll feel fine by tomorrow.'"

"Your captain sounds like my kind of guy," Ray said. "Was he right? Did you feel okay about it the next day?"

"Sure, I felt fine. I mean really fine. I believed what my captain said. I'd done my duty. If the kid's gun had been loaded, I might have gotten a commendation for saving the lives of all those pedestrians standing outside the store to watch all the fireworks. Officer Grant to the rescue. Handshake from the chief. Kudos from the mayor. Champagne all around."

"Tell me about the other times," Ray said huskily.

So I told him about the high-speed pursuit up the FDR Drive, when we managed to bring the driver to a stop, and I stayed by my vehicle to cover my partner while he approached the car, and the driver leapt out brandishing a Rossi 851 .38 Special in blued steel. I had no choice but to bring him down. Captain Feliciano later agreed with my course of action, and everything was okay.

Then there was the out-of-control traffic incident, when a Sikh taxi driver cut off a Jamaican bike messenger at a stoplight, and the messenger retaliated by shattering the driver's side window with his bike lock and beating the driver across the turban with it, and the bloodied driver reached under his seat and pulled out a bright stainless Colt King Cobra .357 Magnum and aimed it at the messenger's head with a shaky trigger finger. I was on the corner and calling for backup when I saw the gun. I pulled out my Glock, identified myself as a police officer, and told the Sikh to throw down his weapon. I gave him more time than I should have, really, but he kept the gun trained on the messenger. Again, I had no choice. I shot the driver dead and charged the messenger with assault as well as criminal damage to property. We later learned that the driver never understood a word of English, but Captain Feliciano insisted that I'd done the right thing. He even bought me a beer.

"I think this captain of yours has the hots for you," Ray said. "He lets you get away with murder because he wants to get into your pants."

"Feliciano? No. If you knew him, you wouldn't say that."

"Yes I would," Ray said. "Isn't that reason enough to go through with killing yourself? I mean, doesn't that just disgust you? You've killed all these people in the line of duty, and you don't even get any suspensions or reprimands because your captain thinks you're a dish. Believe me. I may never have met him, but I know human nature. You're his little buddy, his one special boy. He goes home at night and dreams of you, Tom."

"I doubt that." I laughed nervously. "Feliciano's married."

"As if that meant anything! Tom, don't be so naive!"

"I left him a suicide note," I said.

"You did?" Ray's dark eyebrows rose. "Can I see it?"

"It's sealed, taped to the bathroom mirror."

Ray got up.

"No!" I said. "I told you, it's sealed."

"So we'll reseal it!" Ray said, heading for the bathroom.

"It's for his eyes only," I said, getting up and going after him. I don't want you reading it!"

"I bet it's a love letter!" Ray shot ahead of me.

"It is not!"

Ray got to the mirror first and snatched the middle envelope of the three, the one clearly addressed to Captain Feliciano.

"Ha-ha!" Ray said, backing up to stand in the bathtub. "I've got it." He ripped open the envelope, started reading it, and began to laugh. "Oh, this is great! I love suicide notes!"

"Give it to me!" I said, reaching out for it.

Ray snatched it away and started reading it aloud:

"*Dear Tony*' — Tony, eh? You two are that buddy-buddy? You don't call him captain? Oh, well, never mind — *'Dear Tony, What you see is the end result of my wasted life. I don't know what ever kept me going this long. I guess it was you. You were always there for me when the going got tough. If it weren't for you, I don't think I would have even lasted this far.*' — Oh, Tom, this is a riot! — *'But it's all catching up with me, Tony. I'm a bad cop, and you know it. I can't walk into any situation without my gun going off and leaving somebody dead. No matter what you say, this isn't the way it's supposed to be. Someone should have taken me off into a room somewhere and punished me.'* — Oh, now you're asking Captain Tony for a spanking! Tom's been a bad boy! — *'I don't deserve to wear this badge. But what else can I do? This was my last chance. If I'm a failure at this, I'll be a failure at everything else. I've failed at life. I've got no choice but to end it. Sorry for being such a screwup. Don't bother sending flowers to the funeral. Save the money for yourself and Stella. Good-bye forever — Tom.'*"

"Give that to me," I said, finally snatching it away.

"Tom, that is so precious!" Ray said. "Can I have a copy? I could just run this down to the Kinko's around the corner —"

"No. Get away from me."

"Oh, Tom! Don't be like that!"

"I think you're the one who's got the hots for me, Ray," I said, heading back to the kitchen table.

"*I shall but love thee better after death,*'" Ray said. "That's Elizabeth Barrett Browning, you know."

"I used to own a Browning," I said.

I put the letter back in the envelope, resealed it with cellophane tape, and posted it back up on the bathroom mirror.

"What do the other letters say?"

"More of the same. Don't you dare touch them."

I grabbed Ray's collar and threw him out of the bathroom.

"Hey!" he said.

"In fact, I think you'd better leave."

"Oh, no, Tom. I've got to stay and make sure you follow through with this. You might turn back, for all I know. I'd hate to come back here tomorrow and find you're still alive."

"Beat it. Out. Sayonara. Asti Spumante."

I gave him a push toward the front door.

"I knew it," he said. "You're chicken. You don't want me around because you're too chicken to go through with it. You're not man enough. You don't have what it takes to put that gun in your mouth and blow the back of your head off. You're more of a pansy than I am, Thomas."

"Shut up," I said.

"Pansy, pansy, pansy,"

"I said shut up!"

"The minute I'm out that door, you're going to turn around and pout and say, 'Oh my God! What was I thinking? I can't go through with it! I love life *so* much! Life is *so* good!' And then you're going to put your gun away, lock it up in its box, get it out of your sight, and try to get it out of your mind. You'll go back into your bathroom, rip those suicide notes off the mirror, tear them into confetti, and flush them down the toilet. You'll look at yourself in the mirror and thank your lucky stars that your gun jammed and you're still alive. Only I bet it didn't jam on its own. You fixed it up that way."

"I did not," I protested.

"Did too," Ray said. "It wouldn't be so hard. You knew just what to do to make that bullet lodge there in the chamber. Maybe you did it unconsciously. Whatever, you didn't want to do it. Why not? Because you're weak! You're not a man at all. You're just a fluffy little kitten, playing a fun game with a bright, shiny toy. And when the kitten gets tired of playing, it curls up in its little basket and falls asleep. Beddy-bye. Nighty-night. Sweet dreams, little kitty."

I held Ray by the front of his shirt and gave him a left uppercut to the jaw. He swayed, but I held him up.

"Oh, Tom," he said. "You didn't have to hurt me. But the fact that you did only proves my point. What I'm saying is true. You don't have what it takes to kill yourself. You're pathetic."

I let go of Ray, went back to the kitchen table, and stared at the gun. I picked it up and put the last of the parts in place. I slammed the clip firmly into the grip and loaded one more slug directly into the chamber.

"It's all set to go, now," I said.

Rubbing his jaw, Ray came back and sat down across from me.

"You sure you're going to be able to do it?" he asked.

"Sure, I'm sure."

"If you can't quite manage it, you could let me."

"No thanks. I can do it myself."

"No one would ever know," Ray said. "I could kill you myself, and no one would ever know. Just by putting that gun in my hands and letting me do the job, why, I'd be a murderer. But you've got those notes all neatly prepared — for your landlord, your captain, your mother — and no one would ever suspect a thing. I've got no connection to you. We've never seen each other before. The only person who knows you called is me, and I won't tell anyone!"

"That won't be necessary. I can take care of myself."

"I'm not so sure," Ray said. "Let's see you do it."

"You better stand back," I said, turning the Glock around toward me, just outside my mouth. "It might get messy."

"I know where to sit to get out of the way," Ray said. "I've done this dozens of times."

"You've what?"

"You don't believe me? You think you're the only special person in the universe? That's not the first time I've run that ad, you know. You're a cop, you're probably aware of how many people commit suicide in this city every year. A lot of them call for help. Some call me. I try to talk them through it over the phone, but every once in a while I get a really special case — like you — and no matter what time of day or night it is, I drop what I'm doing and come over to see how I can help. I was asleep when you called tonight, did you know that? Yet I hopped out of bed and came on over. How's that for dedication?"

"Then it's not really a twenty-four-hour help line, is it? When you're over here helping me, you're not taking calls."

"I can only help one person at a time, you know."

I had the muzzle almost to my mouth, but I was curious:

"How many suicides have you witnessed, exactly?"

"I've lost count. Funny, isn't it? You'd think that a guy like me would keep a log or something to keep track, but I don't bother with it. Each customer deserves my undivided attention. I don't want them ending up just another statistic. I don't always just witness, you know. Sometimes I assist. It's perfectly legal, you know."

"Bull."

"Assisted suicide? Of course it is! Dr. Kevorkian paved the way. I bet he's lost count of all his assisted suicides."

"There's a difference," I said. "You're not a doctor, and you're not helping people who are terminally ill."

"Don't pick nits with me, Tom! Dr. Kevorkian helps people who are in great pain and want out. I'm no different. Everyone who calls me is in *excruciating* pain. Aren't you? I mean, Tom, the kind of sickness you have, it just eats at your heart, doesn't it? It's *painful,* and you can hardly *bear* it."

"Something like that," I said, "but —"

"But nothing, Tom! Assisted suicide is the wave of the future. The precedents are set. Soon enough, you're going to see suicide centers spring up all over the country. A whole chain of centers. Suicide superstores, next to every Barnes and Noble."

"You're insane," I said.

"If you're tired of listening to me, why don't you just pull that trigger and get it over with?"

I put the four extending inches of the barrel in my mouth, with my bottom lip resting against the trigger guard. I had it in both hands, with my thumb wrapping around the trigger. There was no chance it would jam this time. It was ready to go.

Ray looked at me with those intense eyes of his. He looked about ready to start slobbering. In fact, he looked lustful.

I shall but love thee better after death . . .

I took the gun out of my mouth.

"Wait a minute," I said, turning the gun on Ray.

Ray's lascivious grin collapsed into a thin red line.

"What's the matter, Tom? I was so proud of you. I thought you were going to make good on your promises."

"Shut up," I said. "I could kill you right now."

"You won't," Ray said confidently. "Everyone else you've killed was armed. I'm helpless, and harmless. You won't do it."

"You want to make a bet?"

"Hey, Tom, come on, buddy! Don't you see it worked?"

"What worked?"

"You were right! I was playing reverse psychology on you all along, and it worked. Another life saved. Damn, I'm good!"

"I don't believe you," I said.

"Don't, then." Ray shrugged.

"You're sick. Death turns you on. Everything about death. It gets you going. Ever since you came over here, you've had this covetous look in your eye —"

"Covetous?" Ray played the innocent. "Covetous of what?"

"Of my body, that's what!"

"Nonsense!" Ray said.

"And you know what? I don't think you're even a pansy or anything. All you care is that it's a body, and that it's dead."

"Tom, I can't believe you're saying that. It's too awful!"

"It's awful because it's true. You don't care how they do it, or why, just so long as you're alone with them afterwards."

"Tom, don't be ridiculous! I do nothing of the sort!"

"Oh yeah? I don't believe you. And I don't believe you have it in you to kill anybody yourself. In this city, you could pick up just about any stranger you saw on the street, if you were clever enough. All you'd have to do is take them home, or to a dark, secluded spot — maybe the park. If you were capable of killing anyone, that's what you'd do."

"Put the gun down, Tom. You're talking crazy! I'm — I'm worried about you. You don't really want to hurt me, do you?"

"Oh, yes, I want to hurt you, Ray. You bet I do. You're scum. You're worse than scum. You're a scavenger. I'd rather hurt you, but I'm going to take you in. Come on, get up."

I stood up and waved the gun at him. Ray got up.

"Take me in? On what charge? You can't prove anything!"

Ray had a point. I had no evidence of his crimes.

"What am I going to do with you, then?" I asked aloud.

"Why don't you just kill me?" Ray suggested.

"No good," I said. "I'd never beat the rap."

"Kill me, then kill yourself. Solves all your problems."

"You have a death wish or something? I'm sorely tempted."

"If that doesn't grab you, why not join me?"

"Join you?" I was incredulous.

"Sure, we'd make a great team! Tom and Ray, the help line boys! Two is better than one. Hey, we could use the good cop, bad cop routine on them! I bet we'd have more successes that way. It's clear to me from that suicide note that you're finished with police work. Well, now Ray's here to hand you back your future on a silver platter. You could quit your job at the police force and come work with me full-time. What do you say?"

"You do this full-time? How do you make a living?"

"Tom. I thought you were brighter than that! I invite myself in. I help them out. I get my kicks, and then I go rooting around for loot. They can't take it with them, and I may as well have it. That's how I collect my fee."

"Your fee," I repeated.

"You think I'd do any of this out of the goodness of my heart? It's a business, Tommy baby. So are you in or out?"

"How much do you make?"

"Some nights are better than others. I bet you don't have much dough lying around. Maybe you got some baseball cards —"

"You're not getting my baseball cards," I said. "Or me."

"And I was so close."

"Your apartment must be filled with stolen goods," I said.

"It's not easy to fence everything so fast."

"Uh-huh." I said, grinning. "That's what I figured."

I emptied my clip into Ray. He fell down all bloody.

I set my Glock down on the kitchen table. I opened my front door, looked up and down the hallway to make sure no one was watching, and went into the hall. I closed my door. I kicked it hard three times with the heel of my boot until I busted the lock and splintered the jamb and the door flew wide open. I went to the bathroom, tore down the suicide notes, and set them aflame using one match. I let them burn in my fingers until I dropped them into the toilet, and I flushed the ashes down and away.

I went to the phone and called the precinct house. Captain Feliciano happened to be the operations officer on duty tonight.

"Tony, it's Tom," I said.

"Hey, Tom!" he said. "You're off tonight, aren't you?"

"Yeah, and I had a bit of a problem here. I was just sitting here watching television in the dark, and some guy broke in through my front door. It looked like he was pointing a gun at me through the pocket of his jacket. He said if I didn't give him all my money, he was going to kill me. I didn't want to take any chances, so —"

Feliciano sighed. "How many times did you shoot him, Tom?"

"That damned trigger jammed on me again, Tony, so I blew the one in the chamber and all seventeen in the clip."

"Eighteen, huh? So I take it he's dead."

I glanced at Ray, not moving. "You take it correctly, sir."

"What kind of a gun did he have on him?"

"It wasn't a gun at all. It must have been his fingers."

"Well, that's okay," my captain said. "Just swear in court that you saw the butt of the gun poking out of his jacket. And you're sure he intended to burglarize you?"

"Oh, I'm positive," I said. "He had his moves down cold, like he's done this dozens of times before. I bet he's got tons of stolen goods at his place. Can we get a warrant?"

"Don't sweat it, Tom. You did the right thing. I'll have dispatch send a car over to take your report. Just relax. You don't have a thing to worry about. I'll see to it myself."

"Thanks, Tony, captain, sir," I said, to cover the bases.

Captain Feliciano laughed good-naturedly and hung up.

Ray lay there darkly staining my carpet.

I looked over at my Glock and smiled. In the end, it hadn't let me down at all. It had given me one last chance to prove I was worthy. I picked it up and found the barrel still warm and smoking. I cooled it off with a nice, long, sloppy kiss.

JAMES CRUMLEY

Hostages

FROM *Measures of Poison*

BETWEEN THE HAMMER of the midwestern sun and the relentless sweep of the bone-dry wind, the small town of Wheatshocker seemed crushed flat and just about to blow across the plains. Long billows of dust filled the empty streets like strings of fog. Male dogs learned to squat or leaned against withered fence posts so the wind wouldn't blow them over when they lifted their legs to pee. The piss dried instantly on the sere dirt, then blew away before the dogs finished. Shadows as black as tar huddled protectively in the shallow dunes that lined the few buildings left on the main street. Most of the windowfronts were as empty as a fool's laugh, while those with glass were etched in formless shapes by the sharp, ghostly wind. The red bricks of the Farmers Bank and Trust had faded to a pallid pink, held in place by desiccated, crumbling mortar. A '32 Ford sedan idled in the bank's alley, as dusty as the rest of the heaps parked in front of the bank. A humpbacked man as small as a child sat behind the wheel, smoking a ready-roll. Only a pro would have noticed the low chortle of the reground cam in his engine. Nothing moved down the street but a mismatched team of mules slowly pulling a wagon with a large Negro in overalls and a canvas-covered bed.

The heat-stunned silence was shattered by a single gunshot. Four armed men backed out of the bank, carrying a canvas laundry bag and pushing along an old lady in a feedsack dress and a young girl in white ruffles.

"And stay down, you damn hayseeds!" the red-headed one shouted. "We've got hostages!"

The group scrambled into the sedan, the last man firing a shot into the bank's front window, then the car sped down the dusty street and around a corner after the wagon with its plodding mules. The crumbling sidewalk in front of the bank slowly filled with a group of confused customers and tellers huddled together like the survivors of a natural disaster. A red-faced man, holding a handkerchief against a bloody knot on his bald head, shoved through the crowd, and stared into the dust cloud into which the bank robbers had disappeared.

"One of you fools get that worthless old bastard out of my bank," he ordered.

"I believe the sheriff's a-dyin'," one of the tellers ventured.

"Not in *my* bank, he isn't," the banker said. "We can't afford to bury the idiot *now.*"

A frail old woman with a hooked nose said to no one in particular, "I believe Mr. Baines was sweet on that poor widow woman."

"How the hell did they know to come today?" the banker muttered, his words lost on the gritty wind.

On the seventh day, Mabel had nearly slipped into an exhausted sleep when she heard the bluegum Geechi boy, Sledge, rack the slide on the sawed-off Ithaca 12-gauge pump. The hard sound slammed through the thin walls of the farmhouse. She knew what that meant. All too well. One of the gang in the nonstop poker game downstairs had pulled a gun. Probably the red-headed prick. Absolutely against all her rules. Mabel sighed, rolled over, and kissed Baby Emma's rosebud lips. Even in her sleep, Baby Emma sucked on Mabel's tongue briefly, then nipped it with her tiny white seed-corn teeth. Mabel wanted to follow the sleepy kiss — even cupped Em's tiny, pert breasts with the rosehip nipples — but she had business to take care of. Baby Emma was twenty but easily passed for ten or eleven. The girl-child seemed built of warm and creamy vanilla scoops, and the blond ringlets curling in a tangle around her face looked like thick caramel drippings. Mabel touched her lips again, softly, not wanting to wake the young woman too quickly. Even smashed on sloe gin and laudanum, the girl's breath reminded Mabel of the soda fountain in Ogallala where her goddammed father had been the local blue-faced, morphine-addicted pharmacist. The memory made what she had to do easier. She wished she could keep the kid out of it this time — Baby Em seemed to like it too much — and she hated to lose the gimp, but they all had to go. "Get ready, sugarplum," she said, then slipped into her clothes piled on a ratty dresser.

The gang had been holed up in the sugarbeeter's house since they had taken down the Farmer's State Bank for almost sixteen thousand. That was the way she always worked. The smart ones didn't run after a job. They holed up nearby for at least two weeks. That was always the hard part, that two weeks of waiting. The easy part was finding a failing farmer with no children and a defeated wife to take them in for a price. It was 1932, and almost anybody would do anything for a price. Of course, the final payment was always a .22 short in the eye and a sack of lime in the root cellar.

As Mabel considered how to deal with this new bunch, she knew she had plenty of time to change into her grandmother clothes. The boys always seemed more likely to obey her when she looked like an old woman rather than a lush ex-whore in her mid-thirties. She gathered her thick red hair into a knot, and stuffed it under a gray wig. She bound her slightly overripe body into an old woman's girdle and a bra stuffed with sand-filled socks to make it seem as if her breasts drooped almost to her waist, all of it covered with a dress sewn from chickenfeed sacks. Her long, slim legs were sheathed in thick gray stockings, and her feet laced into ugly, thick-heeled granny shoes. In this outfit, she and Baby Em made the perfect hostages. Then Mabel added the last touches: a black straw brimless hat, ringed with cloth flowers, attached to the wig with three heavy hatpins, and a .22 Derringer up her sleeve.

Baby Em stripped butt-naked. Either she didn't like blood on her nightclothes, or she liked the warm splatter on her pale, perfect skin.

The scene downstairs was much as Mabel had imagined. The farmer and his wife, as pale as bleached bones, huddled behind the icebox, shaking so badly that the water in the melt tray shimmered as if a cold breeze were sweeping across the worn plank floorboards. A handful of cards had been scattered across the kitchen table, and several stacks of chips tumbled into piles. The largest pile was in front of Fast Freddy Okrentski, the tiny, gimp-legged humpback, who had laid down a false trail for the police and dumped the car while the gang rode out of town in the back of the farmer's wagon covered with a tarp.

The brothers, Crazy Al and Bruno Zale, the muscle, had small neat stacks of chips in front of them covered with their huge hands, hands so large they made their Smith & Wesson .38 revolvers look small. The brothers were large-jawed pug-uglies out of Nutley, New Jersey; men with the kinds of faces who, when they threatened death to the hostages, looked as if they might enjoy the feel of blood, bone chips, and brain matter dripping off their craggy smiles.

Carter Docktrey — the smooth-faced red-headed little shit from Terre Haute, who thought he led the gang, who thought he was God's gift to women, and who thought he knew how to play poker — stood in front of his overturned chair, his chip stack flat and his military Colt .45 semiautomatic pointed at Lindsey. Mabel knew that Carter's rod was mostly for show; the arrogant turd never cleaned the piece so it usually jammed after the first round.

She also knew that Lindsey, whose light blue eyes were as cool as ball bearings in a snowstorm and whose usually smooth forehead was wrinkled slightly, no more than a soft gust of wind across a still pond, was a stone killer. A single drop of sweat slipped off his bald head, over his furrowed brow, to land with a light click on his cards. His hands were under the table and more than likely had the .410 he carried strapped to his calf pointed at Carter. The little shotgun had been cut down to pistol size and loaded with tacks. To be gutshot that way ensured an endlessly painful death, so in a way she'd be doing Carter a favor. The slick little bastard hated Lindsey, who always cased and organized the jobs, because Lindsey was both smarter and calmer than Carter. So this was about them, and had little to do with Freddie the gimp, who probably was dealing seconds. He was as nimble with cards as he was with cars.

The scene was as still as a photograph. Of course, nobody had moved because Sledge stood in the corner, the Ithaca 12-gauge leveled at the table. At this range, a couple of rounds of the double-ought buckshot would have swept the room clean.

Mabel considered the scene, then, smiling, stepped behind Carter and picked up his chair. She grabbed his shoulders firmly and gently eased him into the chair. Then she took the pistol from his hand and set it in front of him.

"You're not going to be needing this, honey," she said softly, then turned to the bluegum and nodded.

Sledge returned the nod with a smile. He and Mabel had been a team since the cathouse in East Memphis where they worked had been burned down by a drunk Baptist preacher, and they went into the bank-robbing business. It had been good to them. Sledge had a small chicken farm outside Tacoma, and Mabel owned a roadhouse north of Bellingham where Canadian whiskey was easy to obtain.

Mabel turned back to Carter, rubbing his neck gently with her left hand, her right hand touching her hat. "Now what's the problem, honey?"

"Goddamned Bohunk has been dealin' seconds all night long," Carter answered.

"I can't believe that," she said, still gentle, "can't believe that any more than I can believe . . ." She paused, then her voice became hard. ". . . that you forgot what I said about no guns, you needle-dicked bug-fucking son of a bitch."

Mabel had done it wrong a couple of times in the past and had to deal with convulsions, confusion, and anger — usually, with the Derringer — so experience had taught her exactly where to put the hatpin at the base of the skull. When she tapped the thick pin with the heel of her hand, it penetrated Carter's dismal brain as easily as it might slip through a round of rat cheese. He was dead before his face hit the meager scattering of chips in front of him.

"I guess you boys will have to play four-handed, now," she said lightly as she picked up Carter's .45 off the table. "Unless you can get the farmer to change his overalls."

Then Mabel lifted the pistol casually and shot Lindsey just where his forehead became his bald pate. He went over like an acrobat. Baby Em stepped around the corner with a nickle-plated .32, pressed it against Freddie's temple, then pulled the trigger twice. She kept pulling the trigger as the gimp toppled sideways out of his chair. Crazy Al went for the piece under his jacket, but Sledge took him down with his first round at such close range that he blew Crazy Al's gun hand off at the wrist and set fire to his dirty tie. Bruno started to raise his hands as if to plead, but Sledge shot him in the face before he could open his mouth.

The sugarbeeter and his wife were shaking and weeping so hard that they had trouble dragging the bodies down to the root cellar, but Mabel kept reassuring them that the lime would destroy the bodies and that with their cut of the bank loot they could start over again in California or Oregon. The tattered couple had stopped shaking by the time they finished dumping the last sack of lime, and the tears had dried from their eyes when Mabel put the two .22 shorts into their brainpans. The couple fell on the pile as neatly as if they had planned it that way.

Sledge finished setting up the house as the women dressed for traveling. He covered the bodies with Bell jars of coal oil and phosphorus, then arranged for a fire. He laid a slow black powder fuse from the root cellar to the kitchen table, where he wrapped it around the base of a three-day candle. Then he washed the Lincoln where the gimp had hidden it in the barn, changed the local plates for real New Jersey ones, and dressed in his driver's uniform.

The guns and money were stashed in a false bottom of the trunk, an obscene amount of luggage piled on top and strapped to the back. The women were lodged in the back seat, draped in traveling dusters, big hats, and dust veils — a wealthy widow and her daughter on their way to the West Coast for a new life.

"Are we set, Mr. Sledge?" Mabel asked as he backed the large car out of the barn.

"Everything but the match, ma'am," he said.

"Well, strike the match, please," she said.

"I wish we were gonna be here to see it," Baby Em said as Sledge headed for the farmhouse. "What's gonna happen next, Momma?"

"There's a plump little bank in Ogallala right next to the drugstore," she answered. "I think we'll pay it a little visit before we go home. I know a couple of old boys in Denver who might help."

"Just no more little red-headed pricks, okay? I'd rather suck a cough drop," Baby Em said as Sledge drove out onto the section road.

"Just a blue-faced monster," Mabel said, "and he'll have plenty of cough drops, and maybe even some hard rock candy. He used to have lots of hard rock candy."

"I wanna gun in the bank next time," Baby Em whined. "Don't you?"

As the sun slipped toward the horizon, the wind paused for a moment, the dust settled, and a fire burned briefly in Mabel's eyes, a fire as brief as her sad smile.

"We don't need guns, Babydoll."

O'NEIL DE NOUX

Death on Denial

FROM *Flesh and Blood: Dark Desires*

The Mississippi. The Father of Waters.
The Nile of North America.
And *I* found it.
   — *Hernando de Soto, 1541*

THE OILY SMELL of diesel fumes wafts through the open window,
filling the small room above the Algiers Wharf. Gordon Urquhart,
sitting in the only chair in the room, a gray metal folding chair,
takes a long drag on his cigarette and looks out the window at a list-
less tugboat chugging up the dark Mississippi. The river water, like
a huge black snake, glitters with the reflection of the New Orleans
skyline on the far bank.

Gordon's cigarette provides the room's only illumination. It's *so*
dark he can barely see his hand. He likes it, sitting in the quiet,
waiting for the room's occupant to show up. Not quite six feet tall,
Gordon is a rock-solid two hundred pounds. His hair turning silver,
Gordon still sees himself as the good-looking heartbreaker he was
in his twenties.

He wasn't born Gordon Urquhart those forty years ago. When
he saw the name in a movie, he liked it so much he became Gordon
Urquhart. He made a good Gordon Urquhart. Since the name
change, he'd gone up in life.

He yawns, then takes off his leather gloves and places them on
his leg. He wipes his sweaty hands on his other pants leg.

The room, a ten-by-ten-foot hole-in-the-wall, has a single bed
against one wall, a small chest of drawers on the other wall, and a
sink in the far corner. Gordon sits facing the only door.

He closes his eyes and daydreams of Stella Dauphine. He'd caught a glimpse of her last night on Bourbon Street. She walked past in that short red dress without even noticing him. As she moved away, bouncing on those spiked high heels, he saw a flash of her white panties when her dress rose in the breeze. He wanted to follow, but had business to take care of.

Sitting in the rancid room, Gordon daydreams of Stella, of those full lips and long brown hair. She's in the same red dress, only she's climbing stairs. He moves below and watches her fine ass as she moves up the stairs. Her white panties are sheer enough for him to see the crack of her round ass.

They're on his ship from his tour in the U.S. Navy. Indian Ocean. Stella stops above him and spreads her legs slightly. He can see her dark pubic hair through her panties. She looks down and asks him directions.

Gordon goes up and shows her to a ladder, which she goes up, her ass swaying above him as he goes up after her, his face inches from her silky panties. Arriving at the landing above, she waits for him atop the ladder. He reaches up and pulls her panties down to her knees, runs his fingers back up her thighs to her bush and works them inside her wet pussy. She gasps in pleasure.

A sound brings Gordon back to the present. He hears footsteps coming up the narrow stairs to the hall and moving to the doorway. Gordon pulls on his gloves and lifts the .22-caliber Bersa semiautomatic pistol from his lap. He grips the nylon stock, slips his finger into the trigger guard, and flips off the safety as the door opens. He points the gun at the midsection of the heavyset figure standing in the doorway.

Faintly illuminated by the dull, yellowed hall light, Lex Smutt reaches for the light switch. Gordon closes one eye. The light flashes on and Smutt freezes, his wide-set hazel eyes staring at the Bersa.

"Don't move, fat boy!" Gordon opens his other eye and points his chin at the bed. "Take a seat."

Smutt moves slowly to his bed and sits. At five-seven and nearly three hundred pounds, Smutt knows better than to think of himself as anything but a toad. He runs his hands across his bald head and bites his lower lip. Wearing a tired, powder-blue seersucker suit, white shirt, and mud-brown tie loosened around his thick neck, Smutt is as rumpled as a crushed paper bag.

"Keep your hands where I can see them." Gordon rises, his knees creaking, and closes the door. In his black suit, Gordon wears a black shirt and charcoal-gray tie.

Yawning again, Gordon says, "Long time, no see."

Smutt lets out a nervous laugh.

Gordon's mouth curls into a cold grin. "Lex Smutt. That's your real name, ain't it? It's a stupid name. You stupid?"

Smutt shakes his head slowly, his gaze fixed on the Bersa.

"You know why I'm here."

Smutt's eyes widen as if he hasn't a clue.

"Give me the fifteen thousand. Or die."

A shaky smile comes to Smutt's thin lips. "I don't have it."

"Then die." Gordon cocks the hammer — for effect — and points the Bersa between Smutt's eyes.

Raising his hands, Smutt stammers, "Come on, now. Gimme a minute."

"You'll have the money in a minute?" Gordon's hand remains steady as he closes his left eye and aims carefully at the small dark mole between Smutt's eyebrows. The loud blast of a ship's horn causes Smutt to jump. Gordon is unmoved.

As long seconds tick by, Gordon takes the slack up in the trigger and starts to pull it slowly. Staring eye-to-eye, Smutt blinks.

"I got six grand," Smutt says.

Gordon's trigger finger stops moving, but his hand remains steady. He blinks and nods.

"Where?"

"On me."

"Where?"

Smutt wipes away the sweat rolling down the sides of his face and exhales loudly. "For a minute there I thought —"

"Where?" Gordon interrupts.

Leaning back on his hands, Smutt looks around the room.

Gordon raises his size-eleven shoe and kicks him in the left shin. Smutt shrieks and grabs his leg. He rocks back and forth twice before Gordon presses the muzzle of the Bersa against the man's forehead.

"Where?" Gordon growls.

"Under the bed." Smutt rubs his shin with both hands. "Under the floorboard."

Gordon grabs the seersucker suit collar with his left hand and yanks Smutt off the bed, shoving the man to the floor. Kicking the bed aside, Gordon orders Smutt to pull up the floorboard.

"Come up with anything except money and you're dead."

On his hands and knees now, Smutt crawls over to where his bed used to stand. Reaching for the loose board, he looks up at Gordon and says, "We have to come to an understanding."

Gordon points the Bersa at the floor next to Smutt's hand and squeezes off a round. A pop is followed by the sound of the shell casing bouncing on the wood floor.

Smutt looks at the neat hole next to his hand, looks back at Gordon, then yanks up the loose board. He reaches inside and pulls out a brown paper bag. He hands it to Gordon without looking up.

Snatching the bag, Gordon takes a couple of steps back. He opens the bag and quickly counts the money. Six grand exactly.

"You're nine thousand short."

Smutt rolls over on his butt and sits like a Buddha, hand on his knees. He wipes the sweat away from his face again and says, "Mr. Happer will just have to understand. You just came into this but it's been goin' on awhile. I need time. Most of the fifteen is vig . . . interest. You know."

Gordon points the Bersa at the mole again. "You're certain this is all you have?"

Smutt nods slowly, looking at the floor now. He waves a hand around. "Does it look like I got more?"

"Try *yes* or *no!*"

"No!" Smutt's voice falters and he clears his throat.

"I heard you won more than this at the Fairgrounds."

"Well, you heard wrong."

Gordon waits.

Smutt won't look up.

So Gordon asks, "Why deny it? You cleared over twenty thousand."

"I had other bills to pay."

"Before Mr. Happer?" Gordon's voice is deep and icy.

"I told you this has been going on awhile. I need time."

"You shoulda thought of that before. Now look at me." Gordon closes his left eye again.

Smutt looks up and Gordon squeezes off a round that strikes just to the left of the mole. Smutt shudders and bats his eyes. Gordon squeezes off another shot, this one just to the right of the mole. Smutt's mouth opens and he falls slowly forward, face first, in his lap.

Gordon steps forward and puts two more in the back of the man's head.

Then he carefully picks up the spent casings, all five of them, and puts them in his coat pocket. The air smells of gunpowder now and faintly of blood. He searches the body and finds another four hundred in Smutt's coat pocket. Still on his haunches, Gordon looks inside the hole in the floor, but there's nothing else there.

He ransacks the room before leaving.

The night air feels damp on his face as he walks around the corner to where he'd squirreled away his low-riding Cadillac.

Gordon checks his watch as he ascends the exterior stairs outside the Governor Nicholls Street Wharf. It's nine o'clock A.M., sharp. He looks across the river at the unpainted Algiers Wharf. Shielding his eyes from the morning sun glittering off the river, he can almost make out the window of Smutt's room.

At the top of the stairs, he enters a narrow hall and moves to the first door. He knocks twice and waits, looking up at the surveillance camera. He straightens his ice-blue tie. This morning Gordon wears his tan suit with a dark blue shirt. Before leaving home, he told himself in his bathroom mirror that he looked "spiffy."

The door buzzes and he pulls it open.

Mr. Happer sits behind his wide desk. Facing the TV at the far edge of his desk, next to the black videocassette recorder, the old man doesn't look up as Gordon crosses the long office. Happer looks small, hunkered down in the large captain's chair behind the desk.

The office smells of cigar smoke and old beer. The carpet is so old it's worn in spots. Gordon takes a chair in front of Mr. Happer's desk and pulls out an envelope, which he places on the desk.

Raising a hand like a traffic cop, Mr. Happer leans forward to pay close attention to the scene on his TV. Gordon doesn't have to look to know what's on the screen. It's Peter Ustinov again and that damn movie Mr. Happer watches over and over. By the sound of it,

Ustinov and David Niven are slowly working their way through the murder on the riverboat. What was the name of that French detective Ustinov plays? Hercules something-or-another.

Mr. Happer suddenly turns his deep-set black eyes to Gordon.

Pushing seventy, Mr. Happer is a skeleton of a man with razor-sharp cheekbones, sunken cheeks, and arms that always remind Gordon of the films of those refugees from Dachau. Mr. Happer reaches with his left hand for the envelope on his desk, picks it up with his spider's fingers, and opens it.

"That's all Smutt had on him," Gordon volunteers.

Mr. Happer nods and says, "Four hundred?" He focuses those black eyes on Gordon and says, "What about the twenty grand from the Fairgrounds."

Gordon is careful as he looks back into the man's eyes. He shrugs. "He said he had other bills to pay."

"Before me?"

"That's what I said to him."

"So?"

"So I took care of him. Tossed the room and that's it."

Mr. Happer shakes his head. Gordon watches him and remembers the man's name isn't Happer either. The old bastard was born Sam Gallizzio and tried for most of his life to become a made man, working at the periphery of La Cosa Nostra. Trying to be a goomba, Happer failed. He did, however, manage to remain alive, which isn't easy for an Italian gangster who's not LCN, even if he's only a semi-gangster.

Shoving the envelope into a drawer, Mr. Happer pulls out another envelope, which he slides across the desk to Gordon.

Gordon picks it up and slips it into his coat pocket. He doesn't have to count it. He knows there's a thousand in there — the old bastard's cut-rate hit fee.

Mr. Happer picks up a stogie from an overflowing ashtray and sticks it in his mouth. He sucks on it and its tip glows red. He shakes his head again.

"It's worth it," Mr. Happer says, as if he needs convincing. "The word'll get out. Make it easier later on. That's what the big boys do."

Gordon nods.

"He woulda never come up with the fifteen," Mr. Happer says, and Gordon wonders if the old man is baiting him. "He woulda never paid me."

Fanning away the smoke from between them, Mr. Happer says, "You sure you tossed the place right, huh? You weren't in no hurry."

"No hurry at all." Gordon feels the old man squeezing him.

Mr. Happer raises a hand suddenly, leans to the side to catch something Ustinov says. He nods, as if he's approving, then props his elbows on the desk. He looks at Gordon.

"You sure?" And there it is. *The* question.

"I'm sure, Mr. Happer." Gordon likes the way his voice is deep and smooth.

"I gotta ask you straight up, you know that, don't you?" The old coot's face is expressionless.

Deny. Deny. Deny. Gordon doesn't even blink. He feels good.

Finally, the old man blinks and Gordon says, "Mr. Happer. I've always been straight with you. You know that."

Mr. Happer waves his hand again as he falls back in his chair.

"Son of a bitch dumped the money awfully fast." Mr. Happer looks again at the TV.

Gordon stops himself from reminding the old bastard that their agreement was simple. Find Smutt, get as much as you can from him, then whack him and leave him where he'll be found. He did his job. A contract is a contract.

Gordon waits. He wants to say, "Well, if that's all —" but knows better. He waits for Mr. Happer to dismiss him.

The old man turns around and looks at the windows that face the river. He takes another puff of his cigar, lets out a long trail of smoke, and then says, "That's what I get for dealing with bums like Smutt. At least he got his."

Turning to Gordon, the old man smiles, and it sends a chill up Gordon's back.

"I was thinking of asking you if you happen to know where Smutt used to hang out. Maybe he had another place. But the money's long gone."

When the old man looks back at his TV, Gordon casually looks at the windows. A gunshot rings out and excited voices, including Ustinov's, rise on the TV. Gordon waits.

Finally, after the commotion on the riverboat calms down, Mr. Happer looks at Gordon and says, "I know where to get you."

Gordon stands and nods at the old man and leaves, Mr. Happer's dismissal echoing in his mind. He knows where to get me. Goodbye and hello at the same time.

Stepping out into the sunlight again, Gordon squints and stretches, then walks down the stairs. He looks at the brown, swirling river water and laughs to himself. Ustinov is still on the riverboat, floating on his own brown water, trying to solve the murder with Mr. Happer watching intently. It strikes Gordon as very, very funny.

Before pulling away in his Caddy, he slips on his sunglasses and looks around. He spots the tail two minutes later, a black Chevy.

Gordon Urquhart's bedroom smells of cheap aftershave and faintly of mildew. Waiting in the darkness, Stella Dauphine sits on Gordon's double bed, her .22 Beretta next to her hand.

She wears a lightweight tan trench coat and matching tan high heels, a pair of skin-tight gloves on her hands. A young-looking thirty, Stella has curly hair that touches her shoulders. For a thin woman, she's buxom, which made her popular in high school but proved a hindrance in the mundane office jobs she held throughout her twenties.

Beneath the trench coat, she wears nothing except a pair of Barely There sheer, thigh-high stockings. She runs a hand over her knee and up to the top of her left thigh-high, pulling it up a little as she waits.

Closing her eyes, she listens intently.

She didn't used to be Stella Dauphine. Born Carla Stellos, she changed her name after a year in New Orleans. After seeing a late-night movie on TV — *A Streetcar Named Desire* — and after parking her car on Dauphine Street, she decided on the change. She felt more like a Stella Dauphine every day.

Her eyes snap open a heartbeat after she hears a distinct metallic click at the back door. The door creaks open. Standing at the foot of the bed, Stella picks up her Beretta, unfastens the trench coat, her gun hidden in the folds of the coat as she waits.

She feels a slight breath of summer air flow into the room and hears a voice sigh and then light footsteps moving toward the bedroom. A figure steps into the doorway.

The light flashes on.

Gordon Urquhart's there, a neat .22 Bersa in his hand.

Stella opens the trench coat and lets it fall off her shoulders.

As Gordon looks down at her naked body, Stella squeezes off a round, which strikes Gordon on the right side of his chest. He's stunned, so stunned he drops his gun. Gordon's mouth opens as he stumbles into the room, falling against the chest of drawers. Blood seeps through the fingers of his right hand, which he's pressed against his wound.

"You shot me!"

"Kick your gun over here."

Gordon's face is ashen. He blinks at her, looks at his chest, and stammers, "You *shot* me!"

"If you don't shut up, I'll shoot you again." Stella's mouth is set in a grim, determined slit. "Now kick the gun."

Gordon swings his foot and the gun slides across the hardwood floor. Stella steps forward and kicks it back under Gordon's bed.

The big man is breathing hard now. Blood has saturated his shirt.

"I think you hit an artery," he says weakly.

"Then we don't have much time, do we?"

"For what?"

Stella points her chin at the bed. "Sit, before you collapse."

Gordon moves to the bed and sits.

Stella moves to the doorway between the bedroom and kitchen, the Beretta still trained on Gordon.

"So," she says. "Where is it?"

He looks at her as if he hasn't the foggiest idea.

"Mr. Happer told me to give you ten seconds to come up with the money you took off Smutt." Stella narrows her eyes, "One. Two. Three —"

"I gave him the four hundred."

"Four. Five. Six —"

Gordon raises his head and says, "Go ahead and shoot me. There's no money."

"Seven. Eight. Nine —"

"If I had it, you think I'd be dumb enough to have it on me? I spotted your Chevy as soon as I left the Governor Nicholls Wharf."

Stella squeezes off another round, which knocks the lamp off the end table next to the bed.

"Dammit!" Gordon groans in pain. "I don't have any more money. Smutt blew it all."

Stella brushes her hair away from her face with her right hand and tells him, "Mr. Happer doesn't believe you and I don't believe you."

Gordon clears his throat and says, "Mr. Happer and me go back a long way, lady. He knows better."

A cold smile crosses Stella's thin lips. "I'll just whack you and toss the place. I'll still get my fee."

"This is crazy. I tell you, there's no more money."

Stella aims the Beretta with both hands again, this time at Gordon's face. She says, "So you and the old man go back a ways, huh? Well, I'm the one he calls when things go badly. And you're as bad as they come."

Gordon nods at her. "I seen you around. I know all about you. And you got me all wrong, lady."

Stella watches his eyes closely as she says, "When Smutt left the Fairgrounds, he went straight to his parole officer's house and paid the man off. Three grand. Stiff payoff, but Smutt figured it was worth it. Then he went to two restaurants, gorged himself. Then dropped some cash at the betting parlor on Rampart."

She watches Gordon's pupils. A pinprick of recognition comes to them as soon as she says the words "Six grand. He had about six grand left. You took it off him."

"No way."

Stella fires again, into Gordon's belly, and he howls.

"That's it." Stella's smile broadens. "Keep denying it."

"I don't have it!" Gordon slumps backward.

Stella levels her weapon, aiming at Gordon's forehead. She pauses, giving him one last chance.

"I don't!" he screams.

She squeezes off a round that strikes Gordon in the forehead. Stepping forward, she puts two more in his head before he falls back on his bed. For good measure she empties the Beretta's magazine, putting two more in the side of the man's head.

She picks up all eight casings and slips them into the pocket of her coat. She leaves his Bersa under the bed. Let the police match it to the Smutt murder. Then, slowly and methodically, she tosses the place.

An hour later, she finds the six thousand in the flour container on Gordon's kitchen counter. The giveaway — what man has fresh flour in a container?

Mr. Happer, sitting back in his captain's chair, bats his eyes at the TV as Peter Ustinov taps out an SOS on his bathroom wall, a large cobra poised and ready to strike the rotund detective. Stella, standing at the desk's edge in the trench coat outfit from last night, recognizes the scene and waits for David Niven to rush in with his sword to impale the snake.

When the scene's tension dies, Mr. Happer turns his deep-set eyes to Stella and says, "Okay. You got the money?"

Stella shakes her head.

Mr. Happer's eyes grow wide. "It wasn't there?"

"I tore the place apart. If he had it, he stashed it."

"Dammit!" Mr. Happer slaps a skeletonic hand on his desk. He picks up the remote control and pauses his movie. His black eyes leer at Stella's eyes as if he can get the truth just by staring. She bites her lower lip, reaches down, and unfastens her coat. She opens it slowly as Happer's gaze moves down her body.

Stella lets the coat fall to the floor and stands there naked except for the thigh-high stockings, which gives her long legs the silky look. Rolling her hips, Stella sits on the edge of the desk. Mr. Happer stares at her body as if mesmerized. It takes a long minute for his gaze to rise to her eyes.

"You sure you tossed the place right?"

Stella nods.

Mr. Happer picks up the remote and looks back at the TV. The riverboat is moored now, against the bank of the wide Nile River.

"Well, the word'll get out. Make it easier later on," Happer says. "That's what the big boys do."

Stella climbs off the desk and picks up her coat. As she closes it, she looks at the old man. Mr. Happer turns those black eyes to her and says, "You *sure* you tossed the place right?"

She's ready, her face perfectly posed. "I'm sure."

"Okay." Mr. Happer looks back at the TV and mouths the words as Peter Ustinov speaks. Without looking, he opens his center desk drawer and withdraws an envelope. He slides it over to Stella, who picks it up and puts it in her purse.

"Good work," Mr. Happer says.

"Thanks." Stella turns and leaves him with his Ustinov and David Niven and riverboat floating down the Nile.

On her way down the stairs she looks at the dark Mississippi water and whispers a message to the dead Gordon. "So you and Mr. Happer go back a long way. Well, we go back a longer way."

And I have tools, plenty of tools to work against this man, against all these men.

Three minutes later she spots the tail, a dark blue Olds.

PETE DEXTER

The Jeweler

FROM *Esquire*

THE OLD MAN ordered the soup of the day again, homemade
noodles and chicken served with bread and a glass of house wine,
and wiped at his nose with his napkin the whole time he ate. It was
February, and everybody on the East Coast had the flu. The old
man looked like he should have been home in bed, but his habits
were set deep. At ten to six every morning, for instance, he stepped
out of his front door in his bathrobe and slippers to retrieve the *In-
quirer.* Two hours later he came out again, dressed in an overcoat,
and walked to the end of his block and caught the SEPTA bus to
work. Twice this week he'd given his seat to young women. Exactly
at one o'clock he left the store, walked the four blocks to the restaurant, and had his soup of the day and wine, always sitting at the
same table near the kitchen. The tab always came to six dollars, and
he always left a dollar for the waitress. She had a snake tattooed
around the fleshy part of her arm, and beneath it the name *Jerry*
was written in script.

The man who had been keeping track of the old man's habits
was named Whittemore, and he noticed the hair in his plate as
soon as the waitress set it on the table. The hair lay across his fish
and was anchored at one end in a little white paper cup of tartar
sauce, moving slightly in the air from the overhead fan, like something dying in bed but not quite dead. He moved closer and saw
that most of the hair was black, but out toward the end, away from
the tartar sauce, there was a bulb of root where it was brown.

The waitress was a blonde, so the hair had come from the
kitchen, which was worse in a way than if it had just belonged to the

waitress herself. She had the tattoo, of course, and a stud in her nose — a small pearl — and a stained blouse, but this was the human being, after all, that they'd sent out to greet the public. Christ knew what they looked like back in the kitchen.

"Is everything all right, hon?" She came back to his table empty-handed from the other side on the way to the kitchen. Whittemore looked up and saw the back of the stud glistening inside her nose. A week ago, when he first walked in and saw the pearl, he thought it was some kind of growth.

"It's fine," he said.

She put a hand on her hip and he noticed her fingers. Cloudy, yellow nails, the skin itself stained dark. He wondered if she was also a photographer, had her hands in chemicals in her off-hours. Or maybe just a Camel smoker. The point was, who could eat the food after they saw her hands? He shuddered suddenly, remembering that he'd been having ideas about this same girl earlier in the week. He remembered the exact words that came into his head: *She looks up for anything.*

"You don't eat much," she said.

"Too much stress."

She nodded, as if that made perfect sense, and then gave him a little wink. "I'm the same way," she said. "I just come in to calm my nerves."

The old man knew he was caught and was no trouble in the parking lot or in the car on the way out of town.

His name was Eisner, and whatever he was stealing, he hadn't been spending any of it on his clothes. He sat in the passenger seat in a suit that must have been fifty years old, wearing a bow tie and a starched white shirt, chewing Smith Brothers cough drops. They passed city hall and he cleared his throat.

"It used to be there were no skyscrapers in the whole city," he said. "It was a local ordinance, nothing taller than the Billy Penn. That was the law." A moment passed, and he shifted in his seat. "The place wasn't as dark then," he said.

A little snot teardrop glistened beneath one of the old man's nostrils, moving up and down as he breathed, and Whittemore felt himself edging away. He tried to remember if he'd touched him in the parking lot. He wasn't worried about the door. He'd followed him out, but he knew he'd covered his hand with his sleeve. He did that without thinking now, and he hadn't shaken hands with anybody since his mother's funeral. Not that it came up much anymore, but when it did, he would cough into his fist and tell whoever it was that he might be coming down with the flu. Nobody got past that, and nothing human had touched him in a long time.

They were on the parkway now, headed toward the river. Whittemore looked up and saw the art museum half a mile ahead, ancient and dead even in the sunlight; it could have been waiting for them both. The old man moved again, the air stirring with germs.

"A tan like that, you must travel a lot," Eisner said. They passed the museum and headed west, along the Schuylkill and past the boathouses. Then he said, "Myself, I'm a creature of habit. I stay put." And then he sneezed into his hands.

Whittemore gave him his handkerchief, which Eisner used to dry his fingers and then his eyes. And when he could see again, he looked out his window, away from the river into Fairmount Park. "During the war," he said, "there were supposed to be Japs that lived back in there in cardboard boxes and ate people's dogs . . ." It was quiet for a little while, and then he said, "I guess they decided they'd rather take their chances in the park."

Against his will, Whittemore began thinking about his visit to the doctor before he left Seattle. The doctor was Japanese — which is what brought it to mind — and said he didn't think the memory lapses were anything to worry about, that they were related to stress. The doctors in Seattle saw a lot of stress, of course, all those fucking owls to worry about, domestic partners who couldn't get on the major medical at Boeing. Whittemore had noticed that it was about twelve years ago when the doctors quit saying *You're fine.* Now it was always *I don't think it's anything to worry about.* Which smelled of insurance. Every day, he saw the world dividing itself into a billion insurance policies, everybody trying to set things up in some way that made them safe.

"Myself, what I don't like is hotels," Eisner said. "Strange mattresses, peepholes in the doors, somebody's always got their hand out. People drool on the pillowcase, it soaks through, even a hundred-dollar hotel." He dabbed at his nose with the handkerchief and said, "Rich people drool as much as anybody else, maybe more, when you think about it. And the strangers walking up and down the halls? No reflection on you, but the more human beings I see from out of state, the less hope I have for the future."

Whittemore had frozen, though, at the mention of hotel pillows. How could he have missed that? It seemed dangerous in some way that the old man had thought of it and he hadn't. Ahead of them, a Rolling Rock delivery truck dropped into a pothole that must have broken half the bottles inside.

"You care to know how this happened?" the old man said a little later.

Whittemore began to say no, that it wasn't any of his business. The old man was popping his toast every two minutes as it was. Instead, he shrugged. He'd been having queer feelings again, even before he left Seattle, like it was all out of his hands.

"There wasn't any reason," the old man said. "That's the big joke. I'm seventy-six years old; they don't have anything I want. Nothing. No reason but the twins themselves. The future-is-ours, dot-com-generation, bastard twins." He looked at him quickly and said, "Kids, I'm talking about. Nothing personal. You want a cough drop?"

Whittemore shook his head no and wondered for the next mile why the old man would think he needed a cough drop.

"Paul and Bonnie, I would cut off my right hand before I took a cent. But then they crashed their car on the Black Horse Pike — going to the shore for a weekend in the middle of winter, for Christ's sake, just like that, they're gone — and the twins take over before they're even in the ground. Forty-two years these people were my friends, they were like my family, but the truth is they didn't spend enough time at home. The business was too important. That's all I'll say about it, end of story. They didn't spend enough time at home."

Whittemore nodded, as if he agreed with that, although he hadn't met the boys himself. That wasn't the way it was done. He worked for himself. There were people in the middle, and everything went through them — the money and the jobs. It was cleaner all the way around.

"Cheating people who've been coming into the store forty years, that's how this happened. Cheating young people come in to buy a wedding ring. Ruining their parents' good reputation. What's that worth? What's the price these days on a good reputation?"

They'd been in the car half an hour now, and the houses in the distance were bigger and had rolling lawns and iron fences. Then a golf course. "You play golf?" the old man said, and a moment later Whittemore grabbed at his knee and ran the outside wheels off onto the shoulder of the road.

The sensation wasn't painful as much as eerie. Like something in there was being unscrewed. It happened on airplanes and in the movies, anywhere Whittemore had to sit still. He took vitamins, rode his bicycle three times a week, did sixty pushups every morning, and never got through the rest of the day without a twinge somewhere, without thinking this might be it.

"You know I taught these little bastards how to play? Did they tell you that?" The old man was warming to the subject now. "They got to have the best clubs, right from the first day. New leather bags, new shoes. God forbid they should play in tennis shoes. Fourteen years old, and they're riding around in carts like old men . . ."

Eisner wiped at his eyes again and then stared out the window, watching someone swing, just wanting to see a golf swing, moving a little in his seat as the swell of the fairway began to eclipse the golfer. "Cheat?" he said. "They embarrass you to death."

The course disappeared, and Eisner sneezed again. Some of it blew out beneath the handkerchief and spotted his pants. "Did you say you played? I get nervous, I can't remember what people tell me."

"A little. I used to play a little."

"Then you know what I'm talking about."

They passed into Lancaster County, and a few minutes later turned off the highway onto a road so faded that there was hardly a road left. Weeds were growing in the lane markers. They saw an Amish pulled to the side who had broken an axle on his buggy. He was up front, calming the horse; a woman was nursing a baby in the shadows of the back seat.

"I hear Titleist is coming out with a new ball, twenty extra yards off the tee," Eisner said.

Whittemore saw the dirt road that he'd picked earlier and began slowing for the turn. The old man's voice was shaking so badly, he could hardly get this out: "Myself," he said, "I wouldn't mind trying it. You get up in years like me, you can use the extra distance."

And that was as close as he came to asking for anything.

Whittemore pulled the car to the side of the road and sat still a minute, thinking it over. "What if you had to go away?"

"Me?" Eisner said. "Where am I going to go?"

"Someplace else," Whittemore said. "The other side of the world."

The old man took a minute putting it together. "You mean like the Poconos?" he said.

Whittemore went to Seventh Street that same afternoon to return the five thousand in person. That was the only chance he saw, to talk to them in person. Something like this — but not exactly this — had happened once before and been negotiated. That was the word the people in the middle used, *negotiated*. It meant they waited three or four months, gave you enough time to think maybe they'd forgotten, and then a couple of guys who laughed at everything came around with their softball bats and their twenty-pound biceps and pimples on their shoulders and brought you back into the world of hospitals and medical science. He couldn't remember now exactly what it had been like. This time, though, unless he could head it off, things would have to be explained, which was a more serious word to the people in the middle.

The jewelers took him upstairs to their office — they seemed to be in a hurry to get him off the showroom floor — and while one of them closed the door, the other one took off his coat, dropped into the chair behind his desk, hung his health-club arms over the sides — the kid wanted him to notice his arms — and stared at him as if he were trying to make up his mind. He was the one who did the talking.

"So?" the kid said.

Right away, he saw for himself what the old man meant.

"We put the five thousand up front, right? I told your people, you're late, you forfeit the back end. That simple."

Whittemore looked from one of them to the other. Identical, but he could already tell who was who.

"No comprende?" the kid said.

He began to tell them that the back end didn't matter, that he hadn't done it anyway, but he stopped himself, waiting to see where this would go. "The deal was ten," he said. "Five in front, five after it's done. That was the agreement."

The kid shook his head, and then he and his brother glanced at each other again. "It's like I told your people. Time constraints have been violated. The agreement's changed."

Whittemore sat dead still, looking from one of the twins to the other.

"I know what you're thinking," the kid said. "I know everything you're thinking, and it's like I told your people, my brother and I have left instructions with our lawyers, sealed instructions to be opened in the event anything unfortunate happens. That occurs, the lawyers open an envelope, which spells out all the details of the whole situation. Names, dates, times, everything. If we so much as slip in the shower."

They waited for him a moment, then smiled as the message settled. One of them, then the other.

"You two shower together?"

"Just a hypothesis, something to consider," the kid said.

Whittemore considered their jewelry: Rolex watches half an inch thick, diamond rings, gold bracelets and neck chains. The one at the bookcase was wearing cuff links. He wondered if it was part of the jewelry business that you had to look like a Gypsy coming out a hotel window, or if these two just liked to twinkle when they moved, separate themselves from the world at large.

The kid in the chair looked at his brother, who had walked over to the window. The little glances reminded him of the way lovers reach out to touch hands without even knowing they're doing it. "I mean, look at yourself," the one in the chair said, "coming in here like this . . ."

Whittemore nodded at him, but the kid misunderstood. But then, he misunderstood everything. "It's a Mexican standoff, man," he said. "Now get your ass out of here before I call the police."

He shot the one at the window first and then turned slowly to the one who did the talking, giving him a moment to reflect on his Mexican standoff.

Afterward, he stayed in the room a little longer than he should have, the cordite stinging his nose, studying the posture of the bodies, down to the exact position of the fingers when everything had stopped moving. He sat down behind the desk in the kid's chair, taking the weight off his knees.

The one at the window had been a nail biter.

He thought of the old man and wondered how long it would be before he got homesick and showed up at the restaurant. His hands had shaken, but that was all. No crying, no regrets. There in the front seat, Whittemore had suddenly remembered how he'd let the guys who laughed at everything position his legs across the kitchen chairs just so and that one of his knees — he wasn't sure even then which one — hadn't dislocated the first time they came down on it, or the second, or the third.

He'd taken Eisner to a bus stop anyway.

Eisner got out and was around the car at Whittemore's window in what seemed like the same instant, tapping at the window, brimming tears, and Whittemore rolled it down to see what he wanted, and he came in like death itself, glistening tears and snot, right through the window, his hands, his head, his shoulders, and shit the sheets if Whittemore didn't just sit there and let the old man hug him.

TYLER DILTS

Thug: Signification and the (De) Construction of Self

FROM *Puerto del Sol*

I THUG.

That's not a grammatical error. I fully intended to use the word "thug" as a verb. I realize, of course, that for you, unless you happen to have some knowledge of hip-hop music and culture or hard-boiled noir fiction, you're probably not familiar with this particular usage. But as I said, I actually meant to use the word "thug" as a verb, rather than in its much more common and familiar usage as a noun. The reasons for this are twofold:

1) I have, of late, been giving a great deal of thought as to how we define both ourselves and each other by what we do.[1] I am fascinated by the subtle yet significant differences between the phrases "I thug" and "I am a thug." The play in signification here seems never to exhaust its ability to keep my intellect bouncing back and forth, questioning the point at which I cease to be the sum of my actions and become the thing itself (i.e., at what point do I cease thugging and simply become thug?).

2) I find this type of nontraditional and playful usage of language to be quite stimulating and more than a little amusing. And I have always imagined it to be exactly the type of intellectual exercise with which my friends and I would ceaselessly amuse ourselves, over postmeal cocktails and cappuccinos at, say, Mum's or Cha Cha Cha, had I, of course, any friends.

At any rate, I thug. And indeed it follows then that I must, to myself at least, pose the following question — since I *do* thug, am I then *a* thug?

Rather than attempting to answer that question presently, though,[2] I reach in front of me to the coffee table, pick up both the television remote control and the current issue of the *TV Guide* on top of which it rests. The *Guide* has been conveniently left open to the proper day but not the proper time, so I find myself flipping past pages of upcoming television "events" to reach the four P.M. listings.[3] Not often having the inclination to watch television in the late afternoon, and curious as to with what I might be able to divert my attention, I find myself pleasantly surprised to see that, in addition to its regular eleven P.M. broadcast, the *Charlie Rose* show is now shown at four in the afternoon. I turn on the 36-inch Mitsubishi to channel 28, anxious to see whom Mr. Rose will be interviewing.[4]

No sooner do I realize that a group of well-known journalists are discussing the ethical ramifications of the recent media coverage of a number of national news events[5] than I hear the unmistakable dull grinding of the garage door opener as it echoes through the kitchen. I turn off the television, slink into the kitchen, and take a position with my back flat against the wall next to the door leading into the garage.[6] I hear Bobby's keys jangling for a moment, and then a click as the door is unlocked. The door opens, concealing me from his peripheral vision as he steps into the room. I slam the door forcefully behind him.

He jumps and spins toward the sound. When he sees me, the expression of fear on his face is very nearly palpable. The reasons for his fear are quite understandable, in fact, even logical, given three significant factors inherent in the situation: 1) there is someone in his kitchen who, for all intents and purposes, has no legal right to be there; 2) the particular someone standing in his kitchen is indeed quite intimidating, due not only to the aforementioned size and bulk,[7] but also to the fact that the particular someone is, save for his eyelashes, completely bald (I suffer from a relatively rare disorder — alopecia areata — that causes, in more extreme cases such as mine, a complete ceasing of hair growth that may or may not be permanent),[8] and 3) he knows precisely who the particular someone is and precisely why he is there. "Hello, Bobby," I say, smiling, friendly, pleasant. It's important to me to make the effort, whenever and wherever possible, to be as polite and courteous as the situation allows. This, I think, has more than a little to do with my particularly imposing physicality. It is an attempt, on both the conscious and, I suspect, subconscious levels, to allay, insomuch as it is possible, people's reactions to my appearance.[9]

"Jesus Fucking Christ!" Bobby yells. "I almost pissed myself, you fucking *bald-headed* freak!" (Italics mine.)

Of the many deprecatory references he might have uttered, he lit upon the single possibility that would undoubtedly cause me, at least momentarily, to lose my composure.[10] I slap him in the face, and as he raises his hands in defense I deliver a forceful uppercut to his solar plexus. The power of the blow lifts him an inch off the floor, and as the wind explodes out of his lungs he collapses like a deboned salmon onto the floor.

I watch him writhe there awhile, gasping for breath, trying to fill his lungs with air. I know I have a few moments before he'll be capable of processing any rational thoughts, so I let him go and take a seat at the kitchen table. It's a nice butcher-block set, very Pottery Barn. The accouterments of the American bottled-water demographic's consumerism were rampant — a two-door stainless restaurant refrigerator, an oversized gourmet stove with industrial-grade grates, a triple oven with convection, microwave, and broiler in one brushed chrome unit, all surrounding a granite-topped island over a rust-colored, antiqued tile floor.

Bobby's desperate writhing begins to slow, and I look down at him. His belted black leather coat is bunched up under his armpits, tufts of his carefully gelled and expensively trimmed yellow hair now jut from his head at odd angles, and he writhes in a semifetal position on the tile. The short gasps of air he is able to take into his lungs grow longer and he looks up at me. I smile affably.

"I'm sorry, Bobby," I say. "That was rather unprofessional of me."

Bobby has a puzzled look in his soft-contacted, artificially blue eyes.

"But, of course, I am more than a little sensitive in regard to my baldness."[11] I pause for emphasis. "So I'll say this only once — do not ever mention it again."

Bobby's breathing approaches normalcy and he sits up.

"Are we clear on that point?"

He tries to answer, but isn't quite able yet. He nods instead.

"Good." I give him a moment to reflect on his situation, watching as he brushes a stiffened lock of hair off his forehead. I wonder if he will stay seated on the floor, or get up and perhaps attempt to join me at the table.

"You, of course, know why I'm here," I say. He stays on the floor and nods again. Good.[12] I pause here, to allow him the option of the next move. He stares dumbly at me for a solid ten seconds. "Where's the money, Bobby?"

He reaches into his inside breast pocket and pulls out a roll of bills. Without even counting, I know it will be short. I take it from his outstretched hand and thumb through the bundle of twenties and fifties.

"You're light, Bobby."

He lowers his eyes to the tile.

"This won't even cover the vig."[13]

"I know."

"You know?"

"Yes."

"Then why even offer it up?"

"I don't know." Bobby looks up at me. Plastic blue eyes pleading. "You seem like a reasonable guy."

"I am a reasonable guy, Bobby."

He looks relieved for a moment. Doesn't realize there's a "but" coming.

"But I'm also an honest guy, Bobby."

Now he looks puzzled.

"What did I tell you last week?"

He hunches his shoulders and spreads his hands.

"You know," I say.

He looks at the tile again. I begin to think he finds it more interesting than our conversation.

"Tell me, Bobby."

Silence.

I reach down and lift his chin, turning his face toward mine. I wonder if this is what mothers of uncooperative children feel. "Tell me what I said would happen if you came up light again this week." More silence.

I grab him by the lapels and stand, raising him to his feet. Letting go of his collar, I palm his face like a basketball and give him a shove. His body slams against the wall, his head bouncing slightly off the ecru-painted drywall.[14] I close the distance between us and look down into his face. I rest my hand gently on his shoulder and whisper. "What did I say, Bobby?"

He mumbles toward my chest. "You told me you'd break my thumbs."

"That's right." I step back a bit, but not enough to let him move away from the wall. "Now what am I supposed to do, Bobby? What should I do?"

"Cut me some slack, man. Please."

I consider the possibility for a moment. "You know I can't do that. You're not the only one accountable here." Making a special effort to soften my voice, as if talking to a child, I say, "But I'll tell you what . . ." I am sorry as soon as I speak. Looking into his eyes, I see I've given him too much hope. "Sit down at the table, hold still, and don't scream. I'll make it as painless as possible."

I can't read his expression. His brows are arched high above his rounded eyes and his teeth are still clenched together, making the cords on his neck stand out.

"Sit at the table," I say.

He looks at me as if I'm speaking a foreign language, so I put my hand on his shoulder and tug him toward the table. I sit him down. He lowers his head again.

"Are you crying?" I ask.

He shakes his head, lying.

"Give me a hand."

He holds both hands a few inches above the table and considers them.

"Come on, Bobby. I'm going to break them both anyway. It's not *Sophie's Choice*."[15] He looks even more confused. So I reach down, grab his left hand, and quickly snap the thumb.[16]

He yelps like a kicked Chihuahua.

Before he can pull the right hand away, I grab it and repeat the process.

Another yelp, more crying. He holds both hands in front of and away from himself as if they are on fire. He looks confused, tears on his cheeks.[17]

I walk around the island to the freezer. Going well above and beyond the call of duty, I pull out a tray of ice and dump it into a Williams-Sonoma kitchen towel. I fold the ice into the green-checkered fabric and carry it back to Bobby.

"Hold this between your palms." I hand it to him. "Not too tight. I'll see you next time, Bobby."

He mutters something incomprehensible.

"You know what happens next time, right, Bobby?"

Bobby nods.

"Look at me, Bobby."

He looks at me.

"You know?"[18]

He nods.

"You should go to the emergency room to have those set."

Another nod.

"Have a nice day, Bobby."

I lock the door behind myself as I walk out into the street. The cool blue of the sky is just beginning to warm where the sun is nearing the horizon. I feel an itch on the back of my head. Reaching up, I gently rub my finger across the spot, hoping to feel a point or two of new hair growth. I don't.

Sitting behind the wheel of my car, again I wonder — verb or noun?

Notes

1. I use the first person plural here to refer to not only the personal "we," but also to the culture at large.

2. An effort at which, I'll readily concede, I have failed on several past occasions.

3. I know they simply must be considered "events" because in at least three of the ads they were identified variously as events of the "special," "important," and "not-to-be-missed" variety.

4. Charlie Rose is, of course, simply the finest interviewer currently working in television; next to him, Barbara Walters's true gossipmonger colors can be seen in all their vivid brightness. Some might argue that Ted Koppel matches Rose's skill, and while this may certainly be true insofar as simple technique is concerned, the broader scope of Rose's interviewees and his encyclopedic knowledge in so many diverse areas clearly give him the edge. I won't even deign to mention Larry King and his all-consuming celebrity nasal/anal interface.

5. I realize, of course, the oxymoronic possibilities of the phrases "ethical ramifications" and "media coverage" being used in the same sentence; that is, in fact, the irony I was looking forward to seeing examined on the program.

6. Surprisingly, for a man of my considerable size and bulk — I stand six-foot-five and weigh 282 pounds — I slink surprisingly well. The skill is something of a requirement for any kind of long-ranging success in the thugging field.

7. See note 6, above.

8. For more information on alopecia areata, visit the National Alopecia Areata Foundation's Web site at www.alopeciaeareata.com.

9. As a closely related corollary to my previously mentioned interest in the manner in which our actions function as determinants in our conception of selfhood, I am also actively seeking some personal understanding of the manner in which our appearances affect our actions and how these dual factors, acting both separately and in concert with one another, influence our conception of self.

10. The reference to my alopecia is the single insult that, from the time I first lost my hair in the eighth grade, I have been completely unable to tolerate. I do, however, consider myself somewhat fortunate in one regard — I have, almost exclusively through both implicit and explicit threats of physical violence, been able to silence the vast majority of those who sought to injure me in this fashion. Those who were not intimidated enough to think better of their actions were moderately to severely injured. I think often of people who suffer from alopecia and other similar disorders which render them, to varying degrees, different in appearance from those in the majority, and wonder how they make it through the day. I like to think I am doing some small service in educating those who would mock and belittle others simply on the basis of their physical appearance.

11. At an alopecia support group meeting recently, one of the members proposed we coin the phrase "follicle-challenged" to describe ourselves. That suggestion was almost comic in its political correctness. The only factor that mitigated my impulse to laugh audibly was the fact that I so clearly understood the pain from which the suggestion arose.

12. Had he risen, it would have signified either a conscious or unconscious desire on his part to challenge my superior position.

13. Vig or vigorish: the exorbitant interest charged by a loan shark (aka shylock; despite the pejorative connotations of this particular term to those of Jewish ancestry, it is still by far the more commonly used). This interest is, in fact, specifically designed to be impossible for the mark to pay. This in turn forces the forfeiture by said mark of any real properties s/he might possess.

14. I cannot state unequivocally that the color of the wall is ecru; it might very well be eggshell, or possibly even Navajo white.

15. I regret at once the literary reference. I think perhaps the relatively wide exposure of the film version of Styron's novel will suffice to effectively convey my intended meaning; it does not.

16. The proper technique for a clean thumbbreak is as follows: grasp the thumb at its base, as close as is possible to the hand itself, wrapping your own thumb and forefinger around the joint. Repeat the process at the upper joint. The idea is to support each of the joints to the greatest extent possible. Once this has been accomplished, snap the thumb sharply sideways, perpendicular to the direction of the thumb's own movement. You should, in most cases, feel the bone snap in your hands. Imagine breaking a pencil wrapped in several slices of bologna for some idea of the sensation.

17. While this reaction veers clearly toward the maudlin, I certainly prefer it to the violent or indignant. At least he stops short of wetting his pants.

18. Next time, just as Bobby's thumbs are about to be severed from his hands, he'll be given the option of releasing his interest in the $38,000 worth of equity he has built up in his home by signing over the deed. We can be fairly sure which option Bobby will choose.

MIKE DOOGAN

War Can Be Murder

FROM *The Mysterious North*

TWO MEN GOT OUT of the Jeep and walked toward the building. Their fleece-lined leather boots squeaked on the snow. One of the men was young, stocky, and black. The other was old, thin, and white. Both men wore olive-drab wool pants, duffel coats, and knit wool caps. The black man rolled forward onto his toes with each step, like he was about to leap into space. The white man's gait was something between a saunter and a stagger. Their breath escaped in white puffs. Their heads were burrowed down into their collars, and their hands were jammed into the pockets of their coats.

"Kee-rist, it's cold," the black man said.

Their Jeep ticked loudly as it cooled. The building they approached was part log cabin and part Quonset hut with a shacky plywood porch tacked onto the front. Yellow light leaked from three small windows. Smoke plumed from a metal pipe punched through its tin roof. A sign beside the door showed a black cat sitting on a white crescent, the words CAROLINA MOON lettered beneath.

"You sure we want to go in here?" the black man asked.

"Have to," the white man said. "I've got an investment to protect."

They hurried through the door and shut it quickly behind them. They were standing in a fair-sized room that held a half-dozen tables and a big bar. They were the only ones in the room. The room smelled of cigarette smoke, stale beer, and desperation. The white man led the way past the bar and through a door, turned left, and walked down a dark hallway toward the light spilling from another open door.

The light came from a small room that held a big bed and four people not looking at the corpse on the floor. One, a big, red-haired guy, was dressed in olive drab with a black band around one biceps that read MP in white letters. The other man was short, plump, and fair-haired, dressed in brown. Both wore guns on their hips. One of the women was small and temporarily blond, wearing a red robe that didn't hide much. The other woman was tall, black, and regal as Cleopatra meeting Caesar.

"I tole you, he give me a couple of bucks and said I should go get some supper at Leroy's," the temporary blonde was saying.

"'Lo, Zulu," the thin man said, nodding to the black woman.

"Mister Sam," she replied.

"What the hell are you doing here, soldier?" the MP barked.

"That's *Sergeant*," the thin man said cheerfully. He nodded to the plump man. "Marshal Olson," he said. "Damn cold night to be dragged out into, isn't it?"

"So it is, Sergeant Hammett," the plump man said. "So it is." He shrugged toward the corpse on the floor. "Even colder where he is, you betcha."

"Look you," the MP said, "I'm ordering you to leave. And take that dinge with you. This here's a military investigation, and if you upstuck it, I'll throw you in the stockade."

"If I what it?" Hammett asked.

"Upstuck," the MP grated.

"Upstuck?" Hammett asked. "Anybody got any idea what he's talking about?"

"I think he means 'obstruct,'" the black man said.

"Why, thank you, Clarence," Hammett said. He pointed to the black man. "My companion is Clarence Jefferson Delight. You might know him better as Little Sugar Delight. Fought Tony Zale to a draw just before the war. Had twenty-seven — that's right, isn't it, Clarence? — twenty-seven professional fights without a loss. Not bad for a dinge, eh?" To the plump man, he said, "It's been a while since I was involved in this sort of thing, Oscar, but I believe that as the U.S. Marshal you're the one with jurisdiction here." To the MP, he said, "Which means you can take your order and stick it where the sun don't shine."

The MP started forward. Hammett waited for him with arms hanging loosely at his sides. The marshal stepped forward and put a hand on the MP's chest.

"Maybe you'd better go cool off, fella," he said. "Maybe go radio headquarters for instructions while I talk to these folks here."

The MP hesitated, relaxed, said, "Right you are, Marshal," and left the room.

"Maybe we should all go into the other room," the marshal said. The others began to file out. Hammett crouched next to the corpse, which lay on its back, arms outflung, completely naked. He was a young, slim, sandy-haired fellow with blue eyes and full lips. His head lay over on his shoulder, the neck bent much farther than it should have been. Hammett laid a hand on the corpse's chest.

"Give me a hand, Oscar, and we'll roll him over," he said.

The two men rolled the corpse onto its stomach. Hammett looked it up and down, grunted, and they rolled it back over.

"You might want to make sure a doctor examines that corpse," he said as the two men walked toward the barroom. "I think you'll find he was here to receive rather than give."

The temporary blonde told a simple story. A soldier had come into her room, given her $2, and told her to get something to eat.

"He said don't come back for an hour," she said.

She'd gone out the back door, she said, shooting a nervous look at the black woman, so she wouldn't have to answer any questions. When she returned, she'd found the soldier naked and dead.

"She told me," the black woman said to the marshal, "and I sent someone for you."

"What did you have to eat?" Hammett asked the temporary blonde.

"Leroy said it was beefsteak, but I think it was part of one of them moose," she said. "And some mushy canned peas and a piece of chocolate cake. I think it give me the heartburn. That or the body."

"That's a story that should be easy enough to check out," Hammett said.

"And what about you, Zulu?" the marshal asked.

"I was in the office or behind the bar all night, Mister Olson," the black woman said. "That gentleman came in, had a drink, paid the usual fee, and asked for a girl. When I asked him which one, he said it didn't matter. So I sent him back to Daphne."

"Seen him before?" the marshal asked.

"Lots of men come through here," Zulu said. "But I think he'd been here before."

"He done the same thing with me maybe three, four times before," the temporary blonde said. "With some a the other girls, too." She shot another nervous look at the black woman. "We talk sometimes, ya know."

"Notice anybody in particular in here tonight?" the marshal said.

"Quite a few people in here tonight," Zulu said. "Some for the music, some for other things. Maybe thirty people in here when the body was found. I think maybe one of them is on the city council. And there was that banker . . ."

"That's enough of that," the marshal said.

"And he could have let anybody in through the back door," Zulu said.

The red-haired MP came back into the barroom, chased by a blast of cold air.

"The major wants me to bring the whore in to the base," he said to the marshal.

"I don't think Daphne wants to go anywhere with you, young man," Zulu said.

"I don't care what a whore thinks," the MP said.

Zulu leaned across the bar and very deliberately slapped the MP across the face. He lunged for her. Hammett stuck a shoulder into his chest, and the marshal grabbed his arm.

"You probably don't remember me, Tobin," Hammett said, leaning into the MP, "but I remember when you were just a kid on the black-and-blue squad in San Francisco. I heard you did something that got you thrown out of the cops just before the war. I don't remember what. What was it you did to get tossed off the force?"

"Fuck you," the MP said. "How do you know so much, anyway?"

"I was with the Pinks for a while," Hammett said. "I know some people."

"You can relax now, son," the marshal said to the MP. "Nobody roughs up Zulu when I'm around. You go tell your major that if he wants to be involved in this investigation he should speak to me directly. Now beat it."

"I'm too old for this nonsense," Hammett said after the MP left, "but you can't have people beating up your partner. It's bad for business."

"There ain't going to be any business for a while," the marshal said. "Until we get to the bottom of this, you're closed, Zulu. I'll roust somebody out and have 'em collect the body. Otherwise, keep people out of that room until I tell you different."

With that, he left.

"I believe I'll have a drink now, Zulu," Hammett said.

"You heard the marshal," the black woman said. "We're closed."

"But I'm your partner," Hammett said, grinning.

"Silent partner," she said. "I guess you forgot the silent part."

"Now there's gratitude for you, Clarence," Hammett said. "She begs me for money to open this place, and now that she has my money she doesn't want anything to do with me. Think what I'm risking. Why, if my friends in Hollywood knew I was half owner of a cathouse . . ."

"They'd all be lining up three deep for free booze and free nooky," Zulu said. "Now you two skedaddle. I've got to get Daphne moved to another room, and I'll have big, clumsy white folk tracking in and out of here all night. I'll be speaking to you later, Mister Sam."

The two men went back out into the cold.

"Little Sugar Delight?" the black man said. "Tony Zale? Why do you want to be telling such stories?"

"Why, Clarence," Hammett said, "think how boring life would be if we didn't all make up stories."

The black man slid behind the wheel and punched the starter. The engine whirred and whined and exploded into life.

"You can drop me back at the Lido Gardens," Hammett said. "I have a weekend pass, and I believe there's a nurse who's just about drunk enough by now."

Hammett awoke the next morning alone, sprawled fully clothed on the bed of a small, spare hotel room. One boot lay on its side on the floor. The other was still on his left foot. He raised himself slowly to a sitting position. The steam radiator hissed, and somewhere outside the frosted-over window a horn honked. Hammett groaned loudly as he bent down to remove his boot. He pulled off both socks, then took two steps across the bare, cold floor to a small table, poured himself a glass of water from a pitcher, and drank it. Then another. He took the empty glass over to where his coat dangled from the back of a chair and rummaged around in the pockets until he came up with a small bottle of whiskey. He poured some into the glass, drank it, and shuddered.

"The beginning of another perfect day," he said aloud.

He walked to the washstand and peered into the mirror. The face that looked back was pale and narrow, topped by crew-cut gray hair. He had baggy, hound-dog brown eyes and a full, salt-and-pepper mustache trimmed at the corners of a wide mouth. He took off his shirt and regarded his pipe-stem arms and sunken chest.

"Look out, Tojo," he said.

He walked to the other side of the bed, opened a small leather valise, and took out a musette bag. Back at the washstand, he reached into his mouth and removed a full set of false teeth. His cheeks, already sunken, collapsed completely. He brushed the false teeth vigorously and replaced them in his mouth. He shaved. Then he took clean underwear from the valise, left the room, and walked down the hall toward the bathroom. About halfway down the hall, a small, dark-haired man lay snoring on the floor. He smelled of alcohol and vomit. Hammett stepped over him and continued to the bathroom.

After bathing, Hammett returned to his room, put on a clean shirt, and walked down a flight of stairs to the lobby. He went through a door marked CAFÉ and sat at the counter. A clock next to the cash register read 11:45. A hard-faced woman put a thick cup down in front of him and filled it with coffee. Hammett took a pair of eyeglasses out of his shirt pocket and consulted the gravy-stained menu.

"Breakfast or lunch?" he asked the hard-faced woman.

"Suit yourself," she said.

"I'll have the sourdough pancakes, a couple of eggs over easy, and orange juice," Hammett said. "Coffee, too."

"Hey, are these real eggs?" asked a well-dressed, middle-aged man sitting a few stools down. The left arm of his suit coat was empty and pinned to his lapel.

The hard-faced women blew air through her lips.

"Cheechakos," she said. "A course they're real eggs. Real butter, too. This here's a war zone, you know."

She yelled Hammett's order through a serving hatch to the Indian cook.

"Can't get this food back home?" Hammett asked the one-armed man.

"Ration cards," the man replied. "Or the black market."

"Much money in the black market?" Hammett asked.

The one-armed man made a sour face.

"Guess so," he said. "You can get most anything off the back of a truck, most of it with military markings. And they say the high society parties are all catered by Uncle Sam. But I wouldn't know for certain." He flicked his empty sleeve. "Got this at Midway. I'm not buying at no goddamn black market."

A boy selling newspapers came in off the street. Hammett gave him a dime and took a newspaper, which was cold to the touch.

"Budapest Surrenders!" the headline proclaimed.

A small article said the previous night's temperature had reached twenty-eight below zero, the coldest of the winter. In the lower right-hand corner of the front page was a table headed "Road to Berlin." It showed that allied troops were 32 miles away at Zellin on the eastern front, 304 miles away at Kleve on the western front, and 504 miles away at the Reno River on the Italian front.

The hard-faced woman put a plate of pancakes and eggs in front of Hammett. As he ate them, he read that the Ice Carnival had donated $1,100 in proceeds to the Infantile Paralysis Fund, the Pribilof Five — two guitars, a banjo, an accordion, and a fiddle — had played at the USO log cabin, and Jimmy Foxx had re-signed with the Phillies. He finished his meal, put a 50-cent piece next to his plate, and stood up.

"Where do you think you are, mister?" the hard-faced woman said. "Seattle? That'll be one dollar."

"Whew!" the one-armed man said.

Hammett dug out a dollar, handed it to the woman, and left the 50-cent piece on the counter.

"Wait'll you have a drink," he said to the one-armed man.

Hammett walked across the lobby to the hotel desk and asked the clerk for the telephone. He consulted the slim telephone book, dialed, identified himself, and waited.

"Oscar," he said. "Sam Hammett. Has the doctor looked at that corpse from last night? Uh-huh. Uh-huh. Was I right about him? I see. You found out his name yet and where he was assigned? A sergeant? That kid was a sergeant? What's this man's army coming to? And he was in supply? Nope, I don't know anybody over there. But if you want, I can have a word with General Johnson. Okay. How about the Carolina Moon? Can Zulu open up again? Come on, Oscar. Be reasonable. They didn't have anything to do with the killing. All right then. I guess we'd better hope you find the killer soon. See you. Oscar. 'Bye."

Hammett returned to his room, put on his overcoat, and went out of the hotel. The air was warmer than it had been the night before, but not warm. He walked several blocks along the street, moving slowly over the hard-packed snow. He passed mostly one- or two-story wooden buildings, many of them hotels, bars, or cafés. He counted seven buildings under construction. A few automobiles of prewar vintage passed him, along with several Jeeps and a new, olive-drab staff car. He passed many people on foot, most of them men in work clothes or uniforms. When his cheeks began to get numb, he turned left, then left again, and walked back toward the hotel. A couple of blocks short of his destination, he turned left again, crossed the street, and went into a small shop with BOOK CACHE painted on its window. He browsed among the tables of books, picked one up, and walked to the counter.

"Whatya got there?" the woman behind the counter asked. Her hair was nearly as gray as Hammett's. "*Theoretical Principles of Marxism* by V. I. Lenin." She smiled. "That sounds like a thriller. Buy or rent?"

"Rent," Hammett said.

"Probably won't get much call for this," the woman said. "How about ten cents for a week?"

"Better make it two weeks," Hammett said, handing her a quarter. "This isn't easy reading."

The woman wrote the book's title, Hammett's name and barracks number, and the rental period down in a register, gave him a nickel back, and smiled again.

"Aren't you a little old to be a soldier?" she asked.

"I was twenty-one when I enlisted," he said, grinning. "War ages a man."

When it came time to turn for his hotel, Hammett walked on. Two blocks later he was at a small wooden building with a sign over the door that read MILITARY POLICE.

"I'm looking for the duty officer," he told the MP on the desk. A young lieutenant came out of an office in the back.

"Sam Hammett of General Johnson's staff," Hammett said. "I'm working on a piece for *Army Up North* about military policing, and I need some information."

"Don't you salute officers on General Johnson's staff?" the lieutenant snapped.

"Not when we're off duty and out of uniform, sir," Hammett said. "As I'm certain they taught you in OCS, sir."

The two men looked at one another for a minute, then the lieutenant blinked and said, "What can I do for you, Sergeant?"

"I need some information on staffing levels, sir," Hammett said. "For instance, how many men did you have on duty here in Anchorage last night, sir?"

Each successive "sir" seemed to make the lieutenant more at ease.

"I'm not sure," he said. "But if you'd like to step back into the office, we can look at the duty roster."

Hammett looked at the roster. Tobin's name wasn't on it. He took a notebook out of his coat pocket and wrote in it.

"Thank you, sir," he said. "Now I'll need your name and hometown. For the article."

Back at the hotel, Hammett removed his coat and boots. He poured some whiskey into the glass, filled it with water, lay down on the bed, and began writing a letter.

"Dear Lillian," it began. "I am back in Anchorage and have probably seen the end of my posting to the Aleutians."

When he'd finished the letter, he made himself another drink and picked up his book. Within five minutes he was snoring.

He dreamed he was working for the Pinkerton National Detective Agency again, paired with a big Irish kid named Michael Carey on the Fatty Arbuckle case. He dreamed he was at the Stork Club, arguing with Hemingway about the Spanish Civil War. He dreamed he was in a watering hole on Lombard with an older Carey, who pointed out red-haired Billy Tobin and said something Hammett couldn't make out. He dreamed he was locked in his room on Post Street, drinking and writing *The Big Knockover*. His wife, Josie, was pounding on the door, asking for more money for herself and his daughters.

"Hey mister, wake up." It was the desk clerk's voice. He pounded on the door again. "Wake up, mister."

"What do you want?" Hammett called.

"You got a visitor downstairs. A shine."

Hammett got up from the bed and pulled the door open.

"Go get my visitor and bring him up," he said.

The desk clerk returned with the black man right behind him.

"Clarence, this is the desk clerk," Hammett said. "What's your name?"

"Joe," the desk clerk said.

"Joe," Hammett said, "this is Clarence 'Big Stick' LeBeau. Until the war came along, he played third base for the Birmingham Black Barons of the Negro league. Hit thirty home runs or more in seven — it was seven, wasn't it, Clarence? — straight seasons. If it weren't for the color line, he'd have been playing for the Yankees. Not bad for a shine, huh?"

"I didn't mean nothing by that, mister," the desk clerk said. "You neither, Clarence." His eyes darted this way and that. "I got to get back to the desk," he said, and scurried off.

"Welcome to my castle," Hammett said, stepping aside to let the black man in. "What brings you here?"

"I've got to get started to Florida for spring training," the black man said. "The things you come up with. I didn't know white folk knew anything about the Birmingham Black Barons. And why do you keep calling me Clarence?"

"It suits you better than Don Miller," Hammett said. "And it keeps everybody guessing. Confusion to the enemy."

"You been drinking?" Miller said.

"A little," Hammett said. "You want a nip?" Miller shook his head. "But I've been sleeping more. The old need their sleep. What brings you here?"

"I was at the magazine office working on the illustrations for that frostbite article when I was called into the presence of Major General Davenport Johnson himself. He said you'd promised to go to a party tonight at some banker's house, and since he knew what an irresponsible s.o.b. you were — those were his words — he was ordering me to make sure you got there. Party starts in half an hour, so you'd better get cleaned up."

"I'm not going to any goddamn party at any goddamn banker's house," Hammett said. "I'm going to the Lido Gardens and the South Seas and maybe the Owl Club."

"This is Little Sugar Delight you're talking to, remember," Miller said. "You're going to the party if I have to carry you. General's orders."

"General's orders," Hammett said, and laughed. "That'll teach me to be famous." He took off his shirt, washed his face and hands, put the shirt back on, knotted a tie around his neck, put on his uniform jacket and a pair of glistening black shoes that he took from the valise, and picked up his overcoat.

"All right, Little Sugar," he said, "let's go entertain the cream of Anchorage society."

Hammett got out of the Jeep in front of a two-story wooden house. Light spilled from all the windows, and the cold air carried the muffled murmur of voices.

"You can go on about your business," he told Miller. "I'll walk back to town."

"It must be twenty below, Sam," Miller said.

"Nearer thirty, I expect," Hammett said. "But it's only a half-dozen blocks, and I like to walk."

Indoors, the temperature was 110 degrees warmer. Men in suits and uniforms stood around drinking, talking, and sweating. Among them was a sprinkling of overdressed women with carefully done-up hair. A horse-faced woman wearing what might have been real diamonds and showing a lot of cleavage walked up to Hammett.

"Aren't you Dashiell Hammett, the writer?" she asked.

Hammett stared down the front of her dress.

"Actually, I'm Samuel Hammett, the drunkard," he said after several seconds. "Where might I find a drink?"

Hammett quickly downed a drink and picked up another. The woman led him to where a large group, all wearing civilian clothes, was talking about the war.

"I tell you," a big, bluff man with dark, wavy hair was saying, "we are winning this war because we believe in freedom and democracy."

Everyone nodded.

"And free enterprise, whatever Roosevelt might think," said another man.

Everyone nodded again.

"What do you think, Dashiell?" the woman asked.

Hammett finished his drink. His eyes were bright, and he had a little smile on his lips.

"I think I need another drink," he said.

"No," the woman said, "about the war."

"Oh, that," Hammett said. "First of all, we're not winning the war. Not by ourselves. We've got a lot of help. The Soviets, for example, have done much of the dying for us. Second, the part of the war we are winning we're winning because we can make more tanks and airplanes and bombs than the Germans and the Japs can. We're not winning because our ideas are better than theirs. We're winning because we're drowning the sonsabitches in metal."

When he stopped talking, the entire room was quiet.

"That was quite a speech," the woman said, her voice much less friendly than it had been.

"You'd have been better off just giving me another drink," Hammett said. "But don't worry. I can get it myself."

He was looking at a painting of a moose when a slim, curly-haired fellow who couldn't have been more than thirty walked up to him. He had a major's oak leaves on his shoulders.

"That was quite a speech, soldier," the major said. "What's an NCO doing at this party, anyway?"

"Ask the general," Hammett said.

"Oh, that's right, you're Hammett, the hero of the morale tour." The major took a drink from the glass he was holding. "You must be something on a morale tour with speeches like that." When Hammett said nothing, the major went on, "I hear you're involved in the murder of one of my sergeants."

Hammett laughed. "I don't know about involved," he said, "but I've got a fair idea who did it."

The major moved closer to Hammett.

"I think you'll find that in the army, it's safer to mind your own business," he said. "Much safer."

Hammett thrust his face into the major's face and opened his mouth to speak, but was interrupted by another voice.

"Ah, Sergeant Hammett," the voice said, "I see you've met Major Allen. The major's the head of supply out at the fort."

"Thanks for clearing that up, General," Hammett said. "I thought maybe he was somebody's kid and these were his pajamas."

The major's face reddened and his mouth opened.

"Sergeant!" the general barked. "Do you know the punishment for insubordination?"

"Sorry, General, Major," Hammett said. "This whiskey just plays hob with my ordinarily high regard for military discipline."

The major stomped off.

"That mouth of yours will get you into trouble one day, Sergeant," the general said. He sounded as if he were trying hard not to laugh.

"Yes, sir," Hammett said. "But he is a jumped-up little turd."

"Yes, he is that," the general said. "Regular army. His father was regular army, too. Chief of supply at the Presidio. Did very well for himself. Retired to a very nice home on Nob Hill. This one's following in the family footsteps. All polish and connections. There, see? See how politely he takes his leave of the hostess. Now you behave yourself." The general looked at the picture of the moose. "Damned odd animal, isn't it?" he said, and moved off.

The general left the party a half hour later and Hammett a few minutes after that. He made his way down the short, icy walkway and, as he turned left, his feet flew out from under him. As he fell he heard three loud explosions. Something whirred past his ear. He twisted so that he landed on his side and rolled behind a car parked at the curb. He heard people boil out of the house behind him.

"What was that?" they called. And, "Are you all right?"

Hammett got slowly to his feet. There were no more shots.

"I'm fine," he called. "But I could use a lift downtown, if anyone is headed that way."

It was nearly midnight when Hammett walked into the smoke and noise of the Lido Gardens. A four-piece band was making a racket in one corner, and a table full of WACs was getting a big play from about twice as many men in the other. Hammett navigated his way across the room to the bar and ordered a whiskey.

"Not bad for a drunk," he said to himself and turned to survey the room. His elbow hit the shoulder of the man next to him. The man spilled some of his beer on the bar.

"Hey, watch it, you old bastard," the man growled, looking up. A broad smile split his face. "Well if it isn't Dash Hammett, the worst man on a stakeout I ever saw. What are you doing here at the end of the earth?"

"Dispensing propaganda and nursemaiding Hollywood stars,"

Hammett said. "Isn't that why every man goes to war? And what about you, Carey? The Pinks finally figure out how worthless you are and let you go?"

The two men shook hands.

"No, it's a sad tale," the other man said. "A man of my years should have been able to spend the war behind a desk, in civilian clothes. But then the army figured out that a lot of money was rolling around because of the war and that money might make people do some bad things." Both men laughed. "So they drafted me. Me, with my bad knees and failing eyesight. Said I had special qualifications. And here I am, back out in the field, chasing crooks. For even less money than the agency paid me."

"War is indeed hell," Hammett said. "Let me buy you a drink to ease the pain." He signaled to the bartender. When both men had fresh drinks, he asked, "What brings you to Alaska?"

"Well, you'll get a good laugh out of this," Carey said. "You'll never guess who we found as a supply sergeant at Fort Lewis. Bennie the Grab. And he had Spanish Pete Gomez and Fingers Malone as his corporals."

"Mother of God," Hammett said. "It's a surprise there was anything left worth stealing at that place."

"You know it, brother," Carey said. "So you can imagine how we felt when all of the paperwork checked out. Bennie and the boys wouldn't have gotten much more than a year in the brig for false swearing when they joined up if it hadn't been for some smart young pencil pusher. He figured out they were sending a lot of food and not much of anything else to the 332nd here at Fort Richardson."

"Don't tell me," Hammett said. "There is no 332nd."

"That's right," Carey said. "The trucks were leaving the warehouses, but the goods for the 332nd weren't making it to the ships. There wasn't a restaurant or diner or private dinner party in the entire Pacific Northwest that didn't feature U.S. Army butter and beef. We scooped up Bennie and the others, a couple of captains, a major, and a full-bird colonel. All the requisitions were signed by a Sergeant Prevo, and I drew the short straw and got sent up here to arrest him and roll things up at this end."

"It seems you got here just a bit late, Michael," Hammett said. "Because unless there are two supply sergeants named Prevo, your man got his neck broken in a gin mill last night. My gin mill, if it matters."

"This damned army," Carey said. "We didn't tell anybody at this end, because we didn't know who might be involved. And it looks like we'll never find out now, either."

"I don't know about that," Hammett said. "I need to know two things. Were the men running the supply operation at Fort Lewis regular army? And what was it a kid named Billy Tobin got kicked off the force in 'Frisco for? If you can answer those questions, I might be able to help you."

Before Hammett went down the hall to the bathroom the next morning, he took a small pistol from his valise and slipped it into the pocket of his pants. He left it there when he went downstairs for bacon and eggs. As he ate, he read an authoritative newspaper story about the Jap army using babies as bayonet practice targets in Manila. He spent the rest of the day in his room, reading and dozing, leaving the room to take one telephone call. He ate no lunch. He looked carefully up and down the hallway before his visit to the bathroom. When his watch read 7:30, he got fully dressed, packed his valise, and sat on the bed. Just at nine P.M., there was a knock on his door.

"Mister," the desk clerk called. "You got a visitor. The same fella."

Hammett walked downstairs and settled his bill with the clerk. He and Miller went out and got into a Jeep. Neither man said anything. The joints on the far side of the city limits were doing big business as they drove past. The Carolina Moon was the only dark building. As they pulled up in front of it, Hammett said, "You might want to find yourself a quiet spot to watch the proceedings."

"What you doing this for?" Miller asked. "Solving murders isn't your business."

"This one is my business," Hammett said. "Zulu's got to eat, and I want a return on my investment. Nobody's making any money with the Moon closed."

"You and Miss Zulu more than just business partners?" Miller asked.

"A gentleman wouldn't ask such a question," Hammett said, "and a gentleman certainly won't answer it."

Hammett hurried into the building. He had trouble making out the people in the dimly lit barroom. Zulu was there, and the temporary blonde. The marshal. The MP. Carey, a couple of tough-looking gents Hammett didn't know, and the major from the party. The MP was standing at the bar, looking at himself in a piece of mirror that hung behind it. Everyone else was sitting. Hammett went around behind the bar, took off his coat, and laid it on the bar. He poured himself a drink and drank it off. The MP wandered over to stand next to the door to the hallway.

"I see you've got everyone assembled," Hammett said to Carey.

The investigator nodded.

"The major came to me," he said. "Said as it was his sergeant that was killed, he wanted to be in on this."

"That's one of the things that bothered me about this," Hammett said. "Major Allen seems to know things he shouldn't. For instance, Major, how did you know I was involved in this affair?"

The major was silent for a moment, then said, "I'm certain my friend Major Haynes of the military police must have mentioned your name to me."

"We'll leave that," Hammett said. "Because the other thing that bothered me came first. Oscar, did you call the MPs the night of the killing?"

The marshal shook his head.

"Then what was the sergeant doing here?"

"Said he was in the neighborhood," the marshal said.

"But Oscar," Hammett said, "don't the MPs always patrol in pairs on this side of the city limits?"

"They certainly do," the marshal said. "What about that, young fella?"

The MP looked at the marshal, then at Hammett.

"My partner got sick," he said. "I had to go it alone. Then I saw all them soldiers leaving here and came to see what was what."

"Michael?" Hammett said.

"Like you said, the duty roster said the sergeant wasn't even on duty that night," the investigator said.

Everyone was looking at the MP now. He didn't say anything.

"This is your case, Oscar," Hammett said, "so let me tell you a story.

"There's a ring of thieves operating out of Fort Lewis, pretending to send food to a phony outfit up here, then selling it on the black market. The ones doing the work were crooks from San Francisco. Tobin here would have known them from his time with the police there.

"Their man on this end, the fellow who was killed the other night, didn't seem to have any connection with them. Michael told me on the telephone today that he was from the Midwest and had never been arrested. He seemed to be just a harmless pansy who used the Moon to meet his boyfriend."

"That's disgusting," the major said.

"That's what happens when the army makes a place the dumping ground for all of its undesirables, Major," Hammett said. "What did you do to get sent here?"

"I volunteered," the major grated.

"I'll bet you did," Hammett said. "Anyway, last night Michael reminded me that Tobin here had been run off the San Francisco force for beating up a dancer at Finocchio's. He claimed the guy made a pass at him, but the inside story was that it was a lovers' quarrel."

"That's a goddamn lie!" the MP shouted.

"It's just one coincidence too many," Hammett said, his voice as hard as granite. "You know the San Francisco mob. They're stealing from the government. Prevo was in on the scheme. He was queer. You're queer. You're sewn up tight. What happened? He get cold feet and you had to kill him?"

The MP looked from one face to another in the room. Then he looked at Hammett.

"I didn't kill the guy," the MP said. "It was him." He pointed to the major.

Everyone looked at the major, then back at the MP. He was holding his automatic in his hand.

"That's not going to do you any good, young man," the marshal said. "This is Alaska. Where you going to run?"

The MP seemed not to hear him.

"I ain't no queer!" he shouted at Hammett. "I hate queers. I beat that guy up 'cause he made a pass at me, just like I said. I'd have killed him if I thought I'd get away with it. Here, I was just giving the major a little cover in case anything happened. Like the place got raided or something. Then the other day he told me some pal of his had warned him that they'd knocked over the Fort Lewis end of the deal and we were going to have to do something about his boyfriend. 'Jerry will talk,' he said. 'I know he will.' I told him I wasn't killing anybody. The stockade was better than the firing squad. So he comes out the back door of this place the other night and says he killed the pansy himself."

"That's a goddamn lie," the major shouted, leaping to his feet. "I don't even know this man. I've got a wife and baby at home. I'm no fairy."

"You're for it, Tobin," Hammett said to the MP. "He doesn't leave anything to chance. Why, he tried to shoot me last night just on the off chance I might know something. I'll bet he does have a wife and child. And I'll bet there's nothing to connect him to either you or the corpse. And there's the love letters Michael found in your footlocker."

"Love letters?" the MP said. "What love letters?"

He looked at Hammett, then at the major. Understanding flooded his face.

"You set me up!" he screamed at the major. "You set me up as a fairy!"

The automatic barked. The slug seemed to pick the major up and hurl him backwards. The temporary blonde screamed. All over the room, men were taking guns from holsters and pockets. They seemed to be moving in slow motion. The MP swung the gun toward Hammett.

"You should have kept your nose out of this," the MP said, leveling the automatic. His finger closed on the trigger.

Don Miller stepped out of the hallway behind the MP and laid a sap on the back of his head. The MP collapsed like he was filled with sawdust.

Miller and Hammett looked at one another for a long moment. Hammett took his hand off the pistol in the pocket of his coat.

"I think that calls for a drink," he said, pouring himself one.

The marshal was putting cuffs on the MP. Carey looked up from where the major lay and shook his head.

"I guess this means you'll be able to open up again, Zulu," Hammett said.

The following afternoon Miller found Hammett lying on a table in the cramped offices of the magazine *Army Up North,* reading Lenin.

"I've got some errands to run in town," he told Hammett.

"Fine by me," Hammett said, sitting up. "I've been thinking I'll put in my papers. The war can't last much longer, and this looks like as close as I'll get to any action."

"You'd have been just as dead if that MP shot you as you would if it'd been a Jap bullet," Miller said.

"I suppose," Hammett said. "This morning the general told me they were going to show Major Allen as killed in the line of duty. They'll give Tobin a quick trial and life in the stockade. The whole thing's being hushed up. The brass don't want to embarrass the major's father, and they don't want the scandal getting back to the president and Congress. This is the country I enlisted to protect?"

Miller shrugged. "I got to be going," he said.

"Right you are," Hammett said. "And by the way, thanks for stepping in last night. I didn't want to shoot that kid, and I didn't want to get shot myself."

Miller turned to leave.

"I suppose I'll just give the Moon to Zulu if I go," Hammett said.

"That'd be real nice," Miller said over his shoulder.

He went out, got into a Jeep, drove downtown, and parked. He walked into the federal building, climbed a set of stairs, walked down a hallway, and went through an unmarked door without knocking. He sat in a chair and told the whole story to a man on the other side of the desk. "That's all very interesting," the man said, "but did the subject say anything to you or anyone else about Marx, Lenin, or communism?"

"Is that all you care about?" Miller asked. "I keep telling you, I've never heard him say anything about communism."

"You've got to understand," the man said. "This other matter just isn't important. The director says we are already fighting the next war, the war against communism. This war is a triumph of truth, justice, and the American way. And it's over."

Miller said nothing.

"You can let yourself out," the man said. Then he turned to his typewriter, rolled a form into it, and began to type.

BRENDAN DUBOIS

Richard's Children

FROM *Much Ado About Murder*

FOR MID-OCTOBER, the weather in London was quite warm and
the sun was out, another rare occurrence in this cloudy town. Kevin
Tanner, assistant professor of English at Lovecraft University in
Massachusetts, sat on a park bench in the middle of a small court-
yard at the Tower of London. He still felt a bit jet-lagged, like everything he saw was too bright and loud, and the scents and sounds
were too strong and forceful. He was near one of the largest stone
buildings in the Tower of London complex, the White Tower, and
there he waited. He had been here once before, as a grad student,
more than sixteen years ago, and it seemed like not much had
changed over the years. There were manicured lawns, sidewalks,
and walls and battlements and towers, all representing nearly a
thousand years of English history. And beyond the Tower complex,
the soaring span of the Tower Bridge — looking ancient, of course,
but less than a hundred years old — and the wide and magnificent
Thames.

At his feet was a small red knapsack, and just a half-hour ago —
after spending nearly twenty minutes in line for the privilege of
spending eleven pounds to gain entry — a well-dressed and polite
security officer had examined his bag and its contents. Inside the
bag was a water bottle, two candy bars, a thick guidebook to London, and secured in a zippered pouch within the knapsack, his
passport and round-trip airline ticket. He supposed that if the security guard had been more on the job, he would have looked at the
airline ticket and inquired as to how an assistant professor at a
small college with a savings account of just over two thousand dol-

lars could have afforded a round-trip, first-class airline ticket. Now that would have been something worth investigating.

Despite the oddity of this whole trip and the arrangements, he had enjoyed the flight over. He had never traveled business class in his life, never mind first class, and he felt slightly guilty at having all the attention and comforts of being up in the forward cabin. But after ten or so minutes, he quickly realized why it was so special. How could anybody not want to fly first class if they could afford it? The wide, plush seats, with plenty of elbow- and legroom, and the flight attendants who were at his beck and call. That's when he felt that familiar flush of anger and embarrassment. Anger at being someone supposedly admired in society, a teacher of children, a molder of future generations, and the only way he could come to England and in first class was through the generosity of strangers. And embarrassment, for he was a grown man, had made grownup choices, and he shouldn't be angry at that.

Still, he thought, looking down at his bag, it was going to be pleasant flying back.

He looked around him, seeing the crowds of tourists. There were two types: those moving about the grounds of the Tower by themselves, with brochures and maps, and those in large groups following one of the numerous Yeoman Warders, dressed in their dark blue and red Beefeater uniforms. Each uniform had *ER* written on the chest in fine script. *Elizabeth Regina.* Kevin crossed his legs, waited, checked his watch. It was 11 A.M., and a man came over to him, wearing a red rose in the lapel of his suit coat. He was tall, gaunt, with thick gray hair combed back in a lionlike mane. The suit and shoes were black, as was the tie, and the shirt was white. The man came to him and nodded.

"Professor Tanner," he said in a cultured English accent that said it all: Cambridge or Oxford, followed by a civil service position at Whitehall, relaxing in all the right clubs, following the cricket matches on the BBC.

"The same," Kevin said. "And Mister Lancaster?"

"As well," he said. "May I join you?"

He shifted on the park bench, turned so he could watch the man sit down and see how he carefully adjusted the pleat of his pants.

"I trust your flight was uneventful?"

"It was," he said.

"And your room is satisfactory?"

Kevin smiled. "The Savoy is just as it's advertised. I think even a broom closet would be satisfactory in that place."

If he was hoping for a response from Mister Lancaster, it didn't happen. The older man nodded and said, "I see. I appreciate you coming here on such short notice. Will your university miss you?"

"No," he said, a note of regret in his voice, he realized. "I'm on sabbatical. Supposedly working on a book. Which is why I was able to drop everything to come here and see you."

"Really, then."

Kevin paused. "All right, I have to admit, you folks raised my curiosity. A round-trip first-class ticket, first-class accommodations, plus a stipend in pounds equal to about a thousand dollars. All to meet with you at the Tower of London. And to discuss what?"

"Quite," Lancaster said, folding his long hands over his knees. "History, if you don't mind. Some history old and history new, all starting here in England."

"Are you sure you want me?" he asked. "I'm an assistant professor of English. Not history."

The older man shrugged. "Yes, I know you're not a professor of history. And yet I know everything there is to know about you, Professor Tanner. Your residence in Newburyport, Massachusetts. Your single life. The courses you teach, your love of Shakespeare and Elizabethan England. Your solitary book, a study of gravestone epitaphs in northern New England, which sold exactly six hundred and four copies two years ago. And the fact that you are currently struggling on another book, one that will guarantee you receive tenure. But that book is nowhere near being completed, am I correct?"

Kevin knew he should be insulted by the fact that this pompous Englishman knew so much about his life, but he was almost feeling honored, that someone should care so much. "All right, you've done some research. To what purpose?"

"To help you with this book you're working on," Lancaster said.

"Excuse me?"

Lancaster turned away and said, "Look about you, Professor Tanner. Hundreds of years of history, turned into a bloody tourist attraction. The other day I was on a tour here, with a visitor from Germany. One of the Beefeaters told the tourists that the *ER* on his chest stood for 'Extremely Romantic.' Imagine that, making sport of our monarch, in this property that belongs to her. And think about all of the people who have been imprisoned here, from Lady Jane Grey to Sir Walter Raleigh to Rudolf Hess. And in this White Tower behind us, do you know what famous black deed happened there?"

He turned on his bench, looked at the tall building, the line of tourists snaking their way in. "The two princes."

"Yes, the two princes. Young Edward the Fourth and his younger brother Richard, the Duke of York. Imprisoned here by Richard the Third. You do know Richard the Third, do you not?"

"If you know my background, you already know the answer to that."

"Ah, yes, Richard the Third. One of the most controversial monarchs this poor, green, sceptered isle has ever seen. Made even more famous by our bard, Mister Shakespeare. 'Now is the winter of our discontent.' Either a great man or an evil man, depending on your point of view. And what happened to the young princes, again, depending on your point of view. What do you think happened, Professor?"

Kevin said carefully, "There's evidence supporting each view, that Richard the Third either had the princes killed, to remove possible claimants to the throne, or that he was ignorant of the whole thing. But the bones of two young boys were found there, buried under a staircase, some years later."

"Very good, you've given me a professor's answer, but not a scholar's answer. So tell me again, Professor, what do you think happened?"

Kevin felt pressure, like he was going up before the damn tenure board itself. "I think he had them murdered. That's what I think."

"And what's your evidence?"

"The evidence is, who profits? After Richard the Third seized the throne, he had to eliminate any possible rivals. Those two boys were his rivals. He did what he had to do. It was purely political, nothing else."

"Hmmm. And your book, the one you're working on, compares and contrasts our Richard, our Duke of Gloucester, with another Richard from your country, am I correct?"

"Jesus," Kevin exclaimed. "Who the hell are you people?"

"Never mind that right now," Lancaster said, leaning in closer to him. "Correct, am I not? Our Richard and your Richard, the Duke of San Clemente. Mister Nixon. Quite the comparison, eh? Richard the Third and Richard Nixon. The use of power, the authority, all that wonderful stuff. But tell me, the book is not going well, is it?"

Kevin thought about lying and then said, "Yeah, you're right. The book isn't going well."

"And why's that?"

"Because it's all surface crap, that's all," he said heatedly. "Sure, it sounds good on paper and in talking at the faculty lounge, but c'mon, Richard the Third and Nixon? Nixon certainly was something else, but he didn't have blood on his hands, like your Duke of Gloucester. And don't start yapping at me about Vietnam. He didn't start that war. Kennedy and Johnson did. And for all his faults, he ended it the best way he could. Messily, but the best way he could. And I think, and so do other historians, that his opening to China balanced that out. And that's why the book isn't going well. Because it's all on the surface, like it came from some overheated grad student's imagination."

Lancaster nodded again, plucked a piece of invisible lint off his suit coat. "Perhaps you're ignoring the rather blatant comparisons."

"What do you mean?"

The older man gestured to the White Tower. "What crime was committed here. The murder of two young princes. And what kind of crime was committed in your own country. In 1963 and 1968. Two young princes, loved and admired, who promised great things to their people. Cut down at a young age."

Kevin was aghast. "The Kennedys?"

"Of course."

"You brought me all the way over here to spout conspiracy theories? Gibberish? Who the hell are you?"

"I told you, in a matter of —"

Kevin grabbed his knapsack. "And I'll tell you, unless you come straight with me, right now, I'm leaving. I'm not here to listen to half-ass Kennedy assassination theories. And you can cancel my room and airfare home, and I don't care. I'll pay my own way."

"And not finish your book?"

"That's the price I'll pay," Kevin said.

Lancaster smiled thinly. "How noble. Very well. Here we go. Leave now and your book will never be completed, you know that, don't you. Leave now and you won't get tenure. In fact, your life will start getting unwound. You will be forced out of your college, perhaps be tossed back into the great unwashed. Teaching English at high schools or what you folks call vocational technical schools. Or perhaps conjugating verbs to prisoners. Is that a better life than teaching at a comfortable university?"

Kevin felt his breathing quicken. "Go on."

"Stay with me and learn what I have to offer, and you'll not only write your book, you'll write a book that will become an instant bestseller. You will be known across your country and ours as well. If you want to stay at your university, that will be fine, but I can tell you, once this book comes out, Harvard and Yale and Stanford and Columbia will come begging at your door. That's your choice now, isn't it. To stay or go."

"Yeah, that's a hell of a choice," Kevin said.

Lancaster smiled. "But a choice nonetheless. It's a pleasant day, Professor Tanner. We're both alive and breathing and enjoying this lovely autumn day in the best city on this planet. Let me continue with what I have to say, and what I have to offer. And then you can leave and decide what to do next. All right? Don't you at least owe me some time, considering the expense that was incurred to bring you over to our fair country?"

Kevin lowered his knapsack to the ground. "All right, I guess I do owe you that. But make it quick and to the point. And I'm not going to do a damn thing until you tell me who you are, and why you spent all this money to have me fly over."

Lancaster nodded, folded his long hands. "Very well. That seems quite fair. Well, let's begin, shall we? Another history lesson, if you prefer. Let's set the stage, that place, as Shakespeare said, where we are all just actors. But this stage has a bloody history. Tell me, who runs the world?"

Kevin hesitated, thinking that he had fallen into the clutches of that odd group of loons and eccentrics who sometimes haunt college campuses. At one faculty luncheon some months ago, he remembered some physics professor bemoaning the fact that a junkyard dealer in New Hampshire had finally come across a Unified Field Theory and wanted the professor's assistance in getting his theory published. So now it was Kevin's turn, and again that temptation came up, to walk away from this odd man.

But . . . like the man said, it was a pleasant day, he had money and a nice room and a ticket back home, and if nothing else, at least he'd have a good story to tell at the next English faculty function.

So he nodded, gestured toward Lancaster. "All right, a fair question. Who does run the world? I'm not sure the world is actually run. If anything, I think it's hard to even come to an agreement as to who actually runs the country. As a conservative, I could say legally elected governments, in most cases, run most countries in the world. As a liberal, I suppose I could make a case that in some nations, corporations or the military have their hands in running things."

"Ah, not a bad answer," Lancaster said. "But let's try another theory, shall we? What would you say if I told you that royal families across this great globe actually . . . as you say it, run things?"

Oh, this was going to be a great story when he got back to Massachusetts, he thought. Kevin said, "All right, that's a theory. An odd one, but still a theory. But I'm not sure I understand you. Royal families, like the House of Windsor, actually run things?" Kevin found himself laughing. "Then you'd think they could do a better job in running their own personal lives, don't you?"

Lancaster didn't return the laughter. "How droll, I'm sure, Professor Tanner. But when I say royal families, I don't restrict myself to Europe. To make you feel more comfortable, let's discuss your own country, shall we?"

"The States?" He tried to restrain a laugh. "What royalty we have resides in Hollywood. Or Palm Springs. Or on Wall Street. They're involved in entertainment or business, and they get their photos in *People* magazine when they become famous, and in the *National Enquirer* when they get arrested or sent into drug rehab. That's our royalty, Mister Lancaster. Your royalty's been written up by Mister Shakespeare himself. Our royalty, if that's what you call it, is a pretty ratty lot, if you ask me."

Lancaster's face seemed more drawn. "This isn't a joke."

"I'm sorry, I wasn't being amusing."

"You certainly weren't. And you're not taking this seriously. Not at all. And I suggest you do."

"Or what? Will you have me arrested?"

Lancaster's look was not reassuring. "That would be easier to accomplish than you think, Professor Tanner. So let's proceed, shall we? I was asking you about royalty in America. I don't care about your tycoons or your entertainers. What I do care about is the royalty involved in politics, the kind that actually, again as you say, 'runs things.'"

Kevin didn't like the threat he had just heard, but he pressed on. "I'm sorry, I don't understand. We don't have any kind of royalty in the United States."

Lancaster's look was imperious. "Really? Look at your own history. What names in the last half of the twentieth century have either been in your Oval Office or nearby in your Congress? Let's try, shall we? Roosevelt, Kennedy, Rockefeller, du Pont, Bush, Gore, Byrd, Russell . . . wealthy families of influence who reside in and maintain the circles of power in your country. Tell me, Professor Tanner, are you really that naive?"

"No, I'm not that naive, and I'm also not that stupid," Kevin said, thinking again of what a great tale this would make once he got back home. "But you're reaching, Mister Lancaster, you're reaching quite a lot. Those families are political families, that's all, just like other families that have their backgrounds in oil, retail, or other kinds of business. Some families pick cattle, others pick politics. That's it."

"Really?" the man asked, his voice filled with skepticism.

"Really," Kevin said.

"These . . . families, as you call them, have been running your government and your lives for many decades, Professor Tanner. Just like the royal families in Shakespeare's time. In public they may show their good works and charities, as they run for office and for influence, but in private, it's quite different. They lie, they cheat, and they steal, and oftentimes they kill. Look at your own news reports over the years, when famed members of these families would often die."

"What do you mean? They kill each other?"

Lancaster made a dismissive motion with a long hand. "Of course. Again, look at the news reports. Many times, members of your royal family — a Kennedy, a du Pont, a Rockefeller — perishes. Sometimes it's called a drug overdose. Other times, an accidental shooting. And in one memorable case a few years ago, a plane crash. Those are the cover stories. The real stories are darker, more malignant, as they kill each other, always vying for power, for influence, for money."

Kevin sighed. The shadows were getting longer, it was getting cooler, and he recalled the size of the bed waiting for him back at the Savoy. He said, "No offense, Mister Lancaster, but I think you're nuts. Again, no offense. The story of royal families in the United States, acting like characters from Shakespeare . . . Well, it's too fantastic."

"Is it, now?" he asked. "Think of young John F. Kennedy, Jr., the one who died in that plane crash. He was a charming young man, of middling intelligence and skills. But what did he have going for him? Any extraordinary talents, any extraordinary gifts? Not really, am I right? He was just a pleasant young man. Yet tell me, Professor Tanner, if he had decided to enter politics, perhaps as a congressman, how long before he would be a leading candidate for president on the Democratic ticket? Two years? Four? Do you doubt that?"

And the truth is, Kevin couldn't doubt what the old man was saying about that particular subject, because it made sense. In his own home state of Massachusetts, old Teddy Kennedy was the proverbial eight-hundred-pound gorilla of politics, swatting down ineffectual opponents every six years, like King Kong on top of the Empire State Building, swatting down aircraft. Not to mention the Kennedy offspring that had been spun off from Massachusetts, setting up their own political dynasties in Rhode Island, New York, and Maryland . . .

"So you're telling me that John-John was murdered, is that it?" Kevin asked.

Lancaster slowly shrugged. "A possibility, that's all I can say. Just a possibility. But there's a reality we need for you to look at. A very real event that happened almost forty years ago. A lifetime, for sure, but the death of your own young princes is still a topic that bestirs the imagination, does it not?"

With this odd talk and the cooling weather and the harsh cries of the ravens — legend had it that if they were ever to leave the Tower, England would fall, which is why they had their wings clipped — Kevin was starting to get seriously spooked. The Tower of London no longer seemed to be the cheery tourist attraction that it had been earlier. His imagination could bring forth all of the bloody and horrible deeds that had taken place among these buildings, among these battlements. He suddenly wished that this gaunt man had never contacted him, had never pulled him away from his comfortable little life at Lovecraft University. He wished now he had tossed away that thick airmail envelope with ROYAL MAIL emblazoned in the upper right corner.

"Yes, the two princes — the two Kennedys — still bestir the imagination," Kevin said. "But I have to ask you again, who are you people? And why me?"

Lancaster shifted his weight. "Very well. A fair question. For the past few hundred years, ever since Shakespeare's time, this poor little globe has been under the influence of these families, who front companies, governments, and armies. As time passes, they have formed two alliances. Not a firm alliance — there are shifts here and there — but groupings of interest."

The old man made a noise like a sigh, as if he had worked hard every day, carrying a heavy burden on those thin shoulders. "Our group believes in the freedom of the individual, in concentrating power in the smallest possible arena. Where you have an open press, a Freedom of Information Act, legitimate elections, you can trust that our group or its allies have been behind it."

"So that's your group," Kevin said. "And the other one?"

"The second group has as its goal power: power of a government over people, a corporation over people, of one group of people over another. When you read about a newspaper in Russia being closed, when you read about Internet software that can track you on-line, when you read about Balkan tribes slaughtering each other, you can be sure this group is behind it. By their actions, by their deeds, they are the offspring of Richard the Third. For lack of a better phrase, we call them Richard's Children."

"You do, do you," Kevin said, now convinced that he was spending the afternoon with a madman. "And what do you call yourselves?"

A thin smile. "You're a bright young man. I'm sure you can figure it out."

Then it struck him. The red rose in the lapel. The last name. "The War of the Roses . . . The House of York fighting against the House of Lancaster. White rose versus red rose. Is that it?"

A crisp nod. "Very good. You're correct. It's been a long struggle, over generations and generations, but now we feel it's time to strike a blow. Despite the fall of the Berlin Wall and communism, Richard's Children and their allies are gathering strength. It's time to bring things out in the open."

"Which is where I come in?"

"Exactly," Lancaster said. "Meaning no offense, but an anonymous professor from an obscure college comes across documentation and facts about the murder of America's two young princes. His book becomes a worldwide bestseller. The evidence he presents is irrefutable. The major news organizations, upset that such a scoop and story have escaped them over the years, perform their own research, based on the leads that this young professor has uncovered. And when these leads are followed, they will end up in some very interesting areas of inquiry. Richard's Children will have to retreat, maybe for decades, maybe long enough so that a true human civilization can emerge, a civilization based on the sanctity of the individual."

Lancaster reached into his coat pocket, withdrew a thick brown envelope. "In here you will find some evidence. But not the whole story, and nothing so directly offered, of course."

Kevin refused to take the offered envelope. "What do you mean, nothing so directly offered?"

"What I mean is that you will be offered leads, avenues to explore," Lancaster said. "It makes sense that way, does it not? For if everything is offered to you on a silver platter, then it will be shown that you performed little or no original research on your part. Your work, your published book, will be roundly criticized and ignored. But if you follow these leads" — he wiggled the envelope back and forth — "all will become clear. Everything. And your life will change in ways you can't imagine."

Kevin waited, watched the man who was offering so much. But what was behind that offer? Lancaster said, "Enclosed in the envelope, of course, is another stipend. About five thousand dollars."

Again, Kevin waited. He finally said, "There's no guarantee, you know. Publishers aren't exactly lining up outside my office to sign me up for a new book. I could write this and nothing would happen."

"I doubt that," Lancaster said. "And speaking of doubts, don't believe that we won't be watching you. Do the research, do the work that goes into this book. Don't entertain any thoughts of going back home to your little place and pretend this meeting didn't happen, that you don't have an obligation. Have I made myself clear?"

His hand seemed to move of its own volition as it grasped the heavy envelope. "Yes. Quite clear."

"Good. We'll be in touch."

Kevin bent over to place the envelope in his knapsack, and when he raised his head, Lancaster was gone. He looked around at the paths, now almost entirely deserted of tourists, and he got up himself and shouldered his bag. Within a few minutes he was on a crowded sidewalk, heading for the Tower Hill tube station, and the knapsack — with the envelope safely inside — felt like a boulder.

Two days later, in his room at the Savoy — which had cost as much as two months' rent in his apartment back home — Kevin looked at his meager collection of luggage. His head was still spinning, for in the two days he had had by himself in London, he tried to put Mister Lancaster and that envelope out of his mind. He had caught an afternoon matinee performance at the London Lyceum of *The Lion King*, had spent an entire day touring the British Museum, and in one surprisingly sunny morning, he had actually caught the changing of the guard at Buckingham Palace. He found himself enjoying London and its people and the black taxicabs and the tube system, even though at night, back in his room, he kept on being drawn to that envelope. He knew he should open it up and examine the evidence and the stipend, but no, he didn't want to spoil what little time he had in London. So the envelope had remained closed, like a tiny cage holding a dangerous reptile, one that he wanted to be very careful while opening up.

"'Lord, what fools these mortals be!'" he quoted. "Yeah, Puck, you had that one right."

And he picked up his bags and left.

On the British Airways flight going home, again he was luxuriating in the comfort and pleasure of flying first class, and he drank a little bit too much champagne. His head and tongue were thick, and he wished he could convince the pilot and crew to keep on flying around the world, stopping only to pick up food and fuel. He was sure that if that would happen, he would gladly spend the rest of his days in this metal cocoon, reading newspapers and magazines, sleeping in luxury, eating the finest food — compared to what he could whip up at home in his own kitchen — served by conscientious helpers and watching the latest movies.

It would be an odd life, a strange life, but one worth it, so long as he could avoid thinking about his knapsack and that envelope, up there in the overhead bin.

He had one more glass of champagne, and then slept the rest of the way home.

His apartment was in an old house, built near the Merrimack River in Newburyport, Massachusetts. He knew he paid an extra hundred dollars a month for the privilege of a river view, and most days he thought it was worth it. He sat in his office, brooding, staring at the piles of papers, books, and file folders that represented a book in progress, a book that was months, if not years, away from being finished. Kevin powered up his computer, looked at the little folder icon that represented his months of work. *Two Richards* was going to be the name of it, contrasting Richard III with Richard Nixon. And damn that Lancaster character — he knew he was nowhere near completing it on time and in the way he wanted it done. At the beginning, he had wanted a dark, brooding book, full of facts and contrasts. A book that would safely secure his tenure, would at last make a mark in the world. And now?

Now it was stuck in the mud, just like Lancaster had said.

Sitting in his dark office, he usually got a feeling of peace and tranquility, here among his books and papers. But not this evening, not after that strange meeting at the Tower. Those people — he doubted Lancaster could have pulled everything off on his own — had poked and pried into his life, knew almost everything about him. He picked up the envelope from his desk. Such a choice. Continue working on *Two Richards,* or dive into the ravings of a lunatic.

He looked up on the wall, where a tiny framed portrait of the Bard looked down at him. "Old Will," he said aloud, "did you ever have days like this? With odd people and noblemen coming to you, demanding you write about them or their families or adventures? Did you?"

The portrait remained silent. Of course. If Will had started talking to him, Kevin would have gotten up and driven to the hospital, demanding to be admitted.

Things were odd, things might be mad, but they weren't that bad.

Not yet.

He picked up the envelope, took a letter opener, and slit open the top.

Inside were three sheets of blank white paper, folded over. Inside was another cashier's check, drawn on the Midlands Bank, for three thousand pounds. About five thousand dollars, give or take. And beside the check and the paper were two 8-by-10 glossy black-and-white prints, also folded over. He switched on the overhead lamp on his desk, flattened out both photos. The air in the office seemed to get suddenly cold and damp. Both photos he recognized, though he had never been at either location in his entire life. The first showed a black open-top Lincoln limousine parked outside a hospital. Police officers and reporters and other people were clustered around the luxury car, their mouths open in shock, some of the people holding up hands to their faces. It looked like a bright and sunny day, and near the car was the emergency room entrance to the hospital.

But of course. Parkland Memorial Hospital in Dallas. November 22, 1963.

The second photo was of a crowded hallway in a building of some sort, people clustered about, some reporters standing on chairs or tables, trying to get a better view, police officers trying to hold the crowd back. A man was on the ground, and only his feet were visible. As in the other photo, the people's faces were almost the same, mirroring shock, disbelief, anger.

And of course, the second photo was the Ambassador Hotel in Los Angeles. June 4, 1968.

America's two young princes. Murdered.

He stared at the photos for a long time, knowing of the official stories, the ones that said both men, both young princes, had been cut down by deranged men with dark passions and grudges. Kevin had never really paid that much attention to the various conspiracy theories and stories, but now, since his meeting with Lancaster . . .

He looked again at the faces of the people in the crowds. Citizens of a nation, confident that their leaders and rulers were freely elected every two, four, or six years. Not a nation as in Shakespeare's time, ruled by royalty and extended families, with long knives and longer memories.

But what was the point of the two photos? What was their meaning? Back at the Tower, Lancaster said that only leads would be provided. Not information. Not direct clues. No, just leads, so that Kevin would have to work and work at it to get the leads to uncovering the story of the century, and perhaps the story of the millennium.

He sighed, went back to looking at each photo, sparing a glance up at the print of Shakespeare.

"What the hell are you looking at?" he grumbled as he picked up the first photo.

Kevin woke with a start, tangled up in his sheets and blankets. A dream had come to him, a dream of running along a muddy path, chased by wraiths armed with long knives and pikes, closing in on him. He rubbed at his eyes and mouth, feeling his legs tremble from the memory of the dream. He rarely ever had nightmares, but this one had been a doozy. He rolled over and sat up, looking out at the night. Like his office, his bedroom had a view of the Merrimack River, and he could make out the red and green navigation lights of a fishing craft, heading out to the cold Atlantic for a hard day of fishing.

He rubbed at the base of his neck, wondering what about the dream had disturbed him so. He had spent several hours holed up in his office before going to bed. He had looked at each photo until he was almost cross-eyed. He had gone on the Internet and had quickly been sucked into the strange world of conspiracies and plots. A few Web sites he had gone to had even hinted at the story Lancaster had been peddling, about powerful interests and families ruling the world, but those sites had gone off the edge with racist nonsense about religious cabals.

After a quick dinner of macaroni and cheese and an hour decompressing before the television, he had gone to bed and had instantly gone to sleep, until that dark dream had come upon him.

What in the hell was he doing? he thought. An obscure English teacher at an even more obscure college, supposedly holding the key to a worldwide conspiracy? Please. No doubt he had fallen in league with some elaborate prank of some eccentric Englishman, trying to gain some amusement by making Kevin run around like a fool, chasing down spirits and ghosts.

Spirits and ghosts, just like the wraiths chasing him in that dream, wraiths that were frightening and uniform in their appearance . . .

Uniform.

That thought stuck with him. Why?

Uniform. Uniform wraiths, armed and heading toward him . . .

He stumbled out of bed, almost fell as a sheet tripped him up, and went back to his office, switching on the lights. The office looked strange, illuminated at such a time in the morning, but he didn't care. He grabbed both photos, took a magnifying glass, and started looking. His chest started thumping, and the hand holding the magnifying glass began shaking. He took deep breaths, tried to calm down, and looked again.

Dallas, Texas. Outside the hospital, holding back part of the crowd. A man dressed in a policeman's uniform, nose prominent, a nice profile shot.

Los Angeles, California. In the hallway of a hotel, holding back part of the crowd. A man dressed in a policeman's uniform, nose prominent, a nice profile shot.

In both pictures, there's an odd expression on the face, different from the crowd about him, those people shocked and scared and horrified.

The expression . . . Happiness? Sadness? Grief?

He blinked his eyes, looked again. It was the same man. Had to be. And what would be the chances that a police officer would be in Dallas the day JFK was killed, and would leave town and get a job in Los Angeles as a police officer, and then be present at the time RFK was killed?

What would be the chances?

He bounced back and forth again to the two photos, and then realized what the expression was on each face, frozen in time almost five years apart.

It was satisfaction.

That's what.

Satisfaction for a job well done.

He slowly got up and left the office, leaving the lights on, and then went back to bed and stayed awake until it was time for breakfast.

Three weeks after the night he had spent with the photos, Kevin was in a rental car, shivering, wondering if he would have the guts to take it this far. For nearly the past month, he had gone down a twisting and turning path, trying to identify the police officer who appeared in both photographs, separated by nearly five years and thousands of miles. Luckily for him, his university had a library that was one of the best in the region. Through its research assistants and some microfilm files and in searching old newspapers and magazines, he had found captions identifying the officer in the Dallas photo as Mike McKenna and the officer in Los Angeles as Ron Carpenter. That had taken almost a week of backbreaking work, sitting in hard chairs, blinking as the black-and-white microfilm reels whirred by, almost like a time machine, taking him back to tumultuous times when it seemed like the two princes would make a difference in the American empire.

Once he had the names, what next?

Then came frustrating contacts with the police departments of Dallas and Los Angeles, trying to find out who Mike McKenna and Ron Carpenter were, and if they were still living. Another couple of days, blocked, for the departments weren't cooperative, not at all. Then, not really enjoying what he had to do next, he delved deeper into the outlands of the Internet, looking into the different conspiracy pages put up by people still investigating the deaths of JFK and RFK. Then, this was followed by flights to Dallas and Los Angeles — spending the latest money from Lancaster — to two separate offices, where obsessive men and women were keepers of what they felt was the real truth, and he made some additional contacts. In turn, they led him to other people, who gave him two interesting facts: the names of Mike McKenna and Ron Carpenter still existed in the systems of the Dallas and Los Angeles police departments, and forwarding addresses for pension and disability information were exactly the same: 14 Old Mast Road, Nansen, Maine.

Unbelievable. So here he was, on a dirt road in a rural part of Maine, and after doing some additional work at the local town hall, looking at tax rolls, he found out who lived at 14 Old Mast Road: one Harold Brown, age seventy-nine. Retired. And that's it.

So here he was, at a place where the driveway intersected Old

Mast Road, waiting in his rental car. The driveway — also dirt — went up to a Cape Cod house on top of a hill, painted gray. Smoke tendriled up from a brick chimney. Kevin rubbed at his chin, kept an eye on the house. Could this be it, right up here? All the years of controversy, investigations, claims, counterclaims, all brought to this one point, this little hill in a remote section of Maine? And all coming about because of him, Kevin Tanner, assistant professor of English?

Insane. It all sounded so insane.

And now what? That he had debated with himself for a couple of days, before he had worked up some courage, rented a car — his old Toyota would have never made it — and spent nearly four hours on the road. All along the way, he had practiced and repracticed his approach, what he would say, what he was going to try to come away with.

Now it was time.

He opened the door, shivered from the early November cold. He walked up the muddy dirt driveway, looking at the old Cape Cod house, one of thousands sprinkled throughout the rural regions of Maine, Vermont, and New Hampshire. A very insignificant house, one easily ignored, except if the book was written and was published and became a bestseller, this sagging collection of wood and windows would become one of the most famous houses in the world.

The front lawn was brown, stunted grass, and Kevin went to the concrete stoop and knocked at the door. There was no doorbell, so he knocked again, harder. He could hear movement from inside. Kevin stood still, feeling his heart race away in his chest. Could this be it? Truly?

The door slowly opened, and an old man appeared, dressed in baggy jeans and a gray sweatshirt. His face was gaunt, his white hair was spread thinly across his freckled scalp, his eyes were watery and filmed, and his prominent nose was lined with red veins. Kevin felt his breath catch. This was him, the man in the photos.

"Yes?" he said, his voice almost a whisper.

Kevin cleared his throat. "Mister Brown? Harold Brown?"

"Yes," the man said. "Are you the tax assessor? Is that it?"

"No, no sir, I'm not," he said. "My name is Kevin Tanner. I'm a professor of English."

The old man blinked. "An English professor? Are you lost, is that it?"

"No, I'm not lost," Kevin said. "I was wondering if I could talk to you, just for a couple of minutes."

Brown looked suspicious. "You're not one of the those door-to-door religious types, are you?"

"No, sir, I'm not. Just a professor of English. That's all."

Brown moved away from the door. "All right, come on in. I guess there won't be no harm in it."

Kevin walked into the house, breathing slowly, trying to calm down. The house had the scent of dust and old cooking odors, and he followed Brown as he moved into the living room. Kevin felt a faint flush of shame, watching the shuffling steps of Brown as he used a metal walker to move into the room. The black bedroom slippers he was wearing made a whispering noise against the carpeting.

Brown settled heavily into an old couch, and Kevin sat near him in an easy chair, balancing an envelope on his knees. The wallpaper was a light blue, and there were framed photos of lighthouses and ships, but nothing that showed people. There were piles of newspapers around the floor of the small living room, and even piles on top of the television set. Brown coughed and said, "So. An English professor. Where do you teach?"

"Lovecraft University, in Massachusetts."

The old man shook his head. "Never heard of it. And why are you in this part of Maine?"

"To see you."

"Me?" Brown said, sounding shocked. "Whatever for?"

"Because I'm working on a book, and I think you have some information I could use," Kevin said.

"Me?" Brown said again. "I think you've come a long way for the wrong reason, young man."

Kevin remembered how he had thought this would go, and decided it was time to just bring it out in the open, just barrel right ahead. He opened up the envelope and took out the two black-and-white photos that Lancaster had provided him and passed them over. Brown looked at the photos and then fumbled in his shirt pocket, to pull out a pair of glasses. With the glasses on, Brown examined each photo, and then there was a quick intake of breath. Kevin leaned forward, wondering if he would have to pull out the other bits of information he had when Brown would deny that it was him in the photos. From the college newspaper research, he had additional photos, showing Brown in a variety of photos at each murder scene. From information supplied by the conspiracy buffs, he had old police department records, placing him at each scene. Kevin waited for the answer, and when the answer came, he was shocked and surprised.

Brown looked up. "Are you here to kill me?"

Kevin said, "No, no, not at all. I really am a college professor, and I really am working on a book. About the deaths of both JFK and his brother. And my research led to these photographs, and then to you, Mister Brown. So that's really you, isn't it? You were present at both assassinations."

Brown's voice lowered to a whisper. "So long ago . . . so very long ago . . ."

Then, Kevin surprised even himself as a burst of anger came up and he said, "Why? Why did you do it?"

Brown looked stunned at the question. "What do you mean, why? I did it because I was ordered to, that's why. I was younger back then, full of energy and purpose, and I did what I thought was right, and did what I was told. It was a different time, a turbulent time."

"And who ordered you to do it?"

Brown shook his head, lowered the photos down on the couch, kept his gaze on them both. "I'm not going to say a word. I'm an old man, living up here nice and quiet, and I'm not going to say another word."

"Was it Richard's Children? Was it?"

Brown's eyes snapped right back at him. "Who told you that?"

"That was part of my research. Richard's Children." Kevin took a breath, thinking, true, all true. That loon Lancaster was right. "I'm working on a book, Mister Brown, and I'm going to reveal your part in it, whether you help me or not."

Brown put his shaking hands in his lap. "It could be dangerous."

"Maybe so, but it'll be the truth."

Brown didn't say anything for what seemed to be a long time, and then he said, "I've been retired, for years . . . but I was a pack rat, you know. Against all orders. I kept documents and papers and photographs . . . lots of information . . ."

"You did?"

A slow nod from the old man. "I certainly did . . . A book. You said you're working on a book?"

"I am."

Brown said, "Would you like to see those materials?"

"God, yes."

Brown nodded, slowly got up off the couch, holding on to the walker with both gnarled hands. "You wait right here. I'll go get them."

Kevin clasped his hands together, his heart thumping yet again, thinking of how he would spend the day with the old man, debriefing him, figuring out all the angles of this story, the biggest story of the millennium, and all belonging to him. Kevin started smiling. Questions of tenure at old shabby Lovecraft U? Lancaster was right. When this book was done, he'd be considering offers from Yale and Harvard and —

Brown came back into the room. He moved quickly. He didn't have a walker with him, not at all, and he moved with the grace of an old man who had kept himself in shape. And there were no papers or books or photographs in his hand. Just a black, shiny, automatic pistol.

"You should have stuck with your Shakespeare," Brown said, his voice even and quite strong, and those words and the sharp report of the pistol were the last things that Kevin ever heard.

After receiving the news from a coded transatlantic phone call, the man who sometimes called himself Lancaster and sometimes called himself York got up from his desk and walked across the room to a thick oaken door. He rapped once on the door and entered at the soft voice that said, "Do come in."

The room was cozy, with long drapes and bookshelves lined with leatherbound volumes, some framed photos on the dull white plaster walls, and a wide window that looked down upon the windswept Thames. From his vantage point, looking over the desk and the comfortable chair that the old man sat in, Lancaster could make out the round shape of the rebuilt Globe Theatre.

The man wore a thick dressing gown, and his black hair was swept back, displaying a prominent nose. One arm was on the desk, and the other one, withered and almost useless, was propped up on the arm of his chair. The old man was known as one of the rich-

est and most philanthropic men in all the world, and on the wall
were photos of him with the president of the United States, Prince
Philip of Great Britain, the prime minister, and several other nota-
bles. Including a small photograph of him with Richard Nixon, and
Nixon was the one smiling the most, as if pleased at what had just
been agreed to. He looked up and said, "You have news?"

"I do," Lancaster said. "The college professor has been removed.
Mister Brown fulfilled our request admirably, and his compensa-
tion is en route."

"Good," the man said. "Any loose ends?"

Lancaster paused, and then proceeded, knowing that the man
before him was always one for direct questions. "No, no loose ends.
But I am concerned about just one thing, sir."

"Which is?"

Lancaster said, "I understand the whole point of this exercise. To
locate those people with sufficient imagination and interest to look
into our activities, and then see how far they can go before we eliminate them. And eliminate those they have contact with, who have
supplied them with damaging information. But there's just one
thing. Mister Brown, our man in Maine."

"Yes?" he asked.

"Don't you think he should be . . . taken care of, as well?"

The man at the desk turned and looked out at the mighty
Thames and sat still. Lancaster knew better than to interrupt him
when he was in such a reverie. Finally, he said, "No. I don't think so.
And you want to know why?"

"Yes, I do."

"Loyalty," he said. "The man has done noble services for us,
many times, over the years. He deserves our loyalty. So he shall remain alive. Understood?"

"Yes," Lancaster said.

"Good," said the man who called himself Richard. "As the Bard
once said of my spiritual ancestor, 'I am determined to prove the
villain, and hate the idle pleasures of these days.' Come, we have
work to do."

"So we do, sir," he said. "So we do."

ELMORE LEONARD

When the Women Come Out to Dance

FROM *When the Women Come Out to Dance: Stories*

LOURDES BECAME Mrs. Mahmood's personal maid when her friend Viviana quit to go to L.A. with her husband. Lourdes and Viviana were both from Cali in Colombia and had come to South Florida as mail-order brides. Lourdes's husband, Mr. Zimmer, worked for a paving contractor until his death, two years from the time they were married.

She came to the home on Ocean Drive, only a few blocks from Donald Trump's, expecting to not have a good feeling for a woman named Mrs. Mahmood, wife of Dr. Wasim Mahmood, who altered the faces and breasts of Palm Beach ladies and aspirated their areas of fat. So it surprised Lourdes that the woman didn't look like a Mrs. Mahmood, and that she opened the door herself: this tall redheaded woman in a little green two-piece swimsuit, sunglasses on her nose, opened the door and said, "Lourdes, as in Our Lady of?"

"No, ma'am, Lour-des, the Spanish way to say it," and had to ask, "You have no help here to open the door?"

The redheaded Mrs. Mahmood said, "They're in the laundry room watching soaps." She said, "Come on in," and brought Lourdes into this home of marble floors, of statues and paintings that held no meaning, and out to the swimming pool, where they sat at a patio table beneath a yellow and white umbrella.

There were cigarettes, a silver lighter, and a tall glass with only ice left in it on the table. Mrs. Mahmood lit a cigarette, a long Virginia Slim, and pushed the pack toward Lourdes, who was saying, "All I have is this, Mrs. Mahmood," Lourdes bringing a biographical data sheet, a printout, from her straw bag. She laid it before the redheaded woman showing her breasts as she leaned forward to look at the sheet.

"'Your future wife is in the mail'?"

"From the Latina introduction list for marriage," Lourdes said. "The men who are interested see it on their computers. Is three years old, but what it tells of me is still true. Except of course my age. Now it would say thirty-five."

Mrs. Mahmood, with her wealth, her beauty products, looked no more than thirty. Her red hair was short and reminded Lourdes of the actress who used to be on TV at home, Jill St. John, with the same pale skin. She said, "That's right, you and Viviana were both mail-order brides," still looking at the sheet. "Your English is good — that's true. You don't smoke or drink."

"I drink now sometime, socially."

"You don't have e-mail."

"No, so we wrote letters to correspond, before he came to Cali, where I lived. They have parties for the men who come and we get — you know, we dress up for it."

"Look each other over."

"Yes, is how I met Mr. Zimmer in person."

"Is that what you called him?"

"I didn't call him anything."

"Mrs. Zimmer," the redheaded woman said. "How would you like to be Mrs. Mahmood?"

"I wouldn't think that was your name."

She was looking at the printout again. "You're virtuous, sensitive, hardworking, optimistic. Looking for a man who's a kind, loving person with a good job. Was that Mr. Zimmer?"

"He was okay except when he drank too much. I had to be careful what I said or it would cause him to hit me. He was strong, too, for a guy his age. He was fifty-eight."

"When you married?"

"When he died."

"I believe Viviana said he was killed?" The woman sounding like she was trying to recall whatever it was Viviana had told her. "An accident on the job?"

Lourdes believed the woman already knew about it, but said, "He was disappeared for a few days until they find his mix truck out by

Hialeah, a pile of concrete by it but no reason for the truck to be here since there's no job he was pouring. So the police have the concrete broken open and find Mr. Zimmer."

"Murdered," the redheaded woman said.

"They believe so, yes, his hands tied behind him."

"The police talk to you?"

"Of course. He was my husband."

"I mean did they think you had anything to do with it."

She knew. Lourdes was sure of it.

"There was a suspicion that friends of mine here from Colombia could be the ones did it. Someone who was their enemy told this to the police."

"It have anything to do with drugs?"

The woman seeing all Colombians as drug dealers.

"My husband drove a cement truck."

"But why would anyone want to kill him?"

"Who knows?" Lourdes said. "This person who finked, he told the police I got the Colombian guys to do it because my husband was always beating me. One time he hit me so hard," Lourdes said, touching the strap of her blue sundress that was faded almost white from washing, "it separated my shoulder, the bones in here, so I couldn't work."

"Did you tell the Colombian guys he was beating you?"

"Everyone knew. Sometime Mr. Zimmer was brutal to me in public, when he was drinking."

"So maybe the Colombian guys did do it." The woman sounding like she wanted to believe it.

"I don't know," Lourdes said, and waited to see if this was the end of it. Her gaze moved out to the sunlight, to the water in the swimming pool lying still, and beyond to red bougainvillea growing against white walls. Gardeners were weeding and trimming, three of them Lourdes thought at first were Latino. No, the color of their skin was different. She said, "Those men . . ."

"Pakistanis," Mrs. Mahmood said.

"They don't seem to work too hard," Lourdes said. "I always have a garden at home, grow things to eat. Here, when I was married, I worked for Miss Olympia. She call her service Cleaning with Biblical Integrity. I wasn't sure what it means, but she would say things to us from the Holy Bible. We cleaned offices in buildings in Miami.

What I do here Viviana said would be different, personal to you. See to your things, keep your clothes nice?"

Straighten her dresser drawers. Clean her jewelry. Mrs. Mahmood said she kicked her shoes off in the closet, so Lourdes would see they were paired and hung in the shoe racks. Check to see what needed to be dry-cleaned. Lourdes waited as the woman stopped to think of other tasks. See to her makeup drawers in the bathroom. Lourdes would live here, have Sundays off, a half day during the week. Technically she would be an employee of Dr. Mahmood's.

Oh? Lourdes wasn't sure what that meant. Before she could ask, Mrs. Mahmood wanted to know if she was a naturalized citizen. Lourdes told her she was a permanent resident, but now had to get the papers to become a citizen.

"I say who I work for I put Dr. Wasim Mahmood?"

The redheaded wife said, "It's easier that way. You know, to handle what's taken out. But I'll see that you clear at least three-fifty a week."

Lourdes said that was very generous. "But will I be doing things also for Dr. Mahmood?"

The redheaded woman smoking her cigarette said, "What did Viviana tell you about him?"

"She say only that he didn't speak to her much."

"Viviana's a size twelve. Woz likes them young and as lean as snakes. How much do you weigh?"

"Less than one hundred twenty-five pounds."

"But not much — you may be safe. You cook?"

"Yes, of course."

"I mean for yourself. We go out or order in from restaurants. I won't go near that fucking stove and Woz knows it."

Lourdes said, "Wos?"

"Wasim. He thinks it's because I don't know how to cook, which I don't, really, but that's not the reason. The two regular maids are Filipina and speak English. In fact, they have less of an accent than you. They won't give you any trouble, they look at the ground when they talk to anyone. And they leave at four, thank God. Woz always swims nude — don't ask me why, it might be a Muslim thing — so if they see him in the pool they hide in the laundry room. Or if I put on some southern hip-hop and they happen to walk in while

I'm bouncing to Dirty South doing my aerobics, they run for the laundry room." She said without a pause, "What did Viviana say about me?"

"Oh, how nice you are, what a pleasure to work here."

"Come on — I know she told you I was a stripper."

"She say you were a dancer before, yes."

"I started out in a dump on Federal Highway, got discovered and jumped to Miami Gold on Biscayne, valet parking. I was one of the very first, outside of black chicks, to do southern hip-hop, and I mean Dirty South raw and uncut, while the other girls are doing Limp Bizkit, even some old Bob Seeger and Bad Company — and that's okay, whatever works for you. But in the meantime I'm making more doing laptops and private gigs than any girl at the Gold and I'm twenty-seven at the time, older than any of them. Woz would come in with his buddies, all suits and ties, trying hard not to look Third World. The first time he waved a fifty at me I gave him some close-up tribal strip-hop. I said, 'Doctor, you can see better if you put your eyeballs back in your head.' He loved that kind of talk. About the fourth visit I gave him what's known as the million-dollar hand job and became Mrs. Mahmood."

She told this sitting back, relaxed, smoking her Virginia Slim cigarette, Lourdes nodding, wondering at times what she was talking about, Lourdes saying "I see" in a pleasant voice when the woman paused.

Now she was saying, "His first wife stayed in Pakistan while he was here in med school. Right after he finished his residency and opened his practice, she died." The woman said, "Let's see . . . You won't have to wear a uniform unless Woz wants you to serve drinks. Once in a while he has some of his ragtop buddies over for cocktails. Now you see these guys in their Nehru outfits and hear them chattering away in Urdu. I walk in, 'Ah, Mrs. Mahmood,' in that semi-British singsongy way they speak, 'what a lovely sight you are to my eyes this evening.' Wondering if I'm the same chick he used to watch strip."

She took time to light another cigarette, and Lourdes said, "Do I wear my own clothes working here?"

"At first, but I'll get you some cool outfits. What are you, about an eight?"

"My size? Yes, I believe so."

"Let's see — stand up."

Lourdes rose and moved away from the table in the direction Mrs. Mahmood waved her hand. Now the woman was staring at her. She said, "I told you his first wife died?"

"Yes, ma'am, you did."

"She burned to death."

Lourdes said, "Oh?"

But the redheaded woman didn't tell her how it happened. She smoked her cigarette and said, "Your legs are good, but you're kinda short-waisted, a bit top-heavy. But don't worry, I'll get you fixed up. What's your favorite color?"

"I always like blue, Mrs. Mahmood."

She said, "Listen, I don't want you to call me that anymore. You can say ma'am in front of Woz to get my attention, but when it's just you and I? I'd rather you called me by my own name."

"Yes?"

"It's Ginger. Well, actually it's Janeen, but all of my friends call me Ginger. The ones I have left."

Meaning, Lourdes believed, since she was married to the doctor, friends who also danced naked, or maybe even guys.

Lourdes said, "Ginger?"

"Not Yinyor. Gin-ger. Try it again."

"Gin-gar?"

"That's close. Work on it."

But she could not make herself call Mrs. Mahmood Ginger. Not yet. Not during the first few weeks. Not on the shopping trip to Worth Avenue where Mrs. Mahmood knew everyone, all the sales-girls, and some of them did call her Ginger. She picked out for Lourdes casual summer dresses that cost hundreds of dollars each and some things from Resort Wear, saying, "This is cute," and would hand it to the salesgirl to put aside, never asking Lourdes her opinion, if she liked the clothes or not. She did, but wished some of them were blue. Everything was yellow or yellow and white or white with yellow. She didn't have to wear a uniform, no, but now she matched the yellow and white patio, the cushions, the um-brellas, feeling herself part of the decor, invisible.

Sitting out here in the evening several times a week when the doctor didn't come home, Mrs. Mahmood trying hard to make it seem they were friends, Mrs. Mahmood serving daiquiris in round crystal goblets, waiting on her personal maid. It was nice to be treated this way, and it would continue, Lourdes believed, until Mrs. Mahmood finally came out and said what was on her mind, what she wanted Lourdes to do for her.

The work was nothing, keep the woman's clothes in order, water the houseplants, fix lunch for herself — and the maids, once they came in the kitchen sniffing her spicy seafood dishes. Lourdes had no trouble talking to them. They looked right at her face telling her things. Why they avoided Dr. Mahmood. Because he would ask very personal questions about their sexual lives. Why they thought Mrs. Mahmood was crazy. Because of the way she danced in just her underwear.

And in the evening the woman of the house would tell Lourdes of being bored with her life, not able to invite her friends in because Woz didn't approve of them.

"What do I do? I hang out. I listen to music. I discuss soap operas with the gook maids. Melda stops me. 'Oh, missus, come quick.' They're in the laundry room watching *As the World Turns*. She goes, 'Dick follows Nikki to where she is to meet Ryder, and it look like he was going to hurt her. But Ryder came there in time to save Nikki from a violent Dick.'"

Mrs. Mahmood would tell a story like that and look at her without an expression on her face, waiting for Lourdes to smile or laugh. But what was funny about the story?

"What do I do?" was the question she asked most. "I exist, I have no life."

"You go shopping."

"That's all."

"You play golf."

"You've gotta be kidding."

"You go out with your husband."

"To an Indian restaurant and I listen to him talk to the manager. How many times since you've been here has he come home in the evening? He has a girlfriend," the good-looking redheaded woman said. "He's with her all the time. Her or another one, and doesn't care that I know. He's rubbing it in my face. All guys fool around at least once in a while. Woz and his buddies live for it. It's accepted over there, where they're from. A guy gets tired of his wife in Pakistan? He burns her to death. Or has it done. I'm not kidding, he tells everyone her *dupatta* caught fire from the stove."

Lourdes said, "Ah, that's why you don't cook."

"Among other reasons. Woz's from Rawalpindi, a town where forty women a *month* show up at the hospital with terrible burns. If the woman survives . . . Are you listening to me?"

Lourdes was sipping her daiquiri. "Yes, of course."

"If she doesn't die, she lives in shame because her husband, this prick who tried to burn her to death, kicked her out of the fucking house. And he gets away with it. Pakistan, India, thousands of women are burned every year 'cause their husbands are tired of them, or they didn't come up with a big enough dowry."

"You say the first wife was burn to death."

"Once he could afford white women — like, what would he need her for?"

"You afraid he's going to burn you?"

"It's what they do, their custom. And you know what's ironic? Woz comes here to be a plastic surgeon, but over in Pakistan, where all these women are going around disfigured? There are no plastic surgeons to speak of." She said, "Some of them get acid thrown in their face." She said, "I made the biggest mistake of my life marrying a guy from a different culture, a towelhead."

Lourdes said, "Why did you?"

She gestured. "This . . ." Meaning the house and all that went with it.

"So you have what you want."

"I won't if I leave him."

"Maybe in the divorce he let you keep the house."

"It's in the prenup, I get zip. And at thirty-two I'm back stripping on Federal Highway, or working in one of those topless doughnut places. You have tits, at least you can get a job. Woz's favorite, I'd come out in a nurse's uniform, peel everything off but the perky little cap?" The woman's mind moving to this without pausing. "Woz said the first time he saw the act he wanted to hire me. I'd be the first topless surgical nurse."

Lourdes imagined this woman dancing naked, men watching her, and thought of Miss Olympia warning the cleaning women with her Biblical Integrity: no singing or dancing around while cleaning the offices, or they might catch the eye of men working late. She made it sound as if they were lying in wait. "Read the Book of Judges," Miss Olympia said, "the twenty-first verse." It was about men waiting for women, the daughters of Shiloh, to come out to dance so they could take them, force the women to be their wives. Lourdes knew of cleaning women who sang while they worked, but not ones who danced. She wondered what it would be like to dance naked in front of men.

"You don't want to be with him," Lourdes said, "but you want to live in this house."

"There it is," the woman who didn't look at all like a Mrs. Mahmood said.

Lourdes sipped her daiquiri, put the glass down, and reached for the pack of Virginia Slims on the table.

"May I try one of these?"

"Help yourself."

She lit the cigarette, sucking hard to get a good draw. She said, "I use to smoke. The way you do it made me want to smoke again. Even the way you hold the cigarette."

Lourdes believed the woman was very close to telling what she was thinking about. Still, it was not something easy to talk about with another person, even for a woman who danced naked. Lourdes decided this evening to help her.

She said, "How would you feel if a load of wet concrete fell on your husband?"

Then wondered, sitting in the silence, not looking at the woman, if she had spoken too soon.

The redheaded woman said, "The way it happened to Mr. Zimmer? How did you feel?"

"I accepted it," Lourdes said, "with a feeling of relief, knowing I wouldn't be beaten no more."

"Were you ever happy with him?"

"Not for one day."

"You picked him, you must've had some idea."

"He picked me. At the party in Cali? There were seven Colombian girls for each American. I didn't think I would be chosen. We married . . . In two years I had my green card and was tired of him hitting me."

The redheaded Mrs. Mahmood said, "You took a lot of shit, didn't you?" and paused this time before saying, "How much does a load of concrete cost these days?"

Lourdes, without pausing, said, "Thirty thousand."

Mrs. Mahmood said, "Jesus Christ," but was composed, sitting back in her yellow cushions. She said, "You were ready. Viviana told you the situation and you decided to go for it."

"I think it was you hired me," Lourdes said, "because of Mr. Zimmer — you so interested in what happen to him. Also I could tell, from the first day we sat here, you don't care for your husband."

"You can understand why, can't you? I'm scared to death of catching on fire. He lights a cigar, I watch him like a fucking hawk."

Giving herself a reason, an excuse.

"We don't need to talk about him," Lourdes said. "You pay the money, all of it before, and we don't speak of this again. You don't pay, we still never speak of it."

"The Colombian guys have to have it all up front?"

"The what guys?"

"The concrete guys."

"You don't know what kind of guys they are. What if it looks like an accident and you say oh, they didn't do nothing, he fell off his boat."

"Woz doesn't have a boat."

"Or his car was hit by a truck. You understand? You not going to know anything before."

"I suppose they want cash."

"Of course."

"I can't go to the bank and draw that much."

"Then we forget it."

Lourdes waited while the woman thought about it smoking her Virginia Slim, both of them smoking, until Mrs. Mahmood said, "If I give you close to twenty thousand in cash, today, right now, you still want to forget it?"

Now Lourdes had to stop and think for a moment.

"You have that much in the house?"

"My getaway money," Mrs. Mahmood said, "in case I ever have to leave in a hurry. What I socked away in tips getting guys to spot their pants and that's the deal, twenty grand. You want it or not? You don't, you might as well leave, I don't need you anymore."

So far in the few weeks she was here, Lourdes had met Dr. Mahmood face-to-face with reason to speak to him only twice. The first time, when he came in the kitchen and asked her to prepare his breakfast, the smoked snook, a fish he ate cold with tea and whole wheat toast. He asked her to have some of the snook if she wished, saying it wasn't as good as kippers but would do. Lourdes tried a piece; it was full of bones but she told him yes, it was good. They spoke of different kinds of fish from the ocean they liked and he seemed to be a pleasant, reasonable man.

The second time Lourdes was with him face-to-face he startled her, coming out of the swimming pool naked as she was watering the plants on the patio. He called to her to bring him his towel from the chair. When she came with it he said, "You were waiting for me?"

"No, sir, I didn't see you."

As he dried his face and his head, the hair so short it appeared shaved, she stared at his skin, at his round belly and his strange black penis, Lourdes looking up then as he lowered the towel.

He said, "You are a widow?" She nodded yes and he said, "When you married, you were a virgin?"

She hesitated, but then answered because she was telling a doctor, "No, sir."

"It wasn't important to your husband?"

"I don't think so."

"Would you see an advantage in again being a virgin?"

She had to think — it wasn't something ever in her mind before — but didn't want to make the doctor wait, so she said, "No, not at my age."

The doctor said, "I can restore it if you wish."

"Make me a virgin?"

"Surgically, a few sutures down there in the tender dark. It's becoming popular in the Orient with girls entering marriage. Also for prostitutes. They can charge much more, often thousands of dollars for that one night." He said, "I'm thinking of offering the procedure. Should you change your mind, wish me to examine you, I could do it in your room."

Dr. Mahmood's manner, and the way he looked at her that time, made Lourdes feel like taking her clothes off.

He didn't come home the night Lourdes and Mrs. Mahmood got down to business. Or the next night. The morning of the following day, two men from the Palm Beach County sheriff's office came to the house. They showed Lourdes their identification and asked to see Mrs. Mahmood.

She was upstairs in her bedroom trying on a black dress, looking at herself in the full-length mirror and then at Lourdes's reflection appearing behind her.

"The police are here," Lourdes said.

Mrs. Mahmood nodded and said, "What do you think?" turning to pose in the dress, the skirt quite short.

Lourdes read the story in the newspaper that said Dr. Wasim Mahmood, prominent etc., etc., had suffered gunshot wounds during an apparent carjacking on Flagler near Currie Park and was pronounced dead on arrival at Good Samaritan. His Mercedes was found abandoned on the street in Delray Beach.

Mrs. Mahmood left the house in her black dress. Later, she phoned to tell Lourdes she had identified the body, spent time with the police, who had no clues, nothing at all to go on, then stopped by a funeral home and arranged to have Woz cremated without delay. She said, "What do you think?"

"About what?" Lourdes said.

"Having the fucker burned."

She said she was stopping to see friends and wouldn't be home until late.

One A.M., following an informal evening of drinks with old friends, Mrs. Mahmood came into the kitchen from the garage and began to lose her glow.

What was going on here?

Rum and mixes on the counter, limes, a bowl of ice. A Latin beat coming from the patio. She followed the sound to a ring of burning candles, to Lourdes in a green swimsuit moving in one place to the beat, hands raised, Lourdes grinding her hips in a subtle way.

The two guys at the table smoking cigarettes saw Mrs. Mahmood, but made no move to get up.

Now Lourdes turned from them and saw her, Lourdes smiling a little as she said, "How you doing? You look like you feeling no pain."

"You have my suit on," Mrs. Mahmood said.

"I put on my yellow one," Lourdes said, still moving in that subtle way, "and took it off. I don't wear yellow no more, so I borrow one of yours. Is okay, isn't it?"

Mrs. Mahmood said, "What's going on?"

"This is *cumbia,* Colombian music for when you want to celebrate. For a wedding, a funeral, anything you want. The candles are part of it. *Cumbia,* you should always light candles."

Mrs. Mahmood said, "Yeah, but what is going on?"

"We having a party for you, Ginger. The Colombian guys come to see you dance."

ROBERT MCKEE

The Confession

FROM *Eureka Literary Magazine*

I PULLED into the Thatcher driveway and shut down my motorcycle. I dropped the sidestand, but I didn't climb off — not yet. When Jane called a half-hour earlier, she told me Charlie was worse and he wanted to see me. She asked me to come right away. I had rushed to their place, but now that I was there, instead of going in, I sat astride my bike taking in deep lungfuls of air. It had just stopped raining, and the night was heavy with the smell of jasmine. Charlie Thatcher took great pride in his yard, and I told myself I just wanted to steal a moment to enjoy the fragrance of his night-blooming jasmine. That was what I told myself, but even before the thought could form, I knew it was a lie.

The porch light came on, but I was parked beyond the reach of its yellow glow. The front door opened, and Jane stepped outside. "Pry?" she called. "Is that you out there?"

"Yeah," I said as I stood and swung my leg over the bike, "it's me."

She came down the steps and met me. "I can't believe you rode a motorcycle," she said. She held her hand palm up. "Didn't you notice it was raining?" She tried to smile, but there was a puffy thickness to her face, and the smile couldn't quite materialize.

"Yeah, I know, but I felt like riding." The truth was that when I got depressed, I liked to ride, and depression that night was as pervasive as the smell of Charlie's jasmine. I gave a little shrug. "Sometimes it makes me feel better."

When I said that, Jane's features came all unscrewed and fell apart. "Oh, Pry," she said, and she rushed to me and threw her arms around my waist. She dropped her head to my chest, and deep, horrible gusts of sound came out of her. She was getting soaked from the water that clung to my oilskin coat, but that didn't seem to matter. "It's happening," she said. "It's happening so fast."

I put my arms around her and pulled her close without saying anything. Charlie had been diagnosed a month earlier with liver cancer. A week ago, he had been admitted to the hospital. Two days ago, against his doctors' advice, he had insisted we bring him home.

"He asked me to call you," Jane said. She lifted her head and looked up at me. "He said it's important that he talk to you right away. He's in terrible pain, but he won't take anything because he wants to have it together when he talks to you."

I gave her a squeeze, and with my hands still on her shoulders, I pushed her back a step and looked down. "It's okay. I'm here now. How are you doing?" I asked.

She wiped her tears away with both hands and said, "I'm not doing so good. I cry constantly, except when I'm around Charlie. I haven't cried in front of him yet. He doesn't need to see my hysteria on top of everything else." She punctuated her comment with another of those not-quite-right smiles.

We walked to the house, and once we were on the porch, I took off my coat, shook the rain from it, and draped it over the railing. "Did he say what's on his mind?" I asked.

"No, he's being secretive as hell, but I could tell that it's important to him." She opened the front door and led me inside. "He said he would explain everything to me and the boys once he's had a chance to talk to you." She nodded toward the staircase and told me to go on up. There was the glint of a scolding mother in her eye. "I'd offer to bring you a beer," she said, "but since you're riding that motorcycle, I won't." Jane never missed an opportunity to let me know she thought motorcycles were dangerous.

I grabbed hold of the thick oak banister and pulled myself up the stairs. The Thatcher home was on Fifth Street, one block from Balboa Park. It was a large, drafty place built in the early 1930s. Charlie had been my number-two man for years, and when I sold my security business, the new owners promoted him to general manager. I assumed when that happened, he and Jane would then sell this place in San Diego and move up to North County, where the main offices were located. When I suggested that, though, Charlie wouldn't consider it. "This is where we raised our two boys," he told me, "and this is where we'll stay."

Once I was at the landing outside Charlie's room, I hesitated again about going inside. I could no longer smell the jasmine, so I was forced to admit the truth. Charlie Thatcher was as close to me as an uncle, and I was not taking this well.

When a hoarse voice called, "Come on in, Father Delaney," I swallowed, gave the door a shove, and stepped inside.

"I've never been mistaken for a priest before," I said. Charlie was in a hospital bed, and it had been adjusted so that he was more or less in a sitting position.

"Oh, Jeez, lookie who's here. It's the biker trash." Charlie was originally from Queens, New York, and to my West Coast ears he sounded exactly like Archie Bunker from that old television series. Except for his size, he even looked like Archie. Charlie was much bigger, though — six-three and well over two hundred pounds. At least before he'd gotten sick he'd been over two hundred pounds. Now he was losing weight fast. It had been only two days since I had seen him, and in that short time, Charlie looked to have taken off twenty pounds and put on twenty years.

I took my best shot at a smile and said, "Good God, Charlie, you look like hell."

"Thanks a lot. I was feeling kinda blue until now, but you really perk a fella up."

I patted his hand. "It's the least I can do."

He growled. "Lately, doin' the least is what you do the most." Charlie liked to give me a hard time about what he considered my life of leisure. I had spent my twenties and early thirties building my business. By the time I sold out, we were doing it all: uniformed security guards, night watchmen, the installation of burglar alarms, private investigations. It had been an all-consuming process for a lot of years. Now I could afford to spend my time doing what I wanted to do, which usually involved riding the motorcycles I had customized myself at my home up the coast. It was not the sort of activity the hard-working Charlie Thatcher considered productive.

We had gotten past our obligatory insults-at-first-sight, and now there was a moment thick with silence. It was Charlie who broke it. "The doc figures less than a week." When he said that, I felt very heavy and allowed myself to drop into the straight-backed chair beside his bed. "Maybe a lot less," he added. "I didn't believe it at first, but I know it's true. It's strange, you know? It's like I can feel myself draining away."

I started to tell him how sorry I was, but he knew that without my saying it. Charlie could always read my mind. We had known each other for eighteen years. Right after he retired from the navy, I hired him as a security guard for a strip mall in National City. It was a tough area, but Big Charlie was perfect for the job. Providing security for that place had been my first contract, so Charlie had been with me since the beginning.

With what looked like a lot of pain, he lifted a hand toward the door. "Close that thing all the way, would you, John?" My name's John Pryor, but most people call me Pry; Charlie always called me John. I shut the door, and as I came back he said, "I thought you might be Father Delaney because I asked Janey to give both of you a call. Since the rectory's only a few blocks away, I expected him to show up first."

"You must have forgotten my disregard for speed limits."

He gave my little joke a quick smile — more than it deserved, really — but I could tell the niceties were over. Charlie had something on his mind. "This is better," he said. "I wanted to talk to you first, anyway."

"What's up?" I asked.

He stared for a long moment at his frail, blotchy hands. Finally he shook his head and said in a weak voice, "I'm not a good man, John."

I sat back down in the chair and leaned my forearms over the bed's rail. "That's crazy. You're the best man I've ever known." And I wasn't just saying that, either. Charlie Thatcher was an honorable, unselfish man. He was a loving father and husband. He was a Boy Scout leader and a Little League coach. He spent one night a week serving soup in a shelter down on Market Street. He had been a Big Brother to dozens of underprivileged kids. "Hell, Charlie," I said, "you're the guy that every sleazeball politician in the country pretends to be. What do you mean, you're not a good man?"

He turned to me, and the rims of his eyes stood out red against his yellowed complexion. "I'm not, John. I wanted to be. I tried to be." He turned his head toward the window and looked into the darkness of his large backyard. "I wanted to make up for what I had done, but there was no making up for it."

"What are you saying?" I asked.

He turned back to me, and the pain I saw in his face was not pain caused by his sickness; it came from something else. "I'm a murderer, John. Thirty-five years ago, I killed a man."

I'm not sure how long it was before I stammered out, "You're kidding, right?" Of course the question was so stupid, Charlie didn't even bother to answer it.

"You're the first person I've ever told. But now it's time I tell everyone. Father Delaney —" His voice broke. "— Jane, the boys. I should have told them long before now."

"What happened, Charlie?" I asked. I still didn't believe him. I couldn't picture Charlie Thatcher being a murderer; the image just wouldn't come.

He dropped his head back to the stack of pillows behind him and stared at some spot on the ceiling. "When it happened," he began, "I was in the navy. I was drinking in a bar in East San Diego, and for some reason — I don't remember why — this guy wanted to fight. I was a tough kid with a hot temper, so we stepped out into the alley."

I asked, "It happened in a fight?"

"Not really. The guy was my size or even bigger, but he wasn't a fighter." Charlie looked at me, and I knew what he was saying was true. "I punched him a couple of times, and he hit the ground hard, smacking the back of his head. It could've ended there, but something in me clicked, you know? I had this — I don't know — this rage, and it took over. There was no stopping it. I knocked this guy down, and then I was on top of him driving my fist into his face over and over and over. When I came to my senses, I started running, and I didn't stop until I was back at the ship. The next day I heard on the radio that the guy was dead."

"Were you ever questioned by the police?" I asked.

"No, I didn't know the man. There was nothing to connect me to him. I don't even remember how the argument started in the first place. We'd only talked for maybe ten minutes in the bar, and I guess no one had noticed us. San Diego was a pretty rough place in those days, especially in that part of town. There was a story in the newspaper a couple of days later. His name was Duane Tragovic. He was a petty criminal. He'd been arrested a dozen times. There wasn't much of an investigation. I don't think this guy's death was real high on the cops' list of things to do."

We both sat silent for a moment. "I tried to just forget about it,"

Charlie finally said, "but I couldn't. Maybe Tragovic was a criminal, but it didn't matter what he was; what mattered was what I was, and I was a murderer.

"The paper said that Tragovic had a wife. Marlee was her name, and for some reason I couldn't get her out of my mind. I'd not only committed a crime against Tragovic, but I had committed a crime against her as well. It got to where I couldn't stand being in San Diego. I thought if I could get out of town, I could put this behind me, so I volunteered for duty on a river patrol boat in Vietnam." He fixed me with his rheumy eyes. "But I could never stop thinking about it, John." He lifted his hand and formed a fist. "Every single day for the last thirty-five years, I have remembered the feel of hitting that man — beating him. Not a day went by that I didn't think of him and his wife. I wanted to find her and tell her how sorry I was, but I couldn't do it. I knew if I ever found her, the truth would come out, and I couldn't face what that would mean. Eventually I had a family of my own, and I couldn't bring myself to tell them." His eyes filled, and he shook his head. "I was too much of a coward to let them know what kind of a man I really am."

As soon as he said that, he gave a gasp, and his body jerked. He clenched his eyes and sucked in a quick, shallow breath. It was clear he was in severe pain.

"Charlie," I said, "what can I do?"

He didn't answer. He just lay there with his eyes clasped and his teeth gritted. After a bit he seemed to relax, but when the pain passed, he looked thinner and even more frail. The angles where the sheet touched his body seemed sharper. In a matter of seconds the pain had come and gone, but when it left, it had taken a piece of Charlie with it. It seemed that there was less of him lying in front of me now than there had been only a moment before.

Slowly he rubbed his eyes, but there was a shadow there — a darkness — he could not rub away. "I tried to be good," he said in a raspy whisper, "but it didn't matter what kind of a man I tried to be, I could never change what I became that night so long ago."

There was a faint rapping at the door, and a middle-aged man wearing a white clerical collar stuck in his head.

"Father Delaney," Charlie said, "give us another second, would you?"

The man nodded. "I'll be right out here when you're ready." He stepped back into the hall and closed the door.

"I need to make my confession, John."

I stood and looked back toward the door that led into the hall-way. "Sure, I'll leave and send the priest right in."

"No, no," he said, "that's not what I mean. I am going to confess to Father Delaney and to Janey and the kids, too, but that wasn't what I meant when I said I need to make my confession. What I meant was I need to make my confession to Marlee Tragovic. I have to tell her what I did to her husband and beg her to forgive me." He lifted his eyes to mine, and I saw the sadness that had always been there. I had seen it before, but I had never recognized it for what it was. "I want you to find her for me," he said. "I want you to bring her here."

I couldn't believe what I was hearing. "My God, Charlie, it's been thirty-five years."

"Yeah," he agreed, and the shadow in his eyes darkened. "Thirty-five long years." He swallowed hard. "You can do it, though, John. I have faith in you. But you better hurry. I'm not getting any young-er." Then he added with a feeble smile, "Or much older, either, for that matter."

I avoided the freeway and went home the long way around Mission Bay, through Pacific Beach, La Jolla, and past the cliffs at Torrey Pines. The constant gear shifting, stopping, and starting provided the activity I needed to prevent myself from thinking. But as I rolled down the ramp into the underground garage at my house in Del Mar, despite my best efforts, the thoughts flooded in.

I doubted I was the right person to do the job Charlie asked. I had been out of the business for over three years, but it was more than that. This was important to Charlie, and I was afraid I would let him down.

I climbed the stairs from the garage into the house, dropped an old Crusaders CD into the player, sloshed some brandy into a glass, and sat down in front of the computer. The e-mail was the usual junk. I trashed it all and clicked on to the 'Net. I did a search for "Marlee Tragovic" and got nothing. It didn't surprise me, really. After so long, if she were still alive, it was likely she had remarried. Even these days, more often than not a woman took her husband's name, and the divorce rate being what it was in the last thirty-five years, it was possible her last name had changed more than once.

The Internet was just coming into common use when I retired, and I never got to take full advantage of all the things it offered private investigators. I knew, though, that the investigations side of my old company used it extensively, and they had access to databases that I didn't. The office was manned twenty-four hours a day, so I fired off an e-mail asking them to run a check for me. I was on my third brandy when they wrote back saying they couldn't find anything either.

So much for the easy way.

My breakfast the next morning consisted of one poached egg, two cups of coffee, and four aspirin. The aspirin was the price I paid for drinking more than one brandy the night before.

I had no confidence in my ability to accomplish what Charlie asked, but I knew that I had to try, so I made a call to Sergeant Al Bruun, a friend of mine on the SDPD. We were the same age and had hit the streets of San Diego at about the same time. The two of us had been trading favors for years.

"Damn, Pry," he said, "I had no idea Charlie was even sick."

"Yeah, it came on fast." Without mentioning Charlie's involvement, I told him about the homicide thirty-five years earlier. He said he would have to send someone to the warehouse to scrounge around for the file, but with any luck, he could have a copy to me by the end of the day.

"Do you still have the same fax number?" Al asked. I told him I did, and we said good-bye.

After one more coffee and a fast shower, I climbed on my bike and rode into San Diego. The city had changed a lot since Charlie was a young man. In those days Broadway was lined with strip bars and clip joints. Slick guys in shiny suits would stand in front of the businesses hawking whatever scam they were trying to work on the sailors. The city fathers had cleaned that up in the '70s and '80s, and, as in all major U.S. cities, they had redirected their efforts to a more sophisticated kind of scam — the kind they worked on the tourists.

I rode up Broadway, and the farther east I got, the seedier things were. The city had dumped millions into cleaning up downtown, but the fringes were apparently invisible to the big-money boys, and these areas had not aged well.

Before I had left Charlie the night before, he had given me a

little more information. There was still a bar where the killing
had taken place. It was located in the middle of the block, and I
whipped a quick U-turn and backed the rear wheel of my bike into
the curb. The place was called the Silk Hat Lounge, and there was
the unlit neon outline of a top hat above the front door — tacky,
maybe, but still the bright spot in an even tackier neighborhood.
The place wasn't opened yet, but I could see through the window
that there was a woman behind the bar counting bottles and making notations on a piece of paper.

I rapped on the window to get her attention, and she called out,
"We open at eleven."

"I'd like to ask you a few questions. It won't take but a minute."

She was a redhead who looked to be in her early sixties. She
had melonlike breasts that threatened the stitching of her nylon
blouse. She had obviously seen me pull up on my chopped Harley-
Davidson. "I don't like bikers," she said. She flipped a backhand
through the air as though shooing a fly. "Beat it."

I dug into the pocket of my jeans and pulled out some bills. I
peeled off a twenty and held it flush to the plate glass. I expect ol'
Andy Jackson had been an accomplished public speaker in his day,
which was only fitting since his picture these days spoke with such
eloquence. She stared at it for a moment, snuffed her cigarette,
and stepped around the bar.

She wore tight, hot-pink slacks and had a surprisingly tiny waist.
"One minute's what you asked for," she said as she opened the
door, "and by a strange coincidence, that's just what you get for a
twenty."

She reached for the bill, but I pulled it back. "This'll be yours in
sixty seconds," I said, "assuming you've got something to sell."

"What are you in the market for, biker?" She said "biker" with a
sour tone.

"Information," I said. "Do you own this place?"

She seemed wary. "Yeah, what's it to you?"

"How long've you had it?"

"'Bout fifteen years. I waited tables here for eight years before
that."

I could tell that at some point in her distant past this woman had
been very attractive. Now, though, she had the kind of face that
harsh morning light did not improve.

I asked who she had bought the bar from, and she said a name but added, "He only had it a couple of years. I got the place at a bargain 'cause he was forced to sell." She gave a smile that multiplied her wrinkles by a factor of three. "He suffered from a common problem in the bar business."

"Yeah, what's that?" I asked.

"He drank his profits." She dug into her front pocket and pulled out a semicrushed pack of Winstons. She lit one with a disposable lighter that was encased in a chrome holder trimmed with plastic jade. "He'd bought the bar from Parker Heath. Parker owned the place for close to thirty years. He built it right after he got back from Korea."

Her eyes cut to the twenty.

"Now, now," I said, "don't get greedy. You have fifteen seconds to go. Is Mr. Heath still around?"

"That depends."

"Let me guess. It depends on why I want to know, right?"

"You're a real smart boy, aren't you?" She gave me a look that communicated she might be inclined to set aside her prejudice against bikers after all. I suspected it was a look she had tossed at more than a few men over the years. When I didn't respond, she shrugged and said, "I worked for Parker a long time. I don't think it would be very nice of me to help just anybody hunt him down."

"All I want is a few answers."

She dragged deep from her smoke and exhaled through her nose. "Twenty bucks," she pointed out, "buys a few answers, but addresses cost extra."

I could hear Charlie's clock ticking, and I didn't have time to haggle. I dug out another twenty and handed her both bills. She tucked them into the pocket with her Winstons, lifted the two fingers that held her cigarette, and pointed at a spot over my left shoulder. I turned around. Across the street was a ratty apartment building, and peering down at us from a second-story window was an old man munching on a sandwich.

Parker Heath's rooms smelled of fried baloney. When he let me in, his sandwich was half gone, and in an apparent defiance of gravity, a dollop of mayonnaise clung to the stubble on his chin. I explained that I did not want much of his time, but I needed to visit with him about something that had taken place thirty-five years before. When I said that, the width of his smile suggested he was a man who enjoyed discussing the past.

I followed him through his living room and into a small kitchen. Waggling his sandwich at one of the two vinyl-covered aluminum chairs beside the table, he said, "Have a seat." I pulled the chair out and sat down. "You're a lucky one," he said as he looked through the fly-spotted window next to the table. He had a perfect view of the bar on the other side of Broadway. "Ain't many fellas able to escape Arlene with their pants still on." He cackled a high-pitched, old man's laugh, and I couldn't help but smile.

"She looks like she might've been a tiger in her day," I allowed.

"In her day, hell. The sun set on her day years ago, and she's still a tiger. I could tell you some tales about Arlene, I could." He took a big gulp of milk from a tumbler beside his plate. "Care for some cow juice?" he asked.

"No, thanks." I jerked my thumb toward the street. "Arlene says you used to own the bar."

"I did. Built it with my own two hands in the summer a '53." He rapped his knuckles against his right temple. "Thanks to a Chinese hand grenade, the army had to stick a steel plate in my noggin. I'd been out of the hospital about six months, but I was still gettin' dizzy spells every time I had ta climb the damned ladder." He looked down at the bar. "I got her built, though," he said. "I surely did." He reached a hoary hand up and wiped the mayonnaise from his chin, then sucked it from his finger. "Sold out in '82, but I moved in here so I could keep an eye on the place." He directed a wistful gaze out the window. "Old habits die hard, I guess."

"Do you remember a time, Mr. Heath, in the late '60s when a man named Tragovic was murdered outside the bar?"

"Sure, I remember."

"What can you tell me about that?"

He shook his head. "Not much to tell, really. Tragovic was just this runt who used to hang around; that's all. I never liked him. No one did."

"Do you remember seeing him the night of the murder?"

"Boy, you're goin' back a ways." He popped the last of the baloney sandwich into his mouth and continued talking without slowing down. "'Bout all I remember is someone found the body, and when the ambulance arrived, all my customers headed out to watch 'em load Tragovic up. That was maybe an hour before closing time.

Once the ambulance left, everybody filed back in. I ended up selling more drinks in that last hour than I ever sold in an hour's time before or since. I reckon death tends to make folks thirsty."

"Was Tragovic talking to anyone that night that you recall — maybe involved in some kind of an argument with a sailor?"

He dug his pinky into his ear and then gave a close inspection to whatever it was he fished out. "I remember the cops asking me that same question the next day. From what I heard, there was some winos sharing a bottle on the street corner who said they had seen a sailor beatin' the hell out of some guy in the alley out back. But, no, I never knew anything was going on. Fights'd happen from time to time. That was just the nature of the business. Hell, sailors were in and out a lot, 'specially then what with Vietnam and all."

"I understand Tragovic was married."

"Yep, he was. His wife came in some, not much, though. She wasn't old enough to drink, which is just as well. Tragovic was the sort of fella who'd use what little drinking money they had on hisself, I'm sure. I don't recall much about her, 'cept she was a mousey little thing. Pretty, I think, but timid, like."

"Whatever became of her? Do you know?"

He gave his head a slow shake. "I've got no idea." He peered again through the window. "She's just one a the many that came and went." A somber cast settled across the old man's brow. "There was thousands of 'em I knew over the years," he said. "Thousands." After a bit, he cleared his throat and turned back to me. With a frown he added, "I don't even remember her name."

"Marlee," I said.

"Was that it? Hell, you coulda fooled me. I do remember she had a couplea brothers who were regulars for a while there. Likable fellas, too, as I recall."

"Do you remember their names?"

He scratched the spot where the army had installed the steel plate. "Boy," he said, "you make a fella shake the dust off, don't ya?"

"Anything you could remember would help."

He pondered it for a moment, then the edges of his mouth crinkled into a smile. "Abbott and Costello," he said.

"Abbott and Costello?"

"Yeah, that's what everyone used to call 'em 'cause their real names was Bud and Lou. Get it? Abbott and Costello."

I nodded. "Sure, I get it. The old comedy team. Do you remember a last name?"

"A last name, huh? Now that's tougher, ain't it?" He gave a long pause, then turned to face me with a sly look on his face. I started to dig into my pocket for another one of the twenties that had worked so well on Arlene across the street. Before I could pull it out, though, Heath smiled and said, "I don't want your money." He then told me the name, and when he did, I realized his long pause was just an old bartender's skill at building a little suspense. He was a man who had shared thousands of chats over the years, and he knew how to make a conversation interesting. "Bickman," he said. "Bud and Lou Bickman. If you don't mind me askin', why is it that you are rummaging around so deep in the long ago?"

I shrugged. "I'm just trying to do a favor for a friend."

"A friend," he said, and with a nod, he added, "That's good."

Even though some of what the old man said didn't add up, it was clear he'd told me all he knew. I had to ask, anyway. "Is there anything else you can remember? I'd like to find Marlee, if I could."

"Find her, huh? I expect the trail's damned cold after thirty-five years."

"Yeah," I agreed, "it is."

"There's nothin' more I can tell you," he said. "People come along, and then they're gone. That's just the way it works. You never see 'em again."

I pushed away from the table and stood. "Well, thanks. Mr. Heath, you've been a lot of help. I appreciate it."

"They come then go. That's what they do — come and go."

I let myself out, and just before I shut the apartment door, I thanked him again. I don't think he heard me, though. He didn't respond. He just sat there drinking his milk and staring out the window at the Silk Hat Lounge.

I called directory assistance on my cell phone. There was a Louis Bickman listed in El Cajon. I got both the address and phone number, but I decided to ride out rather than call. I fired up the Harley, made my way to the freeway, and headed east.

The Bickman residence was a small but tidy place on the outskirts of town. As I pushed the button for the doorbell, I thought I could hear the sound of a television game show coming from somewhere in the house, but no one answered, and I wrote a note saying if the Louis Bickman at this residence had a sister named Marlee, to please give me a call. I said I wished to discuss with her the death of her husband, Duane Tragovic. I gave my name, address, and phone number. I closed the note by writing, "This is an urgent matter. I need to speak to Mrs. Tragovic right away. Please call as soon as possible."

I tucked the note into the Bickman mailbox, climbed on my bike, and headed home.

I noticed Al Bruun's fax when I dropped the chopper's keys onto my computer desk. It consisted of six pages that I could tell had been originally produced by a manual typewriter. Some of the letters were darker or slightly higher on the line than others. It was a nostalgic reminder of a less polished time. The light was flashing on the answering machine, so I pushed "play," and as the tape rewound, I scanned the three-and-a-half-decade-old file on the homicide of Duane Tragovic.

"Hi-ya, Pry," said the tinny voice that came from the answering machine's speaker, "this is Al. I just faxed you what we had on that case you asked about. As you can see from the report, they didn't have much. One of the bar patrons called for an ambulance, but the guy was dead when they showed up. A half-dozen winos had seen a sailor beating on someone earlier that evening. The uniformed boys interviewed as many of the winos as they could round up, but they didn't get much info. Homicide detectives asked a few questions around the neighborhood over the course of the next day or so, but there were no leads. Tragovic had a wife. She was young, only seventeen years old, and apparently pretty hysterical over her husband's killing. They questioned her, of course, but didn't get much from her, either. She said she didn't know any sailors, and as far as she knew, neither did her husband. They kept the file open, but there was nothing to go on, and it doesn't look like they ever did much more with it. I sent along a copy of Tragovic's rap sheet. You can tell by his record that he must have been a real sweetie-pie. I expect the guys doing the investigation knew him pretty well, and it doesn't look like they killed themselves working the case. I also sent along the autopsy report. No surprises there. The mechanism of death was a fractured skull.

"I know it's not much, but it's all we have. If you need anything else, just give me a call. And tell Charlie we're pulling for him." The machine clicked to a stop.

I took what Al had faxed outside to the deck that overlooked the beach. I dropped into a chair, slipped off my boots, and propped my feet on the rail. It didn't take long to read the little that was there, but when I was finished, my palms were sweating and there was a lump in my throat the size of a softball.

I lay the pages in my lap and looked toward the water. There was a young die-hard on a surfboard a few hundred feet out doing his best to snag one of the pathetic waves that stumbled toward shore. He was a very small man — tiny, really; the board was much too big for him, and despite all his effort, he wasn't having any luck. I watched for a while; then I picked up the papers and reread that portion of Tragovic's autopsy report that described the deceased.

I gave Lou Bickman until six o'clock that night to call; when he didn't, I set my telephone to forward calls to my cellular in case he tried while I was out, and I headed back to El Cajon. I parked in front of the Bickman house and made my way up the cracked walk. There was a pickup truck in the carport, and I could hear voices coming from the open windows that lined the front of the house. They must have heard me climb the three steps to the small stoop because the voices went silent, and just as I raised my hand to ring the bell, a large man came to the door.

"What do you want?" he asked. He had wide, heavy shoulders and a neck as thick as my thigh.

I heard a soft voice from behind him say, "It's him, isn't it, Louis?"

"It's okay," the man said over his shoulder. "I'll take care of this." The man was at least two inches taller than my six-one, and he must have outweighed me by sixty pounds. "What's on your mind, mister?" he asked.

"I'm John Pryor," I said. "I'm the guy who left the note in your mailbox this afternoon. I'm looking for a woman by the name of Marlee Tragovic." It was a long shot, but I decided to play a quick bluff. "I know you're her brother, Mr. Bickman. I'd like to talk to her about the death of her husband back in the 1960s." I could tell by the expression that hit his face that I had found the right man. "I don't mean you or your family any harm. I just need to find your sister; that's all."

The voice spoke again. "Please, Louis, let him in."

He turned in the doorway, and I got a look at the woman behind him. If she was who I thought she was, she couldn't have been more than fifty-two, but she looked a decade older. She was thin and frail, and she leaned with both hands on an aluminum walker. "You gotta trust me," Bickman said. "This is a bad idea."

Her voice had an even, resigned tone. "You've been a good brother, Louis, but, please, just let the man in."

Bickman hesitated, but finally he moved back, and I stepped into the house.

"Have a seat," the woman said. She motioned toward a couch across the room, and I sat down. She was wearing a terrycloth bathrobe, and she pulled it tighter around her slight frame. She touched her limp hair and said, "I have a back problem. Sometimes it's worse than others." I took this as an excuse for her appearance. "It's been very bad lately," she added as she eased herself into a chair across from the couch. Bickman continued to stand at the front door, his large arms folded across his chest.

"Your name is Marlee, isn't it?"

She held the lapels of the robe so tightly her knuckles were white. "Yes," she said.

"Is it still Tragovic?" I asked.

"Yes," she said again. "I never married after Duane."

I glanced across the room at Bickman. "Where's Bud?" I asked.

"We don't have to talk to this man, Marlee."

"I know, but it's okay. Bud died of a heart attack in 1983," she said. "Why are you here, Mr. Pryor? What is it you want?"

"What I don't want is to hurt you, Mrs. Tragovic. If it wasn't for a friend of mine, I would not be here at all. I think I understand what happened to your husband, some of it, anyway."

"It's been a long time," she said. "It's been a lifetime."

I waited for her to offer more; when she didn't, I said, "Duane Tragovic was a difficult man to live with, wasn't he?"

She didn't speak; she just gave a quick nod.

"He used to hurt you."

"Yes," she whispered.

"I've seen his record, Mrs. Tragovic. He was charged a half-dozen times with battery against you. Twice he served jail time for it, but he didn't stop, did he?"

She shook her head.

"Finally he did it once too often, and either you or one of your brothers killed him."

Bickman's arms came unfolded, and he moved to the center of the room. "Marlee, you do not have to talk to this man. You don't have to tell him a thing." He turned to me and came to the couch. Looking down, he said, "I don't know who the hell you think you are coming in here like this."

"I'm not the police, Mr. Bickman. I don't intend to go to the police. I'm here for my friend, nothing more. I've read the reports, Mrs. Tragovic, and what I think happened is that your husband was not killed in the alley behind the Silk Hat Lounge as everyone assumed at the time. I think he was dumped there by your brothers." I looked at Bickman. "How big was Bud, Mr. Bickman?"

He hesitated but finally answered. "I don't know. Five-eight, five-nine. Hundred and seventy-five pounds."

I nodded. "I believe that you and your brother wanted to throw the police off. To do that, one of you — and I think it was you, Mr. Bickman — picked a fight with a young, drunk sailor. You wanted the fight to be witnessed, but you also knew who those witnesses would be, and you were confident that they would not be able to give the police a very good accounting of what happened."

The big man stood silent, staring down at me, his eyes wide and unblinking.

"You picked a fight, Mr. Bickman, but it was never your intention to win that fight. You just wanted the winos to see someone getting worked over in that alley, and when Tragovic's body was found, the police would look for a sailor."

"You have no way of knowing that," Bickman said, but he said it softly, without force.

"The sailor you picked for your fight was my friend. He explained to me that the man he fought that night was big, but according to the fella who owned the Silk Hat at the time, Duane Tragovic was a runt. The autopsy report put him at five-foot-four and a hundred and forty pounds. My friend said he hit the man repeatedly in the face, but Tragovic had no injuries to his face. The only injury he had was to the back of the skull, as though he had banged his head against the pavement in a fight, or —" I looked to Marlee Tragovic. "— maybe someone hit him with something from behind."

"He's guessing, Marlee," Bickman said.

Marlee whispered, "He's a good guesser, though, isn't he, Lou?" When she said that, a rush of air escaped from the big man, and he dropped, deflated, to the couch. We were all silent for a long moment.

It was Bickman who broke the silence. "All right, smart guy," he said, "I killed the son of a bitch. You figured it out. Good work."

"Oh, stop, Louis," Marlee said. "Just stop it. You and Bud have taken care of me all my life, even to the point where you had no lives of your own, but it's time I faced what happened." She turned to me. "My brothers would do anything for me, Mr. Pryor. They devoted themselves to me. They would have gladly killed Duane — Bud even threatened to more than once — but they didn't. I did. I was only seventeen, but every time I moved, I ached from Duane's beatings. He would hit me in the small of the back where it was particularly painful, but where the marks wouldn't show. The last time was especially bad, and I have never recovered from it. I've lived in constant pain all these years because of that last beating. But it *was* the last beating, Mr. Pryor. When Duane turned his back, I took a saucepan from the kitchen counter, and I hit him. I just hit him once, but I hit him hard. When I realized he was dead, I called my brothers. They said they would take care of it, and they did. They took care of it then, and together they've taken care of me ever since." She reached over and placed her small hand on her brother's massive forearm. "When one passed on," she added, "the other took care of me by himself."

I nodded and offered a smile that I hoped would show them both that I understood.

Bickman ran his thick fingers through his hair and asked, "What is it you want?"

When he asked that, I turned to his sister and explained what I needed her to do.

Bickman had to carry Marlee up to Charlie's room. She'd had three back surgeries over the years, and it was impossible for her to climb stairs. She lived in constant pain, but both Marlee and her brother agreed that it was a miracle she could still walk at all. Once we were on the landing, Bickman put her down.

"Let me go in first," Janey said. "I'll tell him that you're here, Pry, and that you need to see him." The puffiness in Jane's face was even more pronounced than it had been the night before. She knocked once on the closed door and stepped inside.

"I've got to do this alone, now, Lou," Marlee said. "You wait with

Mrs. Thatcher and don't worry. I'll be fine." Bickman still seemed reluctant to have anything to do with this, but it was clear he was devoted to his sister.

When Janey came back out, she was crying openly. I guessed she had stopped trying to hide her tears from Charlie. "Don't be too long, Pry. He took a turn for the worse today."

I nodded, and she and Bickman started down the stairs. I faced Marlee. "Are you ready?" I asked.

"Yes," she said. And she did seem ready. She even seemed eager.

I put my hand against the door, but before I pushed it open, I said, "This will mean everything to Charlie."

A wisp of a smile tugged at her mouth. "It's funny, isn't it? He was going to make his confession to me, but as it turns out, it'll be the other way around."

"I want to thank you. He's spent his life carrying the guilt of this thing."

Marlee's eyes brimmed with tears. "And guilt is a heavy burden," she said. "Believe me, Mr. Pryor, I know."

WALTER MOSLEY

Lavender

FROM *Six Easy Pieces*

IT WAS a Tuesday morning, about a quarter past eleven. The little yellow dog hid in among the folds of the drapes, peeking out now and then to see if I was still in the reclining living room chair. Each time he caught sight of me, he bared his teeth and then slowly withdrew into the pale green fabric.

The room smelled of lavender and cigarette smoke.

The ticking of the wind-up clock, which I had carried all the way from France after my discharge, was the only sound except for the occasional passing car. The clock was encased in a fine dark wood, its numerals wrought in pale pink metal — copper and tin, most probably.

The cars on Genesee sounded like the rushing of wind.

I flicked my cigarette in the ashtray. A car slowed down. I could hear the tires squealing against the curb in front of our house.

A car door opened. A man said something in French. Bonnie replied in the same language. It was a joke of some sort. My Louisiana upbringing had given me a casual understanding of French, but I couldn't keep up with Bonnie's Parisian patter.

The car drove off. I took a deep drag on the Pall Mall I was nursing. She made it to the front step and paused. She was probably smelling the mottled yellow and red roses that I'd cultivated on either side of the door. When I'd asked her to come live with us she said, "As long as you promise to keep those rosebushes out front."

The key turned in the lock and the door swung open. I expected her to lag behind because of the suitcase. She always threw the door open first and then lifted the suitcase to come in.

My chair was to the left of the door, off to the side, so the first thing Bonnie saw was the crystal bowl filled with dried stalks of lavender. She was wearing dark blue slacks and a rust-colored sweater. All those weeks in the Air France stewardess uniform made her want to dress down.

She noticed the flowers and smiled, but the smile quickly turned into a frown.

"They came day before yesterday."

Bonnie yelped and leapt backward. The little yellow dog jumped out of hiding, looked around, and then darted out through the open door.

"Easy," she cried. "You scared me half to death."

I stood up from the chair.

"Sorry," I said. "I thought you saw me."

"What are you doing home?" Her eyes were wild, fearful.

For the first time I didn't feel the need or desire to hold her in my arms.

"Just curious," I said.

"What are you talking about?"

I took two steps toward her. I must have looked a little off wearing only briefs and an open bathrobe in the middle of a workday.

Bonnie took a half-step backward.

"The flowers," I said. "I was wondering about the flowers."

"I don't understand."

"They been sittin' there since the special delivery man dropped them off. Me and the kids were curious."

"About what?"

"Who sent 'em." The tone of my voice was high and pleasant, but the silence underneath was dead.

"I don't understand," Bonnie said. I almost believed her.

"They're for you."

"Well?" she said. "Then you must have seen the note."

"Envelope is sealed," I said. "You know I always try to teach my children that other people's mail is private. Now what would I look like openin' your letter?"

She heard the *my* in "my children."

Bonnie stared at me for a moment. I gestured with my right hand toward the tiny envelope clipped to an upper stem. She ripped off the top flowers getting the envelope free. She tore it open and read. I think she must have read it through three times before putting it in her pocket.

"Well?"

"From one of the passengers," she said. "Jogaye Cham. He was on quite a few of the flights."

"Oh? He send all the stewardesses flowers?"

"I don't know. Probably. He's from a royal Senegalese family. His father is a chief. He's working to unite the emancipated colonies."

There was a quiet pride in her words.

"He was on at least half of the flights we took, and I was nice to him," Bonnie continued. "I made sure that we had the foods he liked, and we talked about freedom."

"Freedom," I said. "Must be a good line."

"You don't know what you're talking about," she said, suddenly angry. "Black people in America have been free for a hundred years. Those of us from the Caribbean and Africa still feel the bite of the white man's whips."

It was an odd turn of a phrase — "the white man's whips." I was reminded that when a couple first become lovers they begin to talk alike. I wondered if Jogaye's speeches concerned the white man's whips.

I didn't respond to what she said, just inhaled some more smoke and looked at her.

After a brief hesitation, Bonnie picked up her suitcase and carried it into our bedroom. I returned to the big chair, put out the butt, and lit up another, my regimen of only ten cigarettes a day forgotten. After a while I heard the shower come on.

I had installed that shower especially for Bonnie.

If someone were to walk in on me right then, they might have thought that I was somber but calm. Really, I was a maniac trapped by a woman who would neither lie nor tell the truth.

I'd read the note, steamed it open, and then glued it shut. It was written in French, but I used a school dictionary to decipher most of the words. He was thanking her for the small holiday that they took on Madagascar in between the grueling sessions with the French, the English, and the Americans. It was only her warm company that kept his mind clear enough to argue for the kind of freedom that all of Africa must one day attain.

If she had told me that it was a gift from the airlines or the pilot or some girlfriend that knew she liked lavender, then I could have raged at her lies. But all she did was leave out the island of Madagascar.

I had looked it up in the encyclopedia. It's five hundred miles off the West African coastline, almost a quarter million square miles in area. The people are not Negro, or at least do not consider themselves so, and are more closely related to the peoples of Indonesia. Almost five million people lived there. A big place to leave out.

I wanted to drag her out of the shower by her hair, naked and wet, into the living room. I wanted to make her tell me everything that I had imagined her and her royal boyfriend doing on a deserted beach eight thousand miles away.

The bouquet had been sent to her care of the Air France office. Her boyfriend expected them to hold it there. But some fool sent it on, special delivery.

I decided to go into the bathroom and ask her if she expected me to lie down like a dog and take her abuse. My hands were fists. My heart was a pounding hammer. I stood up recklessly and knocked the glass ashtray from the arm of the chair. It shattered. It probably made a loud crashing sound, but I didn't notice. My anger was louder than anything short of a forty-five.

"Easy," she called from the shower. "What was that?"

I took a step toward the bathroom and the phone rang.

"Can you get that, honey?" she called.

Honey.

"Hello?"

"Easy, is that you?"

I recognized the voice but could not place it for my rage.

"Who is this?"

"It's EttaMae," she said.

I sat down again. Actually, I fell into the chair so hard that it tilted over on its side. The end table toppled, taking the lamp with it. More broken glass.

"What?"

"I called Sojourner Truth," she was saying, "and they said you had called in sick."

"Etta, it's really you?"

Bonnie came rushing out of the bathroom.

"What happened?" she cried.

Seeing her naked body, thinking of another man caressing it, holding on to the phone and hearing a woman that I had been searching for for months — I was almost speechless.

"I need a minute, baby," I said to both women at once.

"Hold on a minute," I said to Etta while waving Bonnie back to her shower. "Hold on."

Bonnie stared for a moment. She seemed about to say something and then retreated to the bathroom.

I sat there on the floor with the phone in my lap. If I had had a gun in my hand, I would have gone outside and killed the yellow dog.

The receiver was making noise, so I brought it to my head.

". . . Easy, what's goin' on over there?"

"Etta?"

"Yes?"

"Where have you been?"

"There's no time for that now, Easy. I got to talk to you."

"Where are you?"

She gave me an address on the Pacific Coast Highway, at Malibu Beach.

I hung up and went to the bedroom. Three minutes later I was dressed and ready to go.

"Who was that?" Bonnie called from the bathroom.

I went out of the front door without answering because all I had in my lungs was a scream.

I don't remember the drive from West L.A., where I lived, to the beach. I don't remember thinking about Bonnie's betrayal or my crime against my best friend. My mind kind of shorted out, and all I could do for a while there was drive and smoke.

There wasn't another building within fifty yards of the house, but it looked as if it belonged nestled between cozy neighboring homes. The wire fence had been decorated with clam and mussel shells. The wooden railing around the porch had dozens of different-colored wine bottles across the top. The house had been built on ground below street level so that it would have been possible to hop on the roof from the curb. It was a small dwelling, designed for one or maybe one and a half.

I opened the gate and descended the concrete stairs. She met me at the door. Sepia-skinned and big-boned, she had always been my standard for beauty. EttaMae Harris had been my friend and my lover in turns. I hadn't seen her for almost a year because I was the man who had gotten her husband shot.

"You look wild, Easy," was the first thing she said.

"What?"

"Your hair's all lumpy and you ain't shaved. What's wrong?"

"Where's LaMarque?"

"He's with my people up in Ventura."

"What people?" I asked. My heart skipped, and for an instant Bonnie Shay was completely out of my mind.

"Just a cousin'a mines. She got a little place out in the country around there."

"Where's Mouse?"

Etta peered at me as if from some great height. She was a witch woman, a Delphic seer, and Walter Cronkite on the seven o'clock news all rolled into one.

"Dead," she said. "You know he is."

"But the doctor," I said, almost pleading. "The doctor hadn't made the pronouncement."

"Doctor don't decide when a man dies."

"Where is he?"

"Dead."

"Where?"

"I buried him out in the country. Put him in the ground with my own two hands."

It was certainly possible. EttaMae was the kind of black woman who made it so hard for the rest. She was powerful of arm and iron-willed. She had thrown a full-grown man over her shoulder and carried him from the hospital after knocking out a big white or-derly with a metal tray.

"Can I go to the grave?"

"Maybe one day, baby," she said kindly. "Not soon, though."

"Why not?"

"Because the hurt is too fresh. That's why I ain't called you in so long."

"You mad at me?"

"Mad at everything. You, Raymond. I'm even mad at LaMarque."

"He's just a child, Etta. He ain't responsible."

"The child now will become the man," she preached. "And when he do, you can bet he will be just as bad if not worse than what went before."

"Raymond's dead?" I asked again.

"The only thing more I could wish would be if he would be gone from our minds." Etta looked up over my head and into the sky as if her sermon of man-hating had become a prayer for deliverance from our stupidity.

And we were stupid, there was no arguing about that. How else could I explain being ambushed in an alley when I should have been at home lamenting the assassination of our president? How could I ever tell Mouse's son that he got killed trying to help me out with a little problem I had with gangsters and thugs?

"Come on in, Easy," she said.

The living room was decorated like a sea captain's cabin in a Walt Disney film. A hammock in the corner with fish nets full of glass-ball floats beside it. The floor was sealed with a clear coating so that it looked rough and finished at the same time. The windows were round portals, and the chandelier was made from a ship's wheel.

"Sit down, Easy."

I sat on a bench that could have easily been an oarsman's seat. Etta lowered herself onto a blue couch that had gilded clamshells for feet.

"How have you been?" she asked me.

"No no, baby," I said. "It's you who called me outta my house after more than eleven months of me searchin' high and low. Why am I here?"

"I just wondered if you were sick," she said. "They said at work that —"

"Talk to me, Etta. Talk to me or let me go. 'Cause you know as much as I want to see you and try to make it up to you, I will walk my ass right outta here if you don't tell me why you called after all this time."

Her face got hard and, I imagined, there were some rough words on the tip of her tongue. But Etta held back and took a deep breath.

"This ain't my house," she said.

"I could see that."

"It belongs to the Merchant family."

"Pierre Merchant?" I asked. "The millionaire from up north?"

"Lymon," Etta said, shaking her head, "his cousin runs the strawberry business north'a L.A. I work for his wife. She has me take care'a the house and her kids."

"Okay. And so she let you stay here when you come down to town. So what?"

"No. She don't know I'm here. This is a place that Mr. Merchant has for some'a his clients and business partners when they come in town."

"Etta," I said. "What you call me for?"

"Mrs. Merchant have four chirren," she said. "The youngest one is thirteen and the oldest is twenty-two."

I was about to say something else to urge her along. I didn't want there to be too much silence or space in the room. Silence would allow me to think about what I had just learned — that my best friend since I was a teenager was dead, dead because of me. For the past year I had hoped that he was alive, that somehow EttaMae had nursed him where the hospital could not. But now my hopes were crushed. And if I couldn't keep talking, I feared that I would fall into despair.

But I didn't push Etta because I heard a catch at the back of her throat. And EttaMae Harris was not a woman to show that kind of weakness. Something was very wrong, and she needed me to make it right. I grabbed on to that possibility and took her hand.

A tear rolled down her face.

"It was hard for me to call on you, Easy. You know I blame you for what happened to Raymond."

"I know."

"But I got to get past that," she said. "It's not just your fault. Raymond always lived a hard life an' he did a lotta wrong. He made up his own mind to go with you into that alley. So it's not just that I need your help that I'm here. I been thinkin' for some time that I should talk to you."

I increased the pressure of my grip. EttaMae had a working woman's hands, hard and strong. My clenching fingers might have hurt some office worker, man or woman, but it was merely an embrace for her.

"Mrs. Merchant's second-to-oldest is a girl named Sinestra. She's twenty and wild. She been a pain to her mama and daddy too. Kicked out of school an' messin' around with boys when she was a child. Runnin' from one bad egg to another now that she's a woman."

"She too old for you to look after, Etta," I said.

"I don't care about that little bitch. She's one'a them women that ambush men one after the other. Her daddy think that they doin' to her, but he don't see that Sinestra the rottenest apple in the barrel."

"What's that got to do with me?"

"Sinestra done run away."

"She's twenty," I said. "That means she can walk away without havin' to run."

"Not if her daddy's one of the richest men in the state," Etta assured me. "Not if she done run off with a black boy don't have the sense to come in outta the rain."

"Who's that?"

"Willis Longtree. Hobo child from up around Seattle. He showed up one day with a crew to do some work for the Merchants. You know the foreman of their ranch would go down near the railroad yards in Oxnard whenever he needed to pick up some day labor. They got hobos ride the rails and Mexicans between harvests all around down there. Mr. Woodson —"

"Who?" I asked.

"Mr. Woodson, the foreman," she said. "He brought about a dozen men down to the lower field around four months ago. They was buildin' a foundation for a greenhouse Mr. Merchant wanted. He grows exotic plants and the like. He's a real expert on plants."

"Yeah," I said. "So was my cousin Smith. He could grow anything given the right amount'a light and rainfall."

"Mr. Merchant don't have to rely on nature."

"That's why they build greenhouses instead'a churches," I said.

"Are you gonna let me talk?"

"Sure, Etta. Go on."

"All that Willis boy owned was a guitar and a mouth harp on a harness. Whenever they took a break, he entertained the men playin' old-time tunes. Minstrel, blues, even some Dixieland. I went down there one day after young Lionel Merchant, the thirteen-year-old. The music was so fine that I stayed all through lunch."

"I bet Sinestra loved his barrelhousin'," I said.

"Yes, she did. Everybody did. It took the crew four days to dig the foundation. After that Mr. Merchant himself offered Willis a job. He made him the assistant groundskeeper and had him playin' music for his guests when he gave parties."

"Mighty ungrateful of that boy to think he deserved the boss's daughter," I said.

"It's not funny, Easy. Mr. Merchant got a whole security force work for him. They use it to keep the Mexicans in line on the farms. He told the top man, Abel Snow, that he'd pay ten thousand dollars to solve the problem."

"And he sees the problem as what?"

Etta held up her point finger. "One is Sinestra bein' gone from home, and two," Etta held up the next finger, "is Willis Longtree breathing the same air as him."

"Oh."

"Is that all you got to say? Oh?"

"No," I replied. "I could also say, what's it to you? Boys run away with girls every day. Daddies get mad when they do. Sometimes somebody ends up dead. Most of the time she comes home cryin' and it's all over. That's the way it was in Fifth Ward when we were kids. I remember more than one time that Mouse got jealous'a you. Usually we got the poor fool outta sight before Ray's .41 could thunder."

"Grow up, Easy Rawlins. We ain't in Houston no more, and this ain't no joke I'm tellin' you." There was that catch in her throat again.

"What's wrong, Etta?"

"Willis ain't no more than nineteen. He thinks he's a man but he barely older than LaMarque. And Abel Snow is death in a blue suit."

"You like the boy, huh?"

"He'd come around the kitchen in the afternoon and play for me, tellin' me all the great things he was gonna do. If you just closed your eyes and listened to him, you might believe it'd all come true."

"Like what?"

"All kindsa things. One minute he was gonna be in a singin' band and then he talked about bein' in the movies. He said that he looked like Sidney Poitier and maybe he could play his son in some film. He wanted to be a star. And then Sinestra got her hooks in him. She couldn't help it. It was just kinda like her nature. Girl like that see a man-child beautiful as Willis and she cain't think straight. She just wanna make him crazy, make him run like a dog with her scent in his nose. I saw it happen, Easy. I tried to talk sense to him."

"Maybe you worried about nuthin', Etta," I said. "L.A.'s a big town. The police hardly catch anybody unless they committin' a crime or they just turn themselves in."

"Abel Snow ain't no cop. He's a stone killer. And he got Merchant's money behind him."

"That don't mean he's gonna find Willis. Where would he look?"

"Same place I would if I was him. Jukes and nightclubs on Central. Movie studios and record studios and any place a fool like Willis would look for his dreams. He told everybody his plans, not just me."

"You know I'm still just a janitor, Etta."

"Easy Rawlins, you owe me this."

"If he's big a fool as you say, it's really only a matter of time. You know no matter how hard he try, a fool cain't outrun his shadow."

"All I know is that I got to try," she said.

"Yeah. Yeah," I said. "I know."

I was thinking about Bonnie and her African prince. It still hurt, but the pain was dulled in the face of Etta's maternal desperation. And she seemed to be offering me absolution over the death of her husband.

"I don't even know what the boy looks like," I said. "I don't know the girl. It's a slim chance that I'll even catch a glimpse of them before this Snow man comes on the scene."

"I know that."

"So this is just some kinda blind hope?"

"No. I can help you."

"How?"

"Drive me up to the Merchant ranch outside of Santa Barbara."

I grinned then. I don't know why. Maybe it was the idea of a long drive in the country.

Lymon Merchant was known as the Strawberry King, that's what EttaMae told me. But there wasn't a strawberry field within ten

miles of his ranch. Lymon lived up in the mountains east of Santa
Barbara. The dirt road that snaked up the mountain looked down
on the blue Pacific. We strained and bounced and even slid a time
or two, but finally made it to the wide lane at the top. The dirt boul-
evard was flanked by tall eucalyptus trees. I rolled down my window
to let in their scent.

"This the place?" I asked when we came to a three-story wood
house.

"No," Etta said. "That's the foreman's house."

The foreman's house was larger and finer than many a home in
Beverly Hills. The big front door was oak and the windows were
huge. The cultivated rosebushes around the lawn reminded me of
Bonnie. I felt the pang in my stomach and drove on, hoping I
could leave my heartache on the road behind.

The Merchant mansion was only two floors, but it dwarfed the foreman's house just the same. It was constructed from twelve- and
eighteen-foot pine logs, hundreds of them. It was a fantastic structure looking like the abode of a fairy tale giant — not for normal
mortals at all.

The double front doors were twelve feet high. The bronze handles must have weighed ten pounds apiece.

Before we could knock or ring a bell the front door swung open.
I realized that there must have been some kind of private camera
system that monitored our approach.

A tall white man in a tuxedo appeared before us.

"Miss Harris," the man said in a soft, condescending voice.

"Lawrence," she said, walking past him.

"And who are you?" Larry asked me.

"A guest of Miss Harris."

I followed her through the large foyer and down an extremely
wide hall that was festooned with the heads and bodies of dead animals, birds, and fish. There were boar and swordfish, mountain
lion and moose. Toward the center hall was a rhino head across
from a hippopotamus. I kept looking around, wondering if maybe
Lymon Merchant had the audacity to put a human trophy up on
his wall.

We then came into the family art gallery. The room was twenty
feet square, floored with three-foot-wide planks of golden pine.

Along the walls were paintings of gods and mortals, landscapes, and of course, dead animals. In one corner there stood a white grand piano.

"Easy, come on," Etta said when I wandered away from her lead.

There was something off about the color of the piano. The creamy white seemed natural and I wondered what wood would give off that particular hue. Close up it was obvious that it was constructed completely from ivory. The broad lid and body were made from fitted planks, while the legs were formed from single tusks.

"Easy," Etta said again. She had come up behind me.

"They must'a killed a dozen or more elephants to build this thing, Etta."

"So what? That's not why I brought you here."

"Does anybody ever even play it?" I asked.

"Willis did now and then when they had cocktail parties in here."

"He played piano too?"

"Willis was as talented as he thought he was," Etta said with motherly pride. "That's why it broke my heart when he talked about his dreams."

"If he got the talent, maybe he'll get the dream."

"What drug you takin'?" Etta said. "He's a poor black child in a white man's world."

"Louis Armstrong was a poor black boy."

"And for every one Armstrong you got a string of black boys' graves goin' around the block. You know how the streets eat up our men, especially if they got dreams."

She turned away from me then and made her way toward yet another door. I lagged back for a moment, thinking about a black woman's love being so strong that she tried to protect her men from their own dreams. It was a powerful moment for me, bringing Bonnie once more to mind. She loved me and urged me to climb higher. And now that I was way up there, the only way to go was down.

The next room was a stupendous kitchen. Three gas stoves, and a huge pit built into the wall like a fireplace. Cutting-board tables and sinks of porcelain and a dozen cooks, cooks' helpers, and service personnel. The various workers stared at me, wondering, I supposed, if I was a new member of the hive. A man in a chef's hat actually stopped me and asked, "Are you the new helper?"

"Yes," I said. "But I only work with one food."

"What's that?"

"The jam."

The next room was small and crowded with hampers overflowing with cloth. Even the walls were covered in fabric. The only furniture was a pedal-powered sewing machine built into its own table and two stools, all near a window that was flooded with sunlight.

On one of the stools sat a white woman with long, thick brown hair. She was working her foot on the pedal, pulling a swath of royal-blue cloth under the driving needle.

"Mrs. Merchant," Etta said.

The woman turned from her sewing to face us.

She was in her forties, but young-looking. Etta was in her forties then too, though I always thought of her as being older. Etta's skin was clear and wrinkle-free, but the years she'd lived had still left their mark. Etta was a matron, while the white woman was more like a child. Mrs. Merchant's face was round and her eyes were gray. She'd been crying, was going to cry again.

"Etta," she said.

She rose from her stool. Etta walked toward her and they embraced like sisters. EttaMae was much the larger woman. Mrs. Merchant was small-boned and frail.

"This is the man I told you about, Brian Phillips," Etta said, using a name I had suggested on the drive up.

The white woman put on a smile and held out her hand to me. I took it.

"Thank you for coming, Mr. Phillips," she said.

"I'm here for Etta, Mrs. Merchant."

"Sheila. Call me Sheila."

"What is it you need?" I asked.

"Hasn't Etta told you?"

"Your daughter has run away with one of your employees. That's really about all I know."

"Sin is a full-grown woman," Sheila Merchant said. "She didn't run away, she just left. But she also left a note behind for her father, informing him that she was leaving with Willis. That poor boy has no idea what game she's playing with him."

"Now let me get this straight, Mrs. Merchant," I said. "You're worried about the black man? His well-being?"

"Sin is like a cat, Mr. Phillips. She'll always land on her feet, and on a pile of money too. This is just a game she's playing with her father. She doesn't believe he loves her unless she can make him mad."

"I guess shackin' up with a poor black hobo is about as mad as he's gonna get."

"He loves Sin more than any of the other children," she said. "It's really unhealthy."

I waited for her to say something else; maybe she wanted to, but at the last moment she held back. I noticed then the errant strands of gray in her hair.

"When Etta told me about your daughter and Willis," I said, "I told her that there wasn't much I could do. I mean, L.A.'s a big town. People around there move from house to house like you might go from one room to another."

"I know something," she said. "Something that neither Lymon or Abel are aware of."

"What's that?"

Sheila Merchant looked from side to side as if there might be spies in her sewing room.

"There's a big bush next to the left-hand post that marks the beginning of the eucalyptus drive. It bears red berries."

"I saw it."

"Under that bush is a basket. It's in there."

"What is?"

"A little journal that Willis carried with him. He could barely read or write, but there are some notes and lots of clippings."

"Excuse me, Sheila, but what are you doin' with Willis's diary?"

"He asked me to hold it for him," Sheila Merchant said. "He didn't want somebody to steal it out of the bunkhouse. And we were always talking about music. In my house, when I was a child, we all played an instrument. All except for Father, who had a beautiful tenor voice. None of my children are musical, Mr. Phillips."

"What about that ivory piano I saw?"

"That is an abomination. It cost thirty thousand dollars to build, and the only one who ever played it was Willis Longtree."

"I see," I said. "So you said he was talkin' to you one day . . ."

"Yes. He was telling me about how much he loved music and performing. He showed me his journal, really it was just a ledger book like the accountants use. He had articles clipped about movie stars and L.A. nightclubs."

"If he couldn't read, then how would he know what to clip?" I asked.

"You not here to give nobody the third degree," Etta warned.

"No, I'm not. I'm here to help you. Now if you want me to do that, just button up and let me ask the questions I see fit."

EttaMae glared at me. I'd seen her strike men for less.

"It's all right, Etta," Sheila said. And then to me, "Willis had people read to him. He'd go through the newspaper until he saw words he knew, like Hollywood, or pictures of performers, and then he'd have someone read the article to him."

I got the feeling that she had read to the young man once or twice.

"What do you want from me, Mrs. Merchant?"

"Find Willis before Abel does," she said. "Tell him what Sin did. Try and get him somewhere safe."

Sheila Merchant reached into her apron and came out with a white envelope.

"There's a thousand dollars in here," she said. "Take it and find Willis, make sure that he's safe."

"What about your daughter?"

"She'll come home when she runs out of money."

Sheila Merchant looked away, out the window. I looked too. There was a beautiful pine forest under a pale blue and coral sky. It seemed impossible that someone with all that wealth, surrounded by such natural beauty, could be even slightly unhappy.

"I'll see what I can do," I said.

On the front porch Etta and I were confronted by a sandy-haired man with dead blue eyes.

"Hello, Mr. Snow," Etta said quickly. She seemed nervous, almost scared.

"EttaMae," he replied.

He was wearing gray slacks and a square-cut aqua-colored shirt that was open at the collar. Folded over his left arm was a dark blue blazer. He wore a short-brimmed straw hat, tilted back on his head.

His smile was malicious, but that's not what scared me about him.

EttaMae Harris had lived with Mouse most of her adult life; and Mouse was by far the deadliest man I ever knew. Not once had I seen fear in Etta's face while dealing with Mouse's irrational rages. I had never seen her afraid of anybody. Abel Snow therefore had a unique standing in my experience.

"And who is this?" Abel asked.

"Brian Phillips," I said.

"What are you doing here?"

"Seein' how the other half lives."

I smiled and so did Abel.

"You lookin' for trouble, son?"

"Now why I wanna be lookin' for somethin' when it's standin' right there in front'a me, pale as death?"

Etta cleared her throat.

"You here about Willis Longtree?" Abel Snow asked me.

"Who?"

Snow's smile widened into a grin.

"You got something I should know about in your pocket, Brian?"

"Whatever it is, it's mine."

Snow was having a good time. I wondered if his heart was beating as fast as mine was. We stared at each other for a moment. That instant might have stretched into an hour if Etta hadn't said, "Excuse me, Mr. Snow, but Mr. Phillips is givin' me a ride to L.A."

He nodded and stepped aside, grinning the whole time.

The basket was where Sheila Merchant said it was. I flipped through the ledger for a minute or two and then put it in the trunk.

Etta fell asleep on the long ride back to L.A. I asked her a few more questions about Mouse, but her story never wavered. Raymond was dead and buried by her own hand.

I dropped her off at the mariner's house in Malibu and then drove back home. That was about nine o'clock.

Bonnie was waiting for me at the front door wearing the same jeans and sweater.

"Hi, baby," she said.

"Can I get in?" I asked, and she stepped aside.

The house was quiet and clean. I had straightened up now and then, but this was the first time it had been clean since she was gone.

"Where the kids?"

"They're staying with Mrs. Riley. I sent them because I thought we might want to be alone." Bonnie's eyes followed me around the room.

"No," I said. "They could be here. I don't have anything to say they can't hear."

"Easy, what's wrong?"

"EttaMae called."

"After all this time?"

"Mouse is definitely dead and she knows a young boy who's in trouble." I sat in my recliner.

"What? You found out all that?" Bonnie went to sit on the couch. "How do you feel?"

"Like shit."

"We have to talk," she said in that tone women have when they're treating their men like children.

I stood up.

"Maybe later on," I said. "But right now I got to go out."

"Easy."

I strode into the bathroom, closed the door, and locked it. I showered and shaved, cut my nails, and brushed my teeth. When I went to the closet to get dressed, Bonnie was already in the bed.

"Where are you going?" she asked me.

"Out."

"Out where?"

"Like I told you, to look for that boy Etta wants me to help."

"You haven't even kissed me since I've been home."

I pulled out my black slacks and yellow jacket. Then I went to the drawer for a black silk T-shirt. It wasn't going to be Easy Rawlins the janitor out on the town tonight. A janitor could never find Willis Longtree or Sinestra Merchant.

I had put on dark socks that had diamonds at the ankles. I was tying my laces when Bonnie spoke to me again.

"Easy," Bonnie said softly. "Talk to me."

I went to the bed, leaned over, and kissed her on the forehead.

"Don't wait up, honey. This kinda business could take all night."

I walked to the door and then halted.

Bonnie sat up, thinking I wanted to say more.

But I went to the closet, reached back on the top shelf, and took down my pistol. I checked that it was working and loaded, and then walked out the door.

The Grotto was the first black entrepreneurial enterprise I knew of that cast its net beyond Watts. It was a jazz club on Hoover. Actually, the entrance was down an alley between two buildings that were on Hoover. The Grotto had no real address. And even though the owners were black, it was clear that the Mob was their banker.

Pearl Sondman was the manager and nominal owner of the club. I remembered her from an earlier time in Los Angeles; a time when I was between the street and jail and she was with Mona El, the most popular prostitute of her day.

Mona seduced everybody. She loved men and women alike. If you ever once spent the night with her, you were happy to scrape together the three hundred dollars it cost to do it again — that's what they said. Mona was like heaven on Earth and she never left a John, or Jane, unsatisfied.

The problem was that after one night with Mona, a certain type of unstable personality fell in love with her. Men were always fighting and threatening, claiming that they wanted to save her. It wasn't until Mona met Pearl that that kind of ruckus subsided.

Pearl had a man named Harry Riley, but after one kiss from Mona, or maybe two, Pearl threw Riley out the door. For some reason, most men didn't want to be implicated in trying to free Mona from a woman's arms.

A trumpet, a trombone, and a sax were dueling just inside the Grotto's door. It brought a smile to my face if not to my heart.

"Hi, Easy," Pearl said.

She was wearing a scaly red dress and maybe an extra twenty pounds from the last time we met. Her face was flat and sensual, the color of a chocolate malted.

"I thought you was dead," she told me.

"That was the other guy," I replied.

Pearl's laugh was deep and infectious — like pneumonia.

"How's Mona?" I asked.

"She okay, baby. Thanks for askin'. Had another stroke last Christmas. Just now gettin' around again."

"That's a shame."

"Oh, I don't know," Pearl said. "Mona says that she's lived more than most'a your everyday people by three or four times. You know she once had a prince over in Europe pay her way, first class, every other month for two years."

"What ever happened to him?"

"He wanted her to be his mistress. Offered her all kindsa money and grand apartments, but she said no."

"Why?"

"'Cause she liked the life she was livin'. With me and our two crazy dogs."

I wanted to ask her how she could share a love with some stranger, but I held it back.

"I'm lookin' for a boy named Longtree," I said.

"Pretty boy with a wild white bitch?"

"That's him."

"He come in here Sunday night. Said he could play. When I asked him what, he said, 'Guitar, piano, or whatever.'"

"Not too shy, huh?"

"Not a bit. An' he wasn't wrong neither. He played the afternoon shift for twenty bucks. I think he might'a got twice that in tips. He didn't play nuthin' like bebop, but he was good."

"I need to find him."

"Just look on the sidewalk and follow the trail'a blood."

"It's that bad?"

"That girl's eyes made contact with every dangerous man in the room. She flirted with one of 'em so much that he told Willis that he wanted to borrow her for the night."

"Did they fight?" I asked.

"No. I told that big nigga to sit'own 'fore I shot him. They know around here that I don't play. I told Willis to take his woman outta here, and damn if she didn't give that big man a come-on look while they were goin' out the door."

"You think she might'a told him where they were stayin'?"

"I wouldn't put it past her."

"What was this guy's name?"

"Let's see, um, Art. Yeah, Art, Big Art. Big Art Farman. Yeah, that's him. He lives down Watts somewhere. Construction worker."

I found an address in the phone booth of the Grotto. Listening to jazz and worrying about how big Big Art was made Bonnie fade to a small ache in my heart.

The man who came to the apartment door was not big at all. As a matter of fact, he was rather tiny.

"Art?" I asked.

"No," he said.

"Does Art Farman live here?"

"Do you know what time it is, man?"

I pulled a wad of cash from my pocket.

"It's never too late for a hundred bucks," I said.

The small man had big eyes.

"Wha, what, what do you want?"

"I come to buy somethin' off'a Art. He know what it is." I could be vague as long as the money was real.

"I could give it to him when he comes in," the little man offered.

"You tell him that Lenny Charles got somethin' for him if he come in in the next two hours."

"Why just two hours? What if he don't come in before then?"

"If he don't, then somebody else gonna have to sell me what I need."

"What's that?" the little man asked. His coloring was uneven, running from a dark tan to light brown. He had freckles that looked like a rash and had hardly any eyebrow hair at all.

"I need to find a white girl called Sinestra."

"What for?" The greedy eyes turned suspicious.

"Her daddy asked his maid, my cousin, to ask me to ask her to come back home. He's willin' to pay Art a century if he can help me out."

"What's your name again?"

"Len," I lied. "Yours?"

"Norbert." He was staring at my wad. "What you pay me to find Art?"

"Where is he?"

"No. Uh-uh. I get paid first."

"How much you want?"

"Fifty?" he squeaked.

"Shit," I said.

I turned away.

"Hold up. Hold up. What you wanna pay?"

"Thirty."

"Thirty? That's all? Thirty for me and a hundred for Art?"

"Art can give me the girl, can you?"

"I can give you Art. And she's with him. That's for sure."

I considered taking out my gun but then thought better of it. Sometimes the threat of death makes small men into heroes.

"Forty," I said.

"You got to bring it higher than that, man. Forty ain't worth my time."

"I'll go find Willis myself then," I said.

"You mean that skinny little kid?" Norbert laughed. "Art kicked his ass and took his girlfriend from him."

"He did?"

"Yeah," Norbert bragged. "Kicked his ass and dragged that white girl away. Course she wanted to go."

"She did?"

"Course she did. Why she want that skinny guitar man when she could have Big Art in her bed?"

I handed Norbert a twenty-dollar bill.

"Where was it that Art did this?"

"Next to that big 'partment buildin' down on Avalon. Near the Chevron station with the big truck for a sign."

I handed him another twenty.

"It was the only blue house on the block."

"How do you know all that?" I asked.

"I drove him over there."

"Did Sinestra mind Art beating up her boyfriend?"

"Didn't seem to," Norbert shrugged.

I handed him another twenty-dollar bill.

"Where's Art now?"

"At Havelock's Motel on Santa Barbara. That's where we go when we got a woman, you know, to let the other man get some sleep. I mean, we ain't got but two rooms up in here."

I handed over another leaf of Sheila Merchant's money and went away.

Once in my car I had a small dilemma. Should I go after the girl or Willis? It seemed to me that no one really cared about her, except maybe her father. Willis was the one that Etta was worried about. I knew that if I asked her, she would have told me to make Willis my priority.

But I was raised better than that. No matter what she had done, I couldn't leave Sinestra Merchant at the mercy of a kidnapper and possible rapist. I couldn't take Norbert's word that she maybe wanted some rough action from some big black man in Watts.

Havelock's was a long bungalow in the shape of a horseshoe. When I got there it was closing on midnight. A night clerk was in the office, sitting at the front desk with his back to the switchboard. I parked across the street and considered.

The motel sign said that there was a TV and a phone in each room.

I went to a phone booth and dialed a number that hadn't changed in sixteen years.

"Hola," a sleepy Spanish voice said.

"Primo."

"Oh, hello, Easy. Man, what you doin' callin' me at this time'a night?"

"You got a pencil and a clock?"

I gave Primo a number and asked him to call in seven minutes exactly. I told him who to ask for and what to say if he got through. He didn't ask me any questions, just said "Okay" and hung up the phone.

"Hi," I said to the night clerk five minutes later. "Can you help me with a reservation?"

It was a carefully constructed sentence designed to keep him from getting too nervous about a six-foot black man coming into his office in the middle of the night. Thieves don't ask for reservations. They rarely say hello.

"Um," the white clerk said. He first looked at my hands and then over my shoulder to see if somebody else was coming in behind. "I can't make reservations. I just rent out rooms for people when they come."

"Yeah," I said. "That's what I thought. But you know, I work at a nightclub down the street here, and the only time I can really make it in is after work. Do the daytime people take reservations?"

"I don't know," the clerk said, relaxing a bit. "People usually just look at the sign. If there's a vacancy they drive in, and if not they drive on."

He smiled at me and the phone rang. He turned his back and lifted the receiver.

"Havelock's Motel," he said in a stronger tone than he'd used with me. "Who? Oh yes. Let me put you through."

He pushed the plug into a slot labeled "Number Six." I was smiling honestly when he turned back to me.

"That's really all I can say," he said. "Just look for the sign."

"All right."

I counted the doors on the north side of the building and then I went around the back, counting windows as I went. Number six's curtains were open wide. The only light on in the room was coming from a partially closed door, the bathroom, I was sure. There were two double beds. One was neat, either stripped or made. The other one had something on it, a pair of shoes tilted at an uncomfortable angle.

The window was unlocked.

Big Art — his driver's license said Arthur — Farman had been dead for some hours. The cause of death probably being a bullet through the eye. Before he'd been killed he was bound, gagged, and beaten. A pillow on the floor next to him had been used to stifle the shot.

There was no trace of the girl named Sinestra. But that didn't mean she hadn't been there at the time of Art's death.

I climbed out of the window and made it back to my car. The dead man, who I'd never met in life, was the strongest presence in my mind.

It's hard looking for a blue house at three in the morning. There's white, black, and gray, and that's it. But I saw the big apartment building. It was on a corner with only one house nearby. It helped that the lights were on.

I knocked on the door. Why not? They were just crazy kids. There was no answer so I turned the knob. The house was a mess. Pizza cartons and dirty dishes all over the living room and the kitchen. Half-gone sodas, a nearly full bottle of whiskey; it was the kind of filth that many youths lived in while waiting to grow up.

I couldn't tell if the rooms had been searched. But there wasn't any blood around.

I got home a few minutes before four.

Etta picked up the receiver after the first ring.

"Hello."

I told her about Big Art and Sinestra's games.

"Old Willis don't have to worry about Abel Snow with that girl in his bed," I said.

"She called her daddy," Etta said. "She told him where she was and asked him to come and get her."

"Then she lit out?"

"I don't know. All I know is what Mrs. Merchant said. She told me that Mr. Merchant sent Abel down to get her."

"Did he bring her back?"

"No."

"Damn."

"Do you think he's found 'em, Easy?"

"I'm not sure, but I don't think so. Mr. Snow don't mind leavin' blood and guts behind him."

"Maybe you better leave it alone, Easy."

"Can't do that, Etta. I got to see it through now."

"I don't want you to get killed, baby," she said.

"That's the nicest thing I been told all day."

I slept on the couch for the few hours left of the night.

When I opened my eyes, she was sitting right in front of me.

"We have to talk," Bonnie said.

"I got to go."

"No."

"Bonnie."

"His name is Jogaye Cham," she said. "We, we talked on the plane when everybody else was asleep. He talked about Africa, our home, Easy. Where we came from."

"I was born in southern Louisiana, and I still call myself a Texan 'cause Texas is where I grew into a man."

"Africa," she said again. "He was working for democracy. He worked all day and all night. He wanted a country where everyone would be free. A land our people here would be glad to migrate to. A land with black presidents and black professionals of all kinds."

"Yeah."

"He worked all the time. Day and night. But one time there was a break in the schedule. We took a flight to a beach town he knew in Madagascar."

"You could'a come home," I said, even though I didn't want to say anything.

"No," she said, and the pain in my chest grew worse. "I needed to be with him, with his dreams."

"Would you be tellin' me this if them flowers didn't come?"

"No. No." She was crying. I held back from slapping her face. "There was nothing to tell."

"Five days on a beach with another man and there wasn't somethin' to say?"

"We, we had separate rooms."

"But did you fuck him?"

"Don't use that kind of language with me."

"Okay," I said. "All right. Excuse me for upsetting you with my street-nigger talk. Let me put it another way. Did you make love to him?"

The words cut much deeper than any profanity I could have used. I saw in her face the pain that I felt. Deep, grinding pain that only gets worse with time. And though it didn't make me feel good, it at least seemed to create some kind of balance. At least she wouldn't leave unscathed.

"No," she whispered. "No. We didn't make love. I couldn't with you back here waiting for me."

A thousand questions went through my mind. Did you kiss him? Did you hold hands in the sunset? Did you say that you loved him? But I knew I couldn't ask. Did he touch your breast? Did he breathe in your breath on a blanket near the water? I knew that if I asked one question they would never stop coming.

I stood up. I was dizzy, light-headed, but didn't let it show.

"Where are you going?" she asked.

"I got a job to do for Etta. A woman already paid me, so I got to move it on."

"What kind of job?"

"Nuthin' you need to know about. It's my business." And with that I showered and shaved, powdered and dressed. I left her in the house with her confessions and her lies.

With no other information available to me, I went to see Etta at the Merchants' seaside retreat. She only pulled the door open enough to see me.

"Go away, Easy," she said.

"Open the door, Etta."

"Go away."

"No."

Maybe I had gained some strength of will working for the city schools. Or maybe Etta was getting worn down between losing her husband and working for the rich. All I knew was that at another time she could have stared me down. Instead the door swung open.

Inside, sitting on the blue couch with golden clamshell feet, was a young black man and young white woman, both of them beautiful. They were holding hands and huddling like frightened children. They *were* frightened children. If it wasn't for the broken heart driving me, I would have been scared too.

"They came after you called me, Easy," Etta said.

"Why didn't you call back?"

"You did what I asked you to already. You found them. That's all I could ask."

"I'm Easy," I said to the couple.

"Willis," the boy said. He made a waving gesture, and I noticed that his hands were bloody and bandaged.

"Sin," the girl said. There was something crooked about her face, but that just stoked the fires of her dangerous beauty.

"What happened to Big Art, Sin?"

Her mouth dropped open while she groped for a lie.

"I already know you called your father," I said.

"I was just mad at Art," she said. "He didn't have to beat up Willis and hurt his hands. I thought my father would come and maybe do something." Her eyes grew glassy.

"What happened?"

"I told Art that I was going down to the liquor store and then I called Daddy. I told him that I was with a guy but I was scared to leave, and he said to wait somewhere near at hand. Then I waited in the coffee shop across the street. When I saw Abel, I got scared and went to get Willy. When we came back to get my clothes he was . . ." She trailed off in the memory of the slaughter.

I turned to Willis and said, "You'd be better off holding a gun to your head."

"I didn't mean for him to get killed," Sinestra said angrily.

"What now?" I asked Etta.

"I'm tryin' to talk some sense to 'em. I'm tryin' to tell Sin to go home and Willis to get away before he ends up like that Art fella."

"I'm not going back," Sinestra proclaimed.

"And I'm not leavin' her or L.A."

"She just had a big man break your fingers, and then she went and fucked him."

"She didn't know. She was just flirtin' and it got outta hand. She's just innocent, that's all."

My mouth fell open, and I put my hand to cover it.

Etta started laughing. Laughing hard and loud.

"What are you laughing at?" Sinestra asked.

I started laughing too.

"Shut up, shut up," Sinestra said.

"Yes. Please be quiet," Abel Snow said from a door in the back.

He had a pistol in his hand.

"There's a man in a car parked out front, Sinestra," Snow said. "Go out to him. He'll take you home."

Without a word, the young white woman went for the door.

Etta looked into my eyes. Her stare was hard and certain.

"Sin," Willis said.

She hesitated and then went out the door without looking back.

"Well, well, well," Abel Snow said. "Here we are. Just us four."

Willis was sitting on the couch. Etta and I were standing on either side of the boy. He turned on the blue sofa to see Snow.

"You gonna kill us?" I asked, my voice soaked with manufactured fear.

"You're gonna go away," he said, and smiled.

I took a step to the side, away from Etta.

"You gonna let us go?" Willis asked, playing his part well, though I'm sure he didn't know it.

Snow was amused. He was listening for something.

Etta put her hands down at her side. She raised her face to look at the ceiling and prayed, "Lord, forgive us for what we do."

At a picnic table Snow's grin would have been friendly.

I took another step and bumped into the wall.

"Nowhere to run," Snow apologized. "Take it like a man and it won't hurt."

"Please God," Etta said beseechingly. She bent over slightly.

A car horn honked. That was what Snow was waiting for. He raised his pistol. I closed my eyes, the left one a little harder than the right.

Then I forced my eyes open. Abel Snow brought his left heel off the floor, preparing to pivot after killing me. EttaMae pulled a pistol out of the fold of her dress, aimed it at his head, and sucked in a breath. It was that breath that made Snow turn his head instead of pulling the trigger. Etta's bullet caught him in the temple. He crumpled to the floor, a sack of stones that had recently been a man.

"Oh no," Willis cried. He pulled his legs up underneath himself. "Oh no."

Etta looked at me. Her face was hard, her jaws were clenched in victory.

"I knew you had to be armed, baby," I said. "If he was smart, he would'a shot you first."

"This ain't no joke, Easy. What we gonna do with him?"

"What caliber you use?" I asked.

"Twenty-five caliber," she said. "You know what I carry."

"Didn't even sound that loud. Nobody live close enough to have heard it."

"They gonna come in here sooner or later. And even before that he ain't gonna report in to Mr. Merchant."

"Tell me somethin', Etta."

"What?"

"You plannin' to go back to work for them?"

"Hell no."

"Then call your boss. Tell him that Abel's not comin' home and that there's a mess down here."

"Put myself on the line like that?"

"It's him on the line. I bet the gun in Abel's hand was the one he used on Art. And if that girl of his finds out about any killing in this house, she'd have somethin' on her old man till all the money runs out."

"What about Willis?"

"I'll take care of him. But we better get outta here now."

I drove Etta to a bus station in Santa Monica. She kissed me good-bye through the car window.

"Don't feel guilty about Raymond," she said. "Much as was wrong with him, he took responsibility for everything he did."

"What you gonna do with me?" Willis Longtree asked as we drove toward L.A.

"Take you to a doctor. Make sure your hand bones set right."

"I'm still gonna stay here an' try an' make it in music," he told me.

"Oh? What they call you when you were a boy?" I asked.

"Little Jimmy," he said. "Little Jimmy because my father was James and everybody said I looked just like him."

"Little Jimmy Long," I said, testing out the name. "Try that on for a while. I can get you a job as a custodian at my school. Do that for a while and try to meet your dreams. Who knows? Maybe you will be some kinda star one day."

"Little Jimmy Jones," Willis said. "I like that even better."

I got home in the early afternoon. Bonnie wasn't there, but her clothes were still in the closet. I went to the garage and got my gardener's toolbox. I clipped off all the roses, put them in a big bowl on the bedroom chest of drawers. Then I took the saw and hacked down both rosebushes. I left them lying there on either side of the door.

The little yellow dog must have known what I was doing. He yelped and barked at me until I finished the job.

I went off to work then. I got there at the three o'clock bell and worked until eleven.

When I got home, the bushes had been removed. Bonnie, Jesus, and Feather were all sleeping in their beds. There were no packed suitcases in the closet, no angry notes on the kitchen table.

I lay down on the couch and thought about Mouse, that he was really dead. Sleep came quickly after that, and I knew that my time of mourning was near an end.

JOYCE CAROL OATES

The Skull

FROM *Harper's Magazine*

CONTRARY TO POPULAR BELIEF, the human cranium isn't a single helmet-shaped bone but eight bones fused together, and the facial mask is fourteen bones fused together, and these, in the victim, had been smashed with a blunt object, smashed, dented, and pierced, as if the unknown killer had wanted not merely to kill his victim but to obliterate her. No hair remained on any skull fragments, for no scalp remained to contain hair, but swaths of sun-bleached brown hair had been found with the skeleton and had been brought to him in a separate plastic bag. Since rotted clothing found at the scene was a female's clothing, the victim had been identified as female. A woman, or an older adolescent girl.

"A jigsaw puzzle. In three dimensions." He smiled. Since boyhood he'd been one to love puzzles.

He was not old. Didn't look old, didn't behave old, didn't perceive himself as old. Yet he knew that others, envious of him, wished to perceive him as old, and this infuriated him. He was a stylish dresser. Often he was seen in dark turtleneck sweaters, a wine-colored leather coat that fell below his knees. In warm weather he wore shirts open at the throat, sometimes T-shirts that showed to advantage his well-developed arm and shoulder muscles. When his hair had begun to thin in his mid-fifties he had simply shaved his head, which tended to be olive-hued, veined, with the look of an upright male organ throbbing with vigor, belligerence, good humor. You couldn't help but notice and react to Kyle Cassity: to label such a man a "senior citizen" was absurd and demeaning.

Now he was sixty-seven, and of that age. He would have had to concede that as a younger man he'd often ignored his elders. He'd taken them for granted, he'd written them off as irrelevant. Of course, Kyle Cassity was a different sort of elder. There was no one quite like him.

A maverick, he thought himself. Unlabelable. Born in 1935 in Harrisburg, Pa., a long-time resident of Wayne, N.J.: unique and irreplaceable.

Among his numerous relatives he'd long been an enigma: generous in times of crisis; otherwise distant, indifferent. True, he'd had something of a reputation as a womanizer until recent years, yet he'd remained married to the same devoted wife for four decades. His three children, when they were living at home, had competed for their father's attention, but they'd loved him, you might have said they'd worshiped him, though now in adulthood they were closer to their mother. (Outside his marriage, unknown to his family, Kyle had fathered another child, a daughter, whom he'd never known.)

Professionally, Dr. Kyle Cassity was something of a maverick as well. A tenured senior professor on the faculty of William Paterson University in New Jersey, as likely to teach in the adult night division as in the undergraduate daytime school, as likely to teach a sculpting workshop in the art school as a graduate seminar in the School of Health, Education, and Science. His advanced degrees were in anthropology, sociology, and forensic science; he'd had a year of medical school and a year of law school. At Paterson University he'd developed a course entitled "The Sociology of 'Crime' in America" that had attracted as many as four hundred students before Professor Cassity, overwhelmed by his own popularity, retired it.

His public reputation in New Jersey was as an expert prosecution witness and a frequent consultant for the New Jersey Department of Forensics. He'd been the subject of numerous media profiles, including a cover story in the *Newark Star-Ledger* Sunday magazine bearing the eye-catching caption "Sculptor Kyle Cassity fights crime with his fingertips." He gave away many of his sculptures, to individuals, museums, schools. He gave lectures, for no fee, throughout the state.

As a scientist he had little sentiment. He knew that the individual, within the species, counts for very little; the survival of the species is everything. But as a forensic specialist he focused his attention on individuals: the uniqueness of crime victims and the uniqueness of those who have committed these crimes. Where there was a victim there would be a criminal or criminals. There could be no ambiguity here. As Dr. Kyle Cassity, he worked with the remains of victims. Often these were badly decomposed, mutilated, or broken, seemingly past reconstruction and identification. He was good at his work and had gotten better over the years. He loved a good puzzle. A puzzle no one else could solve except Kyle Cassity. He perceived the shadowy, faceless, as-yet-unnamed perpetrators of crime as human prey whom he was hunting and was licensed to hunt.

This skull! What a mess. Never had Kyle seen bones so broken. How many powerful blows must have been struck to reduce the skull, the face, the living brain, to such broken matter. Kyle tried to imagine: twenty? thirty? fifty? A frenzied killer, you would surmise. Better to imagine madness than that the killer had been coolly methodical, smashing his victim's skull, face, teeth, to make identification impossible.

No fingertips — no fingerprints — remained, of course. The victim's exposed flesh had long since rotted from her bones. The body had been dumped sometime in the late spring or early summer in a field above an abandoned gravel pit near Toms River in the southern part of the state, a half-hour drive from Atlantic City. Bones had been scattered by wildlife, but most had been located and reassembled: the victim had been approximately five feet two, with a small frame, a probable weight of 100 or 110 pounds. Judging by the hair, Caucasian.

Here was a grisly detail, not released to the press: not only had the victim's skull been beaten in, but the state medical examiner had discovered that her arms and legs had been severed from her body by a "bluntly sharp" weapon like an ax.

Kyle shuddered, reading the report. Christ! He hoped the dismemberment had been after, not before, the death.

It seemed strange to him: the manic energy the killer had expended in trying to destroy his victim he might have used to dig a deep grave and cover it with rocks and gravel so that it would never be discovered. For, of course, a dumped body will eventually be discovered.

Yet the killer hadn't buried this body. Why not?

"Must have wanted it to be found. Must have been proud of what he did."

What the murderer had broken Dr. Cassity would reconstruct. He had no doubt that he could do it. Pieces of bone would be missing, of course, but he could compensate for this with synthetic materials. Once he had a plausible skull, he could reconstruct a plausible face for it out of clay, and, once he had this, he and a female sketch artist with whom he'd worked in the past would make sketches of the face in colored pencil, from numerous angles, for investigators to work with. Kyle Cassity's reconstruction would be broadcast throughout the state, printed on flyers and posted on the Internet.

Homicides were rarely solved unless the victim could be identified. Kyle had done a number of successful facial reconstructions in the past, though never working at such a disadvantage. This was a rare case. And yet it was a finite task: the pieces of bone had been given to him; he had only to put them together.

When Kyle began working with the skull in his laboratory at the college, the victim had been dead for approximately four months, through the near-tropical heat of a southern New Jersey summer. In his laboratory, Kyle kept the air-conditioning at 65 degrees Fahrenheit. He played CDs: Bach's "Well-Tempered Clavier" and the "Goldberg Variations," performed by Glenn Gould, most suited him. Music of brilliance and precision, rapid, dazzling as a waterfall, that existed solely in the present moment; music without emotion, and without associations.

The hair! It was fair, sun-bleached brown with shades of red, still showing a distinct ripply wave. Six swaths had been gathered at the crime scene and brought to his laboratory. Kyle placed them on a windowsill, where, when he glanced up from his exceedingly close work with tweezers and bits of bone, he could see them clearly. The longest swath was seven inches. The victim had worn her hair long, to her shoulders. From time to time, Kyle reached out to touch it.

Eight days: it would take longer than Kyle anticipated. For he was working with exasperating slowness, and he was making many more small mistakes than he was accustomed to.

His hands were steady as always. His eyes, strengthened by bifocal lenses, were as reliable as always.

Yet it seemed to be happening that when Kyle was away from the laboratory, his hands began to shake just perceptibly. And once he was away from the unsparing fluorescent lights, his vision wasn't so sharp.

He would mention this to no one. And no one would notice. No doubt it would go away.

Already by the end of the second day he'd tired of Bach performed by Glenn Gould. The pianist's humming ceased to be eccentric and became unbearable. The intimacy of another's thoughts, like a bodily odor, you don't really want to share. He tried listening to other CDs, piano music, unaccompanied cello, then gave up to work in silence. Except, of course, there was no silence: traffic noises below, airplanes taking off and landing at Newark International Airport, the sound of his own blood pulsing in his ears.

Strange: the killer didn't bury her.

Strange: to hate another human being so much.

Hope to Christ she was dead by the time he began with the ax . . .

"Now you have a friend, dear. Kyle is your friend."

The victim had been between eighteen and thirty years old, it was estimated. A size four, petite, they'd estimated her rotted clothing to have been. Size six, a single open-toed shoe found in the gravel pit. She'd had a small rib cage, small pelvis.

No way of determining if she'd ever been pregnant or given birth.

No rings had been found amid the scattered bones. Only just a pair of silver hoop earrings, pierced. The ears of the victim had vanished as if they'd never been; only the earrings remained, dully gleaming.

"Maybe he took your rings. You must have had rings."

The skull had a narrow forehead and a narrow, slightly receding chin. The cheekbones were high and sharp. This would be helpful in sculpting the face. Distinctive characteristics. She'd had an overbite. Kyle couldn't know if her nose had been long or short, a pug nose or narrow at the tip. In the sketches they'd experiment with different noses, hairstyles, gradations of eye color.

"Were you pretty? 'Pretty' gets you into trouble."

On the windowsill, the dead girl's hair lay in lustrous sinuous strands.

Kyle reached out to touch it.

*

Marriage: a mystery.

For how was it possible that a man with no temperament for a long-term relationship with one individual, no evident talent for domestic life, family, children, can nonetheless remain married, happily it appeared, for more than four decades?

Kyle laughed. "Somehow, it happened."

He was the father of three children within this marriage, and he'd loved them. Now they were grown — grown somewhat distant — and gone from Wayne, New Jersey. The two eldest were parents themselves.

They, and their mother, knew nothing of their shadowy half sister.

Nor did Kyle. He'd lost touch with the mother twenty-six years ago.

His relationship with his wife, Vivian, had never been very passionate. He'd wanted a wife, not a mistress. He wouldn't have wished to calculate how long it had been since they'd last made love. Even when they'd been newly married their lovemaking had been awkward, for Vivian had been so inexperienced, sweetly naive and shy — that had seemed part of her appeal. Often they'd made love in the dark. Few words passed between them. If Vivian spoke, Kyle became distracted. Often he'd watched her sleep, not wanting to wake her. Lightly he'd touched her, stroked her unconscious body, and then himself.

Now he was sixty-seven. Not old, he knew that. Yet the last time he'd had sex had been with a woman he'd met at a conference in Pittsburgh the previous April; before that it had been with a woman one third his age, of ambiguous identity, possibly a prostitute.

Though she hadn't asked him for money. She'd introduced herself to him on the street saying she'd seen him interviewed on New Jersey Network, hadn't she? At the end of the single evening they spent together she'd lifted his hand to kiss the fingers in a curious gesture of homage and self-abnegation.

"Dr. Cassity. I revere a man like you."

The crucial bones were all in place: cheeks, above the eyes, jaw, chin. These determined the primary contours of the face. The space between the eyes, for instance. Width of the forehead in proportion to that of the face at the level of the nose, for instance. Beneath the epidermal mask, the irrefutable structure of bone. Kyle was beginning to see her now.

The eye holes of the skull regarded him with equanimity. Whatever question he would put to it, Kyle would have to answer himself.

Dr. Cassity. He had a Ph.D., not an M.D. To his sensitive ears there was always something subtly jeering, mocking, in the title "Doctor."

He'd given up asking his graduate students to call him "Kyle." Now that he was older, and had his reputation, none of these young people could bring themselves to speak to him familiarly. They wanted to revere him, he supposed. They wanted the distance of age between them, an abyss not to be crossed.

Dr. Cassity. In Kyle's family, this individual had been his grandfather. An internist in Harrisburg, Pennsylvania, whose field of specialization had been gastroenterology. As a boy, Kyle had revered his grandfather and had wanted to be a doctor. He'd been fascinated by the books in his grandfather's library: massive medical texts that seemed to hold the answers to all questions, anatomical drawings and color plates revealing the extraordinary interiors of human bodies. Many of these were magnified, reproduced in bright livid color that had looked moist. There were astonishing photographs of naked bodies, bodies in the process of being dissected. Kyle's heart beat hard as he stared at these, in secret. Decades later, Kyle sometimes felt a stirring of erotic interest, a painful throb in the groin, reminded by some visual cue of those old forbidden medical texts in his long-deceased grandfather's library.

Beginning at about the age of eleven, he'd secretly copied some of the drawings and plates by placing tracing paper over them and using a felt-tip pen. Later, he began to draw his own figures without the aid of tracing paper. He would discover that, where fascination gripped him, he was capable of executing surprising likenesses. In school art classes he was singled out for praise. He became most adept at rapid charcoal sketches, executed with half-shut eyes. And later, sculpting busts, figures. His hands moving swiftly, shaping and reshaping clay.

This emergence of "talent" embarrassed him. To obscure his interest in the human figure *in extremis,* he learned to make other sorts of sculptures as well. His secret interests were hidden, he believed, inside the other.

It would turn out that he disliked medical school. The dissecting room had revulsed him, not aroused him. He'd nearly fainted in his first pathology lab. He hated the fanatic competition of medical school, the almost military hegemony of rank. He would quit before he flunked out. Forensic science was as close as he would get to the human body, but here, as he told interviewers, his task was reassembling, not dissecting.

The skull was nearly completed. Beautifully shaped, it seemed to Kyle, like a Grecian bust. The empty eye sockets and nose cavity another observer would think ugly, Kyle saw filled in, for the girl had revealed herself to him. The dream had been fleeting yet remained with him, far more vivid in his mind's eye than anything he'd experienced in his own recent life.

Was she living, and where?

His lost daughter. His mind drifted from the skull and on to her, who was purely abstract to him, not even a name.

He'd seen her only twice, as an infant, and each time briefly. At the time, her mother, manipulative, emotionally unstable, hadn't yet named her; or, if she had, for some reason she hadn't wanted Kyle to know.

"She doesn't need a name just yet. She's mine."

Kyle had been deceived by this woman, who'd called herself "Letitia," an invented name probably, a stripper's fantasy name, though possibly it was genuine. Letitia had sought out Kyle Cassity at the college, where he'd been a highly visible faculty member, thirty-nine years old. Her pretext for coming into his office was to seek advice about a career in psychiatric social work. She'd claimed to be enrolled in the night division of the college, which turned out to be untrue. She'd claimed to be a wife estranged from a husband who was "threatening" her, which had possibly been true.

Kyle had been flattered by the young woman's attention. Her obvious attraction to him. In time, he'd given her money. Always cash, never a check. And he never wrote to her: although she left passionate love notes for him beneath his office door, beneath the windshield wiper of his car, he never reciprocated. As one familiar with the law, he knew: never commit yourself in handwriting! As, in more recent years, Kyle Cassity would never send any e-mail message he wouldn't have wanted to see exposed to all the world.

He hadn't fully trusted Letitia, but he'd been sexually aroused by her, he liked being in her company. She was a dozen years younger than he, reckless, unreliable. Not pretty, but very sexual, seductive. After she vanished from his life he would suppose, sure, she'd been seeing other men all along, taking money from other men. Yet he accepted the pregnancy as his responsibility. She'd told him the baby would be his, and he hadn't disbelieved her. He had no wish to dissociate himself from Letitia at this difficult time in her life, though his own children were twelve, nine, and five years old. And Vivian loved him, and presumably trusted him, and would have been deeply wounded if she'd known of his affair.

Though possibly Vivian had known. Known something. There was the evidence of Kyle's infrequent lovemaking with her, a fumbling in silence.

But in December 1976, Letitia and the infant girl abruptly left Wayne, New Jersey. Even before the birth Letitia had been drifting out of her married lover's life. He'd had to assume that she had found another man who meant more to her. He had to assume that his daughter would never have been told who her true father was. Twenty-eight years later, if she were still alive, Letitia probably wouldn't have remembered Kyle Cassity's name.

"Now: tell us your name, dear."

After a week and a day of painstaking work, the skull was complete. All the bone fragments had been used, and Kyle had made synthetic pieces to hold the skull together. Excited now, he made a mold of the skull and on this mold he began to sculpt a face in clay. Rapidly his fingers worked as if remembering. In this phase of the reconstruction he played new CDs to celebrate: several Bach cantatas, Beethoven's Seventh and Ninth symphonies, Maria Callas as Tosca.

Early in October the victim was identified: her name was Sabrina Jackson, a part-time community college student studying computer technology and working as a cocktail waitress in Easton, Pennsylvania. The young woman had been reported missing by her family in mid-May. At the time of her disappearance she'd been twenty-three, weighed 115 pounds, photographs of her bore an uncanny resemblance to the sketches Kyle Cassity and his assistant had made. In March she'd broken up with a man with whom she'd been living for several years, and she'd told friends she was quitting school and quitting work and "beginning a new life" with a new male friend who had a "major position" at one of the Atlantic City casinos. She'd packed suitcases, shut up her apartment, left a message on her voice mail that was teasingly enigmatic: "Hi there! This is Sabrina. I sure am sorry to be missing your call but I am OUT OF TOWN TILL FURTHER NOTICE. Can't say when I will be returning calls but I WILL TRY."

No one had heard from Sabrina Jackson since. No one in Atlantic City recalled having seen her, and nothing had come of detectives questioning casino employees. Nor did anyone in Easton seem to know the identity of the man with whom she'd gone away. Sabrina Jackson had disappeared in similar ways more than once in the past, in the company of men, and so her family and friends had been hesitant at first to report her missing. Always there was the expectation that Sabrina would turn up. But the sketches of the Toms River victim bore an unmistakable resemblance to Sabrina Jackson, and the silver earrings found with the remains were identified as hers.

"Sabrina."

It was a beautiful name. But Sabrina Jackson wasn't a beautiful young woman.

Kyle stared at photographs of the missing woman, whose blemished skin was a shock. Nor was her skin pale, as he'd imagined, but rather dark, and oily. Her eyebrows weren't delicately arched, as he'd drawn them, but heavily penciled in, as the outline of her fleshy mouth had been exaggerated by lipstick. Still, there was the narrow forehead, a snub nose, the small, receding chin. The shoulder-length hair, wavy, burnished brown, as Kyle had depicted it. When you looked from the sketches drawn in colored pencil to the actual woman in the photographs, you were tempted to think that one was a younger, sentimentally idealized version of the other, or that the two girls were sisters, one very pretty and feminine and the other somewhat coarse, sensuous.

Strange, it seemed to him, difficult to realize: the skull he'd reconstructed was the skull of this woman, Sabrina Jackson, and not the skull of the girl he'd sketched. Always, Sabrina Jackson had been the victim. Kyle Cassity was being congratulated for his excellent work, but he felt as if a trick had been played on him.

He contemplated for long minutes the girl in the photographs who smiled, preened, squinted into the camera as if for his benefit. The bravado of not knowing how we must die, how our most capricious poses outlive us. The heavy makeup on Sabrina Jackson's blemished face made her look older than twenty-three. She wore cheap, tight, sexy clothes, tank tops and V-neck blouses, leather miniskirts, leather trousers, high-heeled boots. She was a smoker. She did appear to have a sense of humor: Kyle liked that in her. Mugging for the camera. Pursing her lips in a kiss. The type who wouldn't ask a man for money directly, but if you offered it she certainly wouldn't turn it down. A small pleased smile would transform her face as if this were the highest of compliments. A murmured "Thanks!" And the bills quickly wadded and slipped into her pocket and no more need be said of the transaction.

The skull was gone from Kyle's laboratory. There would be a private burial of Sabrina Jackson's remains in Easton, Pennsylvania. Now it was known that the young woman was dead, the investigation into her disappearance would intensify. In time, Kyle didn't doubt, there would be an arrest.

Kyle Cassity! Congratulations.

Amazing, that work you do.

Good time to retire, eh? Quit while you're ahead.

There was no longer mandatory retirement at the university. He would never retire as a sculptor, an artist. And he could continue working indefinitely for the State of New Jersey since he was a freelance consultant, not an employee subject to the state's retirement laws. These protests that rose in him he didn't utter.

He'd ceased playing the new CDs. His office and his laboratory were very quiet. A pulse beat sullenly in his head. Disappointed! For Sabrina Jackson wasn't the one he'd sought.

"Officer. Come in."

The face of Sabrina Jackson's mother was as tight as a sausage in its casing. She made an effort to smile, like a sick woman trying to be upbeat but wanting you to know she was trying for your sake. In her dull eager voice she greeted Kyle Cassity, and she would persist in calling him "Officer," though he'd explained to her that he wasn't a police officer, just a private citizen who'd helped with the investigation. He was the man who'd drawn the composite sketch of her daughter that she and other relatives of the missing girl had identified.

Strictly speaking, of course, this wasn't true. Kyle hadn't drawn a sketch of Sabrina Jackson but of a fictitious girl. He'd given life to the skull in his keeping, not to Sabrina Jackson, of whom he'd never heard. But such metaphysical subtleties would have been lost on the forlorn Mrs. Jackson, who was staring at Kyle as if, though he'd just reminded her, she couldn't recall why he'd come, who exactly he was. A plainclothes officer with the Easton police, or somebody from New Jersey?

Gently, Kyle reminded her: the drawing of Sabrina? That had appeared on TV, in papers? On the Internet, worldwide?

"Yes. That was it. That picture." Mrs. Jackson spoke slowly, as if each word were a hurtful pebble in her throat. Her small warm bloodshot eyes, crowded inside the fatty ridges of her face, were fixed upon him with a desperate urgency. "When we saw that picture on the TV . . . we knew."

Kyle murmured an apology. He was being made to feel responsible for something. His oblong shaved head had never felt so exposed and so vulnerable, veins throbbing with heat.

"Mrs. Jackson, I wish that things could have turned out differently."

"She always did the wildest things, more than once I'd given up on her, I'd get so damn pissed with her, but she'd land on her feet, you know? Like a cat. That Sabrina! She's the only one of the kids, counting even her two brothers, made us worry so." Oddly, Mrs. Jackson was smiling. She was vexed at her daughter but clearly somewhat proud of her too. "She had a good heart, though, Officer. Sabrina could be the sweetest girl when she made the effort. Like the time, it was Mother's Day, I was pissed as hell because I knew, I just knew, not a one of them was going to call —"

Strange and disconcerting it was to Kyle, the mother of the dead girl was so young: no more than forty-five. A bloated-looking little woman with a coarse ruddy face, in slacks and a floral-print shirt and flip-flops on her pudgy bare feet, hobbled with a mother's grief like an extra layer of fat. Technically, she was young enough to be Kyle Cassity's daughter.

Well! All the world, it seemed, was getting to be young enough to be Kyle Cassity's daughter.

"I'd love to see photographs of Sabrina, Mrs. Jackson. I've just come to pay my respects."

"Oh, I've got 'em! They're all ready to be seen. Everybody's been over here wanting to see them. I mean, not just the family and Sabrina's friends — you wouldn't believe all the friends that girl has from just high school alone — but the TV people, newspaper reporters. There's been more people through here, Officer, in the last ten, twelve days than in all of our life until now."

"I'm sorry for that, Mrs. Jackson. I don't mean to disturb you."

"Oh, no! It's got to be done, I guess."

The phone rang several times while Mrs. Jackson was showing Kyle a cascade of snapshots crammed into a family album, but the fleshy little woman, seated on a sofa, made no effort to answer it. Even unmoving on the sofa, she was inclined to breathlessness, panting. "Those calls can go onto voice mail. I use that all the time now. See, I don't know who's gonna call anymore. Used to be, it'd be just somebody I could predict, like out of ten people in the world, or one of those damn solicitors I just hang up on, but now, could be anybody almost. People call here saying they might know who's the guilty son of a bitch did that to Sabrina, but I tell them call the police, see? Call the police, not me. I'm not the police."

Mrs. Jackson spoke vehemently. Her body exuded an odor of intense excited emotion. Hesitantly Kyle leaned toward her, frowning at the snapshots. Some were old Polaroids, faded. Others were creased and dog-eared. In family photos of years ago it wasn't immediately obvious which girl was Sabrina, Mrs. Jackson had to point her out. Kyle saw a brattish-looking teenager, hands on her hips and grinning at the camera. As a young adolescent she'd had bad skin, which must have been hard on her, granting even her high spirits and energy. In some of the close-ups, Kyle saw an almost attractive girl, warm, hopeful, appealing in her openness. *Hey: look at me! Love me.* He wanted to love her. He wanted not to be disappointed in her. Mrs. Jackson sighed heavily. "People say those drawings looked just like Sabrina, that's how they recognized her, y'know, and I guess I can see it, but not really. If you're the mother you see different things. Sabrina was never pretty-pretty like in the drawings, she'd have laughed like hell to see 'em. It's like somebody took Sabrina's face and did a makeover, like cosmetic surgery, y'know? What Sabrina wanted, she'd talk about sort of joking but serious, was, what is it, 'chin injection'? 'Implant'?" Ruefully, Mrs. Jackson was stroking her chin, receding like her daughter's.

Kyle said, as if encouraging, "Sabrina was very attractive. She didn't need cosmetic surgery. Girls say things like that. I have a daughter, and when she was growing up . . . You can't take what they say seriously."

"That's true, Officer. You can't."

"Sabrina had personality. You can see that, Mrs. Jackson, in all her pictures."

"Oh, Christ! Did she ever."

Mrs. Jackson winced as if, amid the loose, scattered snapshots in the album, her fingers had encountered something sharp.

For some time they continued examining the snapshots. Kyle supposed that the grief-stricken mother was seeing her lost daughter anew, and in some way alive, through a stranger's eyes. He couldn't have said why looking at the snapshots had come to seem so crucial to him. For days he'd been planning this visit, summoning his courage to call Mrs. Jackson.

Mrs. Jackson said, showing him a tinted matte graduation photo of Sabrina in a white cap and gown, wagging her fingers and grinning at the camera, "High school was Sabrina's happy time. She was so, so popular. She should've gone right to college, instead of what she did do, she'd be alive now." Abruptly then Mrs. Jackson's mood shifted, she began to complain bitterly. "You wouldn't believe! People saying the cruelest things about Sabrina. People you'd think would be her old friends, and teachers at the school, calling her 'wild,' 'unpredictable.' Like all my daughter did was hang out in bars. Go out with married men." Mrs. Jackson's ruddy skin darkened with indignation. Half-moons of sweat showed beneath her arms. She said, panting, "If the police had let it alone, it'd be better, almost. We reported her missing back in May. Over the summer, it was like everybody'd say, 'Where's Sabrina, where's she gone to now?' A bunch of us drove to Atlantic City and asked around, but nobody'd seen her, it's a big place, people coming and going all the time, and the cops kept saying, 'Your daughter is an adult' and crap like that, like it was Sabrina's own decision to disappear. They listened to her tape and came to that conclusion. It wasn't even a 'missing persons' case. So we got to thinking maybe Sabrina was just traveling with this man friend of hers. The rumor got to be, this guy had money like Donald Trump. He was a high-stakes gambler. They'd have gotten bored with Atlantic City and gone to Vegas. Maybe they'd driven down into Mexico. Sabrina was always saying how she wanted to see Mexico. Now — all that's over." Mrs. Jackson shut the photo album, clumsily; a number of snapshots spilled out onto the floor. "See, Officer, things maybe should've been left the way they were. We were all just waiting for Sabrina to turn up, anytime. But people like you poking around, 'investigating,' printing ugly things about my daughter in the paper, I don't even know why you're here taking up my time or who the hell you *are.*"

Kyle was taken by surprise, Mrs. Jackson had suddenly turned so belligerent. "I, I'm sorry. I only wanted —"

"Well, we don't want your sympathy. We don't need your goddamn sympathy, Mister. You can just go back to New Jersey or wherever the hell you came from, intruding in my daughter's life."

Mrs. Jackson's eyes were moist and dilated and accusing. Her skin looked as if it would be scalding to the touch. Kyle was certain she wasn't drunk, he couldn't smell it on her breath, but possibly she was drugged. High on crystal meth — that was notorious in this part of Pennsylvania, run-down old cities like Easton.

Kyle protested, "But, Mrs. Jackson, you and your family would want to know, wouldn't you? I mean, what had happened to . . ." He paused awkwardly, uncertain how to continue. Why should they want to know? Would he have wanted to know, in their place?

In a voice heavy with sarcasm Mrs. Jackson said, "Oh, sure. You tell me, Officer. You got all the answers."

She heaved herself to her feet. A signal it was time for her unwanted visitor to depart.

Kyle had dared to take out his wallet. He was deeply humiliated but determined to maintain his composure. "Mrs. Jackson, maybe I can help? With the funeral expenses, I mean."

Hotly the little woman said, "We don't want anybody's charity! We're doing just fine by ourselves."

"Just a . . . a token of my sympathy."

Mrs. Jackson averted her eyes haughtily from Kyle's fumbling fingers, fanning her face with a *TV Guide.* He removed bills from his wallet, fifty-dollar bills, a one-hundred-dollar bill, folded them discreetly over, and placed them on an edge of the table.

Still, the indignant Mrs. Jackson didn't thank him. Nor did she trouble to see him to the door.

Where was he? A neighborhood of dingy wood-frame bungalows, row houses. Northern outskirts of Easton, Pennsylvania. Midafternoon: too early to begin drinking. Kyle was driving along potholed streets uncertain where he was headed. He'd have to cross the river again to pick up the big interstate south . . . At a 7-Eleven he bought a six-pack of strong dark ale and parked in a weedy cul-de-sac between a cemetery and a ramp of the highway, drinking. The ale was icy cold and made his forehead ache, not disagreeably. It was a bright blustery October day, a sky of high scudding clouds against a glassy blue. At the city's skyline, haze the hue of chewing-tobacco spittle. Certainly Kyle knew where he was, but where he was mattered less than something else, something crucial that had been decided, but he couldn't recall what it was that had been decided just yet. Except he knew it was crucial. Except so much that seemed crucial in his younger years had turned out to be not so, or not much so. A girl of about fourteen pedaled by on a bicycle, ponytail flying behind her head. She wore tight-fitting jeans, a backpack. She'd taken no notice of him, as if he, and the car in which he was sitting, were invisible. With his eyes he followed her. Followed her as swiftly she pedaled out of sight. Such longing, such love, suffused his heart! He watched the girl disappear, stroking a sinewy throbbing artery just below his jawline.

GEORGE P. PELECANOS

The Dead Their Eyes Implore Us

FROM *Measures of Poison*

SOMEDAY I'M GONNA write all this down. But I don't write so good in English yet, see? So I'm just gonna think it out loud.

Last night I had a dream.

In my dream, I was a kid, back in the village. My friends and family from the *chorio,* they were there, all of us standing around the square. My father, he had strung a lamb up on a pole. It was making a noise, like a scream, and its eyes were wild and afraid. My father handed me my Italian switch knife, the one he gave me before I came over. I cut into the lamb's throat and opened it up wide. The lamb's warm blood spilled onto my hands. My mother told me once: Every time you dream something, it's got to be a reason.

I'm not no kid anymore. I'm twenty-eight years old. It's early in June, Nineteen-hundred and thirty-three. The temperature got up to 100 degrees today. I read in the *Tribune,* some old people died from the heat. Let me try to paint a picture, so you can see in your head the way it is for me right now. I got this little one-room place I rent from some old lady. A Murphy bed and a table, an icebox and a stove. I got a radio I bought for a dollar and ninety-nine. I wash my clothes in a tub, and afterwards I hang the *roocha* on a cord I stretched across the room. There's a bunch of clothes, *pantalonia* and one of my work shirts and my *vrakia* and socks, on there now. I'm sitting here at the table in my union suit. I'm smoking a Fatima and drinking a cold bottle of Abner Drury beer. I'm looking at my hands. I got blood underneath my fingernails. I washed real good but it was hard to get it all.

It's five, five-thirty in the morning. Let me go back some, to show how I got to where I am tonight.

What's it been, four years since I came over? The boat ride was a boat ride so I'll skip that part. I'll start in America.

When I got to Ellis Island I came straight down to Washington to stay with my cousin Toula and her husband Aris. Aris had a fruit cart down on Pennsylvania Avenue, around 17th. Toula's father owed my father some *lefta* from back in the village, so it was all set up. She offered me a room until I could get on my feet. Aris wasn't happy about it but I didn't give a good goddamn what he was happy about. Toula's father should have paid his debt.

Toula and Aris had a place in Chinatown. It wasn't just for Chinese. Italians, Irish, Polacks, and Greeks lived there, too. Everyone was poor except the criminals. The Chinamen controlled the gambling, the whores, and the opium. All the business got done in the back of laundries and in the restaurants. The Chinks didn't bother no one if they didn't get bothered themselves.

Toula's apartment was in a house right on H Street. You had to walk up three floors to get to it. I didn't mind it. The milkman did it every day and the old Jew who collected the rent managed to do it, too. I figured, so could I.

My room was small, so small you couldn't shut the door all the way when the bed was down. There was only one toilet in the place, and they had put a curtain by it, the kind you hang on a shower. You had to close it around you when you wanted to shit. Like I say, it wasn't a nice place or nothing like it, but it was okay. It was free.

But nothing's free, my father always said. Toula's husband Aris made me pay from the first day I moved in. Never had a good word to say to me, never mentioned me to no one for a job. He was a son of a bitch, that one. Dark, with a hook in his nose, looked like he had some Turkish blood in him. I wouldn't be surprised if the *gamoto* was a Turk. I didn't like the way he talked to my cousin, either, 'specially when he drank. And this *malaka* drank every night. I'd sit in my room and listen to him raise his voice at her, and then later I could hear him fucking her on their bed. I couldn't stand it, I'm telling you, and me without a woman myself. I didn't have no job then so I couldn't even buy a whore. I thought I was gonna go nuts. Then one day I was talking to this guy, Dimitri Karras, lived in the 606 building on H. He told me about a janitor's job opened up at St. Mary's, the church where his son Panayoti and most of the neighborhood kids went to Catholic school. I put some Wildroot tonic in my hair, walked over to the church, and talked to the head nun. I don't know, she musta liked me or something, 'cause I got the job. I had to lie a little about being a handyman. I wasn't no engineer, but I figured, what the hell, the furnace goes out you light it again, goddamn.

My deal was simple. I got a room in the basement and a coupla meals a day. Pennies other than that, but I didn't mind, not then. Hell, it was better than living in some Hoover Hotel. And it got me away from that bastard Aris. Toula cried when I left, so I gave her a hug. I didn't say nothing to Aris.

I worked at St. Mary's about two years. The work was never hard. I knew the kids and most of their fathers: Karras, Angelos, Nicodemus, Recevo, Damiano, Carchedi. I watched the boys grow. I didn't look the nuns in the eyes when I talked to them so they wouldn't get the wrong idea. Once or twice I treated myself to one of the whores over at the Eastern House. Mostly, down in the basement, I played with my *pootso*. I put it out of my mind that I was jerking off in church.

Meanwhile, I tried to make myself better. I took English classes at St. Sophia, the Greek Orthodox church on 8th and L. I bought a blue serge suit at Harry Kaufman's on 7th Street, on sale for eleven dollars and seventy-five. The Jew tailor let me pay for it a little bit at a time. Now when I went to St. Sophia for the Sunday service I wouldn't be ashamed. I liked to go to church. Not for religion, nothing like that. Sure, I wear a *stavro,* but everyone wears a cross. That's just superstition. I don't love God, but I'm afraid of him. So I went to church just in case, and also to look at the girls. I liked to see 'em all dressed up.

There was this one *koritsi,* not older than sixteen when I first saw her, who was special. I knew just where she was gonna be, with her mother, on the side of the church where the women sat separate from the men. I made sure I got a good view of her on Sundays. Her name was Irene, I asked around. I could tell she was clean. By that I mean she was a virgin. That's the kind of girl you're gonna marry. My plan was to wait till I got some money in my pocket before I talked to her, but not too long so she got snatched up. A girl like that is not gonna stay single forever.

Work and church was for the daytime. At night I went to the

coffeehouses down by the Navy Yard in Southeast. One of them was owned by a hardworking guy from the neighborhood, Angelos, lived at the 703 building on 6th. That's the *cafeneion* I went to most. You played cards and dice there if that's what you wanted to do, but mostly you could be yourself. It was all Greeks.

That's where I met Nick Stefanos one night, at the Angelos place. Meeting him is what put another change in my life. Stefanos was a Spartan with an easy way, had a scar on his cheek. You knew he was tough but he didn't have to prove it. I heard he got the scar running protection for a hooch truck in upstate New York. Heard a cheap *pistola* blew up in his face. It was his business, what happened, none of mine.

We got to talking that night. He was the head busman down at some fancy hotel on 15th and Penn, but he was leaving to open his own place. His friend Costa, another *Spartiati,* worked there and he was gonna leave with him. Stefanos asked me if I wanted to take Costa's place. He said he could set it up. The pay was only a little more than what I was making, a dollar-fifty a week with extras, but a little more was a lot. Hell, I wanted to make better like anyone else. I thanked Nick Stefanos and asked him when I could start.

I started the next week, soon as I got my room where I am now. You had to pay management for your bus uniform, black pants and a white shirt and short black vest, so I didn't make nothing for a while. Some of the waiters tipped the busmen heavy, and some tipped nothing at all. For the ones who tipped nothing you cleared their tables slower, and last. I caught on quick.

The hotel was pretty fancy and its dining room, up on the top floor, was fancy, too. The china was real, the crystal sang when you flicked a finger at it, and the silver was heavy. It was hard times, but you'd never know it from the way the tables filled up at night. I figured I'd stay there a coupla years, learn the operation, and go out on my own like Stefanos. That was one smart guy.

The way they had it set up was, Americans had the waiter jobs, and the Greeks and Filipinos bused the tables. The coloreds, they stayed back in the kitchen. Everybody in the restaurant was in the same order that they were out on the street: the whites were up top and the Greeks were in the middle; the *mavri* were at the bottom. Except if someone was your own kind, you didn't make much small talk with the other guys unless it had something to do with work. I didn't have nothing against anyone, not even the coloreds. You didn't talk to them, that's all. That's just the way it was. The waiters, they thought they were better than the rest of us. But there was this one American, a young guy named John Petersen, who was all right. Petersen had brown eyes and wavy brown hair that he wore kinda long. It was his eyes that you remembered. Smart and serious, but gentle at the same time.

Petersen was different than the other waiters, who wouldn't lift a finger to help you even when they weren't busy. John would pitch in and bus my tables for me when I got in a jam. He'd jump in with the dishes, too, back in the kitchen, when the dining room was running low on silver, and like I say, those were coloreds back there. I even saw him talking with those guys sometimes like they were pals. It was like he came from someplace where that was okay. John was just one of those who made friends easy, I guess. I can't think of no one who didn't like him. Well, there musta been one person, at least. I'm gonna come to that later on.

Me and John went out for a beer one night after work, to a saloon he knew. I wasn't comfortable because it was all Americans and I didn't see no one who looked like me. But John made me feel okay and after two beers I forgot. He talked to me about the job and the pennies me and the colored guys in the kitchen were making, and how it wasn't right. He talked about some changes that were coming to make it better for us, but he didn't say what they were.

"I'm happy," I said, as I drank off the beer in my mug. "I got a job, what the hell."

"You want to make more money, don't you?" he said. "You'd like to have a day off once in a while, wouldn't you?"

"Goddamn right. But I take off a day, I'm not gonna get paid."

"It doesn't have to be like that, friend."

"Yeah, okay."

"Do you know what 'strength in numbers' means?"

I looked around for the bartender 'cause I didn't know what the hell John was talking about and I didn't know what to say.

John put his hand around my arm. "I'm putting together a meeting. I'm hoping some of the busmen and the kitchen guys will make it. Do you think you can come?"

"What we gonna meet for, huh?"

"We're going to talk about those changes I been telling you about. Together, we're going to make a plan."

"I don't want to go to no meeting. I want a day off, I'm just gonna go ask for it, eh?"

"You don't understand." John put his face close to mine. "The workers are being exploited."

"I work and they pay me," I said with a shrug. "That's all I know. Other than that? I don't give a damn nothing." I pulled my arm away but I smiled when I did it. I didn't want to join no group, but I wanted him to know we were still pals. "C'mon, John, let's drink."

I needed that job. But I felt bad, turning him down about that meeting. You could see it meant something to him, whatever the hell he was talking about, and I liked him. He was the only American in the restaurant who treated me like we were both the same. You know, man to man. Well, he wasn't the only American who made me feel like a man. There was this woman, name of Laura, a hostess who also made change from the bills. She bought her dresses too small and had hair bleached white, like Jean Harlow. She was about two years and ten pounds away from the end of her looks. Laura wasn't pretty, but her ass could bring tears to your eyes. Also, she had huge tits.

I caught her giving me the eye the first night I worked there. By the third night she said something to me about my broad chest as I was walking by her. I nodded and smiled, but I kept walking 'cause I was carrying a heavy tray. When I looked back she gave me a wink. She was a real whore, that one. I knew right then I was gonna fuck her. At the end of the night I asked her if she would go to the pictures with me sometime. "I'm free tomorrow," she says. I acted like it was an honor and a big surprise.

I worked every night, so we had to make it a matinee. We took the streetcar down to the Earle, on 13th Street, down below F. I wore my blue serge suit and high-button shoes. I looked like I had a little bit of money, but we still got the fisheye, walking down the street. A blonde and a Greek with dark skin and a heavy black mustache. I couldn't hide that I wasn't too long off the boat.

The Earle had a stage show before the picture. A guy named William Demarest and some dancers who Laura said were like the Rockettes. What the hell did I know, I was just looking at their legs. After the coming attractions and the short subject the picture came on: *Gold Diggers of 1933.* The man dancers looked like cocksuckers to me. I liked Westerns better, but it was all right. Fifteen cents for each of us. It was cheaper than taking her to a saloon.

Afterwards, we went to her place, an apartment in a row house off H in Northeast. I used the bathroom and saw a Barnards Shaving Cream and other man things in there, but I didn't ask her nothing about it when I came back out. I found her in the bedroom. She had poured us a couple of rye whiskies and drawn the curtains so it felt like the night. A radio played something she called "jug band"; it sounded like colored music to me. She asked me, did I want to dance. I shrugged and tossed back all the rye in my glass and pulled her to me rough. We moved slow, even though the music was fast.

"Bill?" she said, looking up at me. She had painted her eyes with something and there was a black mark next to one of them where the paint had come off.

"Uh," I said.

"What do they call you where you're from?"

"Vasili." I kissed her warm lips. She bit mine and drew a little blood. I pushed myself against her to let her know what I had.

"Why, Va-silly," she said. "You are like a horse, aren't you?"

I just kinda nodded and smiled. She stepped back and got out of her dress and her slip, and then undid her brassiere. She did it slow.

"*Ella,*" I said.

"What does that mean?"

"Hurry it up," I said, with a little motion of my hand. Laura laughed. She pulled the bra off and her tits bounced. They were everything I thought they would be. She came to me and unbuckled my belt, pulling at it clumsy, and her breath was hot on my face. By then, God, I was ready. I sat her on the edge of the bed, put one of her legs up on my shoulder, and gave it to her. I heard a woman having a baby in the village once, and those were the same kinda sounds that Laura made. There was spit dripping out the side of her mouth as I slammed myself into her over and over again. I'm telling you, her bed took some plaster off the wall that day. After I blew my load into her I climbed off. I didn't say nice things to her or nothing like that. She got what she wanted and so did I. Laura smoked a cigarette and watched me get dressed. The whole room smelled like pussy. She didn't look so good to me no more. I couldn't wait to get out of there and breathe fresh air.

We didn't see each other again outside of work. She only stayed at the restaurant a coupla more weeks, and then she disappeared. I guess the man who owned the shaving cream told her it was time to quit.

For a while there nothing happened and I just kept working hard. John didn't mention no meetings again though he was just as nice as before. I slept late and bused the tables at night. Life wasn't fun or bad. It was just ordinary. Then that bastard Wesley Schmidt came to work and everything changed.

Schmidt was a tall young guy with a thin mustache, big in the shoulders, big hands. He kept his hair slicked back. His eyes were real blue, like water under ice. He had a row of big straight teeth. He smiled all the time, but the smile, it didn't make you feel good.

Schmidt got hired as a waiter, but he wasn't any good at it. He got tangled up fast when the place got busy. He served food to the wrong tables all the time, and he spilled plenty of drinks. It didn't seem like he'd ever done that kind of work before.

No one liked him, but he was one of those guys, he didn't know it, or maybe he knew and didn't care. He laughed and told jokes and slapped the busmen on the back like we were his friends. He treated the kitchen guys like dogs when he was tangled up, raising his voice at them when the food didn't come up as fast as he liked it. Then he tried to be nice to them later.

One time he really screamed at Raymond, the head cook on the line, called him a "lazy shine" on this night when the place was packed. When the dining room cleared up Schmidt walked back into the kitchen and told Raymond in a soft voice that he didn't mean nothing by it, giving him that smile of his and patting his arm. Raymond just nodded real slow. Schmidt told me later, "That's all you got to do, is scold 'em and then talk real sweet to 'em later. That's how they learn. 'Cause they're like children. Right, Bill?" He meant coloreds, I guess. By the way he talked to me, real slow the way you would to a kid, I could tell he thought I was a colored guy, too. At the end of the night the waiters always sat in the dining room and ate a stew or something that the kitchen had prepared. The busmen, we served it to the waiters. I was running dinner out to one of them and forgot something back in the kitchen. When I went back to get it, I saw Raymond, spitting into a plate of stew. The other colored guys in the kitchen were standing in a circle around Raymond, watching him do it. They all looked over at me when I walked in. It was real quiet and I guess they were waiting to see what I was gonna do.

"Who's that for?" I said. "Eh?"

"Schmidt," said Raymond. I walked over to where they were. I brought up a bunch of stuff from deep down in my throat and spit real good into that plate. Raymond put a spoon in the stew and stirred it up.

"I better take it out to him," I said, "before it gets cold."

"Don't forget the garnish," said Raymond.

He put a flower of parsley on the plate, turning it a little so it looked nice. I took the stew out and served it to Schmidt. I watched him take the first bite and nod his head like it was good. None of the colored guys said nothing to me about it again.

I got drunk with John Petersen in a saloon a coupla nights after and told him what I'd done. I thought he'd get a good laugh out of it, but instead he got serious. He put his hand on my arm the way he did when he wanted me to listen. "Stay out of Schmidt's way," said John.

"Ah," I said, with a wave of my hand. "He gives me any trouble, I'm gonna punch him in the kisser." The beer was making me brave.

"Just stay out of his way."

"I look afraid to you?"

"I'm telling you, Schmidt is no waiter."

"I know it. He's the worst goddamn waiter I ever seen. Maybe you ought to have one of those meetings of yours and see if you can get him thrown out."

"Don't ever mention those meetings again, to anyone," said John, and he squeezed my arm tight. I tried to pull it away from him but he held his grip. "Bill, do you know what a Pinkerton man is?"

"What the hell?"

"Never mind. You just keep to yourself, and don't talk about those meetings, hear?"

I had to look away from his eyes. "Sure, sure."

"Okay, friend." John let go of my arm. "Let's have another beer."

A week later John Petersen didn't show up for work. And a week after that the cops found him floating downriver in the Potomac. I read about it in the *Tribune*. It was just a short notice, and it didn't say nothing else. A cop in a suit came to the restaurant and asked us some questions. A couple of the waiters said that John probably had some bad hootch and fell into the drink. I didn't know what to think. When it got around to the rest of the crew, everyone kinda got quiet, if you know what I mean. Even that bastard Wesley didn't make no jokes. I guess we were all thinking about John in our own way. Me, I wanted to throw up. I'm telling you, thinking about John in that river, it made me sick.

John didn't ever talk about no family and nobody knew nothing about a funeral. After a few days, it seemed like everybody in the restaurant forgot about him. But me, I couldn't forget.

One night I walked into Chinatown. It wasn't far from my new place. There was this kid from St. Mary's, Billy Nicodemus, whose father worked at the city morgue. Nicodemus wasn't no doctor or nothing, he washed off the slabs and cleaned the place, like that. He was known as a hard drinker, maybe because of what he saw every day, and maybe just because he liked the taste. I knew where he liked to drink.

I found him in a no-name restaurant on the Hip-Sing side of Chinatown. He was in a booth by himself, drinking something from a teacup. I crossed the room, walking through the cigarette smoke, passing the whores and the skinny Chink gangsters in their too-big suits and the cops who were taking money from the Chinks to look the other way. I stood over Nicodemus and told him who I was. I told him I knew his kid, told him his kid was good. Nicodemus motioned for me to have a seat.

A waiter brought me an empty cup. I poured myself some gin from the teapot on the table. We tapped cups and drank. Nicodemus had straight black hair wetted down and a big mole with hair coming out of it on one of his cheeks. He talked better than I did. We said some things that were about nothing and then I asked him some questions about John. The gin had loosened his tongue.

"Yeah, I remember him," said Nicodemus, after thinking about it for a short while. He gave me the once-over and leaned forward. "This was your friend?"

"Yes."

"They found a bullet in the back of his head. A twenty-two."

I nodded and turned the teacup in small circles on the table. "The *Tribune* didn't say nothing about that."

"The papers don't always say. The police cover it up while they look for who did it. But that boy didn't drown. He was murdered first, then dropped in the drink."

"You saw him?" I said.

Nicodemus shrugged. "Sure."

"What'd he look like?"

"You really wanna know?"

"Yeah."

"He was all gray and blown up, like a balloon. The gas does that to 'em, when they been in the water."

"What about his eyes?"

"They were open. Pleading."

"Huh?"

"His eyes. It was like they were sayin' please."

I needed a drink. I had some gin.

"You ever heard of a Pinkerton man?" I said.

"Sure," said Nicodemus. "A detective."

"Like the police?"

"No."

"What, then?"

"They go to work with other guys and pretend they're one of them. They find out who's stealing. Or they find out who's trying to make trouble for the boss. Like the ones who want to make a strike."

"You mean, like if a guy wants to get the workers together and make things better?"

"Yeah. Have meetings and all that. The guys who want to start a union. Pinkertons look for those guys."

We drank the rest of the gin. We talked about his kid. We talked about Schmeling and Baer, and the wrestling match that was coming up between Londos and George Zaharias at Griffith Stadium. I got up from my seat, shook Nicodemus's hand, and thanked him for the conversation.

"*Efcharisto, patrioti.*"

"*Yasou, Vasili.*"

I walked back to my place and had a beer I didn't need. I was drunk and more confused than I had been before. I kept hearing John's voice, the way he called me "friend." I saw his eyes saying please. I kept thinking, I should have gone to his goddamn meeting, if that was gonna make him happy. I kept thinking I had let him down. While I was thinking, I sharpened the blade of my Italian switch knife on a stone.

The next night, last night, I was serving Wesley Schmidt his dinner after we closed. He was sitting by himself like he always did. I dropped the plate down in front of him.

"You got a minute to talk?" I said.

"Go ahead and talk," he said, putting the spoon to his stew and stirring it around.

"I wanna be a Pinkerton man," I said. Schmidt stopped stirring his stew and looked up my way. He smiled, showing me his white teeth. Still, his eyes were cold.

"That's nice. But why are you telling me this?"

"I wanna be a Pinkerton, just like you."

Schmidt pushed his stew plate away from him and looked around the dining room to make sure no one could hear us. He studied my face. I guess I was sweating. Hell, I know I was. I could feel it dripping on my back.

"You look upset," said Schmidt, his voice real soft, like music. "You look like you could use a friend."

"I just wanna talk."

"Okay. You feel like having a beer, something like that?"

"Sure, I could use a beer."

"I finish eating, I'll go down and get my car. I'll meet you in the alley out back. Don't tell anyone, hear, because then they might want to come along. And we wouldn't have the chance to talk."

"I'm not gonna tell no one. We just drive around, eh? I'm too dirty to go to a saloon."

"That's swell," said Schmidt. "We'll just drive around."

I went out to the alley where Schmidt was parked. Nobody saw me get into his car. It was a blue, '31 Dodge coupe with wire wheels, a rumble seat, and a trunk rack. A five-hundred-dollar car if it was a dime.

"Pretty," I said, as I got in beside him. There were hand-tailored slipcovers on the seats.

"I like nice things," said Schmidt. He was wearing his suit jacket, and it had to be 80 degrees. I could see a lump under the jacket. I figured, the bastard is carrying a gun.

We drove up to Colvin's, on 14th Street. Schmidt went in and returned with a bag of loose bottles of beer. There must have been a half-dozen Schlitzes in the bag. Him making waiter's pay, and the fancy car and the high-priced beer.

He opened a coupla beers and handed me one. The bottle was ice cold. Hot as the night was, the beer tasted good.

We drove around for a while. We went down to Hanes Point. Schmidt parked the Dodge facing the Washington Channel. Across the channel, the lights from the fish vendors on Maine Avenue threw color on the water. We drank another beer. He gave me one of his tailor-mades and we had a couple smokes. He talked about the Senators and the Yankees, and how Baer had taken Schmeling out with a right in the tenth. Schmidt didn't want to talk about nothing serious yet. He was waiting for the beer to work on me, I knew.

"Goddamn heat," I said. "Let's drive around some, get some air moving."

Schmidt started the coupe. "Where to?"

"I'm gonna show you a whorehouse. Best secret in town."

Schmidt looked me over and laughed. The way you laugh at a clown. I gave Schmidt some directions. We drove some, away from the park and the monuments to where people lived. We went through a little tunnel and crossed into Southwest. Most of the street lamps were broke here. The row houses were shabby, and you could see shacks in the alleys and clothes hanging on lines outside the shacks. It was late, a long time past midnight. There weren't many people out. The ones that were out were coloreds. We were in a place called Bloodfield.

"Pull over there," I said, pointing to a spot along the curb where there wasn't no light. "I wanna show you the place I'm talking about."

Schmidt did it and cut the engine. Across the street were some houses. All except one of them was dark. From the lighted one came fast music, like the colored music Laura had played in her room.

"There it is right there," I said, meaning the house with the light. I was lying through my teeth. I didn't know who lived there and I sure didn't know if that house had whores. I had never been down here before. Schmidt turned his head to look at the row house. I slipped my switch knife out of my right pocket and laid it flat against my right leg.

When he turned back to face me he wasn't smiling no more. He had heard about Bloodfield and he knew he was in it. I think he was scared.

"You bring me down to niggertown, for what?" he said. "To show me a whorehouse?"

"I thought you're gonna like it."

"Do I look like a man who'd pay to fuck a nigger? Do I? You don't know anything about me."

He was showing his true self now. He was nervous as a cat. My nerves were bad, too. I was sweating through my shirt. I could smell my own stink in the car.

"I know plenty," I said.

"Yeah? What do you know?"

"Pretty car, pretty suits . . . top-shelf beer. How you get all this, huh?"

"I earned it."

"As a Pinkerton, eh?"

Schmidt blinked real slow and shook his head. He looked out his window, looking at nothing, wasting time while he decided what he was gonna do. I found the raised button on the pearl handle of my knife. I pushed the button. The blade flicked open and barely made a sound. I held the knife against my leg and turned it so the blade was pointing back. Sweat rolled down my neck as I looked around. There wasn't nobody out on the street. Schmidt turned his head. He gripped the steering wheel with his right hand and straightened his arm.

"What do you want?" he said.

"I just wanna know what happened to John."

Schmidt smiled. All those white teeth. I could see him with his mouth open, his lips stretched, those teeth showing. The way an animal looks after you kill it. Him lying on his back on a slab.

"I heard he drowned," said Schmidt.

"You think so, eh?"

"Yeah. I guess he couldn't swim."

"Pretty hard to swim, you got a bullet in your head."

Schmidt's smile turned down. "Can you swim, Bill?"

I brought the knife across real fast and buried it into his armpit. I sunk the blade all the way to the handle. He lost his breath and made a short scream. I twisted the knife. His blood came out like someone was pouring it from a jug. It was warm and it splashed onto my hands. I pulled the knife out and while he was kicking at the floorboards I stabbed him a coupla more times in the chest. I musta hit his heart or something because all the sudden there was plenty of blood all over the car. I'm telling you, the seats were slippery with it. He stopped moving. His eyes were open and they were dead.

I didn't get tangled up about it or nothing like that. I wasn't scared. I opened up his suit jacket and saw a steel revolver with wood grips holstered there. It was small caliber. I didn't touch the gun. I took his wallet out of his trousers, pulled the bills out of it, wiped off the wallet with my shirttail, and threw the empty wallet on the ground. I put the money in my shoe. I fit the blade back into the handle of my switch knife and slipped the knife into my pocket. I put all the empty beer bottles together with the full ones in the paper bag and took the bag with me as I got out of the car. I closed the door soft and wiped off the handle and walked down the street. I didn't see no one for a couple of blocks. I came to a sewer and I put the bag down the hole. The next block I came to another sewer and I took off my bloody shirt and threw it down the hole of that one. I was wearing an undershirt, didn't have no sleeves. My pants were black so you couldn't see the blood. I kept walking toward Northwest.

Someone laughed from deep in an alley and I kept on.

Another block or so I came upon a group of *mavri* standing around the steps of a house. They were smoking cigarettes and drinking from bottles of beer. I wasn't gonna run or nothing. I had to go by them to get home. They stopped talking and gave me hard eyes as I got near them. That's when I saw that one of them was the cook, Raymond, from the kitchen. Our eyes kind of came together but neither one of us said a word or smiled or even made a nod.

One of the coloreds started to come toward me and Raymond stopped him with the flat of his palm. I walked on.

I walked for a couple of hours, I guess. Somewhere in Northwest I dropped my switch knife down another sewer. When I heard it hit the sewer bottom I started to cry. I wasn't crying 'cause I had killed Schmidt. I didn't give a damn nothing about him. I was crying 'cause my father had given me that knife, and now it was gone. I guess I knew I was gonna be in America forever, and I wasn't never going back to Greece. I'd never see my home or my parents again.

When I got back to my place I washed my hands real good. I opened up a bottle of Abner Drury and put fire to a Fatima and had myself a seat at the table.

This is where I am right now.

Maybe I'm gonna get caught and maybe I'm not. They're gonna find Schmidt in that neighborhood and they're gonna figure a colored guy killed him for his money. The cops, they're gonna turn Bloodfield upside down. If Raymond tells them he saw me I'm gonna get the chair. If he doesn't, I'm gonna be free. Either way, what the hell, I can't do nothing about it now. I'll work at the hotel, get some experience and some money, then open my own place, like Nick Stefanos. Maybe if I can find two nickels to rub together, I'm gonna go to church and talk to that girl, Irene, see if she wants to be my wife. I'm not gonna wait too long. She's clean as a whistle, that one. I've had my eye on her for some time.

SCOTT PHILLIPS

Sockdolager

FROM *Measures of Poison*

1. Upholstery

After cashing the last of the summer's commission checks I had
stopped at home for a shower and a change of clothes, then
headed straight for the Royal Crown Club on East Douglas. I sat for
a while shooting the bull with old Gleason, the prehistoric bartender, and trying in vain to ignore the oppressive, wet heat of the
tail end of a Kansas summer. I was morbidly watching a drop of
sweat work its way down Gleason's piebald temple to his flabby
cheek when a woman walked in through the front door and took a
seat, her perfunctory show of disinterest given lie to by the fact that
she'd planted her nicely upholstered rump a mere two stools to the
right of me. The bar was empty except for me and Gleason, and if
she didn't want company she would have taken a table.

Gleason, who was my father's oldest friend, had been a widower
for twenty years, and he stared enraptured and without shame
at her knockers; she helpfully pretended not to notice. With his
slobbery, loose jowls, his peculiar dusty odor, and earlobes hanging
damn near down to his chin, he was old enough to have tended bar
before the state outlawed booze, and Kansas had done it thirty
years ahead of the rest of the country. It was still contraband in the
Sunflower State, despite the passage of the Twentieth Amendment,
but it could be had with a minimum of effort if you knew where
to look.

The woman shifted her ass on the stool and pulled at the neck-
line of her thin summer dress, giving her tits a quick bounce for old

Gleason. She looked to be about thirty-five, with black hair coiled in a permanent wave, and a little extra baggage at her waist and hips and under her kohl-smeared eyes. None of that bothered me at all, in fact all summer I'd been wondering what it would be like screwing a woman her age. I mean one who liked it, not one of those you hear about who just lies back and goes limp and thinks about something else, waiting for it to be over so she can go back to her bonbons and movie magazines and radio serials. That was too much like the high school girls I'd been nailing since I turned fourteen, girls who traded sex for status, for the sake of being known as the quarterback's or the student council president's girl. Nuts to that.

But I couldn't act on my impulses, despite the many opportunities sales work afforded me. First of all, I was a professional salesman with a code of ethics. Secondly, if such a breach of that code were found out it could have meant the loss of my position, even if it was only a summer job. Thirdly, times were tough, and most of the offers I'd had over the last three summers had involved a quid pro quo, a blow job for a new coffeepot or a plain screw for a cast-iron frying pan. One careworn and brazen mother of five proposed paying me fifty cents on the dollar plus three (3) incidents of sexual intercourse per week all summer for a full set of stainless steel kitchenware, a sort of carnal installment plan that would have wrecked me financially. If I hadn't had a girlfriend from school to take the physical pressure off a couple of nights a week, I might have been tempted.

I wasn't on the job now, though, and the lady to my right wasn't a customer. On top of her fresh permanent and florid perfume I could smell the sauce she'd already downed before coming in, and I calculated I could find out what I wanted to know for the price of two to four more drinks, judging from the thickness of her slur as she'd ordered the first. My wallet had a small fortune in it, thirty-six dollars before I'd started buying drinks, and when she swallowed the last of her drink I pulled out a two-dollar bill and signaled to Gleason.

"Another gimlet for the lady," I said, and she swiveled the stool around to face me, recrossing her legs as she did so. They were long, and her flimsy red and white dress was short enough to reveal a certain slackness of thigh that I found unexpectedly appealing.

"How genteel," she said, softening the "g."

"My pleasure," I said, raising my own glass. "Wayne Ogden."

"Mildred Halliburton. Pleased to meet you, Dwayne." She moved over to the stool next to mine, and when her thigh met my knee she didn't move it away.

"That's Wayne."

She giggled as Gleason served her, his watery blue pupils blatantly following her nipples like twin searchlights. "I'm awfully sorry, Wayne. And what, as they say, is your line?"

"I'm a salesman for the Lanham Company." At least I had been until two days before; I didn't think it would help to mention that the next week I would be starting my senior year of high school.

"Oh. Selling pots and pans, door to door?"

"Kitchenware of all kinds."

"How inneressting," she slobbered. "I myself am a user of kitchenware." I braced myself for the inevitable offer of a trade, but she surprised me. "I got all I need, though, so you can forget about that." She laughed again, and I started to think my one drink might be my ticket into her short-and-silkies.

"I'm not on duty anyway," I said.

She knocked the drink back in a gulp, then placed her palm flat on her breast. "Oh." Her eyes were wide open for a second, and then she laughed again, a melodious, low sound. "These drinks are starting to hit me, I think."

I knocked mine back in the same manner and got straight to business. She now looked like she was a drink or two away from being no fun at all. "How'd you like to join me for a double feature at the Miller?"

She put the tips of the fingers of her left hand on my right knee, and for the first time I noticed her wedding band. "That's real sweet, Wayne, honey," she said, and I steeled myself for rejection on the basis of my being half her age. Instead she confirmed my longheld suspicion that sexual transactions between adults were far less complicated than those between people my age: "I got a better idea, though." She lowered her voice to a hoarse stage whisper. "Why don't we go back to my house and you can manhandle me some."

I picked up my change, leaving a healthy tip for Gleason, and helped her off her stool. As we walked toward the door he nodded to me approvingly, with a slightly wistful air.

*

We jaywalked, or ran, to the other side of the street, and she laughed when she got a good look at my 1916 Hudson Super Six Phaeton.

"Shall we take yours, then?" I asked, careful to hide my irritation. The car had cost me a month's commissions the year before, and I'd spent hundreds of hours since improving it mechanically and cosmetically, but to some people a twenty-year-old car was junk, no matter its condition.

"I came in a taxicab," she said. "So unless you want to spring for another one, this'll do fine. I live in Riverside, on Woodrow, down by the park."

It was even muggier than when I'd arrived at the Royal Crown, and despite that shower my fresh shirt was already sticking to my back. I noted with pleasure that the same thing was happening to her, the cotton dress clinging to her in dark, wet ovals just above and below the back of her brassiere. She brightened visibly when I lowered the top, and when I pulled out onto Douglas she closed her eyes and sighed at the air flowing over her, drying the sweat on her brow before we'd crossed the drainage canal. An airplane droned overhead, descending, and I looked up out of habit to identify it.

"That's a brand-new Collins Airmaster, headed for Collins airfield," I said reflexively.

She opened her eyes and looked sideways at me. "Goody gumdrops," she said, "a brand-new Airmaster."

I didn't let my face give anything away, though what I wanted was to backhand that supercilious smirk right off her mouth. We didn't say anything else until we got to Woodrow and she pointed out her house.

2. *What You Got for a Gin Gimlet in Those Days*

It was a big red brick two-story, just around the corner from my girl's parents on Porter. I wondered if she knew them, and then I got worried about someone who knew me seeing me go into her house at five in the afternoon. It couldn't be helped, though. I opened her garage door and put the readily identifiable Super Six inside. As I helped her out and pulled the garage door down it occurred to me that someone might show up expecting to find the space empty. "You don't have a husband coming home, do you?"

"Hell, no," she said. "I'm not that drunk. Floyd and the kids took off on a camping trip at five this morning. You ever hear of a place called the Garden of the Gods? It's in Colorado." She went around front, despite my craven suggestion that we go in the back door. She had trouble finding the key, and when she did she couldn't quite slip it into the lock at the right angle.

"I've heard of it," I said. "How come you didn't go?"

She laughed that pretty laugh again, only this time it was a little out of control. "I'm supposed to be helping with the goddamned back-to-school church fair. I'm on . . . on . . . the organizing committee." She was nearly hysterical now, bracing herself on the door-frame as the door opened. She practically collapsed entering the front room, and I followed quickly, slamming the door behind me. She fell onto the couch, and I lit a lamp. Spying a radio in the corner, I moved to turn it on for some music.

"Whattaya doing?" she asked, winded, from the couch.

"Thought it might be nice to have some music," I said.

"What the hell for? I have no intention of dancing with you. S'not Christian." She broke up again, doubled over, and I sat on the couch next to her. "Organizing committee. Oh, boy. What I stayed home for was to get drunk and screw for a couple weeks." She finally stopped laughing. "So why don't you get busy and fuck me, Wayne?"

The first time was on the couch, and it was a quick one, with my pants around my ankles and her dress up to her waist. Afterward she led me upstairs, and despite the fact that less than two minutes earlier I had been inside her, I stared at her ass as longingly as old Gleason had as she mounted the steps ahead of me. One of her stockings had rolled down past her knee, and the sight of the backs of her long legs as they climbed, their muscles relaxing and contracting with each step beneath a healthy layer of fat, was enough to get me ready for another roll in the hay without a breather.

The room was pretty bright and not stiflingly hot, since two windows were open and a pretty good cross draft blew through it. The wallpaper was dark green, and there were fresh flowers in a cheap mail-order vase on the dresser.

"You might go a little slower this time," she said as she fell back onto the bedspread. "I'll get a lot more out of it." I didn't take it as an insult. It had been extremely quick, though she had certainly made enough noise to give the impression — probably to the whole neighborhood — that she was having a good time.

I undressed her slowly, exposing what hadn't already been exposed, and in the golden light slanting through the venetian blinds I thought she was the most beautiful woman I had ever seen naked. I shocked her by putting my mouth onto her private parts, but she'd done the same to me downstairs when we were getting started, and pretty soon I had her going so fast and hot she didn't care if it was against the laws of nature or not. After I was pretty sure she'd had her share of the fun I got inside again and rode her slowly but surely to the point where we were both yelling and moaning. Right before I shot my second and more satisfying load she squealed, "Rudy . . . take me, Rudy, take me . . . that's it, Rudy," and then her cries became incomprehensible and animalistic before tapering off as I disengaged and rolled onto the sheets.

I lay there next to her for a little bit, feeling the breeze cool my sweaty torso, and when it seemed like it was time to talk I asked her who Rudy was.

She pointed at the dresser, atop which sat among many framed family pictures a signed portrait of Rudolph Valentino. "I always thought it was a damned shame he died before I got the chance to give myself to him. I coulda made him happy in a way that Russian bitch never could." Her eyes were wet with tears now, though she didn't sound as drunk as she had in the car.

I'd always heard Rudy was queer, but it wouldn't do to say it to her. He was ten years dead anyway. She was swimming in melancholy, luxuriating in it, and I swung my feet off the bed so I could wash up and get away.

"Where the hell are you going?" she asked.

"Thought I'd go and let you have a little peace and quiet."

"The hell with peace and quiet. You and me got more screwing to do."

I must have had a funny look on my face, because she laughed.

"What the hell's the point of picking up a real young sport if you're not going to take full advantage of all that extra horsepower?"

What the hell, I was having a good time. "Okay."

"Anyway, there's plenty of things we haven't done yet. I sure did like that mouth-on-the-pussy business of yours. It's a safe bet Floyd's never gonna put his mouth anywhere near the goddamn thing." She got up on her knees and leaned forward. "Have you ever had sex with a lady's rectum, Wayne?"

I nodded. A very religious girlfriend in my sophomore year was eager for it that way, since she believed that vaginal intercourse was for marriage only, and even then only for the purpose of conceiving future soldiers of the Cross. It had been a year and a half since I'd messed around that way, though, and I missed it.

"Well, we can do some of that if you want, I don't mind. Believe me, there's all kinds of ways to do it we haven't thought of yet." She moved to the edge of the bed and dangled her legs off it, and with a thoughtful look cupped a hand under each breast as though trying to guess their weight. "Last time Floyd took the kids on a camping trip was more than a year ago, and I am just about as goddamn horny as it's possible to be without taking to the streets."

"Floyd doesn't ever give you any?"

"What Floyd gives me happens once a week and takes about ninety seconds, and I could get more satisfaction from a sanded-down dowel rod. I often do, as a matter of fact."

I looked back up at the dresser and saw what I assumed to be a picture of Floyd, a beefy-looking kind of guy with a gap in his front teeth and a receding hairline. Next to that was a picture of him with Mildred, and three little kids. Judging by her apparent age in the picture, and her bobbed hair and flapper dress, it was a few years old. "How old are your kids?"

She thought for a second. "Sylvester's seventeen. Myrtle's fifteen, gonna be sixteen in October, and Herbert's ten. He was a surprise, if you catch my meaning."

Fuck a duck, I thought, and my hands began to tingle as though I'd been hit in the funny bone; I had just put the meat to Sylvester Halliburton's mother. I'd stolen my girl Sally from Sylvester the year before, and he still hated my guts for it. I wondered what he'd do if he found out I'd fucked his dear old mother, and the thought got a laugh out of me.

"What's funny?" she asked, and I said it was nothing. Rather than pursue it, she wondered if I knew where to get a bottle, since neither of us had thought to get one to go at the Royal Crown. "Floyd won't allow me to keep any in the house. It's against the law," she said, mimicking an idiotic hillbilly's voice. I knew a source just a few blocks away, and I decided to walk rather than take the car. "Make it rum," she shouted after me.

3. Rum, Sodomy, and the False Eyelash

The evening was cooling off when I crossed the 11th Street Bridge, and I started thinking maybe I could make this a habit with Mildred. She certainly seemed to be enjoying herself, and I could easily afford the price of a motor court cabin a couple of times a week. I'd be doing her a favor as much as myself, if you thought about it, giving her on a year-round basis the hooch and screwing Floyd was failing to provide.

I was en route to a blind pig on 12th and Bitting, on the upper floor of an old carriage house, across the street from a steep slope leading down to the riverbank. This time of year the bars didn't fill up until the cool of the evening, and the proprietor of the blind pig was so lonely he insisted on giving me a drink on the house before he'd sell me the bottle, just to have someone to talk to. I didn't mind sticking around, and I figured Mildred's reaction on my returning later than expected would give me an indication of what to expect if I pursued her any further.

"Guess school must be about to start. You done yet?"

"One more year and I'm free, Norman."

"What you planning to do after that?"

"I'm going to college. No choice in the matter, my old man's been socking it away since I was born."

"Uh-huh. That's good, Wayne." He emptied his drink. "You getting any lately?" he asked.

"I'm a door-to-door salesman, Norman," I said as if that meant something.

He nodded and poured himself another bourbon. "Married women. Got to watch it, there. Good way to get into trouble."

I agreed with him and asked him the same question.

He held up his right hand and wiggled his fingers. "Since Lisette ran off it's mostly been Madame Palm and her five daughters."

"Lisette?"

"My wife. She took off for warmer climes a couple, three years ago. Before you started coming in."

I wondered what sort of woman she had been. Norman was fifty or so, with hair that always needed cutting. His face seemed perfectly round, an impression accentuated by a pair of round spectacles through which his wide-set eyes gazed sadly at his circumscribed world. In the two years I'd been coming to the blind pig I had never rung the bell without Norman being there to answer, and I knew this was his home as well as his business. If he went anywhere at all, even to get groceries or stamps, I wasn't aware of it.

I got the bottle, and though he wanted me to stay for a second drink I left. It was starting to get dark, and I was ready to go back and give it to Mildred some more. Hell, I thought, maybe I'll give Sylvester another brother, even more surprising than the last one.

The sun was all the way down before I got back, and I went in through the front door into the dark living room like the deed had my name on it and not Floyd Halliburton's. "Darling, I'm home," I bellowed, and I bounded up the steps three at a time and found her sitting up in bed, naked and crying. The tears had made an awful mess of her eye makeup; one fake lash dangled limp from the corner of her left eye and streaks of black ran right down to her tits, with one rivulet describing the border of her right aureola. The enticingly mature woman I had met at the Royal Crown had transformed somehow into a gorgon, and I wondered about making an excuse and leaving her to her boozing.

"What are you crying for?"

"What the hell you think? Give me that goddamn bottle," she said, and I handed it to her. She cracked it and took a long, hard swallow, then clumsily tried to place the bottle on the nightstand. It fell over, and a good portion of it spilled out before I could right it. I didn't want any more myself, but I'd paid for it and her carelessness rankled.

She seemed to feel a little better, and without wiping her face she smiled wickedly at me. "Thanks for getting the booze, sweetheart. You're a real doll. Now, did you see what I got for you?"

I didn't and told her so in a curt manner that didn't seem to put her off at all.

"Went down to the kitchen and got you some of this," she said, and notwithstanding her grotesque appearance I felt my dick be-gin to harden again at the sight of the cardboard can of vegetable shortening. She stuck her hand into the thick white mess, and then I saw her red-nailed middle finger disappear briefly into the puck-ered asterisk of her anus, damned near up to the third knuckle. Ex-tracting it, she gave me a look of such depraved cunning that I had an impulse to bolt for the street, but I managed to ignore it as I vaulted onto the bed, wrestling with my trousers.

My third orgasm of the evening took a while in coming, and half-way through it she reached over clumsily for the bottle, nearly knocking it over again, and I pulled out for a minute to allow her to knock back a decent slug of it. Then I replaced it on the nightstand and started back up. Afterward I washed my dick in the bathtub, despite her whining and pleading that I stay in bed with her. She was afraid I was going to leave, and she was right; in any case, the combined smell of fecal matter, vegetable shortening, and rum needed to be dealt with immediately or I was going to get sick. When I returned she had the bottle in hand again, and rum drib-bled from her lips to her chin. For the first time I considered that getting hooked up with an alcoholic woman might be less amusing than I'd always imagined; the girls I knew at school got silly and playful with a little booze in them, but in her cups Mildred put me in mind of an embittered, middle-aged male wino, full of vitriol and self-pity.

She held out the bottle for me and I waved it away. I had my trou-sers back on again, and she frowned without looking too broken up about it. "Whyncha come back tomorra," she said. "We can think of some more things to do, I bet."

"I'll do that, Mildred," I said over my shoulder as I skipped down the stairs. "I'll bring a bottle."

That brought forth a ghastly cackle, and the question of whether I'd be back or not was very much undecided as I picked Mildred's discarded unmentionables up off her couch and jammed them into my pants pocket for a souvenir. I stepped out the front door and crossed the yard and driveway to the garage, where I stashed the silk shorts in the glove box of the Super Six. Pulling out onto Woodrow, I thought about stopping over at my girl's house, but I imagined I could still smell Mildred's shit on my dick despite my earlier, vigorous ministration of soap and water. Anyway, and this was the curious part, I felt sated for once. A fourth orgasm would have been superfluous, and I realized that if that weren't so I would have stayed with Mildred, who seemed set to go all night long.

I was headed east on Douglas with no particular destination in mind, and as I neared Hillside, I thought I'd stop at the Royal Crown and let old Gleason know how it had gone. I parked at the curb a few doors down and stepped inside to find seven or eight drinkers at the bar and a dozen or more scattered around the tables, mostly men with a few girlfriends or wives thrown in. I greeted Gleason, who nodded and said, "How'd it go, champ?"

"Aces," I said. "Six ways from Sunday."

"You managed to walk out of here with the only unaccompanied female that's been in all week. Congratulations."

"She got what she came in for, all right."

"Uh-huh. You want something to drink?"

I didn't really want any, but I didn't want to look like a lightweight. "Same as before."

He set the drink down in front of me, and a man next to me turned and gave me the eye. He looked like he was in his forties, with thin brown hair on top and an oft-broken nose.

"You want to paint my portrait, Gertrude?" I asked, and his expression got harder.

"Goddamn it, Gleason," the man said. "I told you a million times not to serve kids in here."

"Who's a kid?" I said, self-consciously deepening my voice, fortifying my feeling of adulthood with the thought that I had just had carnal knowledge of a woman in her middle thirties.

"You're a kid," the man said, apparently unable to read my thoughts. He sniffed and wrinkled his nose. "And you smell like shit, too. Go home and wipe your ass and come back when you're twenty-one."

"This is a speakeasy," I protested, feeling my voice rise. "There's no minimum age."

"There sure as hell is. I pay off the law, and one of their conditions for looking the other way is, they don't want to see any goddamn kids in here. You understand me? Now scram."

He took my drink off the table and handed it back to Gleason, and I suddenly felt like I was ten years old.

"Shit, Gleason, I got Stanley Gerard coming down from K.C. to-morrow. I don't want him to see anything like that, got me?"

"Yes, sir, Mister Shelton." Gleason nodded with great dignity as I slid off my stool and headed for the door, my cheeks burning with shame and rage. I went to my car and sat for a while, dreaming of revenge, and then I headed for home.

4. The Duesie

The next day I stayed around the house reading. Around four-thirty in the afternoon I headed over to my girl's house, just a block away from Mildred's. Sally was home and her parents weren't, and they weren't expected back until evening. We screwed furtively in her room upstairs, and as I was zipping back up I said I'd be going.

"Now? But I thought we might go to a picture show," Sally whined.

"I'm feeling a little peaked. I think I'd better go on home," I said with a pout to show what a physical wreck I was. She scowled and turned away from me, and didn't acknowledge me as I left. Outside in the car I laughed out loud. What I was feeling was horny and dirty, still, and what I wanted now was my dirty, drunken, middle-aged gal Mildred.

I stopped by the blind pig for a bottle, and Norman was once again alone, so I let him buy me a drink.

"Shit, these hot days like this it ain't worth staying open. I'm barely making my nut here."

"How big's the nut?" I asked. "If you're paying more than twenty bucks a month rent you're being robbed."

"I pay seventeen-fifty, and that ain't the problem. I have my stock to account for, and I have to pay people to stay in business. In case you ain't heard, this stuff's against the law around here." He knocked his back and poured another.

"Who do you pay? The cops?"

"Them first, and then there's other guys. Guys from out of town. Costs me damn close to a hundred and fifty bucks a month just to open the goddamn door."

Downstairs someone opened the big carriage house doors and started up a car. Then the door shut and the driver tapped the horn, and I looked out the window in time to see a Graham Custom Eight, obviously the pride and joy of the ape behind the wheel, who wheeled out onto the street and burned rubber up 12th, honking his horn again at the corner.

"That's one of the guys I gotta pay to stay in business. He rents the garage space downstairs."

"What's his racket?" I asked.

"His racket is, people pay him so they can stay in business," Norman said, a little irritated. Again he wanted to give me another drink, but I demurred and started to leave. I stopped at the door and asked him if he knew the owner of the Royal Crown.

"Larry Shelton? I know who he is. He don't know me from a snake's dick."

"All right," I said. "See you."

I parked in Mildred's garage again. When I knocked on the front door there was no answer, so I tried the knob. It opened and I went inside.

"Mildred?" She didn't answer, and I wondered if she wasn't passed out upstairs. "I got you a bottle." The downstairs was neat and clean, and so was the upstairs. The bed was neatly made, and turning it down I saw that the sheets had been changed. Mildred wasn't as sloppy a drunk as I'd thought.

I could have gone back to Sally's and made her happy by taking her to a movie like she wanted, but instead I headed for the Royal Crown and hoped I wouldn't have to clash with Larry Shelton.

Parked in front of the Royal Crown was the only Duesenberg SJ I had ever seen outside of the pages of a magazine. I parked a few doors down and hopped out. I stood before the SJ for a minute, wondering where it had come from and to whom it belonged. Its top was down, and shortly a yokel slouching down the sidewalk stopped to join me, whistling in admiration.

"You know what that is?" he asked.

Playing the dope, I scratched my head. "Some sort of convertible?" I said.

"'At there is a Duesie SJ."

"Like the Jesuits?"

"Nuh-uh, it's a Duesenberg. Some of 'em's got a ram's horn manifold'll boost you right up to four hundred horsepower."

"This one?"

"You'd never know unless you drove it, or looked under the hood."

"Golly Moses," I said. "Imagine just leaving it on the street like that. Somebody might just open the hood and take a look inside at the manifold." I was tired of pulling the hillbilly's leg and I left him standing there gaping, tormented by the temptation I had just placed in front of him. I didn't blame him, though. It was a beautiful piece of machinery, black and white with red trim, and it made that Graham I'd spotted earlier look like a galvanized trash barrel on wheels.

The sun was low and the temperature dropping, but the Royal Crown wasn't hopping quite yet. Gleason spotted me at the door and shook his head, jerking it at Shelton, who sat there talking to a swell who looked like he might belong to the Duesenberg. At any rate, the man was wearing a suit that wouldn't have seemed shabby behind the wheel of a car like that. Shelton's back was to me, and two stools down from him sat Mildred, still able to balance on the stool despite the approaching dusk. She had on the same thin sleeveless dress as the day before, probably the only flattering summerweight one she had. I took the stool next to hers despite Gleason's frantic, silent attempts to wave me away, his head shaking so hard his jowls shook like rubber balloons filled with water.

"Gin," I said, "and another gimlet for the lady." He just stood there looking at me, lips tight, and then he turned disgustedly and made a single drink, which he placed in front of me. Then he leaned down.

"Leave the chippie alone," Gleason whispered. "She's with those fellows tonight."

"The hell with that," I said in a normal tone of voice. "I said another gimlet for the lady."

Gleason shook his head disgustedly, and Mildred, sensing that some free booze was on offer, turned my way. She looked nice, I thought, better than she had last night before things got started, and she smiled in recognition. "Hello, there, Wayne." Her eyes promised the foulest of biblically proscribed delights.

"Mildred."

Gleason put the gimlet down in front of her.

"You sure are sweet."

"Thanks. I stopped by your house with a bottle, only you weren't there."

"Nope, I was here."

"You want to go drink it, once you finish that?"

She glanced over at Shelton, still deep in conversation. "What the hell," she said, and she knocked the gimlet back in a gulp and slid off the stool. "Lead on, MacDuff."

I laid down some money on the bar, and Gleason shook his head at me with a very grim look on his face.

We were halfway to the door when Shelton noticed us.

"Hey," he shouted. "Mildred."

"I'm tired of waiting, Larry, and this nice young gentleman offered me a ride home. Wasn't that kind of him?"

Larry Shelton looked at me without much pleasure. "You look like a boy doesn't understand what 'stay the hell away' means."

"You said to stay away until I was twenty-one. Today's my birthday."

He softened a little. "Well, why didn't you say so?" Grinning, he showed off a gap between his front teeth that made Floyd's look like an orthodontist's masterwork, and he stuck out his hand for me to shake. "Come on over here and I'll buy you a drink for your birthday."

I thought for a second, stupidly, that I'd pulled one over on him, and approached him with my hand extended. The man with the snappy suit watched the transaction with bored disinterest, impatient to resume his conversation with Shelton and annoyed at the distraction.

When I was three feet away from Shelton, he grabbed his own drink from the bar and threw it in my face. I stood for a moment, humiliated, with bourbon running down my face and dripping off my chin as he and his friend cracked up laughing.

"You were about to offer the lady a ride home on your bike, junior?" the man in the suit said.

"Come on, Mildred," I said, turning to face her, but she wasn't there. She was leaning against the bar in hysterics, laughing so hard that no sound was coming out, doubled over with her hands resting on her shapely knees. Tears rolled down her cheeks, streaming kohl in their wake as they had yesterday, and my first urge was to throw my fist at her jaw. Instead I put the slug onto

Shelton, and I got him so fast he went down with the first blow to the midriff. Mildred was still laughing, and so was the man in the suit. I gave Shelton a kick to the ribs and another to the belly that knocked the breath clear out of him, and I grabbed my own unfinished drink from the bar. I poured it into his hair and rubbed it in with my hand like scalp tonic.

Everybody was laughing but me and Shelton, and I wanted to, God knows. Gleason stood behind the bar making a valiant effort to keep a straight face, but his eyes shone with joy.

"All right, boy," the man in the suit said. "You've had some fun, now it's time to run along." He was still smiling, but he said it like he meant it.

My honor was restored, and I was happy to go now. "Come on, Mildred," I said.

"Huh-uh. Mildred's not going."

I almost made a smart remark, but Mildred was back on her barstool now, wiping the smeared makeup off her cheeks with a wet bar rag, facing the bar and studiously pretending I wasn't there.

"You with them or with me, Mildred?"

She turned around. "You're a dear sweet boy, Wayne, but tonight's kind of a grown-up night for me, if you don't mind. I'll see you some other time."

"You hear that, Wayne? Now scram."

It was crazy, but at that moment I wanted Mildred more than I had ever wanted any woman before, more than I had ever desired anything in my whole life. I wanted to fuck her, run away with her, marry her, raise a family. I didn't care that she was a lush and a slattern, that she was nearly twenty years older than me, or that she had dropped me for the first prosperous swinging dick that came through the barroom door. I wanted her right then and there, and I took her by the arm.

"Mildred, let's go." I had hoped to keep the pleading tone out of my voice, but I heard it just like everyone else did, high-pitched and boyish.

"Mildred, let's go," the man in the suit mocked in a voice like Mickey Mouse's that deepened to a growl. "Let go of her arm or I'll break yours."

"Screw you, Charlie," I said.

"The name's Stan Gerard, and I own this place." He stood up

and moved toward me, and with no more telegraphing than I'd given Shelton he backhanded me across the face, and then he pulled something metallic out of his pocket and hit me with it, hard, and I closed my eyes for a second. Crazy colors floated before me, and another blow caught me on the ear as I went down. I never quite lost consciousness, but somehow I couldn't open my eyes as they carried me through the bar to the rear and tossed me into the back alley.

"Don't hurt him too bad," I heard my beloved call languidly from her perch at the bar.

I hit the pavement, hard, and Stan Gerard spoke to me in a polite way before he went back inside.

"Can you hear me, Wayne?"

I indicated that I could.

"Like Shelton said, come back when you're twenty-one. I'll even buy you a drink. But not before then, got me?"

I nodded once again, and the door closed. I opened my eyes and looked around. It was getting dark, and I limped around to the side alley and made my way to the street, where my Hudson sat parked a stone's throw from Stan Gerard's Duesenberg.

Idiot, I told myself as I sat there pulling the starter again and again with no result. You've been running all over town, covering twice as much ground as you normally would have, and you didn't stop for gas. With my cheekbone throbbing, I got out and started the humiliating six-block walk to my house and my bicycle.

5. *In Which I Accept My Status, for Now*

I couldn't find my old man's gas can, so I took a milk bottle in a wire basket from the back porch. As I climbed onto my bike with it I had an idea. I went back to the porch and took a second bottle, and then I rode over to the Skelly station on Hillside.

"Ain't putting gas in there, not in a glass bottle." The Skelly man shook his head firmly, letting it stop at the far end of each shake.

"I'll put it in myself."

"Nuh-uh. You take this metal can or nothing. Cost you a nickel extra for deposit, but you can get it back."

Though the evening had cooled considerably, the asphalt beneath our feet still felt warmer than it should have, and the whole station smelled like gas, seeping up through the asphalt and past my nostrils to lodge in the spongy repository of my sinus, where it would slowly leak into my brain for the rest of the night if I didn't get away. I could feel the fumes building up there, thick and nauseating behind my eyes, and I broke.

"Okay, put it in the can," I said.

The Skelly man got up off of his chair and took the can over to the pump. He filled the can and I paid him and rode along the sidewalks back to the Royal Crown. I put the bicycle and the basket with the milk bottles into the rear seat of the Hudson and put some of the gasoline in the tank, and a little slug into the carburator. There was about a quart of it left, and I left it in the can on the seat next to me.

I headed one block east on Douglas and turned left over to First, where I parked in front of a two-story duplex. I got the bike and one of the milk bottles out of the back seat and filled the milk bottle with the can of gas. From the glove compartment I extracted Mildred's purloined drawers, drenching them in the gasoline and stuffing them into the mouth of the bottle. I hopped back onto the bike and rode back to Douglas and, from the safety of a large coniferous shrub outside the Hillcrest apartment building, cased the front of the Royal Crown. The sidewalk was empty, and I pulled out my lighter and went for broke, coasting down the sidewalk with one hand on the handlebars and the other around the bottle. When I got to the Duesenberg, I stopped and propped the bike up on one leg as I flicked the lighter and lit Mildred's gasoline-soaked intimates. They burned bright for a second and in a single action I threw the bottle at the dashboard and kicked the pedals into motion, hearing with no small satisfaction the breaking of the bottle and the whooshing sound of the fire erupting from the interior of the Duesie. I didn't look back, but I could feel the heat at my back, and the sidewalk before me glowed yellow in a way it hadn't a second before.

I tore ass across Douglas against the light. Once safely across, I stopped in the shadowy entryway to a store that sold artificial limbs and settled in to enjoy the show.

The flames were big and bright, eclipsing the streetlights and engulfing the interior of the convertible. From the seat of the bike I watched a disbelieving Stan Gerard race out of the Royal Crown, followed by several others, including Larry Shelton; Mildred straggled out last, a little unsteady on her feet, and had to hold on to the doorframe in order to stay upright. I could hear them shouting, and people started crowding the sidewalk, pouring out of the surrounding buildings and passing cars that had stopped at the sight, all of them keeping a respectful distance from the fire. Finally Gerard, looking scared as hell, ran up to the car to get something out of it. Shelton caught up to him, though, and tackled him and pulled him back, an action that would probably have earned him an asskicking had the Duesie's gas tank not chosen that moment to blow.

The crowd oohed and aahed at the sight of the fireball, of the car's low-slung skeletal frame showing delicately through the flames, and I felt a certain pride of authorship. It was a shame to have to waste such a terrific piece of machinery, but I believed at that moment I had used it to create something even more beautiful, though fleeting. I've read about some odd birds who get a sexual thrill out of watching fires burn, but this wasn't like that; my pleasure was purely aesthetic. This was a spectacle of light and shadow, metal and heat, underwear and gasoline.

It got old quick. When I heard the klaxons of the fire engines hauling it down Hillside I pedaled away on the bicycle, past the businesses across from the Royal Crown and toward College Hill. It felt good to be on the bike after such a long time, and before I returned to the Hudson I rode far out of my way, looking in at the houses and wondering who lived there. It wasn't a neighborhood I'd worked, but I bet there were a dozen women just like Mildred around there, and a hundred boys just like me.

DANIEL STASHOWER

The Adventure of the Agitated Actress

FROM *Murder, My Dear Watson: New Tales of Sherlock Holmes*

"WE'VE ALL HEARD stories of your wonderful methods, Mr. Holmes," said James Larrabee, drawing a cigarette from a silver box on the table. "There have been countless tales of your marvelous insight, your ingenuity in picking up and following clues, and the astonishing manner in which you gain information from the most trifling details. You and I have never met before today, but I dare say that in this brief moment or two you've discovered any number of things about me."

Sherlock Holmes set down the newspaper he had been reading and gazed languidly at the ceiling. "Nothing of consequence, Mr. Larrabee," he said. "I have scarcely more than asked myself why you rushed off and sent a telegram in such a frightened hurry, what possible excuse you could have had for gulping down a tumbler of raw brandy at the Lion's Head on the way back, why your friend with the auburn hair left so suddenly by the terrace window, and what there can possibly be about the safe in the lower part of that desk to cause you such painful anxiety." The detective took up the newspaper and idly turned the pages. "Beyond that," he said, "I know nothing."

"Holmes!" I cried. "This is uncanny! How could you have possibly deduced all of that? We arrived in this room not more than five minutes ago!"

My companion glanced at me with an air of strained abstraction, as though he had never seen me before. For a moment he seemed to hesitate, apparently wavering between competing impulses. Then he rose from his chair and crossed down to a row of blazing footlights. "I'm sorry, Frohman," he called. "This isn't working out as I'd hoped. We really don't need Watson in this scene after all."

"Gillette!" came a shout from the darkened space across the bright line of lights. "I do wish you'd make up your mind! Need I remind you that we open tomorrow night?" We heard a brief clatter of footsteps as Charles Frohman — a short, solidly built gentleman in the casual attire of a country squire — came scrambling up the side access stairs. As he crossed the forward lip of the stage, Frohman brandished a printed handbill. It read: "William Gillette in his Smash Play! Sherlock Holmes! Fresh from a Triumphant New York Run!"

"He throws off the balance of the scene," Gillette was saying. "The situation doesn't call for an admiring Watson." He turned to me. "No offense, my dear Lyndal. You have clearly immersed yourself in the role. That gesture of yours — with your arm at the side — it suggests a man favoring an old wound. Splendid!"

I pressed my lips together and let my hand fall to my side. "Actually, Gillette," I said, "I am endeavoring to keep my trousers from falling down."

"Pardon?"

I opened my jacket and gathered up a fold of loose fabric around my waist. "There hasn't been time for my final costume fitting," I explained.

"I'm afraid I'm having the same difficulty," said Arthur Creeson, who had been engaged to play the villainous James Larrabee. "If I'm not careful, I'll find my trousers down at my ankles."

Gillette gave a heavy sigh. "Quinn!" he called.

Young Henry Quinn, the boy playing the role of Billy, the Baker Street page, appeared from the wings. "Yes, Mr. Gillette?"

"Would you be so good as to fetch the wardrobe mistress? Or at least bring us some extra straight pins?" The boy nodded and darted backstage.

Charles Frohman, whose harried expression and lined forehead told of the rigors of his role as Gillette's producer, folded the handbill and replaced it in his pocket. "I don't see why you feel the need to tinker with the script at this late stage," he insisted. "The play was an enormous success in New York. As far as America is concerned, you *are* Sherlock Holmes. Surely the London audiences will look on the play with equal favor?"

Gillette threw himself down in a chair and reached for his prompt book. "The London audience bears little relation to its American counterpart," he said, flipping rapidly through the pages. "British tastes have been refined over centuries of Shakespeare and Marlowe. America has only lately weaned itself off of *Uncle Tom's Cabin.*"

"Gillette," said Frohman heavily, "you are being ridiculous."

The actor reached for a pen and began scrawling over a page of script. "I am an American actor essaying an English part. I must take every precaution and make every possible refinement before submitting myself to the fine raking fire of the London critics. They will seize on a single false note as an excuse to send us packing." He turned back to Arthur Creeson. "Now, then. Let us continue from the point at which Larrabee is endeavoring to cover his deception. Instead of Watson's expression of incredulity, we shall restore Larrabee's evasions. Do you recall the speech, Creeson?"

The actor nodded.

"Excellent. Let us resume."

I withdrew to the wings as Gillette and Creeson took their places. A mask of impassive self-possession slipped over Gillette's features as he stepped back into the character of Sherlock Holmes. "Why your friend with the auburn hair left so suddenly by the terrace window," he said, picking up the dialogue in midsentence, "and what there can possibly be about the safe in the lower part of that desk to cause you such painful anxiety."

"Ha! Very good!" cried Creeson, taking up his role as the devious James Larrabee. "Very good indeed! If those things were only true, I'd be wonderfully impressed. It would be absolutely marvelous!"

Gillette regarded him with an expression of weary impatience. "It won't do, sir," said he. "I have come to see Miss Alice Faulkner and will not leave until I have done so. I have reason to believe that the young lady is being held against her will. You shall have to give way, sir, or face the consequences."

Creeson's hands flew to his chest. "Against her will? This is outrageous! I will not tolerate —"

A high, trilling scream from backstage interrupted the line. Creeson held his expression and attempted to continue. "I will not tolerate such an accusation in my own —"

A second scream issued from backstage. Gillette gave a heavy sigh and rose from his chair as he reached for the prompt book. "Will that woman never learn her cue?" Shielding his eyes against the glare of the footlights, he stepped again to the lip of the stage and sought out Frohman. "This is what comes of engaging the company locally," he said in an exasperated tone. "We have a mob of players in ill-fitting costumes who don't know their scripts. We should have brought the New York company across, hang the expense." He turned to the wings. "Quinn!"

The young actor stepped forward. "Yes, sir?"

"Will you kindly inform —"

Gillette's instructions were cut short by the sudden appearance of Miss Maude Fenton, the actress playing the role of Alice Faulkner, who rushed from the wings in a state of obvious agitation. Her chestnut hair fell loosely about her shoulders and her velvet shirtwaist was imperfectly buttoned. "Gone!" she cried. "Missing! Taken from me!"

Gillette drummed his fingers across the prompt book. "My dear Miss Fenton," he said, "you have dropped approximately seventeen pages from the script."

"Hang the script!" she wailed. "I'm not playing a role! My brooch is missing! My beautiful, beautiful brooch! Oh, for heaven's sake, Mr. Gillette, someone must have stolen it!"

Selma Kendall, the kindly, auburn-haired actress who had been engaged to play Madge Larrabee, hurried to Miss Fenton's side. "It can't be!" she cried. "He only just gave it — that is to say, you've only just acquired it! Are you certain you haven't simply mislaid it?"

Miss Fenton accepted the linen pocket square I offered and dabbed at her streaming eyes. "I couldn't possibly have mislaid it," she said between sobs. "One doesn't mislay something of that sort! How could such a thing have happened?"

Gillette, who had cast an impatient glance at his pocket watch during this exchange, now stepped forward to take command of the situation. "There, there, Miss Fenton," he said, in the cautious, faltering tone of a man not used to dealing with female emotions. "I'm sure this is all very distressing. As soon as we have completed our run-through, we will conduct a most thorough search of the dressing areas. I'm sure your missing bauble will be discovered presently."

"Gillette!" I cried. "You don't mean to continue with the rehearsal? Can't you see that Miss Fenton is too distraught to carry on?"

"But she must," the actor declared. "As Mr. Frohman has been at pains to remind us, our little play has its London opening tomorrow evening. We shall complete the rehearsal, and then — after I have given a few notes — we shall locate the missing brooch. Miss Fenton is a fine actress, and I have every confidence in her ability to conceal her distress in the interim." He patted the weeping actress on the back of her hand. "Will that do, my dear?"

At this, Miss Fenton's distress appeared to gather momentum by steady degrees. First her lips began to tremble, then her shoulders commenced heaving, and lastly a strange caterwauling sound emerged from behind the handkerchief. After a moment or two of this, she threw herself into Gillette's arms and began sobbing lustily upon his shoulder.

"Gillette," called Frohman, straining to make himself heard above the lamentations, "perhaps it would be best to take a short pause."

Gillette, seemingly unnerved by the wailing figure in his arms, gave a strained assent. "Very well. We shall repair to the dressing area. No doubt the missing object has simply slipped between the cushions of a settee."

With Mr. Frohman in the lead, our small party made its way through the wings and along the backstage corridors to the ladies' dressing area. As we wound past the scenery flats and crated property trunks, I found myself reflecting on how little I knew of the other members of our troupe. Although Gillette's play had been a great success in America, only a handful of actors and crewmen had transferred to the London production. A great many members of the cast and technical staff, myself included, had been engaged locally after a brief open call. Up to this point, the rehearsals and staging had been a rushed affair, allowing for little of the easy camaraderie that usually develops among actors during the rehearsal period.

As a result, I knew little about my fellow players apart from the usual backstage gossip. Miss Fenton, in the role of the young heroine Alice Faulkner, was considered to be a promising ingenue. Reviewers frequently commented on her striking beauty, if not her talent. Selma Kendall, in the role of the conniving Madge Larrabee, had established herself in the provinces as a dependable support player, and was regarded as something of a mother hen by the younger actresses. Arthur Creeson, as the wicked James Larrabee, had been a promising romantic lead in his day, but excessive drink and gambling had marred his looks and scotched his reputation. William Allerford, whose high, domed forehead and startling white hair helped to make him so effective as the nefarious Professor Moriarty, was in fact the most gentle of men, with a great passion for tending the rosebushes at his cottage in Hove. As for myself, I had set out to become an opera singer in my younger days, but my talent had not matched my ambition, and over time I had evolved into a reliable, if unremarkable, second lead.

"Here we are," Frohman was saying as we arrived at the end of a long corridor. "We shall make a thorough search." After knocking on the unmarked door, he led us inside.

As was the custom of the day, the female members of the cast shared a communal dressing area in a narrow, sparsely appointed chamber illuminated by a long row of electrical lights. Along one wall was a long mirror with a row of wooden makeup tables before it. A random cluster of coat racks, reclining sofas, and well-worn armchairs were arrayed along the wall opposite. Needless to say, I had never been in a ladies' dressing room before, and I admit that I felt my cheeks redden at the sight of so many underthings and delicates thrown carelessly over the furniture. I turned to avert my eyes from a cambric corset cover thrown across a ladderback chair, only to find myself gazing upon a startling assortment of hosiery and lace-trimmed drawers laid out upon a nearby ottoman.

"Gracious, Mr. Lyndal," said Miss Kendall, taking a certain delight in my discomfiture. "One would almost think you'd never seen linens before."

"Well, I — perhaps not so many at once," I admitted, gathering my composure. "Dr. Watson is said to have an experience of women which extends over many nations and three separate continents. My own experience, I regret to say, extends no further than Hatton Cross."

Gillette, it appeared, did not share my sense of consternation. No sooner had we entered the dressing area than he began making an energetic and somewhat indiscriminate examination of the premises, darting from one side of the room to the other, opening drawers and tossing aside cushions and pillows with careless abandon.

"Well," he announced, after five minutes' effort, "I cannot find your brooch. However, in the interests of returning to our rehearsals as quickly as possible, I am prepared to buy you a new one."

Miss Fenton stared at the actor with an expression of disbelief. "I'm afraid you don't understand, Mr. Gillette. This was not a common piece of rolled plate and crystalline. It was a large, flawless sapphire in a rose gold setting, with a circle of diamond accents."

Gillette's eyes widened. "Was it, indeed? May I know how you came by such an item?"

A flush spread across Miss Fenton's cheek. "It was — it was a gift from an admirer," she said, glancing away. "I would prefer to say no more."

"Be that as it may," I said, "this is no small matter. We must notify the police at once!"

Gillette pressed his fingers together. "I'm afraid I must agree. This is most inconvenient."

A look of panic flashed across Miss Fenton's eyes. "Please, Mr. Gillette! You must not involve the police! That wouldn't do at all!"

"But your sapphire — ?"

She tugged at the lace trimming of her sleeve. "The gentleman in question — the man who presented me with the brooch — he is of a certain social standing, Mr. Gillette. He — that is to say, I — would prefer to keep the matter private. It would be most embarrassing for him if his — if his attentions to me should become generally known."

Frohman gave a sudden cough. "It is not unknown for young actresses to form attachments with certain of their gentlemen admirers," he said carefully. "Occasionally, however, when these matters become public knowledge, they are attended by a certain whiff of scandal. Especially if the gentleman concerned happens to be married." He glanced at Miss Fenton, who held his gaze for a moment and then looked away. "Indeed," said Frohman. "Well, we can't have those whispers about the production, Gillette. Not before we've even opened."

"Quite so," I ventured, "and there is Miss Fenton's reputation to consider. We must discover what happened to the brooch without involving the authorities. We shall have to mount a private investigation."

All eyes turned to Gillette as a mood of keen expectation fell across the room. The actor did not appear to notice. Having caught sight of himself in the long mirror behind the dressing tables, he was making a meticulous adjustment to his waistcoat. At length, he became aware that the rest of us were staring intently at him.

"What?" he said, turning away from the mirror. "Why is everyone looking at me?"

"I am *not* Sherlock Holmes," Gillette said several moments later, as we settled ourselves in a pair of armchairs. "I am an actor *playing* Sherlock Holmes. There is a very considerable difference. If I did a turn as a pantomime horse, Lyndal, I trust you would not expect me to pull a dray wagon and dine on straw?"

"But you've studied Sherlock Holmes," I insisted. "You've examined his methods and turned them to your own purposes. Surely you might be able to do the same in this instance? Surely the author of such a fine detective play is not totally lacking in the powers of perception?"

Gillette gave me an appraising look. "Appealing to my vanity, Lyndal? Very shrewd."

We had been arguing back and forth in this vein for some moments, though by this time — detective or no — Gillette had reluctantly agreed to give his attention to the matter of the missing brooch. Frohman had made him see that an extended disruption would place their financial interests in the hazard, and that Gillette, as head of the company, was the logical choice to take command of the situation. Toward that end, it was arranged that Gillette would question each member of the company individually, beginning with myself.

Gillette's stage manager, catching wind of the situation, thought it would be a jolly lark to replace the standing set of James Larrabee's drawing room with the lodgings of Sherlock Holmes at Baker Street, so that Gillette might have an appropriate setting in which to carry out his investigation. If Gillette noticed, he gave no sign. Stretching his arm toward a side table, he took up an outsize calabash pipe and began filling the meerschaum bowl.

"Why do you insist on smoking that ungainly thing?" I asked. "There's no record whatsoever of Sherlock Holmes having ever touched a calabash. Dr. Watson tells us that he favors an oily black clay pipe as the companion of his deepest meditations, but is wont to replace it with his cherrywood when in a disputatious frame of mind."

Gillette shook his head sadly. "I am *not* Sherlock Holmes," he said again. "I am an actor *playing* Sherlock Holmes."

"Still," I insisted, "it does no harm to be as faithful to the original as possible."

Gillette touched a flame to the tobacco and took several long draws to be certain the bowl was properly ignited. For a moment, his eyes were unfocused and dreamy, and I could not be certain that he had heard me. His eyes were fixed upon the fly curtains when he spoke again. "Lyndal," he said, "turn and face downstage."

"What?"

"Humor me. Face downstage."

I rose and looked out across the forward edge of the stage.

"What do you see?" Gillette asked.

"Empty seats," I said.

"Precisely. It is my ambition to fill those seats. Now, cast your eyes to the rear of the house. I want you to look at the left-hand aisle seat in the very last row."

I stepped forward and narrowed my eyes. "Yes," I said. "What of it?"

"Can you read the number plate upon that seat?"

"No," I said. "Of course not."

"Nor can I. By the same token, the man or woman seated there will not be able to appreciate the difference between a cherrywood pipe and an oily black clay. This is theater, Lyndal. A real detective does not do his work before an audience. I do. Therefore I am obliged to make my movements, speech, and stage properties readily discernible." He held the calabash aloft. "This pipe will be visible from the back row, my friend. An actor must consider even the smallest object from every possible angle. That is the essence of theater."

I considered the point. "I merely thought, inasmuch as you are attempting to inhabit the role of Sherlock Holmes, that you should wish to strive for authenticity."

Gillette seemed to consider the point. "Well," he said, "let us see how far that takes us. Tell me, Lyndal. Where were you when the robbery occurred?"

"Me? But surely you don't think that I —"

"You are not the estimable Dr. Watson, my friend. You are merely an actor, like myself. Since Miss Fenton had her brooch with her when she arrived at the theater this morning, we must assume that the theft occurred shortly after first call. Can you account for your movements in that time?"

"Of course I can. You know perfectly well where I was. I was standing stage right, beside you, running through the first act."

"So you were. Strange, my revision of the play has given you a perfect alibi. Had the theft occurred this afternoon, after I had restored the original text of the play, you should have been high on the list of suspects. A narrow escape, my friend." He smiled and sent up a cloud of pipe smoke. "Since we have established your innocence, however, I wonder if I might trouble you to remain through the rest of the interviews?"

"Whatever for?"

"Perhaps I am striving for authenticity." He turned and spotted young Henry Quinn hovering in his accustomed spot in the wings near the scenery cleats. "Quinn!" he called.

The boy stepped forward. "Yes, sir?"

"Would you ask Miss Fenton if she would be so good as to join us?"

"Right away, sir."

I watched as the boy disappeared down the long corridor. "Gillette," I said, lowering my voice, "this Baker Street set is quite comfortable in its way, but do you not think a bit of privacy might be indicated? Holmes is accustomed to conducting his interviews in confidence. Anyone might hear what passes between us here at the center of the stage."

Gillette smiled. "I am *not* Sherlock Holmes," he repeated.

After a moment or two Quinn stepped from the wings with Miss Fenton trailing behind him. Miss Fenton's eyes and nose were red with weeping, and she was attended by Miss Kendall, who hovered protectively by her side. "May I remain, Mr. Gillette?" asked the older actress. "Miss Fenton is terribly upset by all of this."

"Of course," said Gillette in a soothing manner. "I shall try to dispense with the questioning as quickly as possible. Please be seated." He folded his hands and leaned forward in his chair. "Tell me, Miss Fenton, are you quite certain that the brooch was in your possession when you arrived at the theater this morning?"

"Of course," the actress replied. "I had no intention of letting it out of my sight. I placed the pin in my jewelry case as I changed into costume."

"And the jewelry case was on top of your dressing table?"

"Yes."

"In plain sight?"

"Yes, but I saw no harm in that. I was alone at the time. Besides, Miss Kendall is the only other woman in the company, and I trust her as I would my own sister." She reached across and took the older woman's hand.

"No doubt," said Gillette, "but do you mean to say that you intended to leave the gem in the dressing room during the rehearsal? Forgive me, but that seems a bit careless."

"That was not my intention at all, Mr. Gillette. Once in costume, I planned to pin the brooch to my stockings. I should like to have worn it in plain view, but James — that is to say, the gentleman who gave it to me — would not have approved. He does not want anyone — he does not approve of ostentation."

"In any case," I said, "Alice Faulkner would hardly be likely to own such a splendid jewel."

"Yes," said Miss Fenton. "Just so."

Gillette steepled his fingers. "How exactly did the jewel come to be stolen? It appears that it never left your sight."

"It was unforgivable of me," said Miss Fenton. "I arrived late to the theater this morning. In my haste, I overturned an entire pot of facial powder. I favor a particular type, Gervaise Graham's Satinette, and I wished to see if I could persuade someone to step out and purchase a fresh supply for me. I can only have been gone for a moment. I stepped into the hallway looking for one of the stagehands, but of course they were all in their places in anticipation of the scene three set change. When I found no one close by, I realized that I had better finish getting ready as best I could without the powder."

"So you returned to the dressing area?"

"Yes."

"How long would you say that you were out of the room?"

"Two or three minutes. No more."

"And when you returned the brooch was gone?"

She nodded. "That was when I screamed."

"Indeed." Gillette stood and clasped his hands behind his back.

"Extraordinary," he said, pacing a short line before a scenery flat decorated to resemble a bookcase. "Miss Kendall?"

"Yes?"

"Has anything been stolen from you?" he asked.

"No," she answered. "Well, not this time."

Gillette raised an eyebrow. "Not this time?"

The actress hesitated. "I'm sure it's nothing," she said. "From time to time I have noticed that one or two small things have gone astray. Nothing of any value. A small mirror, perhaps, or a copper or two."

Miss Fenton nodded. "I've noticed that as well. I assumed that I'd simply misplaced the items. It was never anything to trouble over."

Gillette frowned. "Miss Fenton, a moment ago, when the theft became known, it was clear that Miss Kendall was already aware that you had the brooch in your possession. May I ask who else among the company knew of the sapphire?"

"No one," the actress said. "I only received the gift yesterday, but I would have been unlikely to flash it about, in any case. I couldn't resist showing it to Selma, however."

"No one else knew of it?"

"No one."

Gillette turned to Miss Kendall. "Did you mention it to anyone?"

"Certainly not, Mr. Gillette."

The actor resumed his pacing. "You're quite certain? It may have been a perfectly innocent remark."

"Maude asked me not to say anything to anyone," said Miss Kendall. "We women are rather good with secrets."

Gillette's mouth pulled up slightly at the corners. "So I gather, Miss Kendall. So I gather." He turned and studied the false book spines on the painted scenery flat. "Thank you for your time, ladies."

I watched as the two actresses departed. "Gillette," I said after a moment, "if Miss Kendall did not mention the sapphire to anyone, who else could have known that it existed?"

"No one," he answered.

"Are you suggesting —" I leaned forward and lowered my voice. "Are you suggesting that Miss Kendall is the thief? After all, if she was the only one who knew —"

"No, Lyndal. I do not believe Miss Kendall is the thief."

"Still," I said, "there is little reason to suppose that she kept her own counsel. A theatrical company is a hotbed of gossip and petty jealousies." I paused as a new thought struck me. "Miss Fenton seems most concerned with protecting the identify of her gentleman admirer, although this will not be possible if the police have to be summoned. Perhaps the theft was orchestrated to expose him." I considered the possibility for a moment. "Yes, perhaps the intended victim is really this unknown patron, whomever he might be. He is undoubtedly a man of great wealth and position. Who knows? Perhaps this sinister plot extends all the way to the —"

"I think not," said Gillette.

"No?"

"If the intention was nothing more than to expose a dalliance between a young actress and a man of position, one need not have resorted to theft. A word in the ear of certain society matrons would have the same effect, and far more swiftly." He threw himself back down in his chair. "No, I believe that this was a crime of opportunity, rather than design. Miss Kendall and Miss Fenton both reported having noticed one or two small things missing from their dressing area on previous occasions. It seems that we have a petty thief in our midst, and that this person happened across the sapphire during those few moments when it was left unattended in the dressing room."

"But who could it be? Most of us were either onstage or working behind the scenes, in plain view of at least one other person at all times."

"So it would seem, but I'm not entirely convinced that someone couldn't have slipped away for a moment or two without being noticed. The crew members are forever darting in and out. It would not have drawn any particular notice if one of them had slipped away for a moment or two."

"Then we shall have to question the suspects," I said. "We must expose this nefarious blackguard at once."

Gillette regarded me over the bowl of his pipe. "Boucicault?" he asked.

"Pardon?"

"That line you just quoted. I thought I recognized it from one of Mr. Boucicault's melodramas."

I flushed. "No," I said. "It was my own."

"Was it? How remarkably vivid." He turned to young Henry Quinn, who was awaiting his instructions in the wings. "Quinn," he called, "might I trouble you to run and fetch Mr. Allerford? I have a question or two I would like to put to him."

"Allerford," I said, as the boy disappeared into the wings. "So your suspicions have fallen upon the infamous Professor Moriarty, have they? There's a bit of Holmes in you, after all."

"Scarcely," said Gillette with a weary sigh. "I am proceeding in alphabetical order."

"Ah."

Young Quinn returned a moment later to conduct Allerford into our presence. The actor wore a long black frock coat for his impersonation of the evil professor, and his white hair was pomaded into a billowing cloud, exaggerating the size of his head and suggesting the heat of the character's mental processes.

"Do sit down, Allerford," Gillette said, as the actor stepped onto the stage, "and allow me to apologize for subjecting you to this interview. It pains me to suggest that you may in any way have —"

The actor held up his hands to break off the apologies. "No need, Gillette. I would do the same in your position. I presume you will wish to know where I was while the rest of you were running through the first act?"

Gillette nodded. "If you would be so kind."

"I'm afraid the answer is far from satisfactory. I was in the gentlemen's dressing area."

"Alone?"

"I'm afraid so. All the others were onstage or in the costume shop for their fittings." He gathered up a handful of loose fabric from his waistcoat. "My fitting was delayed until this afternoon. So I imagine I would have to be counted as the principal suspect, Gillette." He allowed his features to shift and harden as he assumed the character of Professor Moriarty. "You'll never hang this on me, Mr. Sherlock Holmes," he hissed, as his head oscillated in a reptilian fashion. "I have an ironclad alibi! I was alone in my dressing room reading a magazine!" The actor broke character and held up his palms in a gesture of futility. "I'm afraid I can't offer you anything better, Gillette."

"I'm sure nothing more will be required, Allerford. Again, let me apologize for this intrusion."

"Not at all."

"One more thing," Gillette said, as Allerford rose to take his leave.

"Yes?"

"The magazine you were reading. It wasn't *The Strand,* by any chance?"

"Why, yes. There was a copy lying about on the table."

"A Sherlock Holmes adventure, was it?"

Allerford's expression turned sheepish. "My tastes don't run in that direction, I'm afraid. There was an article on the sugar planters of the Yucatán. Quite intriguing, if I may say."

"I see." Gillette began refilling the bowl of his pipe. "Much obliged, Allerford."

"Gillette!" I said in an urgent whisper, as Allerford retreated into the wings. "What was that all about? Were you trying to catch him out?"

"What? No, I was just curious." The actor's expression grew unfocused as he touched a match to the tobacco. "Very curious." He sat quietly for some moments, sending clouds of smoke up into the fly curtains.

"Gillette," I said after a few moments, "shouldn't we continue? I believe Mr. Creeson is next."

"Creeson?"

"Yes. If we are to proceed alphabetically."

"Very good. Creeson. By all means. Quinn! Ask Mr. Creeson to join us, if you would."

With that, Gillette sank into his chair and remained there, scarcely moving, for the better part of two hours as a parade of actors, actresses, and stagehands passed before him. His questions and attitude were much the same as they had been with Allerford, but clearly his attention had wandered to some distant and inaccessible plateau. At times he appeared so preoccupied that I had to prod him to continue with the interviews. At one stage he drew his legs up to his chest and encircled them with his arms, looking for all the world like Sidney Paget's illustration of Sherlock Holmes in the grip of one of his three-pipe problems. Unlike the great detective, however, Gillette soon gave way to meditations of a different sort. By the time the last of our interviews was completed, a contented snoring could be heard from the actor's armchair.

"Gillette," I said, shaking him by the shoulder. "I believe we've spoken to everyone now."

"Have we? Very good." He rose from the chair and stretched his long limbs. "Is Mr. Frohman anywhere about?"

"Right here, Gillette," the producer called from the first row of seats. "I must say this appears to have been a colossal waste of time. I don't see how we can avoid going to the police now."

"I'm afraid I have to agree," I said. "We are no closer to resolving the matter than we were this morning." I glanced at Gillette, who was staring blankly into the footlights. "Gillette? Are you listening?"

"I think we may be able to keep the authorities out of the matter," he answered. "Frohman? Might I trouble you to assemble the company?"

"Whatever for?" I asked. "You've already spoken to — Say! You don't mean to say that you know who stole Miss Fenton's brooch?"

"I didn't say that."

"But then why should you — ?"

He turned and held a finger to his lips. "I'm afraid you'll have to wait for the final act."

The actor would say nothing more as the members of the cast and crew appeared from their various places and arrayed themselves in the first two rows of seats. Gillette, standing at the lip of the stage, looked over them with an expression of keen interest. "My friends," he said after a moment, "you have all been very patient during this unpleasantness. I appreciate your indulgence. I'm sure that Sherlock Holmes would have gotten to the bottom of the matter in just a few moments, but as I am not Sherlock Holmes, it has taken me rather longer."

"Mr. Gillette!" cried Miss Fenton. "Do you mean to say you've found my brooch?"

"No, dear lady," he said, "I haven't. But I trust that it will be back in your possession shortly."

"Gillette," said Frohman, "this is all very irregular. Where is the stone? Who is the thief?"

"The identity of the thief has been apparent from the beginning," Gillette said placidly. "What I did not understand was the motivation."

"But that's nonsense!" cried Arthur Creeson. "The sapphire is extraordinarily valuable! What other motivation could there be?"

"I can think of several," Gillette answered, "and our 'nefarious blackguard,' to borrow a colorful phrase, might have succumbed to any one of them."

"You're talking in circles, Gillette," said Frohman. "If you've known the identity of the thief from the first, why didn't you just say so?"

"I was anxious to resolve the matter quietly," the actor answered. "Now, sadly, that is no longer possible." Gillette stretched his long arms. Moving upstage, he took up his pipe and slowly filled the bowl with tobacco from a ragged Persian slipper. "It was my hope," he said, "that the villain would come to regret these actions — the rash decision of an instant — and make amends. If the sapphire had simply been replaced on Miss Fenton's dressing table, I should have put the incident behind and carried on as though I had never discerned the guilty party's identity. Now, distasteful as it may be, the villain must be unmasked, and I must lose a member of my company on the eve of our London opening. Regrettable, but it can't be helped."

The members of the company shifted uneasily in their seats. "It's one of us, then?" asked Mr. Allerford.

"Of course. That much should have been obvious to all of you." He struck a match and ran it over the bowl of his pipe, lingering rather longer than necessary over the process. "The tragedy of the matter is that none of this would have happened if Miss Fenton had not stepped from her dressing room and left the stone unattended."

The actress's hands flew to her throat. "But I told you, I had spilled a pot of facial powder."

"Precisely so. Gervaise Graham's Satinette. A very distinctive shade. And so the catalyst of the crime now becomes the instrument of its solution."

"How do you mean, Gillette?" I asked.

Gillette moved off to stand before the fireplace — or rather the canvas and wood strutting that had been arranged to resemble a fireplace. The actor spent a moment contemplating the plaster coals that rested upon a balsa grating. "Detective work," he intoned, "is founded upon the observation of trifles. When Miss Fenton overturned that facial powder, she set in motion a chain of events that yielded a clue — a clue as transparent as that of a weaver's tooth or a compositor's thumb — and one that made it patently obvious who took the missing stone."

"Gillette!" cried Mr. Frohman. "No more theatrics! Who took Miss Fenton's sapphire?"

"The thief is here among us," he declared, his voice rising to a vibrant timbre. "And the traces of Satinette facial powder are clearly visible upon — Wait! Stop him!"

All at once, the theater erupted into pandemonium as young Henry Quinn, who had been watching from his accustomed place in the wings, suddenly darted forward and raced toward the rear exit.

"Stop him!" Gillette called to a pair of burly stagehands. "Hendricks! O'Donnell! Don't let him pass!"

The fleeing boy veered away from the stagehands, upsetting a flimsy side table in his flight, and made headlong for the forward edge of the stage. Gathering speed, he attempted to vault over the orchestra pit, and would very likely have cleared the chasm but for the fact that his ill-fitting trousers suddenly slipped to his ankles, entangling his legs and causing him to land in an awkward heap at the base of the pit.

"He's out cold, Mr. Gillette," came a voice from the pit. "Nasty bruise on his head."

"Very good, Hendricks. If you would be so good as to carry him into the lobby, we shall decide what to do with him later."

Miss Fenton pressed a linen handkerchief to her face as the unconscious figure was carried past. "I don't understand, Mr. Gillette. Henry took my sapphire? He's just a boy! I can't believe he would do such a thing!"

"Strange to say, I believe Quinn's intentions were relatively benign," said Gillette. "He presumed, when he came across the stone on your dressing table, that it was nothing more than a piece of costume jewelry. It was only later, after the alarm had been raised, that he realized its value. At that point, he became frightened and could not think of a means to return it without confessing his guilt."

"But what would a boy do with such a valuable stone?" Frohman asked.

"I have no idea," said Gillette. "Indeed, I do not believe that he had any interest whatsoever in the sapphire."

"No interest?" I said. "What other reason could he have had for taking it?"

"For the pin."

"What?"

Gillette gave a rueful smile. "You are all wearing costumes that are several sizes too large. Our rehearsals have been slowed for want of sewing pins to hold up the men's trousers and pin back the ladies' frocks. I myself dispatched Quinn to find a fastener for Mr. Lyndal."

"The essence of theater," I said, shaking my head with wonder.

"Pardon me, Lyndal?"

"As you were saying earlier. An actor must consider even the smallest object from every possible angle. We all assumed that the brooch had been taken for its valuable stone. Only you would have thought to consider it from the back as well as the front." I paused. "Well done, Gillette."

The actor gave a slight bow as the company burst into spontaneous applause. "That is most kind," he said, "but now, ladies and gentlemen, if there are no further distractions, I should like to continue with our rehearsal. Act one, scene four, I believe. . ."

It was several hours later when I knocked at the door to Gillette's dressing room. He bade me enter and made me welcome with a glass of excellent port. We settled ourselves on a pair of makeup stools and sat for a few moments in a companionable silence.

"I understand that Miss Fenton has elected not to pursue the matter of Quinn's theft with the authorities," I said after a time.

"I thought not," Gillette said. "I doubt if her gentleman friend would appreciate seeing the matter aired in the press. However, we will not be able to keep young Quinn with the company. He has been dismissed. Frohman has been in touch with another young man I once considered for the role. Charles Chapman."

"Chaplin, I believe."

"That's it. I'm sure he'll pick it up soon enough."

"No doubt."

I took a sip of port. "Gillette," I said, "there is something about the affair that troubles me."

He smiled and reached for a pipe. "I thought there might be," he said.

"You claimed to have spotted Quinn's guilt by the traces of face powder on his costume."

"Indeed."

I lifted my arm. "There are traces of Miss Fenton's powder here on my sleeve as well. No doubt I acquired them when I was searching for the missing stone in the dressing area — after the theft had been discovered."

"No doubt," said Gillette.

"The others undoubtedly picked up traces of powder as well."

"That is likely."

"So Quinn himself might well have acquired his telltale dusting of powder *after* the theft had occurred, in which case it would not have been incriminating at all."

Gillette regarded me with keen amusement. "Perhaps I noticed the powder on Quinn's sleeve before we searched the dressing area," he offered.

"Did you?"

He sighed. "No."

"Then you were bluffing? That fine speech about the observation of trifles was nothing more than vain posturing?"

"It lured a confession out of Quinn, my friend, so it was not entirely in vain."

"But you had no idea who the guilty party was! Not until the moment he lost his nerve and ran!"

Gillette leaned back and sent a series of billowy smoke rings toward the ceiling. "That is so," he admitted, "but then, as I have been at some pains to remind you, I am *not* Sherlock Holmes."

HANNAH TINTI

Home Sweet Home

FROM *Epoch*

PAT AND CLYDE were murdered on pot roast night. The doorbell rang just as Pat was setting the butter and margarine (Clyde was watching his cholesterol) on the table. She was thinking about James Dean. She had loved him desperately as a teenager, seen his movies dozens of times, written his name across her notebooks, carefully taped pictures of him to the inside of her locker so that she would have the pleasure of seeing his tortured, sullen face from *East of Eden* as she exchanged her French and English textbooks for science and math. When she graduated from high school she took down the photos and pasted them to the inside cover of her year-book, which she perused longingly several times over the summer and brought with her to the University of Massachusetts, where it sat, unopened, alongside her thesaurus and abridged collegiate dictionary until she met Clyde, received her M.R.S. degree, and packed her things to move into their two-bedroom ranch house on Bridge Street.

Before she put the meat in the oven that afternoon, Pat had made herself a cup of tea and turned on the television. Channel 38 was showing *Rebel Without a Cause,* and as the light slowly began to rise through the screen of their old Zenith she saw James Dean on the steps of the planetarium, clutching at the mismatched socks of a dead Sal Mineo and crying. She put down her tea, slid her warm fingertips inside the V-neck of her dress, and held her left breast. Her heart was suddenly pounding, her nipple hard and erect against the palm of her hand. It was like seeing an old lover, like remembering a piece of herself that no longer existed. She watched the credits roll and glanced outside to see her husband mowing the lawn. He had a worried expression on his face and his socks pulled up to his knees.

That evening before dinner, as she arranged the butter and margarine side by side on the table — one yellow airy and light, the other yellow hard and dark like the yolk of an egg — she wondered how she could have forgotten the way James Dean's eyebrows curved. *Isn't memory a strange thing,* she thought. *I could forget all of this, how everything feels, what all of these things mean to me.* She was suddenly seized with the desire to grab the sticks of butter and margarine in her hands and squeeze them until her fingers went right through, to somehow imprint their textures and colors on her brain like a stamp, to make them something that she would never lose. And then she heard the bell.

When she opened the door Pat noticed that it was still daylight. The sky was blue and bright and clear and she had a fleeting, guilty thought that she should not have spent so much time indoors. After that she crumpled backwards into the hall as the bullet from a .38-caliber Saturday Night Special pierced her chest, exited below her shoulder blade, and jammed into the wood of the stairs, where it would later be dug out with a penknife by Lieutenant Sales and dropped gingerly into a transparent plastic Baggie.

Pat's husband Clyde was found in the kitchen by the back door, a knife in his hand (first considered a defense against his attacker and later determined as the carver of the roast). He had been shot twice — once in the stomach and once in the head — and then covered with cereal, the boxes lined up on the counter beside him and the crispy golden contents of Captain Crunch, Corn Flakes, and Special K emptied out over what remained of his face.

Nothing had been stolen.

It was a warm spring evening, full of summer promises. Pat and Clyde's bodies lay silent and still while the orange sunset crossed the floors of their house and the streetlights clicked on. As darkness came, and the skunks waddled through the backyard and the raccoons crawled down from the trees, they were still there, holding their places, suspended in a moment of quiet blue before the sun came up and a new day started and life went on without them.

It was Clyde's mother who called the police. She dialed her son's number every Sunday morning from Rhode Island. These phone calls always somehow perfectly coincided with whenever Pat and Clyde had just settled down to breakfast, or whenever they were on the verge of making love.

Thar she blows, Clyde would say, and take his hot coffee with him over to where the phone hung on the wall, or slide out of bed with an apologetic glance at his wife. The coffee and Pat would inevitably cool, and in this way his mother would ruin every Sunday. It had been years now since they frolicked in the morning, but once, when they were first married and Pat was preparing breakfast, she had heard the phone, walked over to where her husband was reading the paper, dropped to her knees, pulled open his robe, and taken him in her mouth. *Let it ring,* she thought, and he had let it ring. Fifteen minutes later the police were on their front porch with smiles as Clyde, red-faced, bathrobe bulging, answered their questions at the door.

In most areas of her life Clyde's mother was a very nice person. She behaved in such a kind and decorous manner that people would often remark, having met her, *What a lovely woman.* But with Clyde she lost her head. She was suspicious, accusing, and tyrannical. Her husband had died suddenly a few years back, and once she got through her grief her son became her man. She pushed this sense of responsibility through him like fishhooks, plucking on the line, reeling him back in when she felt her hold slipping, so that the points became embedded in his flesh so deep that it would kill him to take them out.

She dialed the police after trying her son thirty-two times, and because the lieutenant on duty was a soft touch, his own mother having recently passed, a cruiser was dispatched to Pat and Clyde's on Bridge Street, and because one of the policemen was looking to buy in the neighborhood, the officers decided to check out the back of the house after they got no answer, and because there was cereal blowing around in the yard the men got suspicious, and because it was a windy day and because the hinges had recently been oiled and because the door had been left unlocked and swung open and because one of them had seen a dead body before, a suicide up in Hanover, and knew blood and brain and bits of skull when he saw them, he made the call back to the station, because his partner was quietly vomiting in the rosebushes, and said, *We've got trouble.*

*

Earlier that morning, as Little Mike Findleman delivered Pat and Clyde's *Sunday Globe*, the comics straining around the sections like wrapping on an inappropriate gift, he noticed that the welcome mat was gone. It had been ordered out of an expensive catalog and said, *Home Sweet Home*. Every day when Little Mike rode up on his bicycle and delivered the paper, he looked at the mat and thought of his own home. It was not sweet.

Little Mike's father had recently returned from a minimum-security prison, where he had spent the past three years doing time for embezzlement. With her husband back in the house, Little Mike's mother, a charismatic redhead, was now on antidepressants, and had cooked spaghetti for dinner twenty-eight days in a row. To top it off, Little Mike had not made the cut to junior league baseball, as his friends Norman and Greg Kessler had, and the shame he felt when he checked the list posted outside the gym and later as he told the twins, who squinted into the sun and shrugged their shoulders together as if they were brushing him off their lives like a bug, struck him deeply and confirmed his suspicions of his own lack of greatness. Little Mike enjoyed getting off of his bicycle and kicking Pat and Clyde's welcome mat as he dropped off their paper just after dawn, leaving it askew and glancing back at it as he walked down the front porch steps. It made him feel less alone.

Each morning he would return and find the welcome mat back in place. He wondered sometimes if they complained about their delivery, but Pat and Clyde never said anything, and when the money was due for the paper they left a check in an envelope taped above the doorbell, usually with a few extra bucks for a tip. So when he walked up the porch steps and found the door shut tight and no *Home Sweet Home*, Little Mike paused. Later, when he was interviewed by Lieutenant Sales, he would say that he had sensed that something was wrong. But in that moment, standing on the porch in the smoky light of early morning, he felt angry and cheated, as if this small pleasure of kicking the mat had been plugging up a large and gaping hole inside of him, and now that it was gone he saw through it to all the other empty places in his life. Little Mike threw the *Sunday Globe* off the porch into the bushes with a vengeance, where it would later be found by Buster, the Mitchells' Labrador retriever, and buried in another part of the yard along with some abandoned Kentucky Fried Chicken rummaged from the local barrels. Little Mike did not tell the police that he had done this. He claimed that he had left the paper on the front porch as always. He did not want anyone to think he was a bad delivery boy.

Buster was the kind of dog who knew how to feel at home. He treated all the yards on Bridge Street as if they were his own, making his way leisurely through flower beds, pausing for a drink from a sprinkler, tearing into garbage bags and relieving himself among patches of newly planted rutabagas. When he discovered Pat and Clyde's *Sunday Globe* caught in the low branches of a rhododendron it was after eight. Mrs. Mitchell had let him out that morning with an affectionate pat on his behind. *Don't get into too much trouble,* she said. He had left her with his nose to the ground.

The Kentucky Fried Chicken was a gift. Half a bucket of wings and drumsticks left in an open trash can by a teenager on his way home after a night of near misses. The dog fell upon it like a drunk on whiskey, without remorse or pause or reason, with no more than the sense of *get this in me now.* Be he also caught a whiff of melancholy left on the bucket from the teenager's hands, and the smell told the dog to save some bones for a time when he was not so lucky.

Buster was already digging a hole in Pat and Clyde's yard when he noticed a small golden flake on the grass. It was food, and he followed the promise of more across the lawn, through the back door, and over to Clyde, stiff and covered with flies, the remaining cereal a soggy wet pile of pink plaster across his shoulders. The rug underneath the kitchen table was soaked in blood. Buster left red paw prints as he walked around the body and sniffed at the slippers on the dead man's feet.

The dog smelled fear in the sweat of Clyde's last moment. It had curled in the arch of his foot as he listened to his wife answer their front door. The bell rang just as he pierced the roast with the carving fork, releasing two streams of juice, which ran down the sides of the meat until they were captured by the raised edge of the serving plate. He paused then, as he lifted the knife, waiting to hear and recognize the voices of his wife and whoever had come to their house. When he heard nothing, an uneasiness tightened at the base of his stomach. Their home contained his life, and he realized, suddenly, that he could not imagine something that could not be greeted by name, could not easily become a part of everything they had inside: their potholders in the shape of barnyard animals; the creak in the third stair; the way their bedroom door stuck in the summer heat. When the shot exploded, he felt it all at once and everywhere — in the walls, in his eyes, in his chest, in his arms, in the utensils he was holding, in the piece of meat he was carving, in the slippers that placed him on the floor, in the kitchen, before their evening meal.

Buster pulled off one of the slippers and sank his teeth into it. It was rank, worn, and sour-tasting, cutting the sweetness of the Captain Crunch. He worked on removing the stuffing of the inner sole and kept his eye on the dead man who used to shoo-shoo him away from garbage bags, from munching the daffodils that lined the walk, from humping strays behind the garage. Once, after catching the dog relieving himself in the middle of the driveway, Clyde had dragged him by the collar all the way down Bridge Street. *Listen to me, pooch,* Mr. Mitchell had said after Clyde had left, one hand smoothing where the collar had choked and the other hand vigorously scratching the dog's behind. *You shit wherever you feel like shitting.*

On his way out of the yard Buster found the *Sunday Globe* that Little Mike Findleman had tossed. It held the same scent he'd picked up over the body — anger, fear, and disconnectedness — things that cried out to be buried. He dragged the paper over to the hole he'd already started and threw it in with the slipper and the leftover chicken. The earth had a way of settling things. The dog walked back and forth over the spot once it was filled, then lifted his leg to mark it. He shook some dirt out of his ear and used four paws to take himself home.

The Mitchells had moved into the neighborhood five years before. They brought their dog with them. Three years later, a son arrived — not a newborn baby decked out in bonnets but a thin, dark boy of indiscriminate age. His name was Miguel, and it was unclear to the people living on Bridge Street whether he was adopted or a child from a previous marriage. He called the Mitchells his mother and father, enrolled in the public school for the district, and quietly became a part of their everyday lives.

In fact, Miguel was the true son of Mr. Mitchell, sired unknowingly on a business trip with a Venezuelan prostitute some seven years before. The mother had been killed in a bus accident along with fifty-three other travelers on a road outside Caracas, and the local police had contacted Mr. Mitchell from a faded company card she had left pressed in her Bible. After a paternity test, the boy arrived at Logan airport with a worn-out blanket and duffel bag full of chickens (his pets), which were quickly confiscated by customs officials. Mr. Mitchell drove down Route 128 in his station wagon, amazed and panicked at his sudden parenthood, trying to comfort the sobbing boy and wondering how Miguel had managed to keep the birds quiet on the plane.

When they pulled into the driveway, Mrs. Mitchell was waiting with a glass of warm milk sweetened with sugar. She was wearing dungarees. She took the boy in her arms and carried him immediately into the bathroom, where she sat him on the counter and washed his face, his hands, his knees, and his feet. Miguel sipped the milk while Mrs. Mitchell gently ran the washcloth between his toes. When she was finished, she tucked him into their guest bed and read him a stack of *Curious George* books in Spanish, which she had ordered from their local bookstore. She showed Miguel a picture of the little monkey in the hospital getting a shot from a nurse and the boy fell asleep, a finger hooked around the belt loop of her jeans. Mrs. Mitchell sat on the bed beside him quietly until he rolled over and let it go.

Mr. Mitchell had met his wife in Northern California. They pulled up beside each other at a gas station. He had just completed his business degree, and was driving a rented car up the coast to see the Olympic rain forest. She was in a pickup truck with Oregon plates. They both got out and started pumping. Mr. Mitchell finished first, and on his way back to his car after paying, he watched the muscles in her thick arm flexing as she replaced the hose. She glanced up, caught him looking, and smiled. She was not beautiful, but one of her teeth stuck out charmingly sideways. He started the car, turned out of the station, and glanced into his rearview mirror. He watched the pickup take the opposite road, and as it drove away he felt such a pulling that he turned around and followed it for 150 miles.

At the rest stop, he pretended that he was surprised to see her. Later he discovered that many people followed his wife, and that she was used to this, and that it did not seem strange to her. People she had never met came up and began to speak to her in supermarkets, in elevators, in the waiting rooms of doctors, at traffic lights, at concerts, at coffee shops and bistros. Even their dog, a stray she fed while camping in Tennessee, came scratching outside their door six weeks later. Mr. Mitchell was jealous and frightened by these strangers, and often used himself as a shield between them and his wife. *What do they want from her?* he often found himself thinking. But he also felt, *What will they take from me?*

His wife was a quiet woman, in the way that large rocks just beyond the shore are quiet; the waves rush against them and the seaweed hangs on and the birds gather round on top. Mr. Mitchell was amazed that she had married him. He spent the first few years doing what he could to please her and watched for signs that she was leaving.

Sometimes she got depressed and locked herself in the bathroom. It made him furious and desperate. When she came out, tender and pink from washing, she would put her arms around him and tell him that he was a good man. Mr. Mitchell was not sure of this, because sometimes he found himself hating her. The door was in front of him but the knob wouldn't turn. He wanted her to know what it felt like to be powerless. He found himself taking risks.

When he got the call from Venezuela telling him about Miguel, he was terrified that he might lose his wife and also secretly happy to have wounded her. But all of the control he felt as they prepared for his son's arrival slipped away as he watched her take the strange dark boy into her arms and tenderly wash his feet. He realized then that she was capable of taking everything from him.

The three of them formed an awkward family. Mr. Mitchell tried to place the boy in a home but his wife would not let him. She did this to punish him. He had now been an accidental father for two years. He took the boy to baseball games and bought him comic books and drove him to school in the mornings. Sometimes Mr. Mitchell enjoyed these things, other times they made him angry. One day he walked in on Miguel talking to his wife in Spanish and the boy immediately stopped. He realized then that his son was afraid of him. He was sure his wife had done this too. Mr. Mitchell began to resent what had initially drawn him to her, and to offset these feelings he began an affair with their neighbor, Pat.

It did not begin innocently. Mr. Mitchell walked over to Pat one afternoon as she was planting bulbs in her garden and slid his hand into the elastic waistband of her Bermuda shorts. He leaned her up against the fence, underneath a birch tree, right there in the middle of a bright, spring day where everyone could see. He didn't say anything, but he could tell by her breath and the way she rocked on his hand that she wasn't afraid.

He hadn't known that it was in him to do anything like this. He had never been attracted to Pat; he had never had any conversation with her that went beyond the weather or the scheduling of trash. He had been on his way to the library to return some books. Look, there they were, thrown aside on the grass, wrapped in plastic smeared with age and the fingers of readers who were unknown to him. And here was another person he did not know, panting in his ear, streaking his arms with dirt. Someone he had seen bent over in the sunlight, a slight glistening of sweat reflecting in the backs of her knees, and for which he had suddenly felt a hard sense of lonesomeness and longing. A new kind of warmth spread in the palm of his hand and he tried not to think about his wife.

They had hard, raw sex in public places — movie theaters and parks, elevators and playgrounds. After dark, underneath the jungle gym, his knees pressing into the dirt, Mr. Mitchell began to wonder why they hadn't been caught. Once, sitting on a bench near the reservoir, Pat straddling him in a skirt with no underwear, they had actually waved to an elderly couple passing by. The couple continued on as if they hadn't seen them. Who knows, maybe they were half-blind, but the experience left the impression that his meetings with Pat were occurring in some kind of alternative reality, a bubble in time that he knew would eventually pop.

Pat told him that Clyde had been impotent for years — a reaction, it seemed, from witnessing his father's death. The man had been a mechanic, and was working underneath a bulldozer when the lift slipped, crushing him from the chest down. The father and the son had held hands, and the coldness that came as life left seemed to spread through Clyde's fingers and into his arms, and he stopped using them to reach for his wife. Since the funeral she'd had two lovers. Mr. Mitchell was number three.

There were rumors, later on, that the lift had been tampered with — that Clyde's father had owed someone money. Pat denied it, but Mr. Mitchell remembered driving by the garage and sensing he'd rather buy his gas somewhere else.

Mr. Mitchell's desire increased with the risk of discovery, and he'd started arranging meetings with Pat that were closer to home. In his house he fantasized about the dining room table, the dryer in the laundry room, the space on the kitchen counter beside the mixer. He touched these places with his fingertips and trembled, thinking of how he would feel later, watching his wife sip her soup, fold sheets, mix batter for cookies in the same places.

On the day Pat was murdered, before she put the roast in the oven or reminisced about James Dean or thought about the difference between butter and margarine, she was having sex in the vestibule. The coiled rope of Home Sweet Home scratched her behind and dug into Mr. Mitchell's knees. He had seen Clyde leave for a bowling lesson, and as he waited on the front porch for Pat to open the door, something had made him pick up the welcome mat. When she answered he'd thrown it down in the hall, then her, then himself, the soles of his shoes knocking over the entry table.

Mrs. Mitchell would soon be home with Miguel. Mr. Mitchell brought Pat's knees to his shoulders and listened for the choking hum of his wife's Reliant.

The following day when Lieutenant Sales climbed the stairs of Pat and Clyde's porch he did not notice that there was nothing to wipe his feet on. He was an average-looking man: six feet two inches, 190 pounds, brown hair, brown eyes, brown skin. He had once been a champion deep-sea diver, until a shark attack (which left him with a hole in his side crossed with the pink, puckered scars of new skin) pulled him from the waters with a sense of righteous authority and induced him to join the force. He lived thirty-five minutes away in a basement apartment with a Siamese cat named Frank.

When Sales was a boy, he'd had a teacher who smelled like roses. Her name was Mrs. Bosco. She showed him how to blow eggs. Forcing the yolk out of the tiny hole always felt a little disgusting, like blowing a heavy wad of snot from his nose, but when he looked up at Mrs. Bosco's cheeks, flushed red with effort, he knew it would be worth it, and it was — the empty shell in his hand like a held breath, like the moment before something important happens. Whenever he began an investigation he'd get the same sensation, and as he stepped into the doorway of Pat and Clyde's house he felt it rise in his chest and stay.

He interviewed the police who found the bodies first. They were sheepish about their reasons for going into the backyard, but before long they began loudly discussing drywall and sheetrock and the pros and cons of lanceted windows (all of the men, including Lieutenant Sales, carried weekend and part-time jobs in construction). The policeman who had thrown up in the roses had gone home early. When Sales spoke to him later, he apologized for contaminating the scene.

Lieutenant Sales found the roast on the counter. He found green beans still on the stove. He found a sour cherry pie in the oven. He found the butter and the margarine, softened tubes of yellow, half melted on the dining room table. He found that Pat and Clyde used cloth napkins and tiny separate plates for their dinner rolls. The silverware was polished. The edges of the steak knives turned in.

He found their unpaid bills in a basket by the telephone. He found clean laundry inside the dryer in the basement — towels, sheets, T-shirts, socks, three sets of Fruit of the Loom, and one pair of soft pink satin panties, the elastic starting to give, the bottom frayed and thin. He found an unfinished letter Pat had started writing to a friend who had recently moved to Arizona: *What is it like there? How can you stand the heat?* He found Clyde's stamp albums from when he was a boy — tiny spots of brilliant color, etchings of flowers and portraits of kings, painstakingly pasted over the names of countries Lieutenant Sales had never heard of.

He found the bullet that had passed through Pat's body embedded in the stairs. He found a run in her stocking, starting at the heel and inching its way up the back of her leg. He thought about how Pat had been walking around the day she was going to die, not realizing that there was a hole in her pantyhose. He found a stain, dark and blooming beneath her shoulders, spreading across the oriental rug in the foyer and into the hardwood floors, which he noticed, as he got down on his knees for a closer look, still held the scent of Murphy's Oil. He found a hairpin caught in the fringe. He found a cluster of dandelion seeds, the tiny white filaments coming apart in his fingers. He found a look on Pat's face like a child trying to be brave, lips tightened and thin, forehead just beginning to crease, eyes glazed, dark, and unconvinced. Her body was stiff when they moved her.

There were dog tracks on the back porch. They were the prints of a midsized animal, red and clearly defined as they circled the body in the kitchen, then crisscrossing over themselves and heading out the door, fading down the steps and onto the driveway before disappearing into the yard. Lieutenant Sales sent a man to knock on doors in the neighborhood and find out who let their dogs off the leash. He interviewed the paperboy and Clyde's mother. He went back to the station and checked Pat and Clyde's records — both clean. When he finally went to sleep that night, the small warmth of his cat tucked up behind his knees, Lieutenant Sales thought about the feel of satin panties, missing slippers, stolen welcome mats, dandelion seeds from a yard with no dandelions, and the kind of killer who shuts off the oven.

A month before Pat and Clyde were murdered, Mrs. Mitchell was fixing the toilet. Her husband passed by on his way to the kitchen, paused in the doorway, shook his head, and told her that she was too good for him. The heavy porcelain top was off; her arms elbow deep in rusty water. The man she had married was standing at the entrance to the bathroom and he was speaking to her, but she was not thinking about him, and so she did not respond. She was concentrating on the particular tone in the pipes she was trying to clear. It was this same ability to turn her attention into focus, like a lighthouse whose spinning had unexpectedly stopped, that made people follow her.

Mr. Mitchell went into the kitchen and began popping popcorn. The kernels cracked against the insides of the kettle as his words settled into her, and when, with a twist of the coat hanger in her hand beneath the water, she stopped the ringing of the pipes, Mrs. Mitchell sensed in the quiet that came next that her husband had done something wrong. She had known in this same way before he told her about Miguel. A breeze came through the window and made the hair on her wet arms rise. She pulled her hands from the toilet and thought to herself, *I fixed it.*

When Miguel came into their home, she had taken all the sorrow she felt at his existence and turned it into a fierce motherly love. Mrs. Mitchell thought her husband would be grateful; instead he seemed to hold it against her. He became dodgy and spiteful. Her mind was full of failings, but all she understood was that her husband was having difficulty loving her, because it seemed as if she didn't make mistakes. It was the closest she ever came to leaving; but she hadn't expected the boy.

Miguel spent the first three months of his life in America asking to go home. When the fourth month came he began to sleepwalk. In the dark he wandered downstairs to the kitchen, emptied the garbage can onto the floor, and curled up inside. The next morning Mrs. Mitchell would find him asleep, shoulders in the barrel, feet in the coffee grounds and leftovers. He told her he was looking for his mother's head. She had been decapitated in the bus accident, and now she stepped from the corners of Miguel's dreams at night and beckoned him with her arms, tiny chicks resting on her shoulders, pecking at the empty neck.

Mrs. Mitchell suggested that they make her a new one. She brought materials for papier-maché. The strips of newspaper felt like bandages as she helped Miguel dip them in glue and smooth them over the surface of the inflated balloon. They fashioned a nose and lips out of cardboard. Once it was dry, Miguel described his mother's face and they painted the skin brown, added yarn for hair, cut eyelashes out of construction paper. Mrs. Mitchell took a pair of gold earrings, poked them through where they'd drawn the ears, and said, heart sinking, *She's beautiful.* Miguel nodded. He smiled. He put his mother's head on top of the bookcase in his room and stopped sleeping in the garbage.

Sometimes when Mrs. Mitchell checked on the boy at night she'd feel the head looking at her. It was unnerving. She imagined her husband making love to the papier-maché face and discovered a hate so strong and hard it made her afraid of herself. She considered swiping the head and destroying it, but she remembered how skinny and pitiful the boy's legs had looked against her kitchen floor. Then Miguel began to love her. She suddenly felt capable of anything. She thumbed her nose at the face in the corner. She held her heart open.

Mrs. Mitchell was raised by two of her aunts in a house near the Columbia River. Her mother had her when she was sixteen, then died a few years later of a botched abortion. Mrs. Mitchell kept a picture of her mother next to the mirror in her room, and whenever she checked her reflection, her eyes would naturally turn from her own face to that of the woman who gave birth to her. The photo was black and white and creased near the edges; she was fifteen, her hair in braids, the end of one strand stuck between her lips. It made Mrs. Mitchell think of stories she'd heard of women who spent their lives spinning — years of passing flax through their mouths to make thread would leave them disfigured, lower lips drooping off their faces; a permanent look of being beaten.

The aunts who raised her were expert marksmen. They built a shooting range on an area of property behind the house. As a child, it was Mrs. Mitchell's job to set up the targets and fetch them iced tea and ammo. She kept a glass jar full of shells in the back of her closet, shiny gold casings from her aunts' collection of .22-calibers and .45s. They made a shooting station out of an old shed, two tables set up with sandbags to hold the guns, nestling the shape of heavy metal as the pieces were placed down.

When she was twelve years old the aunts gave her a rifle. She already knew the shooting stances, and she practiced them with her new gun every day after school. She could hit a target while kneeling, crouching, lying down, and standing tall, hips parallel to the barrel and her waist turned, the same way the aunts taught her to pose when a picture was being taken to look thin. She picked off tin cans and old metal signs and polka-dotted the paper outlines of men.

Mrs. Mitchell remembered this when she pulled into her driveway, glanced over the fence, and saw her husband having sex in the doorway of their neighbor's house. She turned to Miguel in the passenger seat and told him to close his eyes. The boy covered his face with his hands and sat quietly while she got out of the car. Mrs. Mitchell watched her husband moving back and forth and felt her feet give way from the ground. She had the sensation of being caught in a river, the current pulling her body outwards, tugging at her ankles, and she wondered why she wasn't being swept away until she realized that she was holding on to the fence. The wood felt smooth and worn, like the handle of her first gun, and she used it to pull herself back down.

Later she thought of the look on Pat's face. It reminded Mrs. Mitchell of the Tin Woodman from *The Wizard of Oz* — disarmingly lovely and greasy with expectation. In the book she bought for Miguel she'd read that the Woodman had once been real, but his ax kept slipping and he'd dismembered himself, slowly exchanging his flesh piece by piece for hollow metal. Mrs. Mitchell thought Pat's body would rattle with the same kind of emptiness, but it didn't; it fell with the heavy tone of meat. As she waited for the echo Mrs. Mitchell heard a small cough from the kitchen, the kind a person does in polite society to remind someone else that they are there. She followed it and found Clyde in his slippers, the knife in the roast.

Hello, she said. *I just shot your wife.* The beans were boiling; the water frothing over the sides of the pan and sizzling into the low flame beneath. Mrs. Mitchell would not let the dinner be ruined. She turned off the oven and spun all the burners to zero.

The aunts never married. They still lived in the house where they raised their niece. Occasionally they sent her photographs, recipes, information on the NRA, or obituaries of people she had known clipped from the local newspaper. When a reporter called Mrs. Mitchell asking questions about Pat and Clyde, she thought back to all the notices her aunts had sent over the years, and said: *They were good neighbors and wonderful people. I don't know who would have done something like this. They will be greatly missed.* The truth was that she felt very little at their loss. It was hard to forgive herself for this, so she didn't try.

She waited patiently through the following day and night for someone to come for her. On Monday morning she woke up and let the dog out. She made a sandwich for Miguel and fit it in his lunchbox beside a thermos of milk. She poured juice into a glass and cereal into a bowl. Then she locked herself in the bathroom and watched her hands shake. She remembered that she had wanted to cover Clyde with something. Falling out of the box, the cereal had sounded crisp and new like water on rocks, but it quickly turned into a soggy mess that stayed with her as she left him, stepped over Pat, and picked up the welcome mat with her gloves. She could still see her husband moving back and forth on top of it. She wanted to make Home Sweet Home disappear, but the longest she could bring herself to touch it was the end of the driveway, and she left it in a garbage can on the street.

She found that she could not say good-bye. Not when her husband pounded on the door to take a shower and not when Miguel asked if he could brush his teeth. She sat on the toilet and listened to them move about the house and leave. Later, she watched a policeman wrap her neighbor's house in yellow tape. To double it around a tree in the yard he circled the trunk with his arms. It was a brief embrace and she thought, *That tree felt nothing.*

In the afternoon, when the sun began to slant through the western windows, Lieutenant Sales crossed the Mitchells' front yard. He was carrying a chewed-up slipper in a bag, jostling the dandelions and sending seeds of white fluff adrift. Mrs. Mitchell saw him coming. She turned the key in the lock, and once she was beyond the bathroom she ran her fingers through her hair, smoothing down the rough spots. The bell rang. The dog barked. She opened the door, and offered him coffee.

Miguel turned nine years old that summer. In the past two years he'd spent with the Mitchells the boy had grown no more than an inch, but with the warm weather that June he'd suddenly sprouted — his legs stretching like brown sugar taffy tight over his new knobby bones, as if the genes of his American father had been lying dormant, biding their time until the right combination of spring breezes and processed food kissed them awake. He began to trip over himself. On his way home from baseball practice that Monday, he caught one of his newly distended feet on a trash can, just outside the line of yellow police tape that closed in Pat and Clyde's yard. Miguel fell to the sidewalk, smacking his hands against the concrete. The barrel toppled over beside him and out came a welcome mat. Home Sweet Home.

Miguel was not the best student, but he had made friends easily once he hit several home runs in gym class. Norman and Greg Kessler, the most popular kids in school, chose him for their team and for their friend, replacing Little Mike Findleman, who had never been that good in the first place. Norman and Greg helped him with English, defended him against would-be attackers, and told him they had seen his father naked.

The boys claimed they had looked down from the window of their mother's minivan and seen Mr. Mitchell drive past, stripped bare from the waist down. There was a woman in the car with him and she was leaning over the gearshift. *It's true,* said the twins. Miguel made them swear on the Bible, on a stack of Red Sox cards, and finally on their grandfather's grave, which they did, bikes thrown aside in the grass and sweaty hands pressed on the polished marble of his years. At dinner that night the boy watched his father eating. The angle of his jaw clenched and turned.

Miguel felt a memory push past hot dogs, past English, past Hostess cupcakes and his collection of Spiderman comic books. He was five years old and asked his mother where his father was. She was making coffee — squeezing the grounds through a sieve made out of cloth and wire. He'd collected eggs from their chickens for breakfast. He was holding them in his hands and they were still warm. His mother took one from him. *This is the world and we are here,* she said, and pointed to the bottom half of the egg. *Your father is there.* She ran her finger up along the edge and tapped the point with a dark red nail. Then she cracked the yolk in a pan and threw the rest of the egg in the garbage. He retrieved it later and pushed his fingertips back and forth across the slippery inner membrane until the shell came apart into pieces.

Miguel picked up the doormat and shook it to get the dust off. It seemed like something Mrs. Mitchell might be fond of. That morning he had kept watch through the bathroom keyhole. She was out of sight, but he caught the scent of her worry. He knew she needed something.

In Caracas he had gone through the trash regularly, looking for things to play with and at times for something to eat. Ever since he heard about his father being naked on the highway, he had been remembering more about his life there, and even reverting to some of his old habits; as if the non sequitur of his father's nudity had tenderly shaken him awake. He lay in bed at night and looked into the eyes of the papier-maché head for guidance. He had two lives now, two countries, and two mothers. Soon he would find another life without his father, and another, when he went away to college, and another life, and another, and another, and another; each of them thin, fragile casings echoing the hum of what had gone before.

The boy walked into the kitchen and found his American mother sitting with a strange man. They both held steaming mugs of coffee. Buster was under the table, waking from his afternoon nap. He saw Miguel and thumped his tail halfheartedly against the floor. The adults turned. *Now what have you got there?*

Lieutenant Sales took Home Sweet Home in his hands. He felt it was what he had been looking for. The twisted pink skin where the shark had bitten him began to itch. It had been tingling all afternoon. He hadn't had sensation there for years — the buildup of scar tissue had left him numb — but there was something in the look of the boy and the feel of the rope that held possibility, and excitement rose like fear within him, alongside the memory of closing teeth. Later, in the lab, the welcome mat would reveal tiny spots of Pat's blood, dog saliva, gunpowder, dead ants, mud, fertilizer, and footprints — but not the impression of Mr. Mitchell's knees, or the hesitation of his lonely wife on the doorstep, or the hunger of his son in the garbage. All of this had been shaken off.

Lieutenant Sales would leave the Mitchells' house that afternoon with the same thrill he'd had when the shark passed and he realized his leg was still there. He was exhilarated and then exhausted, as though his life had been drained, and he knew then that he had gone as far as he could go. Home Sweet Home would lead him back to the beginning of a murder he could not solve. There would be no scar, just the sense that he missed something, and the familiar taste of things not done. For now, he reached out with a kind of hope and accepted the welcome mat as a gift.

Mrs. Mitchell put her arm around Miguel's shoulders and waited for Lieutenant Sales to arrest her. She would continue to wait in the weeks ahead, as suspects were raised and then dismissed and headlines changed and funerals were planned. The possibilities of these moments passed over her like shadows. When they were gone she was left standing chilled.

Clyde's mother arranged for closed caskets. In the pew Mrs. Mitchell sat quietly. Her husband cracked knuckles beside her. He was thinking about the way Clyde's father died — his chest pressed hard into the nothing of concrete. Mr. Mitchell was sure whoever rigged the lift had killed Pat and her husband. He worried that he could be next. He thought, *Who would hold my hand?* He reached for his wife and her fingers were cold.

When Mr. Mitchell first learned what had happened to his lover he had opened his closet and started to pack. His family listened to suitcases being dragged down from the attic, the swing of hangers, zipper teeth, the straps of leather buckles. Things from their home began to go missing. They reappeared when Lieutenant Sales came by. They disappeared again after the funerals. Then Mr. Mitchell said he was leaving, and his wife felt her throat clutch. She wanted to ask him where he would go; she wanted to ask him what she had done this for; she wanted to ask him why he no longer loved her but instead she asked for his son.

She had watched Miguel hand the welcome mat to the detective, and as it passed by her she felt an ache in the back of her mouth, as though she hadn't eaten for days. Lieutenant Sales turned Home Sweet Home over in his hands. He placed it carefully on the kitchen table and Mrs. Mitchell saw the word *Sweet*. She remembered the milk she had made for the boy when he arrived, and sensed that this would not be the end of her. She could hear the steady breathing of her sleeping dog. She could smell the coffee. She felt the small frame of Miguel steady beneath her hand. These bones, she thought, were everything. *Hey sport,* Mrs. Mitchell asked. *Is that for me?* The boy nodded, and she held him close.

SCOTT WOLVEN

Controlled Burn

FROM *Harpur Palate*

IT WAS a bad winter and a worse spring. It was the summer Bill Allen lived and died, the sweltering summer I landed a job cutting trees for Robert Wilson's scab-logging outfit near Orford, New Hampshire. June boiled itself away into the heavy steam of July. Heat devils rose in waves off the blacktop as timber trucks rolled in. By the end of July, we switched gears and started cutting stove wood. I was cutting eight cords a day while Robert worked the hydraulic splitter. Then we'd deliver it in one of our dump trucks. Some men drove to the woodlot to pick up their own. Some of them had white salt marks on their boots and jackets from sweat — some of them smelled like beer. Most of them smelled like gasoline. They didn't say much, just paid for their wood and left with it in their pickup trucks. They were either busy working or busy living their lies, which is work in itself. I knew about that. The hard work crushed one empty beer can day after another, adding to my lifetime pile of empties. Summer moved on, gray in spite of the bright sun.

That Friday, I was Bill Allen. I was Bill Allen all that summer. Bill Allen was what caused me to jump every time the phone rang. I was Bill Allen from Glens Falls, New York, and I was taking a summer off from college. I repeated that story as often and as loudly as possible. And each ring of the phone might be someone asking me to prove I was Bill Allen, which was out of the question. Back in December, in the middle of another, different lie, I tried to rob a gas station near Cape May, New Jersey. It was off-season then, nobody around, and I thought it would be easy. It fit the person I'd lied about being. A high school girl was behind the counter. I wore a ski mask and carried a cheap, semiautomatic pistol. I must have touched the trigger, because the gun went off. Maybe she lived. I really couldn't say. I left fast. My brain was on fire, I hadn't meant to shoot her. But it was too late for that. I took a roll of bills and ended up at Robert's. Robert paid cash at the end of the week, didn't bother with Uncle Sam, didn't ask for references, and had plenty of backbreaking work that needed doing, without his son around to help him. Bill Allen was just the man for the job, and every day I was Bill Allen to the best of my ability. It didn't help — my grim yesterdays cast the longest shadows in the Connecticut River Valley. I watched every car, studied every face. Bill Allen never knew a peaceful day. If it hadn't been for the marathon workload Robert demanded, Bill Allen never would have slept. I'd have probably shot Bill Allen myself if I hadn't been working so hard to keep him going. Some days, he lives on with different names. Allen Williams, Al Wilson, Bill Roberts. Bill Allen probably died in a fire that summer. Leave it at that, with questions about Bill Allen.

The phone at the woodlot rang around noon that Friday. I heard it, had been hearing it most of August. Robert's son John was in jail in Concord, awaiting trial for murderous assault, so there were a lot of phone calls. Robert had rigged the phone with two speakers — one bolted to the stovepipe that stuck out of the roof of our headquarters shack and the other attached by some baling wire to the sick elm on the end of the lot. The sudden scream of the phone spiked my heart rate at least twice a day. Echoing in the alleys between the giant piles of long logs. The woodlot sat surrounded by low, field-grass hills and trees in a natural bowl, just off the highway north of Hanover. Robert's house was on the top of the hill, built with its back to the woodlot, facing a farm field. On a still day, the beauty of the Connecticut River drifted the quarter mile over the farm field and quietly framed all the other sounds, the birds, the trees in the breeze. I was never a part of those days.

The phone rang over the diesel roar of my yellow Maxi-lift, the near-dead cherry picker we kept around to police up the yard. I was working, sweating in the sun, busy shifting a full twelve-ton load of New Hampshire rock maple to the very back of the drying mountains of timber, heat against next year's winter. The phone rang again, not that anyone wanted to talk to me. Most times I'd shut the equipment down, run across the yard, slam into the shed, pick up, and get "Robert there?" and they'd hang up when I said no. Or they wouldn't say anything, just hang up when they knew I wasn't Robert. And I could breathe again, because it wasn't someone looking for me. Just locals, as if I couldn't take a wood order. Or it would be the mechanical jail operator, would I please accept a collect call from inmate John Wilson at the Merrimack Correctional Facility. Then I'd say yes and have to go get Robert anyway. Nobody wanted to talk to me, and I didn't want to talk to anyone, so I let it ring. Robert would get it. Or he wouldn't. They know where to find me, he'd say. Working in the same place for thirty years, if they can't find me, what the hell would I want to talk to them for, he'd say. Must be stupid if they can't get hold of me. Robert's voice was a ton of gravel coming off a truck, years of cigarettes mucking up the inside of his barrel chest. There was no sign at the dirt road entrance to the woodlot. It was Robert Wilson's woodlot, and everyone knew without asking.

Robert came out of the shed and waved at me to shut the cherry picker down. I flipped a switch, turned the keys back a click, and cranked the brake on. I walked over to the shed. Robert had his jean coveralls on. He squinted against the sun, nodded, and spoke.

"That was Frank Lord. He wants his wood tomorrow." Robert took twenty-five dollars out of his pocket and handed it to me. That was our deal — fifty dollars if I had to work on Saturday, twenty-five up front. "You can fix his load today."

I nodded. "What does he get?"

"Two cord, plus half a cord of kiln-dried."

Robert had converted an old singlewide trailer into a kiln and most of his customers ordered mixed loads of both air- and kiln-dried. Kiln-dried wood burns hotter than air-dried. Mixing a kiln-dried log in with every fire produces more heat, allows the air-dried wood to burn more efficiently. People with woodstoves got as much heat out of two air-dried cords mixed with half a cord of kiln-dried as people who burned four straight cords. When a single woodstove is the primary heat source for a whole house, each log has to do its job. Robert charged more for the kiln-dried and nobody kicked about the price.

I took my Texaco ball cap off. "If you don't want it mixed, we'll have to take two trucks." Lord's farm was thirty-five miles north and slightly west, just on the Vermont side of the Connecticut River, near Newbury. The river came straight down through the Northeast Kingdom, and just past Wells River, it made an oxbow, flowing briefly north in a U-shaped collar before returning to its southern course. Lord's farm encompassed all of the oxbow, stretching from Route 5 all the way east to the river, which was the Vermont–New Hampshire border. It was the most beautiful spot on earth, the most amazing fields and woods and sky that Bill Allen had ever seen. Robert and I had driven past once that summer, on the way to Wells River to pick up a chain saw. Looking out of the truck as we drove up Route 5 and seeing Lord's white farm buildings and fields, I thought maybe I could make it through Bill Allen and still have a life, somewhere. On the way back, the view of the green fields sweeping out into the bend of the river made everything stop. I didn't hear the engine of the truck, nor the gears. We floated along the road as my mind took picture after picture, of the farm and the fields and the blue sky with the sun setting. That bend in the river. I came alive for a minute, and as the farm slowly passed by I died again, back into the zombie lie of Bill Allen.

Robert was talking to me, shaking his head. "He's got some extra work. Stobe can drive the small rig."

Stobik lived south of the woodlot, in White River Junction, and did odd jobs for Robert. Stobik's wife was as big as the house they lived in. He didn't have a phone — if Robert needed him for something, I'd drive down first thing in the morning and pick him up. Just pulled my beat-up Bronco into his dooryard and sat there till he came out. Sometimes, a thin, white hand would appear in the dirty window, waving me away. Too drunk to work. He lived in a culvert on the woodlot for about a month when things got tough with his wife. He was skinny as a rail, hadn't showered in about a week, month, year. His teeth were broken brown stumps and his fingers were stained from tobacco. But he could cut and stack firewood faster than two men, and at half the price.

"I'll pick him up in the morning," I said.

"That's okay. I'll get him tonight and let him sleep on the porch," Robert said. "I want to make sure he can work tomorrow." He walked back inside the shed. I fixed Frank Lord's load of wood for the next day and went to the loft of a barn I called home.

*

Next morning, I was at the woodlot at five-thirty. It was pitch black. Robert was already there, sitting in his pickup truck, drinking coffee and eating a hard-boiled egg. He had the running lights on. I drove slowly over to the open driver's side window.

"Thought you overslept," he said.

I climbed out of the Bronco and got into the big white rig. Stobik got behind the wheel of the small one. Robert was driving the big rig.

The floor of the white rig was taken up with logging chains. The last job Robert had used it for was a semicommercial haul, and he'd left the chains in. He had a whole barn full of them up by his house. He'd load them in the truck and then get weighed, toss them out at the job and then leave them there. The customer paid the difference. How many people paid for those chains, only God knows. The fuse box was open on the passenger's side, so that any metal that jumped up during the ride could cause a spark or worse. It made for a tense ride.

We started the drive up to North Haverhill on the New Hampshire side of the Connecticut River. It was beautiful. The sun began to shine. The truck could only make thirty-five fully loaded. Stobik was always right behind us, with the flashers on. Robert wrestled the gears up a hill. Then he lit a cigarette and spoke.

"When I was fifteen, I ran away and ended up on Frank Lord's farm." He looked over at me.

"I didn't know that," I answered.

"Frank Lord worked me so hard I thought I was going to drop. But it straightened me out. Best thing that ever happened to me."

"What was wrong with you?" I asked.

"Bad temper," Robert answered. "Bad temper and drinking." We passed a broken-down barn.

"At fifteen?"

Robert nodded. "Back then, fifteen was like thirty-five. You had a job, a car — they made you live life back then, and if you didn't like it, get the fuck out." He took a drag off his cigarette. He was silent, smoking, for the rest of the ride.

Frank Lord was standing in his driveway as we pulled up. He looked as though we'd just been there yesterday. He had an oxygen mask on and a green tank marked OXYGEN in white letters standing next to him. The fields stretched out behind him all the way to the river. The big white farmhouse behind him needed a coat of paint. There were a couple of barns and buildings. They needed paint too. Parked alongside the main house was a brand-new pickup truck. On top of the main house was a black wrought iron weather vane, the silhouette of a big black stallion. The weather vane pointed north.

"What are you going to do, make something out of yourself or what?" His voice was muffled behind the clear plastic mask. His breath made it fill with mist. He pointed over toward the nearest barn. "Put it over there," he said through the mask. "Don't mix it together." He and Robert walked slowly toward the main house and sat on the porch in kitchen chairs. Stobik and I unloaded and stacked the wood. Stobik worked fast. His stacks were the straightest I've ever seen. His face seemed frozen in a perpetual grin as we worked in silence. The stacks came out perfectly. We went back over to Robert and Frank on the porch. It was just around noon.

"We've got some other work to do," Frank said. He held out a piece of paper.

"What's that?" I asked.

"Yesterday, in the morning, Judge Harris stopped over here. Unofficially. I've known his family for probably, oh, fifty years." The breeze tossed the tops of the corn. "He told me that the State Police got a tip I was growing marijuana. They were trying to get a warrant to search my house and my fields." He held out the paper. "Harris dropped this off." I read the paper. It was a one-day special permit for a controlled burn.

"What do you want us to do?" I asked.

"Burn it, all of it. Right back to the river. I don't want a single thing left alive." He stared at the porch and then looked straight at Stobik and me. "Just in case there's a little Mexican hay that got mixed in with my corn somehow."

Robert came down off the porch to supervise. He and I rigged up a sprayer with some gas and soaked a good portion of the front field. We left a wide strip in the middle completely dry. Then we drove the tractor through a thin line of trees, and there was a huge cornfield that stretched all the way to the river. In the middle of the field, probably six hundred yards away, was a small white shack. Robert spoke up.

"That's where my first wife and I lived." He looked at it.

I looked over at him. "I never think about you being married."

He nodded. "Well I was, for a while." He pointed his chin at the shack. "People that live in places like that don't very often stay married." He stared at the white shack. "I had a bad temper then."

I nodded. "Should we burn it?"

"Oh yeah." Robert wiped his forehead with a red kerchief. Sweat had run down from his forehead and got into his eyes and on his chin.

"What if there are people in it?" I looked over at the shack.

"Then fuck 'em, let 'em burn. Their name isn't Lord and they don't belong on this property." Robert spit into the field. "Frank said burn it, and that's what we're going to do." He looked across the rows of corn toward the river. "Hotter than Hades." He looked over at me. "You'll never be cold again, after this." He started to drive the tractor toward the white shack with me on the back of his seat. "Here, watch this," he shouted over the tractor.

We pulled up next to the shack. The windows on the one side had been broken, but the chicken wire in the glass remained, rusted from the weather. I heard a faint hum.

"Watch this," Robert said. He took the nozzle from the gas sprayer and aimed a fine stream at the window. I saw some wasps beginning to fly out of the broken window. Robert pointed his chin at them and talked above the noise of the tractor. "Wasps," he said. "They're the worst." Some moved slowly, clinging to the chicken wire. I could see their insect heads, sectioned bodies, and stingers. They were getting soaked with gas. "Throw a match," Robert said.

"No," I said. "It'll explode." I pointed at the sprayer and the tank of gas on the tractor.

"Gas doesn't burn," Robert said. "It's wet — nothing that's wet can burn. It's the fumes that burn." He took a wood match out of his pocket and struck it on the tractor, then tossed the small flame into the gas spray.

The air groaned and came alive with fire. The wasps were flying full-bore out of the broken window now, right into the wall of flame and through it. Their wings were on fire, still beating, the air currents lifting them up in the heat even as they burned to nothing. A flaming wasp landed on my work shirt and I smacked it into the corn. Now they were all over, burning and flying. Stinging anything they touched. One lost a wing and kept flying, a coin-sized flaming circle into the corn. I watched one come out of the window whole, coated shiny with gas. It flew over the corn, its wings caught fire and kept beating as the body burned to a cinder, the wings still going until they vanished in tiny ash. Robert smacked some wasps off his arm and backed the tractor up, driving over to the river.

We soaked the corn next to the river and then sprayed it a little thinner up on the bank. "The fire will seek the gas," Robert said. "That patch we left in the middle will burn slower than the rest. We'll be all set."

We decided that the best way to do it would be to have Stobik drive the truck around to the New Hampshire side of the ox-bow. Then I'd light the fire from the riverbank too, so that the onrushing flames wouldn't somehow jump the river. Robert drove the tractor back through the field, leaving me standing right on the bend in the river with a box of matches. I could barely see the white shack over the corn. The river ran behind me, softly laughing its way over the rocks. Everything was still, and my heart almost stopped panting for the first time in a long time. Bill Allen stood on the riverbank and knew he needed to die. He knew he had to go back to the place he was born and answer for the crime that fathered him. I heard the airhorn blow from the big rig, Robert's signal to me that he was clear of the fields. As I lit the corn on fire, Bill Allen decided to throw himself into the blaze.

The flames grew fast, and I jumped out into the Connecticut River. It must have been cool, but I didn't feel it. The heat from the fire seemed to reach across the oxbow and right through the water. I climbed up on the bank on the other side just in time to see Robert's white wedding shack take the flames full force. The walls and roof caught like they were made of rice paper, and in the next instant the shack was gone. The fire was so hot, so intense, I couldn't look at it. I walked farther up on the bank and Stobik was there with the small truck. I got in and we started to drive back toward Vermont. A black cloud grew in the air of the beautiful blue horizon and we watched it for miles. It seemed as if we'd permanently smudged the sky.

When we got back to Lord's farm, Robert was busy fending off several local volunteer fire companies, who had arrived with sirens and lights going. He just kept showing them the permit Judge Harris had given to Frank. Stobik and I stayed in the small truck. At one point, I swear the flames in the field were higher than the farmhouse. Stobik backed the truck up so the windshield wouldn't crack. I finally got out and sat alone in the passenger's side of the big rig. I fell asleep. It was late that night when Robert climbed in to drive and slammed his door, bringing me straight up in my seat. The fields were still burning and all I could smell was smoke. We drove slowly back to the woodlot and I slept there in my Bronco. The next day — Sunday — I was going to drive all day and turn myself in. Bill Allen was dead.

The screaming echo of the phone over the woodlot woke me. I saw Robert go into the headquarters shack to answer it. He came back out shortly, still in his coveralls, and walked over to the Bronco. I got out. He handed me a Styrofoam cup of coffee and pointed his chin at the Bronco.

"Comfy in there last night?" he asked. I nodded and he went on. "That was John on the phone. He's going to plead out tomorrow and take two years." Robert shook his head. "Anyway, you've got tomorrow off. I'm going up to Concord to be at the sentencing." He reached in his pocket and pulled out a roll of bills. He handed it to me.

"What's this for?" I said.

Robert narrowed his eyes and looked at me. "Do you need it or not?" His voice was the hardest love I'd ever felt. I nodded. He turned around and started walking back to the shed. I watched him close the door. I climbed back in the Bronco and headed out onto the highway. I drove north, and crossed over into Vermont. There was still a huge black cloud in the sky over the oxbow. I drove up Route 5 and looked out over the burnt fields, still smoldering, scorched dead. Lord's farm looked gray from the smoke. I drove up into the Northeast Kingdom. I never did find the courage to turn myself in, and things got worse. I spent the winter at a logging camp in Quebec.

I called once, when I hit a jam out in North Dakota. I called from a phone booth outside a diner. I recognized John's voice the second he spoke. I hung up. Later, much later, in another life, with another name, we were driving and someone handed me a road atlas. I flipped through it and found Vermont and New Hampshire were together on the same page. I started tracing their shared border, the Connecticut River, north toward Canada. I dropped the atlas when my finger reached the oxbow. For just that split second, right on the tip of my finger, the surface of the map was scorching hot. I heard the roar of the fire, the little white house burning. The air rushing to be eaten by the flames. I smelled the gasoline. Riding across the top of the fire on a black horse was Bill Allen. Three dark shapes followed swiftly after him, the burning wasps in their long black hair, chasing him. Catching him and dragging him down into the fire, screaming.

Years later, on the security ward at Western State Hospital near Tacoma, I saw a man in a straitjacket, strapped to a gurney. I walked over to him and spoke.

"I didn't know they used straitjackets anymore."

He could barely move his head. "Well, they do." The smell of ether was everywhere. He was quiet as a white-jacketed doctor walked by. "Say, Mac, scratch my shoulder, will you?"

I slowly reached down and began scratching the outside of the thick canvas that bound him. Solid steel mesh covered the ward windows.

"Harder," he said. "I can barely feel it." He looked up at me. "I think they're trying to save on the heat. Aren't you cold?" I shook my head. "I'm cold all the time," he said.

I dug my nails into the canvas on his right shoulder. "My name is John Wilson," I said.

He looked at me, his eyes wide. "That's my name," he said softly.

I stopped scratching the straitjacket. "What's your middle name?" I asked.

He shook his head slightly and closed his eyes. "Same as yours," he said. He shivered. It was cold. But my paper gown was soaked with dry sweat and my face was hot. I could smell smoke.

MONICA WOOD

That One Autumn

FROM *Glimmer Train*

THAT ONE AUTUMN, when Marie got to the cabin, something looked wrong. She took in the familiar view: the clapboard bunga-low she and Ernie had inherited from his father, the bushes and trees that had grown up over the years, the dock pulled in for the season. She sat in the idling car, reminded of those "find the mis-take" puzzles John used to pore over as a child, intent on locating mittens on the water skier, milk bottles in the parlor. Bent in a cor-ner somewhere over the softening page, her blue-eyed boy would search for hours, convinced that after every wrong thing had been identified, more wrong things remained.

Sunlight pooled in the dooryard. The day gleamed, the clean Maine air casting a sober whiteness over everything. The gravel turnaround seemed vaguely disarranged. Scanning the line of spruce that shielded the steep slope to the lake's edge, Marie looked for movement. Behind the thick mesh screen of the front porch she could make out the wicker tops of the chairs. She turned off the ignition, trying to remember whether she'd taken time to straighten up the porch when she was last here, in early August, the weekend of Ernie's birthday. He and John had had one of their fights, and it was possible that in the ensuing clamor and silence she had forgotten to straighten up the porch. It was possible.

She got out of the car and checked around. Everything looked different after just a few weeks: the lake blacker through the part in the trees, the brown-eyed Susans gone weedy, the chairs on the porch definitely, definitely moved. Ernie had pushed a chair in frustration, she remembered. And John had responded in kind, upending the green one on his way out the door and down to the lake. They'd begun that weekend, like so many others, with such good intentions, only to discover anew how mismatched they were, parents to son. So, she had straightened the chairs — she had definitely straightened them — while outside Ernie's angry footsteps crackled over the gravel and, farther away, John's body hit the water in a furious smack.

She minced up the steps and pushed open the screen door, which was unlocked. "Hello?" she called out fearfully. The inside door was slightly ajar. *Take the dog,* Ernie had told her, *she'll be good company.* She wished now she had, though the dog, a Yorkie named Honey Girl, was a meek little thing and no good in a crisis. *I don't want company, Ernie. It's a week, it's forty miles, I'm not leaving you.* Marie was sentimental, richly so, which is why her wish to be alone after seeing John off to college had astonished them both. *But you're still weak,* Ernie argued. *Look how pale you are.* She packed a box of watercolors and a how-to book in her trunk as Ernie stood by, bewildered. *I haven't been alone in years,* she told him. *I want to find out what it feels like.* John had missed Vietnam by six merciful months, then he'd chosen Berkeley, as far from his parents as he could get, and now Marie wanted to be alone. Ernie gripped her around the waist and she took a big breath of him: man, dog, house, yard, mill. She had known him most of her life, and from time to time, when she could bear to think about it, she wondered whether their uncommon closeness was what had made their son a stranger.

You be careful, he called after her as she drove off. The words came back to her now as she peered through the partly open door at a wedge of kitchen she barely recognized. She saw jam jars open on the counter, balled-up dishtowels, a box of oatmeal upended and spilling a bit of oatmeal dust, a snaggled hairbrush, a red lipstick ground to a nub. Through the adjacent window she caught part of a rumpled sleeping bag in front of the fireplace, plus an empty glass and a couple of books.

Marie felt a little breathless, but not afraid, recognizing the disorder as strictly female. She barreled in, searching the small rooms like an angry, old-fashioned mother with a hickory switch. She found the toilet filled with urine, the back hall cluttered with camping gear, and the two bedrooms largely untouched except for a grease-stained knapsack thrown across Marie and Ernie's bed. By the time she got back out to the porch to scan the premises again, Marie had the knapsack in hand and sent it skidding across the gravel. The effort doubled her over, for Ernie was right: her body had not recovered from the thing it had suffered. As she held her stomach, the throbbing served only to stoke her fury.

Then she heard it: the sound of a person struggling up the steep, rocky path from the lake. Swishing grass. A scatter of pebbles. The subtle pulse of forward motion.

It was a girl. She came out of the trees into the sunlight, naked except for a towel bundled under one arm. Seeing the car, she stopped, then looked toward the cabin, where Marie uncoiled herself slowly, saying, "Who the hell are you?"

The girl stood there, apparently immune to shame. A delicate ladder of ribs showed through her paper-white skin. Her damp hair was fair and thin, her pubic hair equally thin and light. "Shit," she said. "Busted." Then she cocked her head, her face filled with a defiance Marie had seen so often in her own son that it barely registered.

"Cover yourself, for God's sake," Marie said.

The girl did, in her own good time, arranging the towel over her shoulders and covering her small breasts. Her walk was infuriatingly casual as she moved through the dooryard, picked up the knapsack, and sauntered up the steps, past Marie, and into the cabin. Marie followed her in. She smelled like the lake.

"Get out before I call the police," Marie said.

"Your phone doesn't work," the girl said peevishly. "And I can't say much for your toilet, either."

Of course nothing worked. They'd turned everything off, buttoned the place up after their last visit, John and Ernie at each other's throats as they hauled the dock up the slope, Ernie too slow on his end, John too fast on his, both of them arguing about whether or not Richard Nixon was a crook and should have resigned in disgrace.

"I said get out. This is my house."

The girl pawed through the knapsack. She hauled out a pair of panties and slipped them on. Then a pair of frayed jeans, and a mildewy shirt that Marie could smell across the room. As she toweled her hair it became lighter, nearly white. She leveled Marie with a look as blank and stolid as a pillar.

"I said get out," Marie snapped, jangling her car keys.

"I heard you."

"Then do it."

The girl dropped the towel on the floor, reached into the knapsack once more, extracted a comb, combed her flimsy, apparitional hair, and returned the comb. Then she pulled out a switchblade. It opened with a crisp, perfunctory snap.

"Here's the deal," she said. "I get to be in charge, and you get to shut up."

Marie shot out of the cabin and sprinted into the dooryard, where a bolt of pain brought her up short and windless. The girl was too quick in any case, catching Marie by the wrist before she could reclaim her breath. "Don't try anything," the girl said, her voice low and cold. "I'm unpredictable." She glanced around. "You expecting anybody?"

"No," Marie said, shocked into telling the truth.

"Then it's just us girls," she said, smiling a weird, thin smile that impelled Marie to reach behind her, holding the car for support. The girl presented her water-wrinkled palm and Marie forked over the car keys.

"Did you bring food?"

"In the trunk."

The girl held up the knife. "Stay right there."

Marie watched, terrified, as the girl opened the trunk and tore into a box of groceries, shoving a tomato into her mouth as she reached for some bread. A bloody trail of tomato juice sluiced down her neck.

Studying the girl — her quick, panicky movements — Marie felt her fear begin to settle into a morbid curiosity. This skinny girl seemed an unlikely killer; her tiny wrists looked breakable, and her stunning whiteness gave her the look of a child ghost. In a matter of seconds, a thin, reluctant vine of maternal compassion twined through Marie and burst into violent bloom.

"When did you eat last?" Marie asked her.

"None of your business," the girl said, cramming her mouth full of bread.

"How old are you?"

The girl finished chewing, then answered: "Nineteen. What's it to you?"

"I have a son about your age."

"Thrilled to know it," the girl said, handing a grocery sack to Marie. She herself hefted the box and followed Marie into the cabin, her bare feet making little animal sounds on the gravel. Once inside, she ripped into a box of Cheerios.

"Do you want milk with that?" Marie asked her.

All at once the girl welled up, and she nodded, wiping her eyes with the heel of one hand, turning her head hard right, hard left, exposing her small, translucent ears. "This isn't me," she sniffled. She lifted the knife, but did not give it over. "It's not even mine."

"Whose is it?" Marie said steadily, pouring milk into a bowl.

"My boyfriend's." The girl said nothing more for a few minutes, until the cereal was gone, another bowl poured, and that, too, devoured. She wandered over to the couch, a convertible covered with anchors that Ernie had bought to please John, who naturally never said a word about it.

"Where is he, your boyfriend?" Marie asked finally.

"Out getting supplies." The girl looked up quickly, a snap of the eyes revealing something Marie thought she understood.

"How long's he been gone?"

The girl waited. "Day and a half."

Marie nodded. "Maybe his car broke down."

"That's what I wondered." The girl flung a spindly arm in the general direction of the kitchen. "I'm sorry about the mess. My boyfriend's hardly even paper-trained."

"Then maybe you should think about getting another boyfriend."

"I told him, no sleeping on the beds. We didn't sleep on your beds."

"Thank you," Marie said.

"It wasn't my idea to break in here."

"I'm sure it wasn't."

"He's kind of hiding out, and I'm kind of with him."

"I see," Marie said, scanning the room for weapons: fireplace poker, dictionary, curtain rod. She couldn't imagine using any of these things on the girl, whose body appeared held together with thread.

"He knocked over a gas station. Two, actually, in Portland."

"That sounds serious."

She smiled a little. "He's a serious guy."

"You could do better, don't you think?" Marie asked. "Pretty girl like you."

The girl's big eyes narrowed. "How old are *you*?"

"Thirty-eight."

"You look younger."

"Well, I'm not," Marie said. "My name is Marie, by the way."

"I'm Tracey."

"Tell me, Tracey," Marie said. "Am I your prisoner?"

"Only until he gets back. We'll clear out after that."

"Where are you going?"

"Canada. Which is where he should've gone about six years ago."

"A vet?"

Tracey nodded. "War sucks."

"Well, now, that's extremely profound."

"Don't push your luck, Marie," Tracey said. "It's been a really long week."

They spent the next hours sitting on the porch, Marie thinking furiously in a chair, Tracey on the steps, the knife glinting in her fist. At one point Tracey stepped down into the gravel, dropped her jeans, and squatted over the spent irises, keeping Marie in her sights the whole time. Marie, who had grown up in a different era entirely, found this fiercely embarrassing. A wind came up on the lake; a pair of late loons called across the water. The only comfort Marie could manage was that the boyfriend, whom she did not wish to meet, not at all, clearly had run out for good. Tracey seemed to know this, too, chewing on her lower lip, facing the dooryard as if the hot desire of her stare could make him materialize.

"What's his name?" Marie asked.

"None of your business. We met in a chemistry class." She smirked at Marie's surprise. "Premed."

"Are you going back to school?"

Tracey threw back her head and cackled, showing two straight rows of excellent teeth. "Yeah, right. He's out there right now paying our preregistration."

Marie composed herself, took some silent breaths. "It's just that I find it hard to believe —"

"People like you always do," Tracey said. She slid Marie a look. "You're never willing to believe the worst of someone."

Marie closed her eyes, wanting Ernie. She imagined him leaving work about now, coming through the mill gates with his lunch bucket and cap, shoulders bowed at the prospect of the empty house. She longed to be waiting there, to sit on the porch with him over a pitcher of lemonade, comparing days, which hadn't changed much over the years, really, but always held some ordinary pleasures. Today they would have wondered about John, thought about calling him, decided against it.

"You married?" Tracey asked, as if reading her mind.

"Twenty years. We met in seventh grade."

"Then what are you doing up here alone?"

"I don't know," Marie said. But suddenly she did, she knew exactly, looking at this girl who had parents somewhere waiting.

"I know what you're thinking," the girl said.

"You couldn't possibly."

"You're wondering how a nice girl like me ended up like this." When Marie didn't answer, she added, "Why do you keep doing that?"

"What?"

"That." The girl pointed to Marie's hand, which was making absent semicircles over her stomach. "You pregnant?"

"No," Marie said, withdrawing her hand. But she had been, shockingly, for most of the summer; during John's final weeks at home, she had been pregnant. Back then her hand had gone automatically to the womb, that strange, unpredictable vessel, as she and Ernie nuzzled in bed, dazzled by their change in fortune. For nights on end they made their murmured plans, lost in a form of drunkenness, waiting for John to skulk through the back door long past curfew, when they would rise from their nestled sheets to face him — their first child now, not their only — his splendid blue eyes glassy with what she hoped were the normal complications of adolescence, equal parts need and contempt.

They did not tell him about the pregnancy, and by the first of September it was over prematurely, Marie balled into a heap on their bed for three days, barely able to open her swollen eyes. "Maybe it's for the best," Ernie whispered to her, petting her curled back. They could hear John ramming around in the kitchen downstairs, stocking the cupboards with miso and bean curd and other things they'd never heard of, counting off his last days in the house by changing everything in it. As Ernie kissed her sweaty head, Marie rested her hand on the freshly scoured womb that had held their second chance. "It might not have been worth it," Ernie whispered, words that staggered her so thoroughly that she bolted up, mouth agape, asking, "What did you say, Ernie? Did you just say something?" Their raising of John had, after all, been filled with fine wishes for the boy; it was not their habit to acknowledge disappointment, or regret, or sorrow. As the door downstairs clicked shut on them and John faded into another night with his mysterious friends, Marie turned to her husband, whom she loved, God help her, more than she loved her son. *Take it back*, she wanted to tell him, but he mistook her pleading look entirely. "She might've broken our hearts," he murmured. "I can think of a hundred ways." He was holding her at the time, speaking softly, almost to himself, and his hands on her felt like the meaty intrusion of some stranger who'd just broken into her bedroom. "Ernie, stop there," she told him, and he did.

It was only now, imprisoned on her own property by a skinny girl who belonged back in chemistry class, that Marie understood that she had come here alone to find a way to forgive him. What did he mean, not worth it? Worth what? Was he speaking of John?

Marie looked down over the trees into the lake. She and Ernie had been twenty years old when John was born. You think you're in love now, her sister warned, but wait till you meet your baby — implying that married love would look bleached and pale by contrast. But John was a sober, suspicious baby, vaguely intimidating; and their fascination for him became one more thing they had in common. As their child became more and more himself, a cryptogram they couldn't decipher, Ernie and Marie's bungled affections and wayward exertions revealed less of him and more of themselves.

Ernie and Marie, smitten since seventh grade: it was a story they thought their baby son would grow up to tell their grandchildren. At twenty they had thought this. She wanted John to remember his childhood the way she liked to: a soft-focus, greeting card recollection in which Ernie and Marie strolled hand in hand in a park somewhere with the fruit of their desire frolicking a few feet ahead. But now she doubted her own memory. John must have frolicked on occasion. Certainly he must have frolicked. But at the present moment she could conjure only a lumbering resignation, as if he had already tired of their story before he broke free of the womb. They would have been more ready for him now, she realized. She was in a position now to love Ernie less, if that's what a child required.

The shadow of the spruces arched long across the dooryard. Dusk fell.

Tracey got up. "I'm hungry again. You want anything?"

"No, thanks."

Tracey waited. "You have to come in with me."

Marie stepped through the door first, then watched as Tracey made herself a sandwich. "I don't suppose it's crossed your mind that your boyfriend might not come back," Marie said.

Tracey took a big bite. "No, it hasn't."

"If I were on the run I'd run alone, wouldn't you? Don't you think that makes sense?"

Chewing daintily, Tracey flattened Marie with a luminous, eerily knowing look. "Are you on the run, Marie?"

"What I'm saying is that he'll get a lot farther a lot faster without another person to worry about."

Tracey swallowed hard. "Well, what I'm saying is you don't know shit about him. Or me, for that matter. So you can just shut up."

"I could give you a ride home."

"Not without your keys, you couldn't." She opened the fridge and gulped some milk from the bottle. "If I wanted to go home, I would've gone home a long time ago."

It had gotten dark in the cabin. Marie flicked on the kitchen light. She and Ernie left the electricity on year-round because it was more trouble not to, and occasionally they came here in winter to snowshoe through the long, wooded alleys. It was on their son's behalf that they had come to such pastimes, on their son's behalf that the cabin had filled over the years with well-thumbed guidebooks to butterflies and insects and fish and birds. But John preferred his puzzles by the fire, his long, furtive vigils on the dock, leaving it to his parents to discover the world. They turned up pine cones, strips of birch bark for monogramming, once a speckled feather from a pheasant. John inspected these things indifferently, listened to parental homilies on the world's breathtaking design, all the while maintaining the demeanor of a goodhearted homeowner suffering the encyclopedia salesman's pitch.

"Why don't you want to go home?" Marie asked. "Really, I'd like to know." She was remembering the parting scene at the airport, John uncharacteristically warm, allowing her to hug him as long as she wanted, thanking her for an all-purpose "everything" that she could fill in as she pleased for years to come. Ernie, his massive arms folded in front of him, welled up, nodding madly. But as John disappeared behind the gate Ernie clutched her hand, and she knew what he knew: that their only son, their first and only child, was not coming back. He would finish school, find a job in California, call them twice a year.

"My father's a self-righteous blowhard, if you're dying to know," Tracey said. "And my mother's a doormat."

"Maybe they did the best they could."

"Maybe they didn't."

"Maybe they tried in ways you can't know about."

Tracey looked Marie over. "My mother's forty-two," she said. "She would've crawled under a chair the second she saw the knife."

Marie covered the mustard jar and returned it to the fridge. "It's possible, Tracey, that your parents never found the key to you."

Tracey seemed to like this interpretation of her terrible choices. Her shoulders softened some. "So where's this son of yours, anyway?"

"We just sent him off to Berkeley."

Tracey smirked a little. "Uh-oh."

"What's that supposed to mean?" Marie asked. "What do you mean?"

"Berkeley's a pretty swinging place. You don't send sweet little boys there."

"I never said he was a sweet little boy," Marie said, surprising herself. But it was true: her child had never been a sweet little boy.

"You'll be lucky if he comes back with his brain still working."

"I'll be lucky if he comes back at all."

Tracey frowned. "You're messing with my head, right? Poor, tortured mother? You probably don't even have kids." She folded her arms. "But if you do have a kid, and he's at Berkeley, prepare yourself."

"Look, Tracey," Marie said irritably, "why don't you just take my car? If you're so devoted to this boyfriend of yours, why not go after him?"

"Because I'd have no idea where to look, and you'd run to the nearest police station." Tracey finished the sandwich and rinsed the plate, leading Marie to suspect that someone had at least taught her to clean up after herself. The worst parent in the world can at least do that. John had lovely manners, and she suddenly got a comforting vision of him placing his scraped plate in a cafeteria sink.

"The nearest police station is twenty miles from here," Marie said.

"Well, that's good news, Marie, because look who's back."

Creeping into the driveway, one headlight out, was a low-slung, mud-colored Valiant with a cracked windshield. The driver skulked behind the wheel, blurry as an inkblot. When Tracey raced out to greet him, the driver opened the door and emerged as a jittery shadow. The shadow flung itself toward the cabin as Marie fled for the back door and banged on the lock with her fists.

In moments he was upon her, a wiry man with a powerful odor and viselike hands. He half-carried her back to the kitchen as she fell limp with panic. Then, like a ham actor in a silent movie, he lashed her to a kitchen chair with cords of filthy rawhide.

"You wanna tell me how the fuck we get rid of her?" he snarled at Tracey, whose apparent fright gave full flower to Marie's budding terror. That he was handsome — dark-eyed, square-jawed, with full, shapely lips — made him all the more terrifying.

"What was I supposed to do?" Tracey quavered. "Listen, I kept her here for a whole day with no —"

"Where's your keys?" he roared at Marie.

"Here, they're here," Tracey said, fumbling them out of her pocket. "Let's go, Mike, please, let's just go."

"You got money?" he asked, leaning over Marie, one cool strand of his long hair raking across her bare arm. She could hardly breathe, looking into his alarming, moist eyes.

"My purse," she gasped. "In the car."

He stalked out, his dirty jeans sagging at the seat, into which someone had sewn a facsimile of the American flag. He looked near starving, his upper arms shaped like bedposts, thin and tapering and hard. She heard the car door open and the contents of her purse spilling over the gravel.

"The premed was a lie," Tracey said. "I met him at a concert."

She darted a look outside, her lip quivering. "You know how much power I have over my own life, Marie?" She lifted her hand and squeezed her thumb and index finger together. "This much."

He was in again, tearing into the fridge, cramming food into his mouth. The food seemed to calm him some. He looked around. He could have been twenty-five or forty-five, a man weighted by bad luck and a mean spirit that encased his true age like barnacles on a boat. "Pick up our stuff," he said to Tracey. "We're out of this dump."

Tracey did as he said, gathering the sleeping bag and stuffing it into a sack. He watched her body damply as she moved; Marie felt an engulfing nausea but could not move herself, not even to cover her mouth at the approaching bile. Her legs were lashed to the chair legs, her arms tied behind her, giving her a deeply discomfiting sensation of being bound to empty space. She felt desperate to close her legs, cross her arms over her breasts, unwilling to die with her most womanly parts exposed. "I'm going to be sick," she gulped, but it was too late, a thin trail of spit and bile lolloping down her shirtfront.

Mike lifted his forearm, dirty with tattoos, and chopped it down across Marie's jaw. She thumped backward to the floor, chair and all, tasting blood, seeing stars, letting out a squawk of despair. Then she fell silent, looking at the upended room, stunned. She heard the flick of a switchblade and felt the heat of his shadow. She tried to snap her eyes shut, to wait for what came next, but they opened again, fixed on his; in the still, shiny irises she searched for a sign of latent goodness, or regret, some long-ago time that defined him. In the sepulchral silence she locked eyes with him, sorrow to sorrow. He dropped the knife. "Fuck this, you do it," he said to Tracey, then swaggered out. She heard her car revving in the dooryard, the radio blaring on. Now her eyes closed. A small rustle materialized near her left ear; it was Tracey, crouching next to her, holding the opened blade.

"Shh," Tracey said. "He's a coward, and he doesn't like blood, but he's not above beating the hell out of me." She patted Marie's cheek. "So let's just pretend I've killed you."

Marie began to weep, silently, a sheen of moisture beading beneath her eyes. She made a prayer to the Virgin Mary, something she had not done since she was a child. She summoned an image of

Ernie sitting on the porch, missing her. Of John scraping that plate in the college cafeteria. With shocking tenderness, Tracey made a small cut near Marie's temple just above the hairline. It hurt very little, but the blood began to course into her hair in warm, oozy tracks. Tracey lifted the knife, now a rich, dripping red. "You'll be okay," she said. "But head wounds bleed like crazy." The horn from Marie's car sounded in two long, insistent blasts.

"You chose a hell of a life for yourself, Tracey," Marie whispered.

"Yeah," Tracey said, closing her palm lightly over the knife. She got up. "But at least I chose."

"You don't know anything about me."

"Ditto. Take care."

For much of the long evening Marie kept still, blinking into the approaching dark. She had to pee desperately but determined to hold it even if it killed her, which she genuinely thought it might. She was facing the ceiling, still tied, the blood on her face and hair drying uncomfortably. She recalled John's childhood habit of hanging slothlike from banisters or chair backs, loving the upside-down world. Perhaps his parents were easier to understand this way. She saw now what had so compelled him: the ceiling would make a marvelous floor, a creamy expanse you could navigate how-ever you wished; you could fling yourself from corner to corner, unencumbered except for an occasional light fixture. Even the walls looked inviting: the windows appeared to open from the top down, the tops of doors made odd, amusing steps into the next room, framed pictures floated knee-high, their reversed images full of whimsy, hard to decode. In time she got used to the over-turned room, even preferred it. It calmed her. She no longer felt sick. She understood that Ernie was on his way here, of course he was, he would be here before the moon rose, missing her, full of apology for disturbing her peace, but he needed her, the house was empty and their son was gone, and he needed her as he steered down the dirt road, veering left past the big boulder, entering the dooryard to find a strange, battered car and a terrifying silence.

"Oh, Ernie," she said when he did indeed panic through the door. "Ernie. Sweetheart. Untie me." In he came, just as she knew he would.

And then? They no longer looked back on this season as the autumn when they lost their second child. This season — with its

gentle temperatures and propensity for inspiring flight — they recalled instead as that one autumn when those awful people, that
terrible pair, broke into the cabin. They exchanged one memory
for the other, remembering Ernie's raging, man-sized sobs as he
worked at the stiff rawhide, remembering him rocking her under a
shaft of moonlight that sliced through the door he'd left open, remembering, half laughing, that the first thing Marie wanted to do,
after being rescued by her prince, was pee. This moment became
the turning point — this moment and no other — when two long-
married people decided to stay married, to succumb to the shape
of the rest of their life, to live with things they would not speak of.
They shouldered each other into the coming years because there
was no other face each could bear to look at in this moment of
turning, no other arms they could bear but each other's, and they
made themselves right again, they did, just the two of them.

Contributors' Notes

Other Distinguished Stories of 2002

Contributors' Notes

Born and raised in northern Michigan, **Doug Allyn** studied the Chinese language at Indiana University and served in Southeast Asia during the Vietnam War.

Returning to school on the GI Bill, Allyn studied creative writing and criminal psychology at the University of Michigan while moonlighting as a guitarist and a poet and lyricist in the rock group Devil's Triangle. He later taught creative writing at Mott Community College and presently reviews books for the *Flint Journal* while maintaining a full writing schedule.

From the beginning, critical response to Mr. Allyn's work has been remarkable. His first published story won the Robert L. Fish award from the Mystery Writers of America. Subsequent works have won the Edgar Allan Poe Award, the American Mystery Award, the Derringer Award for best novella, and the Ellery Queen Readers' Award five times. His career highlights include drinking champagne with Mickey Spillane and waltzing with Mary Higgins Clark. The Allyns live in frenetic bliss in Montrose, Michigan.

• "The Jukebox King" is based on the reality of the Detroit nightclub scene. Rap didn't introduce gangsters to the music business; the Mob has been in the game since Prohibition. Drawn to the nightlife and easy money, hoods had financial interests in dance clubs, jukeboxes, and even recording studios.

This wasn't necessarily a negative. Some very bad guys had very good taste. But as rhythm and blues began evolving into rock 'n' roll, even the Mafia developed a generation gap.

Christopher Chambers was born in Madison, Wisconsin, and has since lived in North Carolina, Michigan, Minnesota, Florida, Alabama, and Louisiana. He received a degree in English at the University of Wisconsin at River Falls in 1984, and over the following ten years worked as a salesman, bus driver, meat cutter, farmhand, carpenter, journalist, photographer, bartender, dockworker, lifeguard, screenwriter, and editor. He taught martial arts in Minneapolis, high school physical education in South Florida, and writing at the University of Alabama, where he received an M.F.A. degree. His work has appeared in such journals as the *Gettysburg Review, Washington Square, Hayden's Ferry Review, Quarter After Eight, Notre Dame Review, Exquisite Corpse, Controlled Burn, Quarterly West,* and the *Carolina Quarterly.* His short story collection, *Aardvark to Aztec,* was short-listed for the Mary McCarthy Prize. His short fiction has received four Pushcart Prize nominations, the Scott and Zelda Fitzgerald Literary Award for Short Fiction, and is included in the recent anthology *French Quarter Fiction: The Newest Stories from America's Oldest Bohemia.* He lives in New Orleans, where he teaches at Loyola University.

▪ "Aardvark to Aztec" was written on an old Royal portable, in the summer, as I recall. I was living in a cabin outside Tuscaloosa, Alabama. I dragged a wooden table onto the porch that overlooked a ravine that was overgrown and unremarkable most of the time, but became unexpectedly beautiful each spring with an abundance of dogwood blossoms, and on those summer nights when fireflies lit up like a distant metropolis. It was on one of these nights, on that porch, sitting at my typewriter, to a chorus of nocturnal insects, that I tapped out the first sentence. The writing began with the character of Miranda and her vague discontent, so I guess it should have been no surprise for me to discover in the end that it is indeed her story. The clown, like much of the story, came out of nowhere. There may have been a small glass of whiskey, and an inexpensive cigar on the table as well. Perhaps strains of Hank Williams drifting out through the screen door, the drone of the firefly beyond the ravine. I realized quickly that someone was going to die in this story. I didn't know who, but it saddened me, because I was already coming to grow fond of each of these characters.

Christopher Cook lives in Prague, Czech Republic. He previously lived in France and Mexico but grew up in East Texas, the Bible-thumping South. The persistent pounding spurred escape and his incurable nomadism.

Cook decided early to become a writer but soon discovered he didn't know how. To learn, he became a daily newspaper reporter in several southern states of disrepair. Odious bosses caused him to pursue subsequent work as a trade union activist. He later fell into a U.S. think tank, where he thought a lot and recognized that smart public policy is difficult to incite, almost impossible. Writing became his private refuge. Otherwise his life has been ordinary. There are unaccountable gaps in his biography.

Cook's award-winning novel, *Robbers* (2000), was published in the United States and abroad, as was his second book, *Screen Door Jesus & Other Stories* (2001). He is completing a third book.

▪ While living in Paris, and commuting on the underground Métro, I often wished for something interesting to happen, anything at all. Having my pocket picked, for example. Even better, seeing another's pocket picked. Best yet, what if I became a pickpocket? I noodled the idea. But a jail cell is more boring than the subway. So I decided to become one in a story instead.

"The Pickpocket," quickly completed, was eagerly rejected without comment by numerous magazines and literary journals in the U.S.A. In France, however, it won first prize in a literary contest sponsored by the Sorbonne University and Transcontinental Paris. That was 1995. It was finally published stateside in the Dennis McMillan anthology *Measures of Poison* (2002) after a biblical period in exile.

John Peyton Cooke was born in Amarillo, Texas, and grew up in Laramie, Wyoming. He is the author of five novels and several short stories and has collected the typical writer's résumé of odd jobs: literary book shelver, data entry operator, office assistant at the American Institute of History of Pharmacy, and police report typist with the Madison (Wisc.) Police Department. His current, and oddest, job is as editorial director of a medical communications agency in New York City. He lives in Ketonah, New York, with his partner, Keng, and their two dogs: Ricky, a toy poodle and petty thief; and Quilty, a whippet and occasional poet.

▪ I would like to dedicate this appearance of "After You've Gone" to the memory of my father, William Peyton Cooke, author of mystery novels *The Nemesis Conjecture* and *Orion's Shroud*, who died on January 16, 2003, in Amarillo, Texas. When I asked him what he thought of this story, he said, "I liked it. But of course I knew all along how it was going to end." There is nothing like a father to keep egging you on to do better.

This story may be thematically similar to my novel *The Chimney Sweeper*, in that both deal with violence that erupts when their young male protagonists face sudden, unexpected sexual confusion. I would like to think that sex and violence in my stories are inextricably linked, so that you could not remove one without the other. Since I am not a violent person by nature, it is a mystery to me where this impetus comes from in my stories. However, it is almost certainly related to my own identity as a gay man, which developed during my adolescence, during which I was simultaneously indulging my interest in horror, fantasy, science fiction, and mysteries.

I grew up in Laramie, Wyoming, where the only information I could find about gay people like me was in the Albany County Public Library (where I worked as a book shelver) and at the Coe Library on the campus of the University of Wyoming. Laramie, as everyone knows, is the town where Matt Shepard was murdered because he was gay. Although I was out of the closet to my closest friends from the age of fifteen, I never felt personally threatened by my environment. Still, it gives me pause to consider that Matt's murderers are fellow graduates of Laramie Senior High School. The violence they perpetrated on Matt was certainly gratuitous, and it is ironic to me that it is also representative of what I've written about — the unreasonable, unwarranted, and sadistic violence that can easily manifest itself when certain young men feel threatened by the very existence of someone who is sexually different from them.

"After You've Gone" is the result of numerous inputs, including those aforementioned. The initial spark was a passage in a story by Robert W. Chambers, "The Repairer of Reputations," written in the 1890s but set in a future New York of 1920:

> In the following winter began the agitation for the repeal of the laws prohibiting suicide which bore its final fruit in the month of April, 1920, when the first Government Lethal Chamber was opened on Washington Square.

I wanted to write a tale in which a government agent of that weird future goes around helping people commit suicide. I was going to call it "The GAS Man," with GAS standing for government-assisted suicide. This evolved into the rogue agent of "After You've Gone," to whom I now needed to supply some kind of motivation. I got to thinking, naturally, about Dr. Jack Kevorkian, the death-obsessed pathologist who creatively assisted a number of suicides of the terminally ill and is currently in prison on murder charges. What if his own motives were not so altruistic? What if he, quite simply, got off on it? The many disturbing newspaper accounts of inexplicable police suicides (in New York City), usually by male officers who had not quite measured up, helped me develop the "victim" of my assisted-suicide fiend. Given my usual bent, sexual confusion (in one form or another) was bound to enter the story, and it serves here as a trigger for the violence (or whatever) is to come.

Born in New Orleans, **O'Neil De Noux** is a former homicide detective and organized-crime investigator. He has also worked as a private investigator, U.S. Army combat photographer, criminal intelligence analyst, journalist, magazine editor, and computer graphics designer. As a police officer, De Noux received seven commendations for solving difficult murder cases. In 1981 he was named Homicide Detective of the Year for the Jefferson Parish Sheriff's Office. In 1989 he was proclaimed an expert witness on the homicide crime scene by the Criminal District Court in New Orleans.

Mr. De Noux's published novels include *Grim Reaper, The Big Kiss, Blue Orleans, Crescent City Kills, The Big Show* and *Hollow Point / The Mystery of Rochelle Marais.*

O'Neil De Noux has also had over 150 short stories published in the United States, Canada, Denmark, England, France, Germany, Italy, Scotland, and Sweden. He teaches mystery writing at the University of New Orleans. He is the founding editor of two fiction magazines, *Mystery Street* and *New Orleans Stories.*

▪ The inspiration for "Death on Denial" came when my wife, Debra Gray De Noux (editor of *Erotic New Orleans* anthology), peeked into the living room and said, "Are you watching *Death on the Nile* again?" It occurred to me that a play on words was called for. So I came up with a title first, which I've done often, then filled in the blanks, including a character who likes to watch *Death on the Nile* over and over again.

Pete Dexter lives on an island in Puget Sound with his dogs, Pansy and Fred, and his wife, Dian. He has just finished his sixth novel, *Train*. The Dexters have a daughter, Casey, who lives in Phoenix, Arizona, with a kid named Tate, and they have a cat named George, who is originally from Tucson. Due to bad behavior, he is not let out of the house (George, not Mr. Dexter).

▪ "The Jeweler" was the first few pages of a novel, something I wrote to help myself make sense of a character. I was cutting it out of the manuscript later, which is what always happens in this kind of deal, when my brother Tom — who lives in Montana with his wife Jane and his daughters Molly, Annie, and the beautiful but eerie identical twins Phoebie and Elizabeth, and their dog, Gretta — when Tom called out of the clear, blue, Montana sky and said he thought I ought to write some short stories. So instead of throwing the pages away I sent them to my agent, Esther Newberg, who would like to have a dog but is allergic and has a cat instead, who obeys her instantly. But then, don't we all?

A Southern California native, **Tyler Dilts** received his M.F.A. in fiction from California State University, Long Beach, where he now teaches writing in the English and Theater Arts Departments. He is a winner of the Associated Writing Programs' Intro Award, and his short fiction has appeared in a number of literary journals, including *RipRap, The Circle,* and *Puerto Del Sol.* He recently completed his first novel, *A King of Infinite Space,* and is currently hard at work on his second, in which the nameless narrator of "Thug: Signification and the (De) Construction of Self" makes a return appearance.

▪ The protagonist of "Thug" is a character who circled around the edges of my writing consciousness for quite a while before finally finding his place. I had tried using him in a number of different ways, first as a supporting character in other people's stories, then in his own. He never really seemed to fit, though. I just couldn't find the right voice, the right tone, to give him his due. But he was always there, waiting patiently for his chance. I'd almost given up on him, when, during a particularly busy month in graduate school, in the course of which I found myself reading a profoundly odd juxtaposition of works by Dashiell Hammett, Raymond Chandler, Thomas Pynchon, David Foster Wallace, and a half-dozen or so postmodern literary theorists (the two new Jacques — Derrida and Lacan, and the rest of their gang), he bubbled back up to the surface of my awareness and asserted himself. Sitting down to write a critical essay on deconstruction for one of my classes, something else entirely emerged — the first lines of this story.

Mike Doogan is a third-generation Alaskan who lives in Anchorage with his wife of thirty-two years, Kathy. He writes a metro column for the *Anchorage Daily News*. He has won several journalism awards and shared in the newspaper's 1989 Pulitzer Prize. Doogan is the author of two books of nonsense about Alaska and the editor of a collection of essays about living in the far north. "War Can Be Murder" is his first mystery story.

▪ I've been a Dashiell Hammett fan for as long as I can remember, and at one time did quite a bit of research into his service in Alaska with the U.S. Army during World War II. When Anchorage mystery writer Dana Stabenow asked me to write a story for her anthology *The Mysterious North*, which grew immediately out of the Left Coast Crime Conference, I thought immediately of Hammett.

Fortunately, my research had been summarized in an article for the *Armchair Detective* ("Dash-ing Through the Snow," Winter 1989), so the material was readily to hand. The story that resulted is an amalgam of fact and fiction. The Hammett character is as true to life as I could make him, as is World War II Anchorage. The rest of it I made up.

I also did my best to be true to Hammett's writing style and the ethos of his work. I am satisfied with the result, keeping in mind that he was Dashiell Hammett and I'm only me.

Brendan DuBois is the award-winning author of short stories and novels. His short fiction has appeared in *Playboy, Ellery Queen's Mystery Magazine, Alfred Hitchcock's Mystery Magazine, Mary Higgins Clark Mystery Magazine*, and numerous other anthologies. He has twice received the Shamus Award from the Private Eye Writers of America for his short fiction and has been nominated three times for an Edgar Allan Poe Award by the Mystery

Writers of America. This is his fourth appearance in the yearly Houghton Mifflin Best American Mystery Stories series edited by Otto Penzler; one of his short stories was also included in the *Best American Mystery Stories of the Twentieth Century.*

He's also the author of the Lewis Cole mystery series — *Dead Sand, Black Tide, Shattered Shell,* and *Killer Waves.* His novel *Resurrection Day,* a suspense thriller that looked at what might have happened had the Cuban Missile Crisis of 1962 erupted into a nuclear war, received the Sidewise Award in 2000 for best alternative history novel, and it has been published in seven other countries.

His latest novel, a suspense thriller called *Betrayed,* was published this year in both the United States and Great Britain. He lives in Exeter, New Hampshire, with his wife, Mona, where he is at work on a new novel. Please visit his new Web site, www.brendandubois.com.

▪ "Richard's Children" originally appeared in an anthology edited by Anne Perry, *Murder by Shakespeare.* When I was invited to contribute a story to this anthology by Marty Greenburg, I knew that most — if not all — of the stories would take place during the time of William Shakespeare. Being a contrary sort, I decided that my story, while inspired and influenced by Shakespeare's *Richard III,* would take place in contemporary times. One of the aspects of *Richard III* that fascinates me is the back story of influential families, murdering and betraying each other and their rivals for power. Another fascination of mine, of course, is American history, and it's fun — and sometimes unsettling — to realize just how many royal families this democratic nation boasts, from the Kennedys to the Gores to the Bushes and beyond. These two fascinations of mine became the basis of "Richard's Children," and the fact that I was able to use Shakespeare's work to write a modern story is once again proof — as if any more demonstration were needed — of the Bard's enduring genius.

Elmore Leonard, described by the *New York Times Book Review* as "the greatest crime writer of our time, perhaps ever," is the best-selling author of more than forty novels, including *Tishomingo Blues, Pagan Babies, Get Shorty, Be Cool, Maximum Bob, Stick, Bandits,* and *Hombre.* He has also written many short stories and screenplays and has been named a Grand Master by the Mystery Writers of America. He lives with his wife in Birmingham, Michigan.

▪ I was watching a documentary on television about Russian mail-order brides, big, good-looking women, and wondered if I could use one of them in a book or story.

But wait a minute. Would I be able to make her talk? English, but with a hint of a Russian accent? I asked my researcher, Gregg Sutter, to get me some mail-order brides who weren't Russian, and he came up with the Colombian girls in a stack of photos, all quite attractive and anxious to meet some nice gringos.

About the same time I happened to read about the astonishing number of Indian and Pakistani women who suffer severe accidental burns, their *dupattas* catching fire from the stove. They lose face, so to speak, and are discarded by their husbands, disfigured.

Could these story elements somehow be combined in a homicide situation?

Why not?

Robert McKee lives in Douglas, Wyoming, with his wife, Kathy, and their two children, Kent and Jessica. He works as a court reporter and reported the trial involving the murder of the gay University of Wyoming student Matthew Shepard.

He has received a Wyoming Arts Council Literary Fellowship, has twice won first place in the National Writers' Association's short fiction contest, and has three times won the annual fiction contest held by Wyoming Writers, Inc. His short stories have appeared in more than twenty literary and commercial publications.

When not in the courtroom or at his computer, writing, he is rummaging through antiques stores in search of vintage fountain pens or on the back roads of Wyoming riding his BMW motorcycle at what he admits are "excessive rates of speed."

About his story "The Confession," McKee says, "These days it seems that life is cheap. The body count in fiction and movies is staggering, and the characters never seem to give this mayhem a second's thought. In this story, I attempted to create a character, who, while a young man, kills another man and then struggles with the guilt of that act for the rest of his life. Perhaps I thought a character capable of shame might provide the story with an unaccustomed twist."

Joyce Carol Oates is the author most recently of the novel *The Tattooed Girl* and the short story collection *Small Avalanches*. She has frequently written works of suspense and psychological horror, among them the novella *Beasts* and, under the pseudonym Rosamond Smith, *The Barrens, Starr Bright Will Be With You Soon, Double Delight,* and *Snake Eyes.* Her short stories have been nominated for Edgar Awards, and one of her stories is included in *The Best American Mystery Stories of the Century.* She is a member of the American Academy of Arts and Letters.

• "The Skull" is one of those stories generated by an image. A man labors, rather like an artist, to recreate the facial features of a murder victim.

He might tell himself, as an artist must tell himself, that he is the only living person who can achieve this particular goal. There is something magical in his mission, unless there is something obsessive, too. By degrees, the "personality" of the skull exerts its power over him, which is, of course, the irresistible power of the unconscious to seduce us, as we are all vulnerable to seduction by obsessions. In a longer version of the story, pragmatically edited out at *Harper's*, the forensic scientist endangers his marriage in his pursuit of the skull's identity. When he travels to the murder victim's home, he learns who she "really" was — or does he? "The Skull" he pursues with such single-minded devotion is, in a sense, his own skull, his impending mortality.

George P. Pelecanos is an award-winning journalist, screenwriter, independent film producer, and the author of eleven highly regarded crime novels, the latest of which is *Soul Circus*. He is currently writing for the HBO television series *The Wire* and has recently completed his next novel, *Hard Revolution*, to be published in 2004. *Esquire* magazine called Pelecanos "the poet laureate of the D.C. crime world."

■ "The Dead Their Eyes Implore Us" describes that time in our history when European immigrants flocked from their homelands to the American cities. Many were eased into the culture by seasoned relatives who had preceded them. Others found loneliness, prejudice, and confusion. My father's family settled in D.C.'s Chinatown, which housed not only Chinese but poor immigrants of all backgrounds. These men and women typically worked as kitchen help, pushcart vendors, and day laborers. Like today's immigrants, they did the kind of work that native-born Americans were no longer willing to do.

One night, a great-uncle of mine was walking through a pedestrian tunnel after coming home from his stint as a hotel busboy. A man attacked him from the shadows and attempted to rob him of his day's wage. My uncle, a semiprofessional boxer, was in the habit of carrying a knife; what happened next haunted him for the rest of his life. The idea for this story comes, very loosely, out of that event.

Most Greeks came to this country with no formal education or knowledge of the English language; not only did they survive, they excelled. This is the story of one young man who slipped through the cracks. It is my attempt to get inside his head.

Scott Phillips was born in Wichita, Kansas, in 1961. He is the author of *The Ice Harvest* and *The Walkaway* and the forthcoming *Cottonwood*. He has been nominated for, and lost, the Edgar Award, the Hammett Prize, the CWA Gold and Silver Daggers, the John Creasey Memorial Dagger, the Anthony

Award, and the Barry Award. He won a California Book Award for Best First Fiction. He has a wife and daughter, with whom he lives somewhere west of the Mississippi River.

▪ Wayne Ogden is a character from my second novel, *The Walkaway,* and his grandfather Bill Ogden narrates *Cottonwood,* the novel I'm finishing now. When Dennis McMillan asked me to contribute a story set in the 1930s to *Measures of Poison,* I was stumped until he suggested I use a teen-aged Wayne as a protagonist; I was delighted for the chance to get back to that depraved voice and persona, and to see Wayne as a much younger and unformed character. Other characters in the story walked out of my novels as well: Mildred Halliburton appears very briefly in *The Walkaway* at the age of ninety-five, and Gleason the elderly bartender shows up in *Cottonwood* as a twenty-year-old. Bar owner Stan Gerard is the father of Bill Gerard, the strip-joint owner from *The Ice Harvest.* The climactic event in "Sockdolager" is loosely based on a real firebombing that happened in Wichita in the late sixties, and I'm told the perpetrator's motivations were much as I've described Wayne's herein.

Daniel Stashower is the author of five mystery novels and two biographies. His most recent book is *The Boy Genius and the Mogul: The Untold Story of Television,* and he won an Edgar Award in 2000 for *Teller of Tales: The Life of Arthur Conan Doyle.* Stashower is also a past recipient of the Raymond Chandler Fulbright Fellowship in Detective and Crime Fiction Writing. A freelance journalist since 1986, he has written articles for the *New York Times,* the *Washington Post, Smithsonian Magazine, National Geographic Traveller,* and *American History.* He lives in Washington, D.C., with his wife, Alison, and his son, Sam.

▪ When I was thirteen years old, I tried out for the part of Billy the Page in a revival of William Gillette's play *Sherlock Holmes.* I didn't get the part, so I went home and wrote a play of my own, entitled *Sherlock Holmes Versus the Lizard People.* It found Holmes and Watson struggling to fend off an invasion by a formidable army of lizard people, who, if memory serves, had the advantage of hovering spaceships and laser pistols. I was inordinately pleased with it, and in many ways "The Agitated Actress" is the same story again, only without the laser pistols.

Hannah Tinti grew up in Salem, Massachusetts. Her work has appeared in *Story, Epoch, Story Quarterly, Alaska Quarterly Review, Sonora Review,* and the anthology *Lit Riffs* (Simon and Schuster, 2003). She earned her M.A. from New York University's Graduate Creative Writing Program and has been awarded residency fellowships from Blue Mountain Center, Hedgebrook, and the New York State Writers Institute. She is currently the editor of *One Story* magazine and teaches fiction at the Gotham Writers Workshop. Her short story collection, *Animal Crackers,* is forthcoming from Dial Press in March 2004.

- My parents are both huge mystery fans. When I started writing fiction they told me: *If you want to make any money doing this you have to write a mystery.* "Home Sweet Home" was my first attempt. I wanted my murderer to be sympathetic. I also wanted to see if I could drift from point of view to point of view while solving the crime. Michael Koch, the editor of *Epoch,* gave his great insight to finish the piece. It's an honor to be included in this anthology, among such talented writers. Mom and Dad — you were right — about this, and so many things.

Scott Wolven is finishing an M.F.A. at Columbia University. He currently teaches creative writing at Binghamton University (SUNY) and lives in upstate New York with his wife. His story "The Copper Kings" was selected for *The Best American Stories 2002.* Other recent short fiction has appeared in the Crime Issue of the *Mississippi Review* and at Plotswithguns.com.

- "Controlled Burn" started out just as the title (taken from a radio program on forestry and farm techniques) and some thoughts about the nature of fire. The story ended up being about a lot of things, a combination of the elements and various depths of mystery, of crime and the truth about lies. And the story is partially about working, especially at a woodlot or as a farmer, both of which I have heard described in typical New England Yankee fashion as "an easy way to make a hard living." The story went through a lot of revision, and I'm grateful to Toiya Kirsten Finley, fiction editor at *Harpur Palate,* for her great editorial comments.

  This story is dedicated to my grandfather. Special thanks to all the men and women serving in our armed forces. Very special thanks to Ray and Renate Morrison, Colin Harrison, Anthony Neil Smith of Plotswithguns .com, David Bartine, Sloan Harris, and the remarkable team at WSBW.

Monica Wood is the author of three novels, *Secret Language, My Only Story,* and the forthcoming *Any Bitter Thing;* a book of stories, *Ernie's Ark;* and two books for aspiring writers, *Description* and *The Pocket Muse: Ideas and Inspirations for Writing.* Her short stories have been widely published and anthologized, most recently in *Manoa, Glimmer Train,* and *Confrontation.*

- "That One Autumn" is part of *Ernie's Ark,* a collection of linked stories. It is the only one in the book that takes place in the past. In the present, Ernie is nursing Marie through her cancer. They have a beautiful marriage, marred only, perhaps, by Ernie's tendency to mythologize it. I decided to go back thirty years and find out where the myth began for them. That's where the story was born. Tracey turns up later in the book, too, in case you're curious about what happens to her.

Other Distinguished Mystery Stories of 2002

KING, TABITHA
  The Women's Room. *Stranger,* ed. Michele Slung (HarperCollins/Perennial)

LAVID, LINDA
  The Accident. *Southern Cross Review,* January-February
LEHANE, DENNIS
  Gone Down to Corpus. *The Mighty Johns,* ed. Otto Penzler (New Millennium)
LONG, LAIRD
  Sioux City Express. *HandHeldCrime,* September
LUPICA, MIKE
  No Thing. *The Mighty Johns,* ed. Otto Penzler (New Millennium)

MCBREARTY, ROBERT GARNER
  Transformations. *The Green Hills Literary Lantern,* No. 13
MALAE, PETER NATHANIEL
  Turning Point. *Cimarron Review,* Fall

NAYLER, RAY
  The Bat House. *Ellery Queen's Mystery Magazine,* April

O'CONNELL, CAROL
  The Arcane Receiver. *The Mighty Johns,* ed. Otto Penzler (New Millennium)

STEWART, KEVIN
  Red Dog. *Shenandoah,* Spring

TALLEY, MARCIA
  Too Many Cooks. *Much Ado About Murder,* ed. Anne Perry (Berkley)

WEBB, DON
  Our Novel. *The Magazine of Fantasy & Science Fiction,* May
WEISMAN, JOHN
  A Day in the Country. *Playboy,* August
WESTON, JULIE
  Hunter Moon. *River Styx,* No. 62

ZELTSERMAN, DAVID
  More Than a Scam. *Mysterical Bizland*

THE B·E·S·T AMERICAN SERIES ™

THE BEST AMERICAN SHORT STORIES® 2003
Walter Mosley, guest editor • Katrina Kenison, series editor

"Story for story, readers can't beat the *Best American Short Stories* series" (*Chicago Tribune*). This year's most beloved short fiction anthology is edited by the award-winning author Walter Mosley and includes stories by Dorothy Allison, Mona Simpson, Anthony Doerr, Dan Chaon, and Louise Erdrich, among others.

0-618-19733-8 PA $13.00 / 0-618-19732-X CL $27.50
0-618-19748-6 CASS $26.00 / 0-618-19752-4 CD $35.00

THE BEST AMERICAN ESSAYS® 2003
Anne Fadiman, guest editor • Robert Atwan, series editor

Since 1986, the *Best American Essays* series has gathered the best non-fiction writing of the year and established itself as the best anthology of its kind. Edited by Anne Fadiman, author of *Ex Libris* and editor of the *American Scholar*, this year's volume features writing by Edward Hoagland, Adam Gopnik, Michael Pollan, Susan Sontag, John Edgar Wideman, and others.

0-618-34161-7 PA $13.00 / 0-618-34160-9 CL $27.50

THE BEST AMERICAN MYSTERY STORIES™ 2003
Michael Connelly, guest editor • Otto Penzler, series editor

Our perennially popular anthology is a favorite of mystery buffs and general readers alike. This year's volume is edited by the best-selling author Michael Connelly and offers pieces by Elmore Leonard, Joyce Carol Oates, Brendan DuBois, Walter Mosley, and others.

0-618-32965-X PA $13.00 / 0-618-32966-8 CL $27.50
0-618-39072-3 CD $35.00

THE BEST AMERICAN SPORTS WRITING™ 2003
Buzz Bissinger, guest editor • Glenn Stout, series editor

This series has garnered wide acclaim for its stellar sports writing and top-notch editors. Now Buzz Bissinger, the Pulitzer Prize–winning journalist and author of the classic *Friday Night Lights,* continues that tradition with pieces by Mark Kram Jr., Elizabeth Gilbert, Bill Plaschke, S. L. Price, and others.

0-618-25132-4 PA $13.00 / 0-618-25130-8 CL $27.50

THE B·E·S·T AMERICAN SERIES

THE BEST AMERICAN TRAVEL WRITING 2003
Ian Frazier, guest editor • Jason Wilson, series editor

The Best American Travel Writing 2003 is edited by Ian Frazier, the author of *Great Plains* and *On the Rez*. Giving new life to armchair travel this year are William T. Vollmann, Geoff Dyer, Christopher Hitchens, and many others.

0-618-11881-0 PA $13.00 / 0-618-11881-0 CL $27.50
0-618-39074-X CD $35.00

THE BEST AMERICAN SCIENCE AND NATURE WRITING 2003
Richard Dawkins, guest editor • Tim Folger, series editor

This year's edition promises to be another "eclectic, provocative collection" (*Entertainment Weekly*). Edited by Richard Dawkins, the eminent scientist and distinguished author, it features work by Bill McKibben, Steve Olson, Natalie Angier, Steven Pinker, Oliver Sacks, and others.

0-618-17892-9 PA $13.00 / 0-618-17891-0 CL $27.50

THE BEST AMERICAN RECIPES 2003–2004
Edited by Fran McCullough and Molly Stevens

"The cream of the crop . . . McCullough's selections form an eclectic, unfussy mix" (*People*). Offering the very best of what America is cooking, as well as the latest trends, time-saving tips, and techniques, this year's edition includes a foreword by Alan Richman, award-winning columnist for *GQ*.

0-618-27384-0 CL $26.00

THE BEST AMERICAN NONREQUIRED READING 2003
Edited by Dave Eggers • Introduction by Zadie Smith

Edited by Dave Eggers, the author of *A Heartbreaking Work of Staggering Genius* and *You Shall Know Our Velocity,* this genre-busting volume draws the finest, most interesting, and least expected fiction, nonfiction, humor, alternative comics, and more from publications large, small, and on-line. *The Best American Nonrequired Reading 2003* features writing by David Sedaris, ZZ Packer, Jonathan Safran Foer, Andrea Lee, and others.

0-618-24696-7 $13.00 PA / 0-618-24696-7 $27.50 CL
0-618-39073-1 $35.00 CD

HOUGHTON MIFFLIN COMPANY   www.houghtonmifflinbooks.com